D1557246

Fire Ants

FIRE ANTS

and Other Stories

GERALD DUFF

NEWSOUTH BOOKS
Montgomery | Louisville

NewSouth Books
P.O. Box 1588
Montgomery, AL 36102

Library of Congress Cataloging-in-Publication Data

Duff, Gerald.
Fire ants / Gerald Duff.
p. cm.
ISBN-13: 978-1-58838-208-5
ISBN-10: 1-58838-208-7
I. Title.
PS3554.U3177F57 2007
813'.54--dc22
2007011910

Printed in the United States of America

Some of these stories have appeared, often in different form, in the following publications, to whose editors grateful acknowledgment is made: "Fire Ants" in *Ploughshares* and in *Editors' Choice: New American Stories*; "The Way a Blind Man Tracks Light" in *Kenyon Review*; "A Mouth Full of Money" in *A Critique of America*; "Bad Medicine" in *Missouri Review* as "The Motions of the Animals"; "Believing in Memphis" in *Southern Hum*; "Charm City" and "The Bliss of Solitude" in *storySouth*; "The Apple and the Aspirin Tablet" in *Florida Quarterly*; "Texas Wherever You Look" in *Southwest Review*; and "The Road to Damascus" and "The Angler's Paradise Fish-Cabin Dance of Love" in *Coasters*.

This book is for Hilda Lopez and
in memory of Johnny Lopez, Warren Murphy,
and those days together at Lamar.

CONTENTS

And what the dead had no speech for, when living,
They can tell you, being dead: the communication
Of the dead is tongued with fire beyond the language of the
    living.

         — T. S. ELIOT, "Little Gidding"

A quick-tempered but sensual and playful people, they often
dressed provocatively, acted with a volatile belligerence, drank to
excess, engaged in constant and open competition in every form,
and adamantly defied the attempts of outsiders to control them.

         — JAMES WEBB, *Born Fighting*

Fire Ants

Fire Ants

She had kept the bottle stuck down inside a basket of clothes that needed ironing, and throughout the course of the day whenever she had a chance to walk through the back room where the basket was kept, she would stop for the odd sip or two. By the middle of the afternoon, she had stopped feeling the heat even though she had cooked three coconut pies, one for B. J.'s supper and two for the graveyard working, and had ironed dresses for her and Myrtle. And by suppertime with Myrtle and B. J. and Bubba and Barney Lee Richards all around the table waiting for her to bring in the dishes from the kitchen, MayBelle had reached the point that she couldn't tell if she had put salt in the black-eyed peas or not even when she tasted them twice, a whole spoonful each time.

"Aunt MayBelle," B. J. was saying, looking up at her with a big grin on his face, "where's that good cornbread? I bet old Barney Lee could eat some of that." He reached over and punched at one of Barney Lee's sides where it hid his belt. "He looks hungry to me, this boy does."

"Aw, B. J.," said Barney Lee and hitched a little in his chair. "I shouldn't be eating at all, but I save up just enough to eat over here at your Mama's house."

"Well, you're always welcome," said Myrtle from the end of the table by the china cabinet. "We don't see enough of you around here. Used to, you boys were always underfoot. I wish it was that way now."

"Barney Lee," said MayBelle, and waited to hear what she was going to say, "your hair is going back real far on both sides of your head. Not as far as B. J.'s, but it's getting on back there all right." She moved over and set the pan of hot cornbread on a pad in the middle of the table. "You gonna be as bald as your old daddy in a few years."

MayBelle straightened up to go back to the kitchen for another dish, and the Bear-King winked at her and lifted a paw, making her not listen to what Myrtle was calling to her as she walked through the door of the dining room. Maybe I better go look at that clothes basket before I bring in that bowl of okra, she thought to herself, and made a little detour off the kitchen. The foreign bottle was safe where she had left it, and she adjusted the level of the vodka inside to where it came just to the neckline of the white bear on the label.

When she came back into the dining room with the okra, everybody was waiting for B. J. to say grace, sitting quiet at the table and cutting eyes at the pastor at the head of it. "Sit down for a minute, Aunt MayBelle," B. J. said in a composed voice and caught at her arm. "Let's thank the Lord and then you can finish serving the table."

MayBelle dropped into her chair and looked at a flower in the middle of the plate in front of her. It was pounding like a heart beating, and it did so in perfect time to the song of a mockingbird calling outside the window. It's the Texas State Bird, she thought, and Austin is the State Capital. The native bluebonnet is the State Flower and grows wild along the highways every spring. But it's hard to transplant, and it smells just like a weed. If you got some on your hands, you can wash and wash them with heavy soap, and the smell will still be there for up to a week after. But they are pretty to look at, all the bluebonnets alongside the highway. There were big banks of them on both sides of the dirt road for as far as you could see, and when the car went by them it made enough wind to show the undersides of the flowers, lighter blue than the tops of the petals.

He stopped the car so they could look at all of them on both sides of the road, and a little breeze came up just when he turned the engine off, and it went across the bluebonnets like a wave. It was like ripples in a pond; they all turned together in rings and the light blue traveled along the tops of the darker blue petals as if it wasn't just the west wind moving things around, but something else all by itself.

He asked her if she didn't think it was the prettiest thing she ever saw, and she said yes and turned in the seat to face him. And that's when he reached out his hand and put it on the back of her head and said her eyes put him in mind of the color on the underside of the bluebonnets, and he had always wanted to tell her that. It was hot, early May, and there was a little line of sweat on his upper lip and when he came toward her she watched that until her eyes couldn't focus on it anymore he was so close and then his mouth was on hers and it was open and there was a little smell of cigarette smoke.

She could hear the hot metal of the car ticking in the sun. It was hers, the only one she ever owned, and that was only for a little over a year. It set high off the road and could go over deep ruts and not get stuck and it could climb any hill in Coushatta County without having to shift gears. The breeze was coming in the car window off the bluebonnets and it felt cool, but his hands were hot wherever they touched her and she kept her eyes closed and could still see the light blue underside of the flowers and the thin line of sweat on his lip and she was ticking all over just like the new car sitting still between the banks of bluebonnets in the sun.

"All this we ask in Thy Name, Amen," said B. J. and reached for the plate of cornbread. "You can go get the mashed potatoes now, Aunt MayBelle."

"Yes," said Myrtle, looking across the table at her, "and another thing too while you're in the kitchen. You poured me sweet milk in my glass, and you know I've got to have clabbermilk at supper."

Everybody allowed as how the vegetables were real good for this late in the season, but that the blackberry cobbler was a little tart. It was probably because of the dry spell, Barney Lee said, and they all agreed that the wild berries had been hard hit this year and might not even make at all next summer unless they got some relief.

After supper Myrtle and Barney Lee went into the living room to catch the evening news on the Dumont, and B. J. put on his quilted suit and went out with Bubba and the cattle-prod to agitate the Dobermans and German shepherds.

From where she stood by the sinkful of dishes, MayBelle could hear the dogs begin barking and growling as soon as they saw B. J. and Bubba coming toward the pen. She ran some more water into the sink, hot enough to turn her hands red when she reached into it, and she almost let it overflow before she turned off the faucet and started washing. She didn't break but one dish, the flowered plate off which she had eaten a little okra and a few crowder peas at supper, but dropping it didn't seem to help the way she felt any.

She stood looking down at the parts it had cracked into on the floor, feeling the heat from the soapy water rising into her chest and face and hearing the TV set booming two rooms away, and decided she would look into the clothes basket again as soon as she had finished in the kitchen.

Outside a dog yipped and Bubba laughed, and MayBelle lifted her eyes to the window over the sink. The back pasture was catching the last rays of the setting sun, and it looked almost gold in the light. But when she looked closer, she could see that the yellow color was in the weeds and sawgrass itself, not just borrowed from the sun, and what looked like haze was really the dry seed pods rattling at the ends of the stalks.

Further up the hill yellowish smoke was rising from one of the cabins in the quarter, perfectly straight up into the sky as far as she could see, not a waver or a bit of motion to it. She stood watching it for a long time, dishcloth in one hand and a soapy glass in the other, until finally her eye was caught by a small figure moving slowly across the back edge of the pasture and disappearing into the dark line of pines that enclosed it.

That's old Sully, she said to herself, probably picking up kindling or looking at a rabbit trap. Wonder how he stands the heat of a wood cookstove this time of the year. Keeps it going all the time, too, Cora says.

In the living room Barney Lee asked Myrtle something, and she answered him, not loud enough to be understood, and MayBelle went back to the dishwashing, rinsing and setting aside the glass she was holding. It had a wide striped design on it, and it felt right in her hand as she set it on the drainboard to dry.

Picking up speed, she finished the rest of the glassware, the knives and forks, the cooking pots and the cornbread skillet, and then wiped the counters dry and swabbed off the top of the gas stove. By the time she finished turning the coffee pot upside down on the counter next to the sink, the striped glass on the drainboard had dried and a new program had started on the television set. The sounds of a happy bunch of people laughing and clapping their hands came from the front part of the house as MayBelle picked up her glass and walked out of the kitchen toward the back room.

She filled the glass up to the top of where the colored stripe began and took two small sips of the clear bitter liquid. She stopped, held the foreign bottle up to the light and watched the Bear-King while she drained the rest of the glass in one long swallow. A little of the vodka got up her nose, and she almost sneezed but managed to hold it back, belching deeply to keep things balanced. As she did, the Bear-King nodded his head, causing a sparkle of light to flash from his crown, and lifted one paw a fraction. "Thank you, Mr. Communist," MayBelle said, "I believe I will."

A few minutes later, Bubba looked up from helping B. J. untangle one of the German shepherds which had got a front foot hung in the wire noose on the end of the cattle-prod, barely avoiding getting a hand slashed as he did, and caught sight of something moving down the hill in the back pasture. But by the time he got around to looking again, after getting the dog loose and back in the pen and the gate slammed shut, whatever it was had got too far off to see through his sweated-up glasses.

"B. J.," he said and waved toward the back of the house, "was that Aunt MayBelle yonder in the pasture?"

"Where?" said B. J. in a cross voice through the Johnny Bench catcher's mask. He laid the electric prod down in the dust of the yard and pulled the suit away from his neck so he could blow down his collar. He felt hot enough in the outfit to faint, and the dust kicked up by the last dog had got all up in his face mask, mixing with the sweat and leaving muddy tracks at the corners of his cheeks. "What would she be doing in that weed patch? She's in the house last I notice."

"Aw, nothing," said Bubba. "If it was her, she just checking out the blackberries, I reckon. It don't make no difference."

"Bubba," said B. J. and paused to get his breath and look at the pen of barking dogs in front of him. "I believe Christian Guard Dogs, Incorporated, has made some real progress in the last few days. Look at them fighting and snapping in there. Why, they'd tear a prowler all to pieces in less than two minutes."

"B. J.," Bubba answered, "watch this." He picked up the dead pine limb and rattled the hog wire with it, and immediately the nearest Doberman lunged at the fence, snapping and foaming at the steel wire between its teeth, its eyes narrow and bloodshot.

"That dog there," Bubba announced in a serious flat voice, "would kill a stray nigger or a doped-up hippie in a New York minute."

"I figure you got to do what you can," said B. J., "and if there's a little honest profit in it for a Christian, it's nothing wrong with that." B. J. took off the catcher's mask and stood for a minute watching the worked-up dogs prowl up and down the pen, baring their teeth at each other as they passed, their tails carried low between their legs and the hair on their backs all roughed up. Then he turned toward his brother and clapped him on the shoulder.

"Let's go get a drink of water and talk about your business problems, Bubba. The Lord'll find an answer for you. You just got to give Him a chance."

THE HOUSES WERE LINED UP on each side of a dirt road that came up from the patch of weeds to the south and stopped abruptly at the edge of the pasture. In front of the first one on the left, a cabin with two front doors opening into the same room and a window in between them with a pane of unbroken glass still in it, was the body of a '54 Chevrolet up on blocks. All four wheels had been taken off a long time ago and fastened together with a length of log chain and hung from the lowest limb of an oak tree. The bark on the oak had grown over and around the chain, and the metal of the wheels had fused together with rust.

MayBelle took another sip straight from the bottle and stepped around a marooned two-wheeled tricycle, grown up in bitter weeds, careful not to trip herself up. She walked up on the porch of the next shotgun house and leaned over to peer through a knocked-out window. Her footsteps on the floorboards sounded like a drum, she noticed, and she hopped up and down a couple of times to hear the low boom again. There was enough vodka left in the bottle to slosh around as she did so, and she shook it in her right hand until it foamed. It didn't seem to bother the Bear-King any.

The only thing left in the front room was a two-legged wood stove tilted over to one side and three walls covered with pictures of movie stars, politicians, and baseball players. "Howdy, Mr. and Mrs. President," MayBelle said to a large photograph of JFK and Jackie next to a picture of Willie Mays and just below one of Bob Hope. "How y'all this evening?" She took another little sip and had a hard time getting the top screwed back on, and by the time she had it down tight, it was getting too difficult in the fading light to distinguish one face on the wall from another, so she quit trying.

The back of the next cabin had been completely torn off, so when MayBelle stepped up on the porch and looked through the door all she could see was a framed scene of the dark woods behind. A whip-poor-will called from somewhere deep inside the picture, and after a minute was answered by another one further off. MayBelle held her breath to listen, but neither bird made another sound, and after a time, she stepped back down to the road and looked at the clear space around her.

She felt as though it was getting dark too quickly and she hadn't been able to see all she wanted. Already the tops of the bank of pines around the row of houses were vanishing into the sky, and one by one the features of everything around her, the stones in

the road and the discarded jars and tin cans, the bits and pieces of
old automobiles, the broken furniture lying around the porches
and the shiny things tacked up on the wall and around the edges
of the eaves, were slipping away as the light steadily diminished.
Whatever it was she had come to see, she hadn't discovered yet,
and she shivered a little, hot as it was, feeling the need to move on
until she found it. I waited too late in the day again, she thought,
and now I can't see anything.

It was like the time at Holly Springs she had been playing in
the loft of the barn with some of the Stutts girls and had slipped
down between the beams and the shingles of the roof to hide. Papa
had found her there at supper time, passed out from the sting of
wasps whose nest she had laid her head against, her face covered
with bumps and her eyes swollen shut from the poison. He had
carried her down to Double Pen Creek, the coldest water in the
county, running with her in his arms two miles through the cotton
fields and the second-growth thickets until he was able to lay her
in the water and draw off the fire of the wasp stings. She hadn't
been able to see for six days after that, even after the swelling went
down and she was able to open her eyes finally. The feeling of the
light fading and the dark creeping up came on her again as she
stood in the road between the rows of ruined houses, the bottle
tight in her hand.

"You looking for Cora, her place down yonder."

MayBelle lifted her gaze from the Bear-King and focused in
the direction from where the voice had come. In a few seconds she
picked him out of the shadow at the base of a sycamore trunk two
houses down. He was a little black man in a long coat that dragged
the ground and his hair was as white as cotton.

"You Sully," declared MayBelle and took a drink from her
quart bottle.

"Yes, ma'am," said the little black man and giggled high up through his nose. "That be me. Old Sully."

"You used to do a little work for Burton Shackleford. Down yonder." She waved the bottle off to the side without looking away from the sycamore shadow.

"That's right," he called out in a high voice to the empty houses, looking from one side of the open space to the other and then taking a couple of steps out into the road. "You talking about me, all right. I shore used to do a little work for Mister Burton. Build some fence. Dig them foundations. Pick up pecans oncet in a while."

"Uh-huh," said MayBelle and paused for a minute. Two whippoor-wills behind the backless house traded calls again, further away this time than before.

"I heard a lot about you. Cora she told me."

"Say she did?" said Sully and kicked at something in the dust of the road. "Cora you say?"

"That's right," MayBelle said, addressing herself to the Bear-King and lifting the bottle to her mouth. The liquor had stopped tasting a while back and now seemed like nothing more than water.

"She says," MayBelle said and paused to pat at her lips with the tips of her fingers, "Cora says you're still a creeper."

"She say that?" Sully asked in an amazed voice and scratched at the cotton on top of his head. "That's a mystery to me. She a old woman. Last old woman in the quarter." He stopped and looked off at the tree line, then down at whatever he had kicked at in the sand and finally at the bottle in MayBelle's hand.

"What that is?" he said.

MayBelle raised the bottle to eye level and shook its contents back and forth against the Bear-King's feet, "That there liquor is Communist whiskey."

Then both regarded the bottle for a minute without saying

anything as the liquid moved from one side to the other more and more slowly until it finally settled to dead level in MayBelle's steady grasp.

"Say it is?" Sully finally said after a while.

"Uh-huh. You ever drink any of this Communist whiskey?"

"No ma'am, Miz MayBelle. I a Baptist," Sully said. "If I's to vote, I vote that straight Democrat ticket."

MayBelle unscrewed the lid, took a hard look at the level of the side of the bottle, and then carefully sipped until she had brought the liquid down to where the Bear-King appeared to be barely walking on the water beneath his feet.

"You don't drink nothing then," she said to Sully, carefully replacing the metal cap and giving it a pat.

"Nothing Communist, no ma'am, but I do like to sip a little of that white liquor that Rufus boy bring me now and again. Somebody over yonder in Leggett or Marston, they makes that stuff."

"Is it hot?"

"Is it hot?" declared Sully. "Sometimes I gots to sit down to drink from that Mason jar."

"Tell you what, Sully," said MayBelle and gave the little black man a long look over the neck of the bottle.

"Yes, ma'am," he said and straightened to attention until just the edges of his coat were touching the dust of the road. "What's that?"

"You go get yourself a clean glass and bring me one too, and I'll let you have a taste of this Communist whiskey." Sully spun around to leave and she called after him: "You got any of that Mason jar, bring it on, too."

"It be here directly," Sully answered over his shoulder and hopped over a discarded table leg in his way.

MayBelle walked over to the nearest porch and sat down to

wait, her feet stuck straight out in front of her, and began trying
to imitate the whip-poor-will's call, sending her voice forth into
the darkness in a low quavering tone, but not a bird had answered,
no matter how she listened, by the time Sully got back with two
jelly glasses and a Mason jar full of yellow shine, the sheen and
consistency of light oil.

"YOU GONE FELL DOWN again in amongst all the weeds, Miz May-
Belle," Sully said, "you keep on trying to skip."

"I have always loved to skip," said MayBelle, moving through
the pasture down the hill at a pretty good clip. She caught one foot
on something in the dark and stepped high with the other one,
bobbing to one side like a boxer in the ring.

"Watch me now," she said. "Yessir. Goddamn."

"You sho' do cuss a lot for a white lady," said Sully, dodging and
weaving through the rank saw-grass and bull nettles.

"I know it. Damn. Hell. Shit-fart."

"Uh-huh," said Sully, hurrying to catch up and trying to see how
far they had reached in the Shackleford back pasture. The moon
was down, and he was having a hard time judging the distance to
the stile over the back fence, what with his coat catching on weeds
and sticks and the yellow shine thundering in his head.

He bent down to free his hem from something that had snagged
it, felt the burn of bullnettle across his hand, and recognized a
clump of trees against the line of the night sky.

"I'se you," he called ahead in a high whisper. "I'd keep to the left
right around here. Them old fire ants' bed just over yonder."

"Where?" said MayBelle, stopping in the middle of a skip so
abruptly that she slipped on something which turned under her foot
and almost caused her to fall. "Where are them little boogers?"

"Just over yonder about fifteen, twenty feet," Sully said, glad to stop and take a deep breath to settle the moving shapes around him. "See where them weeds stick up, look like a old cowboy's hat? Them ants got they old dirt nest just this side." He paused to smooth his coat around him and rub his bullnettle burn. "That there where they sleep when they ain't out killing things."

"You say they tough," said the skinny white lady. "It burns when they bite?"

"Burns? Lawdy have mercy. Do it burn when they bites? Everywhere one of them fire ants sting you it's a little piece of your hide swell up and rot out all around it. Take about a week to happen."

Sully felt the ground begin to tilt to one side, and he lifted one foot and brought it down sharply to level things out. The earth pushed back hard, but by keeping his knee locked, he was able to hold it steady. "I don't know how long I can last," he said to his right leg, "but I do what I can."

"Shit, goddamn," said MayBelle, "let's go see if they're all asleep in their bed."

"You mean them fire ants? They kill the baby birds and little rabbits in they nests. Chop 'em up, take 'em home and eat 'em. I don't want no part of them boogers. I ain't lost nothing in them fire ants' bed."

"Well, I believe I did," said MayBelle. "Piss damn. I'm going to go over there and go to bed with them."

Sully heard the dry weeds crack and pop as the white lady began moving toward the cowboy hat shape, and he lifted his foot to step toward the sound. When he did, the released earth flew up and hit him all down the right side of his body and against his ear and jaw. "I knowed it was going to happen," he said to his right leg as he lay, half-stunned in the high weeds, "I let things go too quick."

By the time he was able to get up again, scrambling to first one knee, then the other, and then flapping his arms about him to get all the way off the ground and away from its terrible grip, the skinny white lady had already reached the fire ant bed and dropped down beside it. Sully moved at an angle, one arm much higher than the other and his ears ringing with the lick the ground had just given him, until he came up close enough to see the dark bulk of the old woman stretched out in the soft mound of ant-chewed earth.

"You got to get up from there, Miz MayBelle," he said and began to lean toward her, hand outstretched, but then thought better of it as he felt the earth begin to gather itself for another go at him.

She was speaking in a crooning voice to the ant bed, saying words he couldn't understand and moving herself slowly from side to side as she settled into it.

"Miz MayBelle," Sully said, "crawl on up out of there now. They gonna eat you alive lying there. That ain't no fun."

"Don't you put a hand on me, Papa," she said in a clear hard voice, suddenly getting still, "I'm right where I want to be."

"I see I got it to do," Sully said and threw his head back to look around for somebody. He couldn't see a soul, and every star in the night sky was perfectly clear and still.

"You decide to get up while I'm gone," he said to the dark shape at his feet, "just go on ahead and do it."

Running in a half-crouch with one arm out for balance against the tilt the earth was putting on him, Sully started down the hill toward the back fence of the Shackleford place, proceeding through the weeds and brambles like a sailboat tacking into the wind. About every fifty feet, he had to lean into a new angle and cut back to keep the ground from reaching up and slamming him another lick, and the dirt of the dry field and the hard edges of the saw-grass were working together like a charm to slow and trip him up.

He went over the stile on his hands and knees, and the earth popped him a good one again on the other side of the fence, but he was able to get himself up by leaning his back against the trunk of a pine tree and pushing himself up in stages. There was a dim yellow light coming from a cloth tent right at the back steps of the house, and Sully aimed for that and the sounds of a man's voice coming from it in a regular singing pattern. He got there in three more angled runs, the last one involving a low clothesline that caught him in the head just where his hairline started, and he stopped about ten feet from the tent flap, dust rising around him and the earth pushing up hard against one foot and sucking down at the other one.

Barney Lee Richards lifted the tent flap and stuck his head out to see what had caused all the commotion in the middle of B. J.'s prayer against the unpardonable sin, but at first all he could make out was a cloud of suspended dust with a large dark shape in the middle of it. He blinked his eyes, focused again, and the form began to resolve itself into somebody or something standing at an angle, an arm extended above its head, which looked whiter than anything around it, and the whole thing wrapped in a long hanging garment. The clothesline was making a strange humming sound.

"Aw naw," he said in a choked disbelieving voice, jerked his head back inside the lighted tent, and spun around to look at B. J., his eyes opened wide enough to show white all around them.

"B. J.," he said, "it's something all black wearing an old long cape and it's got white on its head and it's pointing its hand up at the sky.

"At the sky?" said B. J. and began to fumble around in the darkness of the tent floor with both hands for his Bible. "You say it's wearing a long cape?"

"That's right, that's right," said Barney Lee in a high whine and began to cry. He heaved himself forward onto his hands and knees and lurched into a rapid crawl as if he were planning to tear out the back of the mountaineer's tent, colliding with B. J. and causing him to lose his grip on the Bible he had just found next to a paper sack full of bananas.

"Hold still, Barney Lee," B. J. said. "Stop it now. I'm trying to get hold of something to help us if you'll just set still and let me."

To Sully on the outside, standing breathless and stunned next to the clothesline pole, the commotion in the two-man tent made it look as though the shelter was full of a small pack of hounds fighting over a possum. First one wall, then the other bulged and stretched, and the ropes fastened to the tent stakes groaned and popped under the pressure. The stakes themselves seemed to shift and glow in the dark as he watched.

"White folks," Sully said in a weak voice and then, getting a good breath, "white folks. I gots to talk to you."

The canvas of the tent suddenly stopped surging, and everything became quiet. Sully stood tilted to one side and braced against the pull of the earth, his mouth half open to listen, but all he could hear for fully a minute was the sound of the yellow shine seeping and sliding through his head and from far off somewhere in the woods the call of a roosting bird that had waked up in the night.

Finally the front flap of the tent opened up a few inches and the bulk of a man's head appeared in the crack.

"Who's that out there?" the head asked.

"Hidy, white folks," said Sully. "It's only just me. Old Sully. Just only an ordinary old field nigger. Done retire."

The flap moved all the way open, and B. J. crawled halfway out the tent, straining to get a better look.

"It's just an old colored gentleman, Brother B. Lee," he said over his shoulder. "Like I told you, it ain't nothing to worry about."

"Well," said Barney Lee from the darkness behind him, "I was afraid it was something spiritual. Why was it standing that way with its hand pointing up, if it was a colored man?"

"Hello, old man," said B. J., all the way out of the tent now and standing up to brush the dirt off his pants. "Kinda late at night to be calling, idn't it?"

"Yessir," said Sully. "It do be late, but a old man he don't sleep much. He don't need what he use to."

"Uh-huh," B. J. said and turned back to help Barney Lee who had climbed halfway up but had gotten stuck with one knee bent and the other leg fully extended.

"Why," Barney Lee addressed the man in the long coat, "Why you standing that way with your arm sticking way up like that?"

"Well sir," said Sully and turned his head to look up along his sleeve. "It seem like it help me to stand like this." The shine made a ripple in a new little path in his head, and he had to lift his hand higher to keep things whole and steady.

"I just wish you'd listen to that, Barney Lee," B. J. said in a tight voice.

"What? I don't hear nothing."

"That's exactly what I'm talking about. Here's this old nig— colored gentleman—come walking up in the dead of night, and what do you hear from them dogs? Not a thing."

Everybody stopped to listen and had to agree that the dog pen was showing no sign of alert.

"And I thought the training was going along so good the last few days. I'm getting real discouraged about Christian Guard Dogs." B. J. sighed deeply, kicked at the ground, and coughed at the dust hanging in the air. "I don't know. I just don't know."

"However," said Sully, "what it is I come up here and bother you white folks about it be up yonder in the pasture." He swung a hand back in the direction he had come, almost lost the hold he was maintaining against the steady pull of the earth, and staggered a step or two before he found it again.

"Say it helps you to stand like that?" asked Barney Lee and shyly stuck one arm above his head until it pointed in the direction of the Little Dipper. "Reckon it helps circulation or something?"

"Didn't make one peep," said B. J. "I didn't hear bark one, much less a growl."

"Yessir, white folks, it up yonder in the pasture. What I come here to your pulp tent for." Sully's arm was getting heavy so he ventured to lean against the pole supporting the clothesline and found that helped him some. Things were tilted, but not moving.

"A few minute ago, I was outside my house walking to that patch of cane. You know, tending to my business and that's when I heard her yonder."

"Who?" said B. J., making conversation as he looked over at the dark outline of the Christian Guard Dog pen as though he could see each individual Doberman and shepherd.

"Miz MayBelle."

"MayBelle? Aunt MayBelle Holt?" B. J. turned back to look at the little black man leaned up against the pole. "You say you heard her up in the nigger quarters?"

"Naw sir, white folks, not rightly in the quarters. She in that back pasture lying down in that fire ant bed."

"The fire ant bed?"

"Yessir, old Sully was in the quarters and she in the bed of fire ants."

"What's Aunt MayBelle doing in the fire ant bed? Did she fall into there?"

"I don't know about that," said Sully and adjusted his pointing arm more precisely with relation to the night sky. "I only just seed her in there a talking to them boosters."

"Come on, Brother B. Lee," B. J. said and broke into a trot

toward the back fence. "We got to see what's going on. Them things will eat her up."

"Thata's just the very thing I thought," said Sully, lurching away from the clothesline pole, and stumbling into a run after B. J., his gesturing right arm the only thing keeping him away from another solid lick from the ground. "I thought it sure wasn't no good idea for a white lady to lie down in amongst all them biting things."

"I'm coming, B. J.," called Barney Lee, a few steps behind Sully but close enough that the old man's flapping coat-tail sent puffs of dust up into his face. As he ran through the fence at the bottom of the hill, he raised an arm above his head and immediately felt his wind get better and his speed increase a step or two.

"I believe," Barney Lee said between breaths to the tilted sidling figure moving ahead of him, "that it's doing me good, too. Pointing my arm up at the sky like this."

"Yessir, white folks," Sully said to the words coming from behind him, fighting as best he could against the yearn of the earth beneath his feet. It was going to get him at the stile again, he knew, but he had to live with that fact. *I just get them fat white folks to the ant bed, I quit,* he said to the clouds of dust floating up before him. *You can have all of it then. I give it on up.* He ran on, changing to a new tack every few feet, the pointing arm dead in the air above him, and listened to the shine rumble and slide through all the crannies of his head.

"It's gonna be hard times in the morning," he said out loud and aimed at the fence stile coming up. *It most always is.*

You've got to say something to me, she said. You don't talk to me right. Now you got to say something to me.

I'm talking to you, he said. I'm talking right now to you. What you want me to say? This?

And he did a thing that made her eyes close and the itching start in her feet and begin to move up the back of her legs and across her belly and along her sides down each rib. Oh, she said, it's all in my shoulders and the back of my neck.

She let him push her further back until her head touched the green and gold bedspread, and one of her hands slipped off his shoulder and fell beside her as though she had lost all the strength in that part of her body. The arm was numb, but tingling like it did in the morning sometimes when she had slept wrong on it and cut off the circulation of blood. She tried to lift it and something like warm air ran up and down the inside of her upper arm and settled in her armpit under the bunched-up sleeve of the dress.

No, she said, it's hot and I'm sweating. It's going to get all over her bed. It'll make a wet mark, and it won't dry and she'll see it.

He said no and mumbled something else into the side of her throat that she couldn't hear. Something was happening to the bottoms of her feet and the palms of her hands. It was crawling and picking lightly at the skin. Just pulling it up a little at a time and letting it fall back and doing it over again until it felt like little hairs were raising up in their places and settling back over and over.

Talk to me, she said into his mouth. Say some things to me. You never have said a thing yet to me.

I'll say something to you, he said, and moved against her in a way that caused her to want to try to touch each corner of the bed.

If I put one foot at the edge down there and the other one at the other corner and then my hands way out until I can touch where the mattress comes to a point, then if somebody was way up above us and could look down just at me and the way I'm laying here, it would look like two straight lines crossing in the middle. That makes an X when two lines cross. And in the middle where they cross is where I am.

Please, she said to the little burning spots that were beginning to start at each end of the leg of the X and to move slowly towards the intersection, come reach each other. Meet in the middle where I am.

But the little points of fire, like sparks that popped out of the fireplace and made burn marks on the floor, were taking their own time, stopping at one place for a while and settling there as if they were going to stay and not go any further and then when something finally burned through and broke apart, moving up a little further to settle a space closer to the middle of the X.

Just a word or two, she said to him, that's all I want you to say.

He said something back to her, something deep in his throat, but her ears were listening to a dim buzz that had started up deep inside her head, and she couldn't hear him.

What? she said. What? One foot and one hand had reached almost to the opposite corners of the bed and she strained, trying to make that line of the X straight and true before she turned her mind to the other line.

He moved above her, and suddenly the first line fell into place and locked itself, and the little burning spots along that whole leg of the X began to gather themselves and move more quickly from each end toward the middle where they might meet.

The buzz inside her head that wouldn't let her hear suddenly stopped the way you would click off a radio, and the sound of a mockingbird's call somewhere outside came twice and acted like something being poured into her head. It moved down inside like water and made two little points of pressure which were the bird calls and which stayed, waiting for something.

You talk to her, she said to him, her mouth so close to the side of his head when she spoke that her lips moved against the short hairs growing just behind his ear. I hear you say things to her. In the night. I hear you in the night. Lots of times.

Her other foot and hand were moving now on their own, and she no longer had to tell them what to do. The fingers of the hand reached, stretched, fell short, tried again and touched the edges of the mattress where the two sides came together. The green and gold spread moved in a fold beneath the hand, and as it did, the foot which formed the last point of the two legs of the X finally found its true position, and the intersecting lines fell into place at last, straight as though they had been drawn by a ruler. And whoever was looking at her from above could see it, the two legs of the X drawing to a point in the middle where they crossed and touched, and something let the burning points know the straight path was clear, and they came with a rush from each far point of the two lines, racing to meet in the middle where everything came together.

Say it, she managed to get the words out just before all of it reached the middle which was where she was, and he said something, but she couldn't hear anything but the fixed cry of the mockingbird and she blended her voice with that, and all the burning points came together and touched and flared and stayed.

A Mouth Full of Money

Nancy saw him first, way up beyond where the heat rising from the surface of the highway made everything look wavy like water. But I told her it was just a large cow or maybe Wylie Knight's young bull standing in the middle of Farm-to-Market Road 1276.

"Nuh-uh," my sister said, coming to a dead stop on the shoulder of the road. "That's Weldon Overstreet, and I'm going back home."

She was wearing shoes, sandals I remember, and so could afford to stand in one place for longer than a second or two at a time while she thought about something other than her feet. But I was barefoot, like always in the summer, and I had to stay in motion to keep the asphalt from burning clean through the skin on the bottom of my soles, tough though they were by the middle of August in East Texas.

"It's not him, neither," I said, lifting first one foot then the other like a soldier marching in place. "It's just that Brahma bull, and he'll go off in the woods when he sees us coming. Let's get to moving."

"Stand in the gravel if your feet're burning. Get off the road."

She knew I couldn't do that because of the grass burrs up and down every roadside in that part of the country, so I didn't even bother to answer.

"I'm going back home," Nancy said. "You can go on by yourself if you're so sure it ain't Weldon."

"No, you're not," I said. "You know Mama'll just send us back out again, and we'll have all this road to do over. Let's just go on a little closer."

I reached over and took the empty two-gallon jug out of her hands to carry, and that got her going again, not nearly as fast this time, but at least my feet were spending more time in the air and less on the black asphalt after I took up the burden she'd been carrying. But I knew my doing that would make Nancy even more nervous because she would realize we hadn't come to the halfway point between our house and Sleetie Cameron's, and so we hadn't yet passed the big longleaf pine with its top shaped like a chicken's head. That was what we used to mark the spot where the other person's turn to carry began. On the way back after Sleetie had filled the jug up with the skimmed milk, we would both have to keep a hold on the wire handle to be able to carry the thing home.

"Weldon held Barbara Ann upside down in a tub of rinse water last Saturday," Nancy said. "Mrs. Overstreet had to hit him on the back of the head with a bleach bottle to make him quit."

"He was probably just trying to worry her some," I said and shifted the milk jug from one side of my chest to the other. I wasn't wearing a shirt, of course, and I didn't like the way the sweat felt between my skin and the glass of the jug. It would catch and slide against my flesh with no warning, and every time it did it made my skin crawl like I'd seen a snake.

"He was trying to drown her," Nancy said. "Not just worry her some. He was out to drown his own sister in a tub of rinse water that had done had several loads of clothes run through it."

"Well," I said. "Maybe. But Maggie Lee got him loose from her with that bleach bottle."

"Had to hit him four times, Maggie Lee told Mama. Until Weldon forgot about Barbara Ann and looked back to see what was stinging him."

The chicken's head-shaped pine was coming up on the left, and up ahead through the heat waves rising off the highway whatever it was that was standing in the middle of the road hadn't moved a peg. It was there like it had been bolted to the ground by somebody with a big wrench, and he had leaned back hard and taken a couple of extra turns to make sure it was fastened for good.

"It's that young bull," I told Nancy. "That's all. See, I can tell it's got horns on its head." I turned my face sideways and squinted through an eye, and it did look like I could see something sticking up from the top of the dark bulk beyond the shimmering curtain of heat.

"Could be a hat," said Nancy. "Or some sticks tied to his head."

"Weldon don't do that no more," I said. "Tie things to his head with string. Not since Brother James told him it was what heathens did."

"He'd sneak off and do it," Nancy said. "I know he won't wear it to Sunday school or church no more, but he'd do it off in the woods or when he's off by himself walking the highways and roads."

I knew my sister was right about that, so I didn't say anything back to her. Weldon Overstreet would do one thing inside the Camp Ruby Baptist Church building and then another one just the opposite of it outside. Everybody knew that.

Like the time he began praying out loud for the boys on the battlefield and kept that up for several months each Sunday whenever the preacher would call for voluntary offerings to the Lord.

When we told Daddy about it, he said Weldon must have heard something about the war in Vietnam on the radio and it had caught his imagination.

"I expect that's not the last you church folks are going to hear from Weldon about the boys on the battlefield," my father said. "He'll be praying for them long after LBJ sends all those Vietcong back to their rice paddies. Weldon likes the sound of those words. Boys on the battlefield. It's got a ring to it."

"If he cares so much about them," I said, "why did he thump that soldier's ears in the Fain Theatre in Livingston, then? He did that until the popcorn girl had to call the deputy sheriff to make him stop."

"He held that soldier from behind with one hand and thumped his ears with the other one," Nancy said. "Delilah Ray saw him do it. Said that soldier's ears was as red as fire by the time Weldon got through with them."

"That Fain Theatre has been a major drawing card to Weldon Overstreet," Daddy said and laughed real big. "It seems to get him all excited and makes him want to do things. I think his daddy is still paying some every month for all those seat backs he sliced up that time in the Fain."

"You know what Weldon told them about that?" I said. "Said he liked the way the cotton stuffing popped out through the holes when his knife went through the plastic."

"It was a feature showing Weldon didn't care nothing about that time he got to using his pocketknife," Nancy said. "He didn't look back once at the screen after the first two minutes had passed, Delilah Ray said."

But that had been all talked about back in our house there across the road from Estol Collins's store, and right now there was something big up ahead bulked up in the middle of the highway.

I wanted a better look at it, and I wanted it before we got much further on up Farm-to-Market 1276.

"Hold this for a minute," I said to Nancy. "I'm going to try a trick way of seeing things way off."

"Just set that jug down on shoulder of the road," Nancy said. "It's not my turn to carry it."

She backed off with her arms close to her sides and kept a close watch on me as I found a smooth place to set the jug down. I understood and didn't blame her. Several times before she got old enough to be wary, I had tricked her into holding something for me and then run off at top speed, leaving her to carry it the rest of the way to wherever we were going at the time.

"It comes from a book," I said, setting the milk jug down and twisting it in the sand of the shoulder to make sure it wouldn't tump over when I let loose.

"You get down real low like this and look under the heat rising off the water and you can see whatever you're looking at a whole lot better."

"It ain't water. It's a blacktop highway," Nancy said, watching me lie down on the edge of the road in a push-up position to keep from getting burned on my bare chest and legs by the rocks and sand.

"Same thing, same thing," I said and tried to sight along the stretch of highway running up to the thing way off in the middle of it.

"Is not, is not," Nancy chanted. "Is not, is not."

What I had read in the book was right. I could see better under the heat waves rather than through them, but just as I was zeroing my sight in on the bottom of the thing bolted to the road ahead, it moved off at a pretty good clip to the left, and I lost it in the stand of pines it walked into.

"He's gone off the road," Nancy said. "Now he's hiding in the woods to jump out and catch us when we walk by on the way to Sleetie's."

"I doubt that," I said, hopping up and brushing my hands together to knock off the sand and gravel. "Since he had four legs that I counted."

"Did he?" said Nancy. "Was it four you counted? Don't tell me no story again, brother."

"Four," I lied. "I counted them. Nothing but a cow or Wylie Knight's bull."

"I hope that's what it is, all right," Nancy said. "I hope that thing's chewing on grass and leaves instead of quarters and nickels."

What she was talking about was Weldon Overstreet in church on Sundays, the way he would carry his money in his mouth while he waited for the collection plate to come around. If one of the younger deacons was passing the plate, he'd make Weldon take all the coins out and wipe them off with his handkerchief before he'd let him put them in the collection.

But I had seen times when one of the old men was in charge, Mr. Collins or Milton Redd, say, and Weldon would just lean forward in the pew and urp a whole mouthful of currency into the plate, spit and all.

"Look at that crazy thing," my mother would say, "mouth just full of money. Sit back in your seat and don't look at him, Harold. It just encourages him to try himself."

One Sunday, by the luck of the draw having to sit by Weldon, I couldn't hear a word of what Brother James was saying during his whole sermon because all the money hadn't come out of Weldon's mouth when the plate came by, and he sat there for the full hour rattling a couple of leftovers, pennies or dimes by the sound of them, up against his teeth on both sides of his mouth, top and bottom. I remember I kept wondering the whole time whether he had saved those coins back on purpose or whether they had lodged under his tongue or behind a molar when he leaned forward to puke his money into the pie plate coming through. I knew one thing, though. When Weldon's money hit that tin bottom it sounded different from everybody else's. More like a rock than metal. The spit did something to the sound.

"I wish it was a watermelon we were going after," I said to Nancy. "Instead of that old raw milk."

"I don't like to drink it," she said. "It ain't pasteurized. It's liable to give you rabies."

"Well, it don't cost nothing," I said.

"Ain't worth nothing, neither."

About then I stepped on a grass burr, not looking where I was going, and had to stop to pull it out of the sole of my foot. This time my sister consented to hold the milk jug while I operated on my foot, so I didn't have to find a safe place to set it. When I finished, we fought briefly over whose turn it still was, but the argument was mainly a matter of principle so it didn't last long.

"It's some buzzards up there," Nancy said, pointing toward where a sweetgum tree had fallen on the shoulder of the road several weeks back during a high wind. "I wonder what they're after."

"Maybe it's a rattlesnake," I said. "Or a piney-woods rooter."

"Naw," she said. "It'll just be a run-over armadillo."

I hoped against hope, but she was right when we got to it. The odds were in her favor by about a million to one, I knew, but it would have been nice to see something else dead on the road besides a swelled-up armadillo with its feet in the air and its shell worked over by bird beaks.

"Look how its tongue's stuck out to the side of its mouth," I said, leaning over to take a good close look at last night's kill. "That's just the way an armadillo will do the second it dies. Stick that tongue out like greased lightning. It's armadillo instinct."

"Frankie poked a stick at a dead one's belly last Wednesday and a bird flew out of its neck," Nancy said. "Living up in there."

"Oh, it was not," I began telling her. "You don't know anything. Birds don't live up inside dead armadillos. That's just a fool superstition. That bird was just eating around inside there after the thing was already dead."

I had already set the milk jug down again, well away from the armadillo for the sake of hygiene, and was leaning over to pick up a small piece of broken lumber that had bounced off somebody's truck there on the highway, thinking to use it as a surgical instrument on the dead armadillo, when the first bellow came.

He had hidden down behind a big pine stump left from when the highway department men had cut down the dead tree itself to keep it from falling on the highway in case a big wind came up. Nancy and I hadn't even noticed where we had got to on the road because of watching for what the buzzards were after, and when I looked up at the sound, Weldon Overstreet was about fifty feet away, standing flatfooted in the middle of the road with his head thrown back, yelling straight up into the sky like he was trying to make the noon-day sun itself hear him.

"Uh-oh," Nancy said and began to cry, "I knew you was lying about counting four feet on that thing. It's him, all right."

One of the straps on Weldon's overalls had come unfastened so that it was dangling, and I could see that the laces on his work-shoes were loose and he wasn't wearing any socks. His straw hat had fallen off when he jumped out from behind the stump and was lying in the road ditch propped up against a rock like the rock was wearing it. I looked at that hat so hard I can still see it today whenever I want to, that yellow straw with one side curled up so you could see the sweatband dark with where it had been around Weldon's sweaty head.

"We got to run," Nancy said. "Come on. Don't you bust that milk jug."

"No," I said, watching Weldon lower his gaze from that hot blue sky and look directly at me with a big smile on his face. "If we turn our backs to run, he'll catch one or both of us. We got to get on by him somehow."

"Hot," Weldon said, and then, "Woo wee. Y'all didn't see me then. Y'all didn't see me until I hollered."

And then he threw his head back and did it again. I could hear the echoes from it ringing on down through the woods on both sides of the road, bouncing off sweetgums and stands of pines and moving further off toward the creek bottoms and wetlands.

Weldon's face was as red as I'd ever seen it, clear from his hairline on down to where his neck was covered by his blue shirt and overalls, and it was glistening with sweat like it had just been rubbed with a wet dishrag. The shade of his face was an important thing. I knew it, and Nancy knew, and anybody living around Camp Ruby and acquainted with the Overstreets knew it.

"He looks just like fire," Nancy said, beginning to ease into a backwards shuffle. "He looks like he's fixing to have a fit any minute now."

"Don't you run back," I told her. "Listen to what I said now. Backing up won't do it, I flat guarantee you."

By this time Weldon had moved out almost into the exact center of the highway and was standing facing us with his arms stretched out like a human barricade. His fingers all looked the same length to me and as big as pork sausages dangling there from the palm of each plate-sized hand.

"Y'all are going after milk," Weldon yelled in a voice loud enough for a deaf man to hear. "Up at Miss Sleetie Cameron's."

The echoes came back from both sides of the road, *Cameron's, Cameron's, Cameron's*, like a Houston station fading out on the radio.

"Yeah, we are," I said, picking up the milk jug and reaching out to grab Nancy's hand. "We got to go and do it now."

"Y'all got to get by me first, you kids," Weldon yelled in a voice loud enough this time to spook the two buzzards that were perched in a dead tree waiting for us to get away from their armadillo. All three of us watched them flap off, slow at first and then catching an updraft, beginning to circle up and up into that blazing sky until finally they were just two black marks against the blue background.

"I wish I was a buzzard," Nancy said in a whisper.

Weldon had thrown his head so far back watching the birds rise up that I could see the roof of his mouth, pink instead of red, the lightest shade of skin I could see anywhere on his body.

"Nancy," I said out of the side of my mouth, "when I say so, you run toward that left ditch over yonder and I'll run toward the right one. That way he won't know which direction to jump and we can slip on by him to Sleetie's."

"Say it quick," said my sister. "Before I pass out here on the shoulder of the road."

"Now," I said, and we broke like a covey of quail in opposite directions, Nancy going to the left with her sandals slapping the pavement like rifle shots and me aiming for the far right ditch, the grass burrs I had been avoiding no longer a consideration.

We'd have both made it, too, if it hadn't been for the milk jug. It began to slip because of the sweat all down my right side and when I looked down to grab it with my left hand, I took my eyes off where I was going and stubbed my right foot against a sweetgum root and started to fall. As I did I got my left hand under the milk jug and turned sideways in the air as I went down in full gallop, sending the milk jug flying like I was deliberately trying to throw it up after the buzzards.

The sun caught it in its rise, and it glittered in the air like a block of clear ice in a blue lake. That's what took Weldon Overstreet's eye, and he went to his left like an outfielder after a line drive and speared it with one hand as it started down for the roadbed of Farm-to-Market 1276. With the other hand, he scooped me up and in what seemed less time than a lightning bolt I was opening my eyes about two inches from the side of Weldon Overstreet's head and looking deep into his right ear which I could see had a tangle of stiff red hairs growing right in the middle of it.

"Uh-huh," Weldon said, and I could feel his voice rumble all through my chest and stomach where he had me grabbed up against him, "uh-huh, I caught you and the milk jug both."

That close to him, the main thing that came to my mind was the way I was afraid Weldon was going to smell when I finally had to take a breath. I tried to push away from him with my free arm, the one that wasn't stuck under his, but when I did he just tightened up, and I took that breath I was dreading before I realized it.

It wasn't much at all, the smell, even hot and sweaty and worked up as Weldon was. It was like hot metal, maybe a pan that had been left out in the sun all afternoon and I had to pick it up and bring it in the house to wash. Just flat and even, not a stink to it at all.

I looked over the top of Weldon's head for Nancy and saw her about twenty feet away, walking back toward me and Weldon and the milk jug at a steady pace, her bangs down in her eyes and a frown on her face that made her bottom lip stick out.

"Run," I started to tell her, but about then Weldon cut loose with a bellow that filled up the pines and the yaupons and the sweetgums and the underbrush on both sides of the road, and my voice got lost in his and the echoes he set ringing.

"Holler," was what he was hollering. "Holler, holler, holler."

"Weldon Overstreet," Nancy said after about the eighth or ninth bellow, "quit saying *holler*, and put him down on the road."

She was standing right in front of him when I turned my eyes away from looking down into Weldon's mouth where all the noise was coming from, and she was reaching up to grab at the bib of his overalls to get his attention.

"Put my brother down and hush up that racket," she said in the crossest voice I ever heard her use.

"Nuh-uh, Nancy," Weldon said. "I ain't. I got him and the milk jug both. HOLLER."

"All right, then. If you won't, you got to pick me up, too," said Nancy and put her arms down stiff by her sides to be lifted up.

"Take the milk jug and don't let it tump over and bust," Weldon told her, leaning forward to hand it to her and then after Nancy had taken it and put it on the blacktop, sweeping her up in the air on his other side.

I didn't know anything to say. I just hung there, smelling hot metal and looking back and forth from the wad of red hair in Weldon's ear to the pooched-out lower lip of my sister.

"Hum," Weldon said. "Hot, hot."

"Yeah, it is," Nancy answered and twisted around to get more comfortable underneath Weldon's left arm. "Weldon," she said, "I know that wreck you had with your daddy's pickup wasn't your fault."

"No," Weldon said in a long drawn-out syllable and the woods came back with the same sound, "Noooo."

"I was coming to where the little road runs into the big road," he said, "and I looked and there wasn't nobody either way. No truck and no car. So I speeded up and put in the clutch just like Daddy said I was always supposed to do when I shifted them gears. It was to make them smooth. And then I turned the wheel to go to Livingston, but the pickup wanted to go straight off into the woods. And then the trees came up and hit at the bumper and the fenders and made the pickup stop and not run no more."

"I don't know nothing about shifting gears yet," said Nancy and threw her head back to get the bangs out of her eyes, "but I know it wasn't your fault, Weldon, that the trees hurt the pickup."

"I bumped my head when it happened," Weldon said. "It made the bleed come out and made a mark. Mama made me put a big bandaid on it. It was a sore place for a long old time."

"Where?" Nancy said. "Right there where the scar is?"

She reached out her hand and touched a finger to a white line right in the middle of all that red skin on Weldon's forehead and then she leaned forward and kissed the spot. Just a touch of her lips that made a little smacking sound in the center of that hot day on Farm-to-Market 1276.

"Now," she said, "I kissed it and made it well. Let us get down to go get our milk, Weldon."

"Harold's got to make it well, too," Weldon said and leaned his forehead toward my face. I never said a word. I just kissed that white spot, smelled metal, tasted Weldon's sweat, and felt the heat rising from his big red head.

"Don't drop this milk jug," Weldon said, setting us down and handing the jug to Nancy. "It's hard to find a bottle this big with a screw-on lid that fits it."

"We won't," Nancy said. "Come on, brother."

"I like to get off in the woods," Weldon called after us as we walked off on up the road toward Sleetie Cameron's. "I like to walk on to where there's a bunch of high trees. I like to see where the squirrels have their nests. I like to watch the squirrels play on the tree limbs. I like to lean my back up against a big oak tree. I like to let my belly rest."

"That bird was too living down inside that armadillo," Nancy said to me as we pushed on up the highway. "Just like Frankie said. It flew out of its neck when she poked it with a stick. It was alive inside that dead thing."

"All right," I said to my sister as we walked together side by side. "O.K., fine. Here, give me the milk jug. It's still my turn to carry it."

Bad Medicine

That one yonder is the head dog then?" said B. J., looking at the black and tan hound curled up in the dust by one of the sections of oak stump supporting the front porch of the house. It was getting on toward evening, and the long shadows of the afternoon sun fell across all of the dog but his head and part of one front leg.

"Yeah," said Uncle Putt Barlow, "he ain't gonna lie to you on trail."

As they watched, the sun-lit leg kept up a steady pawing motion at the red dust beneath it, maintaining a regular measured beat as though it were moving in time to some song that only the dog could hear.

"Why's he scratching like that?" said one of the other men standing in Uncle Putt's front yard. "Is he killing fleas?" The man was called Mr. Hall, he was up on the weekend from Beaumont for one of Putt Barlow's cat hunts, and he was wearing brand new clothes of a camouflage design: boots, trouser, jacket, and hat. The jacket had zippers, pockets, and openings arranged in symmetrical patterns all over it. Each piece of metal on the clothing was tinted dull gray to avoid giving any kind of reflection. Mr. Hall's boots had left perfect impressions of their tread wherever he had stepped in the skinned-off yard in front of Uncle Putt's double-log house.

"Naw," said Uncle Putt and leaned over to spit a big wad of Cotton Boll tobacco juice into the center of one of the boot-tracks Mr.
Hall had made. "He ain't scratching no fleas. Nor ticks neither."

He rolled the cud of tobacco from one jaw to the other and
looked over at the black and tan.

"Name's Elvis," he said. "I'll show you why."

At the sound of the words the hound flopped his tail in the
dust once and looked up at Uncle Putt from under the ridges of
tan markings over his eyes. He took a deep breath, expelled it with
a sigh and advanced three steps away from his spot under the edge
of the porch, ending up standing about eight or ten feet in front
of and facing Uncle Putt. Although the dog had come to a stand-
still, the front half of his body continued to bob up and down at
a rhythmical pace, first to the left and then the right, his forelegs
flexing and working, now and then one foot or the other leaving
the ground briefly to paw gently at the dusty yard.

"Why, I swear he looks like he's dancing," said Mr. Hall's friend
in a Gulf Coast voice.

"Can't help but do it," Uncle Putt said. "He's jitterbugging.
That's why he's named what he is. Elvis."

The circle of cat hunters watched for a while without saying
anything, until finally Elvis sat back on his haunches to scratch at
an ear. Even during this operation, though, he kept up a steady
movement, holding to his established rhythm and not missing a
beat.

"How'd you teach him that?" asked Mr. Hall, fumbling at one
of the zippers in his jacket.

"Didn't," said Uncle Putt. "Distemper when he was a pup left
him with that movement. It's a natural dance, that thing is. You
can't learn a dog nor a human being neither to do nothing like

that. You got to be give something like that. Just like Elvis Presley had a natural gift."

Uncle Putt spit again and then lifted a carved cow horn hung around his neck with a rawhide string to his lips and blew two notes on it. Elvis got to all four feet and increased the tempo of his beat by about a quarter, and three other spotted dogs came surging into the front yard from under the house, two yipping in high voices and one baying in a low mournful tone.

"That blue tick there," B. J. said to Mr. Hall, pointing to the last dog out from under the porch, "him with that low voice, you know what Uncle Putt calls him?"

"No," said Mr. Hall. "This is my first time to hunt up here with the old gentleman. Isn't he a character?" He smiled and pulled a hand away from one zipper on his jacket and made for another. "What is that speckled one named?"

"Johnny Cash," said B. J. "He talks so low on trail. The other one there is Johnny Ray because he sounds like he's crying when he's got something treed. And that one yonder, well . . ." B. J. paused and studied the fourth dog in the pack, a small blue tick with one ear gone and long scars running all the way from the tip of its nose halfway down its back. "Uncle Putt calls him a curse word which I can't repeat. I'm a Baptist minister, you understand."

"Why me and my wife are members of First Baptist in Port Neches," said Mr. Hall and stuck out his hand. "Pleased to be hunting with you, Reverend."

"Just call me B. J.," said B. J. "I'm just one of the boys when I get out in the woods."

"I hope you don't mind us taking a drink now and then tonight, preacher," said the other man, overhearing.

"No, no," B. J. answered him, looking over at the little man who seemed to have a basketball badly hidden under the front of his red plaid shirt. "It's not for me to judge the weakness of other folks."

"You fellers," called Uncle Putt from over by Mr. Hall's pickup truck-house trailer combination, "we got to get into the woods."

The vehicle was a Nomad Home-on-Wheels, and as Mr. Hall watched, Uncle Putt spit a load onto the rear hubcap and opened the door to the housing compartment for the dogs. The hounds swarmed the little set of steps that had flopped down as the door opened, Elvis jiving in the lead, and surged aboard in one big clot of black and tan and blue-tick spots, giving voice all the way in.

"I believe that's the first time they ever been in a house afore," said Uncle Putt and clicked the door shut, the pickup rocking back and forth on its springs as the pack tumbled from one side to the other of the living compartment. "I was kinda afraid Goddamn Son-of-a-Bitch wouldn't take to a place with beds and a stove in it."

"That's the name of the other blue-tick," B. J. said to Mr. Hall who stood with the corners of his mouth turned down and his eyes popped, watching the dogs fighting to get their muzzles up against each window in turn in the Nomad camper.

"You ain't got nothing in that little room to ruin their noses, have you?" Uncle Putt asked Mr. Hall.

"No, I . . ."

"'Cause if you have they ain't gonna be able to scent no bobcat." He paused to shift his cud of Cotton Boil and spit. "Hell, they couldn't smell skunk piss if you got something like loose cigarettes to eat or a opened sardine can for them to get into in yonder."

"No, I don't think so. I hope the dogs won't . . ." Mr. Hall paused for a minute. "Do nothing in my Nomad."

"They ain't gonna hurt theyselves if they ain't nothing loose," said Uncle Putt. "Let's get in the woods."

Uncle Putt directed and Mr. Hall drove, taking the Nomad down a series of logging roads, each one fainter than the one before. The last one looked as though it had not been used in a year. Pulpwooders had cut it long before, and except for occasional hunters and lost berrypickers, the last real traffic had stopped a decade ago. Pine saplings up two and three feet grew in the space between the ruts, and three or four times B. J. and the man in the red plaid shirt had to dismount and pull fallen timber out of the roadway before the pickup could go on. Each time they did, the pack of cat hounds in the living compartment broke into a storm of baying, the deep bass of Johnny Cash setting the tune and the high clamor of Johnny Ray picking out the melody.

Whenever it happened, Uncle Putt would spin around where he was sitting crammed up against Mr. Hall and hammer on the rear of the truck cab, cussing the dogs by name and spraying Cotton Boll fumes over the side of Mr. Hall's head. Mr. Hall had broken a good sweat under his camouflage suit and was beginning to feel increasingly nervous about the cat-hunting pack swarming in among all the portable beds, canned goods and kitchen utensils in the Nomad living compartment.

"They certainly are lively," he remarked at one point to Uncle Putt just after the old hunter had called Goddamn Son-of-a-Bitch every kind of a goddamn son-of-a-bitch for causing a major collapse of several objects just behind the heads of the people riding in the pickup cab.

"Yeah," said the old man, "they having a time. I believe they purely love being in that little house back yonder. Just listen at them tussling with one another."

About then, the dim logging road petered out completely in a burned-out clearing covered with blackened pine stumps, waist-high huckleberry bushes and saw-briers. Mr. Hall killed the engine, and everybody unloaded and began looking around in the rapidly fading light. The tops of the long-needle pines were already disappearing into the night sky, and by the time Uncle Putt had let the dogs out of the back of the pickup there was barely enough light left to make out details in the burned-over clearing.

"So this is the forest primeval," said Mr. Hall's friend and lifted a pint of whiskey to his lips.

"What did he say?" asked B. J.

"He reads a whole lot," said Mr. Hall, switching on the light in the rear of the Nomad and cautiously sticking his head inside to estimate the damage. It wasn't as bad as he thought it would be and he came out in a minute, smiling, and reached for the whiskey bottle.

"He says things like that all the time. Gets them out of books."

"Uh-huh," said B. J. and checked the action of his .22 rifle. Satisfied, he set it against a stump and began watching Uncle Putt tying a rope around Johnny Ray's neck. He had finished with the curse-word dog and Johnny Cash, and Elvis waited on his haunches near the old man, patiently bobbing and weaving in time to the music only he could hear.

"Some people question a Baptist preacher hunting," B. J. announced to the clearing, "but the reason I like to come on cat-hunts with Uncle Putt every year about this time is to get out into nature and look around for signs of God."

Nobody said anything. The book-reader took a measured sip of whiskey.

"You can sense His presence out in the woods like this," B. J. went on. "He talks to us in the movement of the breeze and the motions of the animals."

"You fellers," said Uncle Putt, getting the last rope tied and beginning to fiddle with the carbide light attached to his hat by an elastic strap, "get your pants stuck down inside your boots. They're crawling tonight, and I don't want to have to call off my dogs to take one of y'all to the hospital for snake-bite."

He let the four dogs pull him toward the thicket at the edge of the clearing and called back over his shoulder. "I'm fixing to cast these here dogs now, and when y'all hear Elvis sing out, come a running with your lights on."

"How'll we know it's Elvis and not one of the other ones?" asked Mr. Hall in an anxious voice and zipped something.

"Don't come for the other ones. They just background for Elvis. He got a pure sweet voice. Starts up high and then comes way down low."

The pack of hounds reached the thicket, whining, and the darkness closed around Uncle Putt two steps behind them. The beam of his carbide light bobbed for a few seconds through the dense brush and was gone.

"What kind of snakes?"

"Well, up on the ridges it's rattlers," B. J. said to Mr. Hall. "Timber rattlers mainly, but I have seen a diamond-back now and then. And if the bobcat takes the dogs down into the river bottoms, why you can run into water-moccasins along in there."

"I sure hope not," said Mr. Hall and turned toward the glow of his friend's cigarette end. "Where is that Old Granddad?"

B. J. walked away from the Nomad toward the far edge of the clearing. "I'm just going to step over here and listen to the woods. See if I can hear the Master at work."

When he came back from taking a leak and perusing the night sky for signs of order and regularity, the two men from the Gulf Coast were squatting in front of the headlights of the pickup making sure their boots were firmly fastened. Those poor fellows are depending on the courage that comes from a bottle, B. J. said to himself, and are afraid of the natural creatures God put in these woods. And one of them a declared Baptist. He ought to be ashamed of himself.

"I tell you what scares me," he said loudly, and the book-reader jumped. "It's not the serpent that crawls on his belly in God's forest." B. J. paused, and both men straightened up in his direction, blinking in the beams from the headlights. Mr. Hall had tied the ear flaps of his cap under his chin tight enough to cut into the soft flesh of his throat, and when he turned to look at B. J., the material of the cap strained under the pressure.

"No," said B. J., "it's not the rattler who warns you with the sound of his tail before he strikes or the moccasin who hisses before he bites. What I fear is the serpent who stands on two feet and comes in the night with no announcement to take your goods and the lives of you and your family."

"Oh," said Mr. Hall's friend. "You're talking about sin."

"Not exactly," answered B. J. "I'm talking about communists and hippies and doped-up colored people." He clicked the safety on and off the .22 rifle and reached in his pants pocket for the box of hollow-point cartridges. "What you might call the physical presence of sin. That's what I mean."

"You get many of them up here in these woods?" asked Mr. Hall and coughed because of the tightness of the strap fastening his hat to his throat.

"Well, not yet," B. J. admitted. "But, you see, I live in Corpus Christi. I'm just up here up to preach at the Big Caney graveyard working on Sunday. Where I'm talking about the communists and dope-fiends being is down in the cities. That's where they do all their crimes."

Mr. Hall switched off the pickup's headlights and the clearing plunged into darkness again, so total this time that it was a half a minute until B. J. could make out the difference between the tree line and the night sky. He could hear Mr. Hall's book-reading friend pull the cork from the bottle of Old Granddad in the silence and then make a swallowing sound.

"Was that a dog bark?" the man asked.

"No," said B. J. "You'll know when they start up." He paused for a minute. "But speaking of dogs, you fellows ever hear of Christian Guard Dogs, Incorporated?"

"What did he say?" the book-reader asked Mr. Hall. "Christian dogs?"

Before Mr. Hall could say anything, from the direction in which Uncle Putt had plunged into the thicket came a drawn-out high pitched howl, softened by distance but definitely touched by a good measure of hysteria. It hung in the air above for a few seconds and then was joined by another sound, lower in tone and divided into a series of chopping notes.

"Goddamn," said one of the Gulf Coast citizens. "Excuse me preacher. What's that?"

"That first one's Johnny Ray," said B. J., "and the other one is the curse-word dog. They've hit a cat track."

The racket started up again, and within a few seconds was joined by another voice, this one beginning with a high note, descending the scale a space, hesitating, going back up for the first note, reaching it and then a bit beyond, and suddenly sliding rapidly all the way down to an ultimate bass where it held for three seconds, chopped abruptly off into silence, and then began the whole sequence all over.

"That's Elvis, and he's hot," B. J. said, fumbling with the elastic strap on his carbide light. "That's how he talks when he's close on to one. Uncle Putt says he sings just the same way Elvis Presley does in that old 'Don't Be Cruel' song."

B. J. got the carbide light fastened around his head on the outside of his cap, hit the switch, and the chemicals began to fizz and pop, sending a weak beam of light through the reflector which grew stronger and reached its most intense at about the time he plunged from the clearing into the thicket, his rifle held chest high.

"Hold onto what you got, and let's go," he yelled back at the two lights bobbing behind him. "We want to get there before they tree him."

Heading as best they could toward the sound of Uncle Putt's pack of hounds, the three men moved through the pine thicket, stumbling over fallen logs and underbrush, catching their rifles and pieces of clothing on saw vines and creepers, stepping into rotted-out stump holes with brackish water in the bottoms, and trusting to the pale white light of the carbide.

At one point B. J. came to a brief open space and called back over his shoulder to Mr. Hall and Norman, twenty or thirty yards behind, making thrashing sounds as they tore through a clump of saw briers and scrambled in turn over the trunk of a fallen sweetgum nearly four feet in diameter.

"Lord," he said, "don't you love this? I can just sense the eternal presence of God in this thicket."

But the cat hunters from Beaumont seemed to be too busy to answer, so B. J. spoke a couple of words in his heart to the Master and turned back toward the sounds of Elvis and Johnny Cash, louder and more impatient now as they got closer to what they were after.

In another ten minutes, B. J. reached the crest of a small hill covered with a stand of virgin pine and looked back at the two lights bobbing behind him, working their way slowly up the rise against a tide of huckleberry and yaupon bushes. Mr. Hall was saying something to Norman in a ragged voice, but was having a hard time making himself understood because of his need to pause for a deep quavery breath after every word he uttered.

"Come on," said B. J. to the carbide beams, "they're just across this next little creek. I can see Uncle Putt's light, and I can hear the dogs real good."

The sound from the cat pack was now a storm of howls, bays and yips, compounded by the noises of the dogs crashing through the underbrush lining the bed of the creek as they worked the scent of the bobcat not a hundred yards ahead. Now and then came a faint yip from Uncle Putt himself as he urged the dogs on by name, calling out encouragement to Goddamn Son-of-a-Bitch and Johnny Ray mainly, trusting Elvis to take care of business by himself at the head of the pack.

B. J. launched himself down the hill full-tilt, crashing through brambles and sliding on pine straw, the light from his carbide light jerking from earth to sky to water as he struggled to catch up to the action. By the time he splashed through the knee-deep creek and reached the other bank, the voices of the cat-pack reached a new tone, one deeply touched with urgency and hysteria, and the progress of the dogs slowed, sped up for a few yards and then stopped altogether.

"He's treed," B. J. yelled back toward the men following him, just now reaching the creek and beginning to slow down for the crossing. "Look up yonder at the light on the sweetgum."

When B. J. arrived at Uncle Putt's side and tilted his head back to allow the carbide beam of his lamp to shine up into the limbs of the tree which the bobcat had been forced to climb, the pack of dogs at its base was swarming around the trunk like a school of gar fish. Of the two men behind, Norman came up first, just in time to see Goddamn Son-of-a-Bitch run up the bole of a fallen sycamore leaning toward the trunk of the sweetgum with no hesitation as though he expected to be able to sink his claws into the bark and scramble up the tree after the bobcat.

At this maneuver, Johnny Cash and Johnny Ray went beyond madness to a new state, baying with every breath, and beginning alternately to dig at the ground at the foot of the sweetgum and to claw at its bark as high up as they could reach. Elvis moved away three or four steps and sat back upon his haunches, peering up into the clusters of leaves and branches where the carbide lights jerked in little starts and twitches as the four hunters looked for the red eyes of the bobcat.

Every few seconds the head dog barked in a low regular tune to keep the cat notified he was indeed treed, his dancing front legs moving in a quick measure, fairly close in rhythm to the beat of "That's All Right, Mama."

"Yonder he is," said Uncle Putt as a beam of light picked up two blood-red fiery points about halfway up the sweetgum just above where a large limb intersected with the trunk. "He's grinning at us."

"Where? Where?" said Mr. Hall, the light from his carbide lamp wobbling from one side of the mass of leaves and branches to the other as his head shook with his heavy breathing.

"Yonder," said Uncle Putt and held his light steady on the face of the bobcat. "See them tushes? That thing'd eat a feller up."

"What do we do now?" asked Norman, staring up at the animal and stroking the basketball-shaped belly under the front of his plaid shirt gently with one hand.

"I'm half a mind to climb up in there and punch him out in among these here dogs."

Elvis groaned deep in his throat at Uncle Putt's words and increased the time of his jitterbug step close to that of "Jailhouse Rock."

"But he's a big un," the old man continued, "and I'm scared he might cut one of them boosters up pretty bad." Uncle Putt directed his light down at the pouch on the front of his bib overalls and drew out a cut of Cotton Boll tobacco. He bit off a good-sized chunk and threw his light back up into the bobcat's eyes. "Yeah, I reckon one of y'all's gonna have to shoot him on out of there."

"Which one of us gets to shoot him?" asked Mr. Hall in an eager voice, spinning around to look at Uncle Putt so that the carbide beam of his lamp shone on the old man's face.

"Y'all got to settle that for yourselves," said Uncle Putt and held up a hand to keep the light out of his eyes. "It ain't nothing to me. Just aim for one of them eyes."

The bobcat in the fork of the sweetgum had just made a spitting sound at the three dogs clamoring at the base of the trunk and B. J. had cleared his throat to enter the negotiations about who was to get to shoot when the first voice came from across the creek:

"You palefaces leave that bobcat where he is."

"Yeah," said somebody a little further down the creek bed from the first, "don't any of you fuckers shoot up in that tree."

"Lord," said B. J. and dropped his rifle into the darkness at his feet as though it had become suddenly red-hot, "who is that? Niggers?"

"I don't know," said Uncle Putt, aiming the beam of his lamp toward the trees and brush across the stream and beginning to lift his .22 to his shoulder. "But I'm gonna see."

The light picked up nothing but a mass of leaves and sawvines and hardwood trunks, and the first voice spoke again. "Old man," it said in deep tones which sounded definitely foreign to B. J., "you better lay that rifle down if you don't want your dogs shot full of arrows."

Clear on the opposite side of the sweetgum where the bobcat was treed somebody laughed in a high cackle which cut off abruptly in the middle.

"Oh, Jesus," said Mr. Hall and moved up a step closer to Uncle Putt, "I knew it was a mistake to come out here in these woods. Yvonne tried to get me to stay home."

"What?" said Norman. "What?"

Uncle Putt moved up between Johnny Cash and Johnny Ray and leaned his rifle against the hole of the sweetgum. He stepped back to where he had been, and the dogs stopped barking for a minute, sniffing at the discarded .22 and whining as though puzzled. First one, then all of the pack sat back on their haunches and looked up into the sweetgum toward the bobcat, hidden in the darkness now that the carbide beams on the men's hats had dropped to head level.

"Don't shoot no arrows into none of my dogs, niggers," said Uncle Putt, directing his beam into the thicket across the creek again.

"We ain't niggers," a voice from a different location announced. "We are a war party of the Alabama-Coushatta, and this is your personal Little Big Horn, palefaces."

"Right," said the first one who had spoken. "You have done fucked with our totem, our brother the bobcat. Now you're going to have your famous last stand."

The high cackling laugh broke out again from behind the sweetgum and kept on for a full half minute this time.

"I wasn't going to shoot him," said Norman to the darkness, facing one direction and then shifting to the other. "Look, my rifle's empty. It's not even loaded." He held the weapon so that the beam of light from his carbide lamp shone on it and then jerked his hands away and let it fall to the ground in front of him.

"Here," he said, "you can have these shells." He fumbled in his pocket for his box of cartridges, found it and threw it toward the creek. It made a splash and a tinkle. "We was going to let the preacher shoot the bobcat, me and my buddy was. I mean that sincerely."

"Wait just a minute," B. J. spoke up. "I'm not here to kill anything. I just come out into the woods to study nature and praise God."

"A preacher," said one of the war party. "That means they got to have some whiskey with them."

"Hey," called another voice from a new point of the compass. "We want your firewater, palefaces."

"Here it is," Mr. Hall volunteered, pulling out what was left of the pint of Old Granddad and taking the new unopened one from Norman. "Here's all the whiskey we got."

"Put it over there on that sycamore trunk," somebody said, and Mr. Hall moved to obey, his carbide light jiggling as though he had fever. "Don't throw it in the creek like the other dumb fuck did to the shells."

"A bunch of damn reservation Indians," Uncle Putt said. Elvis whined deep in his throat and barked once at the sweetgum. Two of the other dogs had flopped down to pant in the dead leaves and pine needles, and the other one, Johnny Ray, was lapping water out of the creek.

"Naw, old man," said the first voice that had spoken, "we just come in off a buffalo hunt, and our medicine's been bad."

"Shit," said Uncle Putt and spit a stream of tobacco juice.

"Hush, Uncle Putt," said B. J. "Don't get them mad at us."

"That's right. Listen to the preacher."

"Blessed are the peacemakers," said the Indian who had been doing all the laughing and then he laughed again.

Encouraged, B. J. spoke up. "Now what that young man just said shows you all have gone to Sunday school. Now, is this right? I ask you."

"Shut up, preacher," said somebody across the creek, making snapping noises as he moved through the brush. "We been to Sunday school and we also have seen that video, what's it called, He Who Watches Films?"

"*Deliverance*," said He Who Watches Films and sniggered.

"That's right. It's all about what you rednecks do to one another when you get off in the woods together."

"Palefaces are a nasty bunch," somebody else said.

"Disgusting," came an answer in what sounded to B. J. like a put-on English accent.

"Brave, though."

"You got it," said the first voice. "Tell you soldiers what. We as the Alabama-Coushatta war party want all y'all to take off all your clothes. All them camouflage jackets and boots and them suspenders and Fruit-of-the-Loom jockey shorts and all the rest of it."

"Oh, no," said Norman and began to sob, having seen the video and read the book, too. "What? What?"

"Don't worry, corporal," said the voice across the creek. "We ain't going to cornhole you. We ain't rednecks."

The laugher cackled again and called out: "But our necks are red."

"That sounds like a song. Our necks are red, but we ain't rednecks."

The war party began to guffaw and shake bushes, and up in the sweetgum the bobcat moved down to the next lower limb. Elvis stirred in the dead leaves and whined.

"But back to business," called the voice from across the creek. "After you palefaces get naked, call your dogs off our brother bobcat and haul ass out of here."

Mr. Hall and Norman were already pulling at their clothes, unzipping and unbuttoning as fast as they could in the wavery light from the carbide lamps, scattering garments as each piece came free. In a second B. J. joined them, bending over to untie his boots and almost tripping over the rifle he had dropped when he heard the first voice coming out of the thicket.

"You too, old man," the leader said. "What are you? Some kind of a guide to these fuckers? Get your overalls off, and all of you put your stuff in a big pile. And preacher . . ." the voice paused. "You the biggest man of the bunch, looking at your light. The war party wants you to carry everybody's stuff out of these woods. I mean all of it. We don't want you to leave a single damn paleface thing in these woods."

"Except for the firewater," said somebody, and the rest of them laughed.

"What about their little headlights, chief?" said the voice behind the sweetgum.

"Y'all can wear them on out of here. You look like a bunch of one-eyed men from Mars with them things on anyway."

By this time Uncle Putt's pack of hounds had noticed the bobcat's progress back down the tree and had surged forward to bay at the base of the sweetgum again, only Elvis lagging back a little.

"Shut up them dogs, old man," said the main speaker. "We got arrows trained on them just aching for their blood."

Uncle Putt kicked the last leg of his overalls loose from a foot and began tying lengths of cotton rope around the neck of each dog. "Come on, dogs," he said to the cat pack. "Let him go. Let's get the goddamn hell out of this thicket."

"You tell them, Davy Crockett," said one of the war party and let out a series of high-pitched yips.

Stripped to his carbide light and boots, B. J. leaned over to scoop up his and the other's clothes and rifles, and found it difficult to get everything balanced on one arm while he loaded with the other. A jacket fell off one side as he was feeling around in the dry leaves for a shirt, and somebody's rifle slipped loose when he began to straighten up.

"One of you men help me," he said in the direction of a carbide beam, and the person behind it backed off.

"They said for just you to do it," Mr. Hall warned in a shaking voice. "Uh uh. They might put an arrow through me."

"Goddamn it," said B. J., "come on and help me get out of these fucking woods."

"All right, preacher," said Mr. Hall in a shocked voice and began draping clothes over B. J.'s outstretched arm. Norman had already started off, close in the wake of Uncle Putt and the four dogs, his light veering neither to the right nor left.

B. J. and Mr. Hall caught up within fifty yards, branches and vines slashing at their bare chest and legs like switches as they ran, but they didn't feel a thing. When they reached the top of the ridge paralleling the creek, they could hear sounds of splashing and yelling behind them as the war party waded across after the whiskey. They didn't look back.

Lord, prayed B. J. as he stumbled after the men and dogs in front of him, his arms dead from the weight of the clothes and guns he was carrying, you got to forgive me for taking your name in vain, but there was a whole host of devils all around me. Just get me home. Out loud he called to the naked cat hunters fleeing ahead of him:

"You got to let me tell you about Christian Guard Dogs, Incorporated. It's just this kind of thing they're a real use for." Nobody slowed, and nobody answered him all the way through the moonless thickets back to the burned-over clearing and the Nomad camper parked in the middle of it. The only sound was that of Elvis in the low bushes, moving in a steady jive.

The Angler's Paradise Fish-Cabin Dance of Love

obby Shepard smelled bad. He could tell it himself as he leaned over to push the head of the mop up under the table in the kitchen area of the fishing cabin. It was the third time he had gone back over the linoleum on the floor with a mixture of water and ammonia, and from what he could tell, not only did the dun-colored covering still look as stained and nasty as it did when he had started cleaning four hours ago, it also seemed to be dissolving at various points into small fragments from the power of the ammonia. Everything looked a whole lot more damp now, though, and he figured that was an advance.

The one-room structure did smell different, too, from the large amounts of cleaner and disinfectant and insect repellent Bobby had sloshed around, so much so that a steady stream of tears had been dripping down his cheeks for more than an hour. He paused in his mopping to rub a worn-out T-shirt across his face again, wincing as the cloth irritated his inflamed nose through which he had given up trying to breathe soon after he had started the ammonia treatment of all exposed surfaces in the house.

Despite having switched to puffing in air through his mouth, Bobby could still detect the powerful funk being thrown off in all directions from his body, and he made a mental note to pay extra special attention to deodorizing himself all over in every crease and cavity when he finished with cleaning the fish cabin and turned to the problem of personal hygiene. Bobby remembered from his youth how funny older people smelled to teenagers, anyway, even in a cleanly condition, and he was determined not to offend on the olfactory level. A good hard scrub with a mild bar soap, say Ivory, and a shampoo with a moisturing balsam-based hair product, followed by a heavy spraying of scent-free men's deodorant—Mitchum, maybe, certainly not one of those heavy types with a musk odor—should give him good protection and make his physical aura as inoffensive as it could be, given his age location in the middle years.

No way you could hide the evidence of time's passage, completely, of course, from the sense of smell. Bobby knew that and had to live with it. Standing in line, say, at a checkout counter in a grocery store, he might find himself waiting behind an older woman with another one with a cart behind him, pushing at him with the front end of it so she could start stacking her stuff on the conveyor belt well before it was her turn. The woman in front of him wasn't even finished yet, and here he was with his pile of canned goods and egg plant and onions and what-have-you not even being processed yet by the checkout girl with Edna or Barb or Debbi on her nametag, and the old biddy behind was already nudging away at his butt and the small of his back with the steel edge of her carrier.

And then he would yield finally to the steady pressure of the wire shopping cart chewing away at him from the rear and take a step forward, moving despite himself into the smell-field of the woman ahead with her eyes fixed on the numbers Edna or Barb or Debbi was ringing up, as though she were watching for a signal from God about how many days she had left to live on this earth. Standing there paralyzed and rooted to the floor, that smell rising off of her saying old, old, old, no matter how much Secret or Mum or other old-lady deodorant she was using to try to mask it. All those gray years swarming and seething and working beneath the chemicals.

So smell, that was the first thing he knew he had to tackle and try to defeat when he had decided to do what he was going to do with the fishing cabin on Smith's Point, the last one still standing on that bend of the Gulf of Mexico in the group of eight that had once been the destination of people from Port Arthur and Winnie and Orange and Port Acres and wherever else weekend fishermen used to live in the Golden Triangle of Texas.

It had been a long time ago when Arden Hooks's Angler's Paradise was a going concern, however. It had reached its heyday in the late fifties back before everybody from the level of apprentice oiler in a refinery on up to foreman came to own his personal boat and a pickup truck to pull it around with. As soon as the price of enough horsepower in an outboard motor to push a boat got down to where a man could buy him a rig in installments, the Angler's Paradise on Smith's Point was doomed. These days, you could hardly even find what was left of the old road to it anymore, especially considering what Hurricane Audrey had done to that section of the coast back in the sixties.

Bobby himself hadn't thought of the fish camp in years, in fact, though for a while back there he had spent probably every other weekend in one of Arden Hooks's little cabins, drinking Ancient Times bourbon at night and waiting for enough daylight to come so he could get out on the water in one of Arden's little green boats with a twenty-five horsepower Johnson churning behind.

That experience was gone and had been gone, and it wasn't until he had that dream that the scene of the fishing cabins clustered at the edge of the Gulf rose up before him again. But when the vision came, it arrived as though he had opened a door and discovered himself staring directly into the molten center of the sun. And it had settled into his mind like Portland cement hardening into stone. There for the centuries, no matter how high the tide rose or the wind drove or the rain beat down.

In the dream, Bobby Shepard was sitting in his BarcaLounger, the chair magically transported from his living room in Port Arthur where it always rested before the Sony Tru-Image to a new location in the center of a one-room cabin in Arden Hooks's collection at Smith's Point. The back of the lounger was tilted partway into the reclining option, but not so far back that Bobby was at full repose. He was relaxed, certainly, the muscles of his neck and back not needing to maintain any flex to support himself, but not kicked back so far that he was in danger of feeling the urge to drift into slumber. At ease, but alert was the way he remembered his posture as being in the opening sequence of his dream, when he went over it later in his mind and when he jotted down notes on paper so he could keep the events intact and whole against the onslaught of living in reality in the everyday world.

Music was playing at a low decibel level as the scene opened up, much like it does at the beginning of a movie after the credits have rolled by and before the real action kicks off. The performer was Jimi Hendrix, Bobby recognized immediately, but his guitar was not wailing and he was not screaming directly into the ears of his listeners as he always seemed to be doing in the clips from the music festival appearances Bobby had seen over the years on television. Instead, he was stating over and over again in a soft, deep syrupy tone, "I won't do you no harm, I won't do you no harm, I won't do you no harm."

Before Bobby Shepard, in the cleared space his BarcaLounger occupied in the fishing cabin, all eight members of the Thomas Jefferson High School Cheerleading Squad were standing in a single line, their maroon and gold pompoms shaking to one side and then the other as they spun, dipped, and twisted in elaborate dance, precisely in time and on the beat as they worked every note

and nuance of Jimi's repeated chant. Sometimes forward, sometimes back, sometimes left, sometimes right, high up, low down,
but precisely together in every patterned movement, the squad of
young women swayed, turned and dipped, their individual gazes
burning and fixed as one on Bobby's face as he reclined at ease in
the best chair in the house.

Lulled by the insistent rhythm of Jimi Hendrix's chant and the
moist murmur of his guitar, Bobby allowed his eyes to close for
a second, and when he opened them with a start, desperate not
to miss a single step of the Angler's Paradise cabin dance of the
Thomas Jefferson High cheerleaders, he could count only seven of
the squad still at move before him, one somehow vanished from
his dream of perfect choreography.

There was no let-up from the hypnotic power of Jimi's song,
however, no matter how strongly Bobby struggled to maintain the
concentration of his vision, twisting from side to side in the hold of
the BarcaLounger and drawing deep draughts of air into his lungs
in an attempt to fight off his doze. Inevitably, battle though he did,
the lids of his eyes would slowly drift shut, and when he forced
them open again at great cost to his fading energy, another of the
cheerleading squad would have vanished with no evidence of her
ever having taken part in the fish-cabin dance of his dream.

At last, their number had dwindled to two, a petite blonde
with string-straight hair and eyes the color of an empty Coca-Cola
bottle, and the other the head cheerleader with the kinky dark curls
and the languid hip thrusts, each occurrence of which added a soft
boom, like distant thunder over the Gulf of Mexico, to the music
Jimi Hendrix played.

Bobby Shepard, with his last waning strength, began turning
his hands inward and attempted to lift his arms toward his face in
order to prop his eyes open physically to preserve these last two

before him, but his muscles would not function and his bones would not move and the lids of his eyes slid together once more, touching closed for an instant until he forced them open briefly again by sheer will.

Left alone in single dance in the center of the fish-cabin floor was the final cheerleader, Celia Mae Adcock, her dark hair floating above her head in twisting curls, the rhythm of her movements in strict time to the increased beat and decibel count of Jimi's wailing guitar and guttural shout.

"The last," she said in a deep voice like that of Kathleen Turner's in any love scene from one of her early movies, "shall be first."

"What's the matter, honey?" his wife Myrlie had asked in the bed beside him as Bobby sat bolt upright, groaning and shaking as though in fever chill as he tried to prize his eyes apart with both hands. "Did you have a nightmare that something was going to get you?"

"No," Bobby had said, listening to the sound of cool air pounding through the vents of the dark bedroom and out on the Beaumont highway a clot of trucks laboring through each of their many gears. "It wasn't no nightmare. It was just a dream, just a dream. Go on back to sleep."

Bobby stopped mopping and straightened up, leaning a little of his weight on the wooden handle as he looked about him at the one room of the fish camp cabin. It couldn't get any cleaner, he decided, at least on the floors and walls, not unless he used a blow-torch to sear over every surface, and he didn't have the time or energy to try that. Or the faith, either, he considered, sniffing at first one armpit then the other. It might just set fire to everything and burn down the last cabin left still standing from the original Angler's Paradise. Then where would he be?

The bed, though, he thought, balefully regarding the metal

frame and stained mattress against the far wall of the room, now that I have to do something about, for sure. The red marks all over it are mainly just from rust coming off the frame in all this humidity over the years, and that wouldn't bother me none to lie down on, especially with a sheet or some kind of cloth pulled up over it. But now, a young girl like that curly-headed one, she might think it was where somebody drunk or sick had nastied up the bed or something. She wouldn't want to lie down on that, not even for a nap, whether it was covered up with a nice clean sheet or not.

"A mattress," Bobby Shepard said out loud in the empty room, his words ringing hollow in the enclosed space. He had not spoken aloud until then, during the whole day and a half he had spent mopping and scrubbing and deodorizing and spraying for insect life in the cabin, and his own voice had become strange to him. Too loud and abrupt and a little hurried somehow in its delivery, and he thought he would try it again, this time in a lower register and at a slower rate.

"A mattress," he said again, cocking his head to judge how what he was saying might be received by a person other than himself. "A new mattress," he uttered, curling his lips and tongue around the words to soften and smooth their delivery. Better, at least a little bit. "With a plastic cover nobody's ever slept on." He tried the combination again, then a third time, and then again. By the time he had practiced making the sounds for several minutes and judging them critically as they fell upon his ear, Bobby was fairly convinced anybody who might have happened up, say outside the door of the cabin, and chanced to hear what he was saying would have believed they were listening to a regular person, who talked to other people on occasion or at least knew how to, and who was saying his piece aloud in a perfectly normal way.

He practiced for a while longer, maybe as long as half an hour, before his throat started getting tired, and he had to stop to drink some water from the gallon milk jug he had brought with him from Port Arthur. Standing near the table, his thirst slaked and the mingled odors of ammonia, Raid, and air freshener rising around him, Bobby looked slowly around the room from point to point, item to item, doorjamb to window, oil cloth to nail hole, bed frame to kerosene stove, paint fleck to water stain, from smallest detail to largest feature of the cleansed and cleared space where soon the head cheerleader of Thomas Jefferson High would be performing for him the Angler's Paradise fish-cabin dance of love.

A SEAGULL HAD MADE a bombing run over the new mattress tied to the top of Bobby Shepard's Thunderbird right before the turn-off to the ruins of Arden Hooks's Angler's Paradise and had scored a direct hit just at the point where two lines would intersect if drawn from top to bottom and side to side of the Beauty Rest. But Bobby had chuckled to himself, unconcerned, when he saw the bird swoop and then stall above as it hovered to lay its load.

The nasty mess would have done no harm to his purchase, Bobby knew, since he had covered the mattress with clear heavy-gauge plastic taped down for the trip. The fact the gull had hit its target was nothing but further demonstration of the careful planning Bobby had put into the project and a certain sign that by thinking ahead about any and everything that might go wrong a man could make a dream a reality.

Bobby had sat down for long hours. He had pondered, he had studied, he had put questions to himself that scared him even to conceive of, much less to force himself to answer. And he had undergone this searing self-examination in the service of a final conclusion that he could only sense was somewhere out there before him, waiting like a stalled eighteen-wheeler in the middle of a one-lane road at the heart of a Gulf Coast fog bank.

But he had kept his mind in gear, he had refused to touch the clutch, and he had maintained a steady pressure on the accelerator which fed fuel to the engine of his dream.

And by so doing, he had been allowed that insight which only his gut told him was out there and which his mind could only shrink from. When the fog cleared, its last wisps of gray whipping away as though in a sudden coastal gale, the stalled eighteen-wheeler sat there not as an immobile obstacle which would rip apart the vehicle of faith and daring in which he rode. No, its rear door opened as if by signal, shining ramps extended to receive the wheels he drove, and Bobby Shepard steered his perfected Thunderbird of thought up into the protection of steel-sided and be-roofed certitude.

He knew.

And what he had come to know was this: when a man fails in the endeavor to realize his joy and hope, it is because he loses himself in the need for the goal, in the end of the accomplishment, in the love object itself. Thus his forgetfulness, his ignoring of details, his slighting of process and way. Thus his doom; thus his loss.

And it was this reasoning that led Bobby Shepard to put to himself the painful questions, the second-guessing of every decision, the humbling of himself before the smallest and grossest of each material detail, the learning of and the discipline to a deep patience.

If he had had the space of weeks, days and hours commensurate to the depth of his devotion, Bobby would have spent a year deciding on the brand of mattress alone. He would have driven to Houston to Mattress Warehouse Discounters simply to compare colors and coil count. He would have flown to New Orleans to browse the aisles of Maison Blanc for designer sheets and pillow cases, to Dallas to shop for dust ruffles at Neiman Marcus.

But Bobby Shepard lived on a Pure Oil gauger's salary in this world and in the Golden Triangle of Texas with its side streets and the driveways to many of its dwellings still made of oyster shells, its sidewalks unpaved except right downtown where no one ever went anymore anyway, and its atmosphere a rich brew of congeners, carcinogens, humidity, and high levels of ozone. The air much of the time looked faintly blue. It smelled tartly addictive. In the summer, a rain shower came each day for thirty minutes, beginning precisely at two o'clock in the afternoon, except during hurricane season when all schedules became irregular and nothing could be counted on.

Steam would rise for an hour from the pavement of the streets and all flat surfaces and roof tops, after each shower had ended, and to a person caught outside during the rain, the water felt as warm as a hot bath, and did not refresh.

Therefore, Bobby Shepard shopped at the Wal-Mart on Oleander Boulevard in Port Arthur for all that was needful to prepare the last remaining fish cabin at Angler's Paradise at Smith's Point for its true and fit purpose. The choice of name-brand products there was wide and varied, and it was from this stock he chose that which would be visible to a consumer. The Beauty Rest Magic Coil. The floral sheets with matching pillow case. The ruffled window dressings. The stressed-polyethylene patio chair, collapsible and imprinted with representations of hermit crabs and tiny sea horses. The case of Classic Coke in small bottles. The canned ham from Denmark. The four-pack of herbal-flavored Pringle's chips. The quart jar of fat-free salad dressing. The box of floral-print Kleenex tissue.

It was only with the products not evident to the eye that Bobby stinted. And these he purchased not solely with a view toward economy. The cleaning materials, the insecticides, the room deodorizers, the oils and polishes, all these Bobby subjected to a nose wary and experienced in the manufacture of chemical vehicles, reagents and catalysts, and none was selected, regardless of cost, unless its appropriateness and potency was certified by sense of smell. If it did not speak of origin in a prime first-run barrel, the unguent, ointment, stripping agent, buffing compound, color enhancer or anti-coagulant was passed over, no matter how cheap its price or minor its mission in the transformation of the last standing structure at Smith's Point into the Angler's Paradise Fish-Cabin of Love.

BOBBY SHIFTED DOWN to first gear to maneuver the Thunderbird around a water-filled hole in the road ahead, leaning forward to peer closely at its edge as he approached. One of the few times he had driven the one-lane shell road on a supply trip during the first week, he had let the right front wheel come too close to a similar hole and had dropped what felt like over a foot, bringing the car to a lurching stop. He was afraid he might have broken a tie rod, but hadn't, luckily, and he had learned from the experience not to trust anything on Arden Hooks's abandoned road that was covered with water.

Managing to miss this hole, he steered toward the center of the road and felt a twinge in his back just above his right kidney area as he removed his hand from the gear shift knob. No way he could sit in the bucket seat that it didn't hurt him.

He had to give her credit, he thought to himself. Celia Mae Adcock had caught him with one hell of a kick, even though it was through the seat back itself and therefore cushioned from most of its force. It was the heavy-toed shoes she wore, he knew, and the fact that she exercised all the time to be able to cheerlead that accounted for the lasting effect he was suffering.

It was a good thing the drug, whatever the capsules were his wife kept in large amounts in the medicine cabinet, had begun

phasing in so strongly when it did. Otherwise, the head cheerleader
of Thomas Jefferson High might have kicked him in the small of
his back so hard and so often on the trip from Port Arthur that his
kidneys would've been permanently damaged. Might've ended up
making water through a tube run up into his privates long before
old age put him into a nursing home with all the attachments they
hooked up to you in a place like that.

It was just the one good one she had got off, though, he thought,
looking through the rearview mirror into the backseat where she
lay snoring and pretty much covered up by a silver-colored ground
cloth purchased from Wal-Mart. Before she got groggy enough
from that medicine to doze on off and stop all that lamming and
jerking and kicking around was when she had landed it. And curse?
Lord God, where did a beautiful young girl like that dressed up in
a maroon and gold cheerleading costume learn all those bad words
she had called him?

Actually, Bobby considered, as he drove on at a steady, though
slow, pace through the afternoon sun toward the fish camp, he did
know all the nouns she had used. He had heard them delivered in
his direction before lots of times. It was the modifiers, as Old Lady
Chambliss had called them back in senior English class, that had
puzzled him after she had gotten into the Thunderbird and begun
to feel sleepy. Asshole, O.K. Cocksucker, yes. Shithead, naturally.
But what was a rimjobbing such and such? What did it mean when
somebody called you *poncified?*

She couldn't have learned all those bad words off of TV. Bobby
had cable, the extended sixty-four channel package, and he looked
at each and every one of them, late night, that might show naked
women with men or with other women and even once out of an
open-access outlaw deal in Matamoros, Mexico, two women with a
small donkey and a border collie. They never talked much, anyway,

the people working on each other on those shows. They just tended to business, got the job done and never looked up.

Maybe that stuff she knew how to say Celia Mae Adcock had picked up from having to go to school with blacks or Chicanos or Hispanics or whatever they called themselves these days, and it was not really the language a squad of cheerleaders would use among themselves. Bobby hoped not. He hated to think of girls that looked the way they did, their hair all washed and shining and springy and their skin like brand new, freshly extruded latex just out of the machine, standing around in their costumes calling their boyfriends rimjobbing cool dudes and primo slitlappers.

It was a puzzle, and it was deeply bothering to Bobby, that kind of language, dropping from those lips, and he shook his head hard as though to clear it of such profanity as he drove the Thunderbird down the narrow track between the banks of palmetto and sawgrass and scrub pine.

Two more hard rights, he told himself, then that little swale and another half-mile, and I'll be able to see the water and we'll be there, me and her in the backseat in her cheerleader's outfit with the applique megaphone and the four gold stars sewed on it to show she's the head one. She's Celia Mae Adcock. She stands in the middle of all of them and starts up every yell by clapping her hands together three times and saying all by herself while the rest of the cheerleaders wait, "O.K.," clap clap, "Let's go."

Bobby stood breathing hard in the middle of the one-room cabin, winded after all he'd been doing: untying the mattress on the roof of the Thunderbird, getting it inside the building and its plastic covering all taken off, laying it as fairly square as possible on the bedstead (The frame was not a standard size. He had been afraid of that.), placing the floral sheets on the mattress and the case on the pillow and using a hospital tuck to get everything smooth and tight, wrestling the snoring Celia Mae Adcock up and out of the backseat of the car and walking her inside to lie down on the mattress and sheets as the first person ever to touch them in their role as a bed, unloading everything else from the trunk of the car and putting these things where they belonged with the rest of the stuff already there in the fish cabin, and finally looking around him in a slow revolution as he turned at the center to face each aspect of the scene of his creation in its proper and duly appointed place.

He wanted a cigarette. Bad. But he would deny himself that reward, as he had been doing for the entire week before this day, not knowing what Celia Mae Adcock's response might be to the smell of smoke on his clothes and person, much less the reek of smoker's breath.

He knew she hadn't noticed him or his hygenic condition or anything else in her fish-cabin surroundings as she walked in earlier from the Thunderbird, through the door and toward the pristine Beauty Rest waiting in the middle of the room. She had moved like a drunk being led to a bathroom to puke, her eyes half-closed and her mouth semi-open as though poised in anticipation of action to come, not resisting his aid in her progress at all. In fact, Bobby had been touched by the way she leaned against his shoulder as she proceeded, lifting her feet an extra amount as if she were being presented with a series of eight-inch high wooden blocks she had to step over in her path, though he knew, of course, it was the drug working and not Celia Mae Adcock being friendly on purpose that had led her to accept his help and guiding hand.

As he sat in the plastic lawn chair worked with the hermit crab and sea horse design, watching her lie on her back with her arms perfectly straight down by her sides and listening to her snore at the ceiling, Bobby considered how all events had conspired so well back at Drake's Drive Inn. He still couldn't believe how everything had come together at a little after three o'clock in the afternoon, each part joining up with the one next to it as though machined and polished by a master tool pusher in a Texaco lab.

There was a lesson in it for the thoughtful man, and Bobby promised himself there in the fish cabin where Celia Mae Adcock herself lay dreaming in the full costume of maroon and gold that at a later time when he was calm and unflustered and conditions were right he would figure on this conjunction of events and puzzle out what the larger meaning might be. He owed it to himself to understand. Never before had the details of an event in his life seemed to speak to him in one voice, and he would be a fool not to listen. Maybe if he could comprehend this one thing and how it came to be, he could know how to do next time, get a streak going, find a pattern that worked and just lay it over the rest of his life like a template.

Why, for example, had it come to him that very morning to take apart the blue and yellow capsules in Myrlie's medicine cabinet, pour their granulated contents into a plastic baggie and stick it in his shirt pocket? He hadn't planned that. It just announced itself to him when he saw the label on the bottle picturing a woman sleeping on a cloud bank with a big smile on her face.

Then, after his shift ended at the refinery and he had gotten in his forty hours for the week, and was off for seventy-two, Bobby had decided to choose that afternoon to pick up the Beauty Rest and transport it to Smith's Point. That very afternoon. A real hot day, such a scorcher he had felt like he needed to stop by Drake's Drive Inn on the way out of town for a big cup of root beer slush, which he could have just as well picked up at some place on the coast highway itself, and not had to go out of the way to Drake's to get it. But he hadn't done that, even though he had been afraid somebody might have seen him parked at Drake's with the mattress tied to the roof of the Thunderbird and started giving him shit about it. Jess Hardy, maybe, or Toppy LeBlanc, stopping by for a shrimp burger or ice cream cone after their shifts and catching him looking like a Mexican on moving day with furniture tied to his car top.

But Bobby had chanced it, run the risk of being hoorawed by dumbshits, all because of his loyalty to Drake's, the watering hole of his youth and the hangout of Thomas Jefferson High kids for over forty years, and it had paid off, just as though another of the smoothly polished parts of the machine under construction had clicked snugly into place as he drove up, thirsty for his root beer slush.

Because there she was, in full costume. Her lower lip was stuck out, she was jiggling a set of keys in her hand as though she was trying to decide whether or not to throw them up against some wall, and her mass of black curls was floating above her head with a life of its own.

Bobby Shepard felt a sudden jump in the middle of his chest like a small thing afraid, but he pulled the Thunderbird in beside the Buick anyway, marveling at how his hands knew to kill the engine, put the transmission into Park and engage the emergency brake all on their own without his having to tell them a single step in the operation. "Hello there," he heard himself saying out the driver's window. "Where's the rest of your outfit?"

Still jiggling her keys, Celia Mae Adcock turned her head slowly and looked at Bobby as though she had just been spoken to by one of the two-by-fours supporting the roof overhang of Drake's Drive Inn or by a double order of fried onion rings.

"You're looking at it, mister," she said deliberately. "That's all there is."

"No, no," Bobby said, shocked and apologizing, "I didn't mean what you're wearing, your cheering outfit you got on. I was talking about the other girls, the rest of the TJ cheerleaders. Them other ones."

He stopped talking, but his lips continued to move in a series of dry clicks as he tried desperately to think of another way to identify the people he meant by the use of spoken language. "The ones," he said, "the ones you got to tell how to do when y'all are out there on the field."

"That's what I'm trying to figure out," Celia Mae Adcock said, shifting her clump of keys to the other hand. "They knew to meet me at Drake's, but you can see they're not here."

"No," Bobby said, carefully looking up and down the whole range of the front structure of the building as though the seven missing girls in the maroon and gold of TJ High might have managed to conceal themselves successfully on the premises, maybe behind the menu board, and were about to jump out and yell surprise at him. "I sure don't see a one of them."

"And this old car of Daddy's won't start back up," Celia Mae said, "because the battery's dead or something, and I haven't got a cent of money with me to call him, and Heather's supposed to have brought me my purse."

"Huh," Bobby said, thinking to himself that the madder Celia Mae got the more her hair seemed to want to puff up and swell over her forehead. It looked to him two inches higher than when he'd first pulled the Thunderbird up under the Drake's Drive Inn service shed.

"Listen," he said, wondering what he was about to say to the head cheerleader, "I'll loan you a quarter to call your daddy, and while you're doing that I'll buy you a root beer. I'll be glad to."

"Make it a diet Sprite," Celia Mae said, sticking out her hand toward the window of the Thunderbird, "with extra ice. Large."

As Bobby stood by the serving window of Drake's and watched Celia Mae Adcock work the pay phone at the far corner of the parking lot, the gold satin of her cheerleader's underpants softly shining beneath the maroon of her skirt as it broke over her high-set behind, he could feel the plastic baggie full of dope for sleeping give a little jerk in his shirt pocket. Moving in tiny fits and starts from one side of its enclosure to the other, the baggie rubbed against his chest hairs hard enough to make them tickle as though a drop of sweat was rolling down from his collarbone toward his left nipple.

"Which one of these drinks," he said hoarsely to the woman waiting on the other side of the counter for her money, "is the diet Sprite?"

"Why, what do you think?" she said in a cross voice. "The clear-looking one, of course. The one that ain't root beer."

"Thank you," Bobby Shepard had breathed, turning reverently toward the car with the plastic-wrapped Beauty Rest mattress tied to it, the drink cups held before him like chalices and the plastic baggie moving in a slow squirm in the pocket above his heart. "Oh, thank you."

HE HAD THOUGHT the worst time would be when she first came to, there on the Beauty Rest covered with the floral sheets, and that if she was going to lose it completely it would be then and there at that first moment she opened her eyes and saw where she was. Not riding along in a vintage Thunderbird sipping at a large diet Sprite and ice and starting to feel so sleepy she couldn't hold her head up, but lying on her back in a one-room fish cabin looking up at the ceiling where dirt-dauber wasps had put mud nests in every corner and along the sills of each window right up to the edge of where the wood ran out.

Bobby Shepard hadn't even noticed the clumps of gray mud hardened into a material as tough as concrete until he was sitting in the plastic chair worked with a sea horse and crab design waiting for Celia Mae Adcock to rouse from her nap, and he would have sworn he had cleaned every surface of the cabin thoroughly. That's what comes of just looking down at the floor and worrying about mopping it, he had thought to himself, instead of lifting up your eyes once in a while to see what might be above head-level. Too late to do anything about it now, he had concluded, but one thing was comfortingly for sure: Celia Mae Adcock wouldn't get her feet dirty from walking on the floor, wood or linoleum part either. Bobby had scrubbed it to a state of sterility.

But he had been mistaken in his dread of the instant when the head cheerleader of Thomas Jefferson High would wake from her doze and realize the strangeness of where she was and undoubtedly start screaming and crying in stark terror, convinced that great harm was about to come to her from the man sitting in the light blue high-impact plastic chair with the sea creature motif worked all through its surface.

He had anticipated the look Celia Mae would have on her face. Horror, fear, unreason, all mixed up into a compound announcing her intention to break from the hold of the Beauty Rest and run in any direction. What might slow her down, he had asked himself, and delay her going so mad with fear she wouldn't be able to listen to any calming words or assurances from him, but just simply flee for the outdoors like something caught in the woods, run into the walls like a trapped bird?

Bobby Shepard thought long, he thought hard, he turned on a battery-powered boom box programmed to play the same song over and over as Celia Mae lay in her stupor, lost in the drug-induced dreams of a head cheerleader of one of the most powerful high schools in the Golden Triangle of Texas. That musical offering, purring away in the tape drive, was Engelbert Humperdinck singing "Delilah" again and again directly into her ear.

Surely, Bobby felt, that hymn to the mystery and power of a woman able to conquer the strongest man in the Holy Bible would feed into Celia Mae's unconscious mind, delivered as only Engelbert could bring it, and soak into her head a message of appreciation and awe for the kind of prime high school senior she was. It would show her, even while she was asleep against her will, the nature and depth of feeling the man who had captured her and brought her to the fish cabin was capable of. Whether she was interested in that fact or even cared to know it, she would have to hear it. Engelbert, chanting his tribute to her kind of woman over and over, would bring it on home.

When Celia Mae woke up, she woke up fast. Her eyes popped open, she sat up in bed, the brand new floral sheet cascading from off her uniformed chest to reveal the maroon and gold applique of megaphone, stars and bright letters, and she put both hands to her head and began to fluff her hair.

"What," she said, looking not toward Bobby in his chair or about her at the one-room space of the fish cabin, but at the boom-box beside her pouring forth "Delilah," "is that shit on the radio?"

"Engelbert," Bobby said, swallowing hard and instinctively tensing to run toward the door should Celia Mae suddenly come flying at him with her fingernails held out, "Engelbert Humperdinck."

"Is that a name?" Celia Mae said, still working at her hair with both hands to get out the tangles and the telltale signs of bed-head. "Or something you'd call a retard?"

"He's a vocal stylist," Bobby said, still poised on the edge of the sea horse and crab chair, enough so that the plastic was cutting into the underside of his thighs. It would leave deep red marks, he knew, and it was already putting his feet to sleep. "He does what they call romantic ballads. Or did. He might be dead by now, I don't know."

"Right," Celia Mae said. "Sure. Where's the eject?" She leaned over the edge of the bed and began punching buttons on the boom box, hiking up her cheerleading sweater as she turned to do so, high enough that Bobby could see a flash of bare skin. Something twisted a little somewhere deep in his belly, and he felt as though a meal he had really wanted when he was eating it was announcing now that it might be deciding to come back up.

"It's got a mark on it," he said. "It says E on top of the button."

Now Celia Mae Adcock was examining the Engelbert Humperdinck cassette and reading the words on its label out loud. "*Engelbert Sings Tom Jones: Smoky Bars and Dark Cabarets*. Now who's this one? Tom Jones. He must be using a consumed name."

"Tom Jones sung all them tunes hard, kind of hard-sounding like," Bobby said. "Then Engelbert he made them pretty."

"Hadn't you got anything else?" Celia Mae said, tossing the cassette toward the foot of the bed where it bounced high into the air off the new Beauty Rest mattress and then landed on the floor with a rattling sound. "Why hadn't you got a CD player?"

"Yeah," Bobby said, ignoring the question about the nature of his music system, "I got some other ones. Jimi Hendrix. Jim Morrison. Elvis."

"I've heard that last one's name," Celia Mae said. "But I don't want to listen to him. Haven't you got anything by somebody that's still alive? What about Spent Wad? Love Straddle? Tattooed Babies? They got a new CD out. Tattooed Babies does. *Kiss It Where I Can't Reach*. You heard it? It reminds you of early Suck Puppy. Totally bad."

"No," Bobby admitted. "I guess I missed that one." He was right. His left foot was asleep because of the way the sharp edge of the plastic chair bit into his thigh muscle. Maybe it was destroying a nerve, he thought, and shifted to allow his weight to favor his left buttock. I ought to stand up, but what if she does, too, then? Will she think I'm fixing to try something and then come at me?

A scene rose up instantly in Bobby's head of Celia Mae Adcock hopping off the Beauty Rest, holding the boom box in one hand by its antenna, and charging toward him with the same look on her face she always had when she was beginning the first part of one of the yells in the Thomas Jefferson High arsenal. Determined to do it, to do it loud, and to get a big audience response.

It would be one of the newer yells, not like the ones from Bobby Shepard's own days in high school, say one like T-rah, E-rah, A-rah, M-rah, T-E-A-M, team, rah, rah, rah, but a shorter, punchier one, a yell that showed the influence of minority-group presence in the student body. Probably the one that made all the kids go crazy at TJ High football games these days, the one that urged "Whomp'm up-side the head, whomp'm up-side the head" in a strange and varied tempo just a hair off the beat.

"I'm about to stand up," Bobby announced clearly, "to stretch my legs."

"So?" Celia Mae said. "I'm about to locate 98 Rock on the FM band of this old radio if I can find it." She pushed a couple of buttons, twirled a knob and looked about her finally at the interior of the fish cabin's one room as a rap song began to pour from the speakers.

"Where am I?" she said. "What is this crappy old place?"

"It's a," Bobby began and then paused for a space, still half-crouched before the blue plastic chair, his left foot tingling from the pinched nerve he had suffered while sitting and watching Celia

Mae Adcock snoring away amid the floral sheets, "it's a kind of a resort."

"Really? Is it a beach out there?"

"Yeah," Bobby said. "It sure is."

"Is it in Mexico? Is it Cancun?"

"Well, no," Bobby said. "It's at Smith's Point. Arden Hooks's Angler's Paradise, what's left of it. This here cabin's all there is."

"Well, shit," Celia Mae Adcock said and hopped off the bed into a slightly spread-eagle stance with both fists planted on her hipbones just at the point where the top of the gold pleats began on her cheerleading skirt. "You mean to tell me you slipped dope into my Sprite and only just hauled me as far as Smith's Point?"

"Well, yeah," Bobby admitted, "my old Thunderbird sure wouldn't go as far as some place in Mexico. Not even to Matamoros. I wouldn't trust the transmission."

"Smith's Point," Celia Mae said and began striding around the room in big steps with her hands still balled up into fists. "Smith's fucking Point. Why, we used to come down here sophomore year to make out and smoke grass. Didn't you like know that?"

"No, I sure didn't."

"But we outgrew all that old stuff. What did you think you were doing, Mister, hauling me down here in that old hot car with the sticky seats? Did you think I was going to put out for you at Smith's Point in a damned old shack? I mean, really. Like forget it!"

"I never thought nothing like that at all," Bobby said in a shocked and strangled voice. His left foot was almost back to normal, but he felt like he needed to stomp it on the floor hard a time or two to restore feeling but was afraid to try it. What if Celia Mae thought he was acting mad at her or working himself up into a loner's rage?

If she did, she might shift into a Far Eastern martial arts stance and, using one of her hard-soled black shoes, put his lights out with a spinning roundhouse kick. At the mere idea, Bobby touched his hand to his mouth and patted at his front teeth through the flesh of his lip, assuming as he had his whole life that someday somebody would turn them into a handful of bloody Chiclets. Not yet, please Lord, not now.

"What did you want to do with me, then?" Celia Mae said. "Besides giving me a dope headache. What'd you put in my diet Sprite, anyway? Downers? That's what the fuck it feels like."

"I didn't go to make you feel bad," Bobby protested. "I just wanted to bring you out here to the Angler's Paradise and get you to dance some."

"Dance?"

"Yeah, you know. Dance a dance. It come out of a dream." Bobby shrugged his shoulders up to earlobe level and took a step backward, favoring his left leg to lessen the danger of full pressure causing it to fold and send him sprawling to the scrubbed and sterilized floor of the fish cabin.

"Dance a dance?" Celia Mae Adcock said back to him. "What kind of a dance you talking about?"

"Well, I didn't have nothing particular in mind. I just figured you could make one up. Just do, you know, whatever come to you."

"To that music?" Celia Mae said, pointing toward the boom box as though indicating to someone new in a strange location where not to step. "The kind of tune you had on when I came to while ago? Humperdump, that old retarded dude, his stuff?"

"Humperdinck," Bobby corrected softly. "Engelbert Humperdinck. No, not him. That wasn't the one I had in mind for you to dance to. I just had his tape playing for sleeping music while you was still knocked out."

"That's a relief," Celia Mae said. "Not that I would've done it. I can just see me trying to find some kind of a beat to shake my butt to in that old moaning and groaning. No way, Jose."

"Like I said," Bobby reassured the TJ High head cheerleader, taking another step back to increase the range between his incisors and Celia Mae's footwear. "I wasn't planning on Engelbert's music none for you to dance to, not a bit."

"Like I should hope not," Celia Mae said and began doing a set of deep knee bends, expelling a chuff of air at the end of each repetition. "What then?"

"What music?" Bobby said, observing her surging up and down like a piston in the clear space of the floor.

"Yeah, what music?" Celia Mae said in a tone that sounded to Bobby as though she was trying to imitate the way he sounded when he was talking and at the same time make fun of it.

Bobby cleared his throat, careful to make a good thorough job, really getting some breath behind it, and tried to speak from his diaphragm like Clark Gable does as Rhett Butler in *Gone With the Wind*.

"Jimi," he said forcefully, "Jimi Hendrix, singing 'Purple Haze.'" As he said the words, he could see Jimi working the strings on his left-handed guitar, squeezing the notes out through the amplifier and speakers and forcing them to hang in the air like colored smoke, his huge mouth dropped open like a gar fish.

"My main man," Bobby added in a voice brought down as low as he could get it. Not too shabby, but not nearly as gravelly and dark as Rhett Butler could make it whenever he felt the need to, time after time, depending on the female he happened to be addressing.

"Everything you think about," Celia Mae Adcock said, pausing in the squat position in one of her set of knee bends, "is just real old, isn't it? I've noticed that about what all you say."

"Old?" Bobby said in his normal voice. "Jimi Hendrix? He don't never get old."

"I'm not going to argue with you," Celia Mae said, "I learned not to, because it never does any good with people your age. Forget it."

Her knee-bend set complete, she was now moving into a stretching exercise which required that her feet remain planted straight ahead while she twisted her body sharply from side to side as though trying to face the opposite direction without letting her lower half know about her plans. In the ongoing process, Celia Mae's midriff was again flashing into view at the division between her skirt and her head cheerleader sweater, and Bobby averted his eyes from the display in dread. Good God, what if she misinterpreted and took offense? Thought he was trying to look up underneath.

"Suppose," Celia Mae said, speaking first to one side of the fish cabin, then to the other as she put her body through its paces, "just suppose I was to go on ahead and do a dance to that purple phase song you been talking about. You know, make up some moves and shit. Then what?"

With the last statement, she brought her gyrations to a sudden and full stop and stood facing directly toward Bobby Shepard where he had gradually backed himself over the last few minutes as far as he could go without climbing all the way up on the table biting into the back of his legs and barring his further progress.

"Then what?" Bobby repeated weakly in a voice far from that of Rhett Butler's in resonance and weight.

"Yeah, then what? What you going to want then? You going to want to like do the deed and stuff?"

"The deed?" Bobby said. "The deed?"

"Duh. Yeah, the deed," Celia Mae said, her eyes settled as steadily in Bobby's direction as two dark stones. "You gonna get all wound up from watching me work and want to bump uglies?"

"You mean," Bobby said, extending both arms in front of him, palms in the position a man might hopelessly assume while trying to fend off a hail of lead about to come his way from a shotgun pointed in his direction. "You mean . . ."

"I mean," Celia Mae said in a level tone, "after all the dancing's done, are you going to want to fuck?"

"Oh, no," Bobby Shepard said, "no."

"That's what I figured," Celia Mae said and bent forward to shake her shoulder muscles loose in the cool-down phase of her calisthenics session. "Ho-kay. You got anything to eat around this shack?"

Bobby slid away from the table and moved toward the area of the fish cabin where a sink and a kerosene range used to be. "It's a whole little ham," he said, pointing toward a cardboard box full of provisions. "In a can. It's from Denmark it says on the side of it. And some bread from a bakery, not out of a plastic bag."

"Nuh-uh," Celia Mae said. "I don't need the fat calories. It's a Wendy's in High Island with a salad bar. We can stop there afterwards."

"Afterwards?" Bobby said, looking mournfully at the brightly colored ham-shaped tin can in the box.

"Yeah, after I get through dancing. Crank up Jimi Hendrix. Let me see what the dude's got."

"A twelve-pack of Classic Coke," Bobby began listing, his gaze still fixed on his cardboard box. "Some Nutter Butters. Two packs of Old Slim's Spicy Beef Jerky, a double Tastee Cake."

"Yeah, you eat that junk while you watch," Celia Mae Adcock said. "I got to get back to Port Arthur in time for the Rainbow Girls meeting tonight. I got to do a committee report."

"A committee report?" Bobby said, cueing up "Purple Haze"

and beginning to tear at the plastic of a beef jerky package with his side teeth. The covering was slick, and his teeth slid on it and couldn't find a purchase. Still gnawing, he moved toward his special plastic chair, careful to give Celia Mae plenty of room to find her place to start.

"Uh-huh, about the visit we all made to Moms and Pops in Need. It's for old people who're broke and don't have nothing. We cheered them up."

"'Scuse me," Jimi Hendrix began to wail from twin speakers as Celia Mae Adcock, the head cheerleader for the Thomas Jefferson High Yellow Jackets, stamped one foot, lifted both arms above her head and went into her first move of her ad hoc fish-cabin dance, a hip-hook to the left which caused the satin insets in her maroon skirt to flash a golden shimmer in a highlighting beam of late afternoon light, "while I kiss the sky."

Bobby Shepard, his eyes popped as wide as he could make them, leaned back in his colorful seaside chair, chewed his first salty bite of jerked beef, and prepared to watch that evening sun go down.

A Perfect Man

I have always thought if you live the right kind of life you wouldn't need to pray. To my way of thinking God would already know what you need, anyway, and He would've already figured up how much he was willing to part with to satisfy you. And if it wasn't enough, according to your way of calculation, for you to make do and get by on, well just lump it, then. Like Arnold is always saying, suck it up and bear down.

After all, God is a perfect man. That's what it says in the Bible, I forget which verse and whether it's Old or New Testament, but somewhere in there one of the prophets or wise men or apostles lets it out that we are made in His image. Which means, of course, we look like God but only real bad copies of Him. Say like a Hummel figurine made in Korea instead of in Germany where the real ones come from.

You're going to say wait a minute, though, Mrs. Arnold Dowden, you said perfect man, right? And then I'd answer back, if we were sitting down together talking where we could see each other's faces as we did it—maybe in my kitchen across the table or in yours, but of course I haven't seen your kitchen and don't even know, naturally, if you've even got one. You might live in a studio apartment, or in a cave in the woods, or even be as homeless as one of these bag people you see everywhere you go these days. I don't know your situation. How could I?

Anyway, I'd say yes, right, I said a perfect man, and if you're a woman reading this, you'd come right back at me like this here. "I never have seen a perfect man. I don't even believe there is any such a thing." And then me, I'd say "I did say God. I did say that," and before you could get the words out of your mouth to contradict what I was saying about the nature of being a man, I'd go on a little further and say something that would slow you down and satisfy your curiosity to argue.

"I know," I'd say, "I know. There is no such a thing as a perfect man. There's good ones, there's fine ones, there's ones you could trust with your grandchildren's insurance policies, but of course none of them's perfect enough they don't need a woman to tell them how to do and what's what now and then. Not even God, if he really is a man, perfect or not, and I believe on the Bible He is because that's what it says in there, not even God," I'd say, "doesn't need a little advice from the female side of His nature one time or another."

That would do the job, I imagine, what I just got through saying that I'd say if you raised any objections, and you'd be able to sit back in your chair and enjoy your coffee right there at the table in my kitchen out of one of my set of blue mugs. Or in your kitchen, if we were there. Whatever.

So I didn't start in to praying every fifteen minutes of the night and day when I heard the news that morning right after the *Today Show* got on over with. I did pray some, of course, just a short little address to the Lord, but I let Him know He needn't get concerned with me fixing to begin launching pleas for help every time the clock ticked. He's got plenty to deal with overseas and everywhere here in America, especially California and the East Coast, without having to listen to me say the same thing over and over while he's sorting out plagues, pestilence, and moral breakdowns worldwide. And whatever Michael Jackson and Madonna're up to next.

Besides, I said to myself while I was sending that first one on up and out of the house toward Heaven, maybe through the window or maybe right through the roof itself, who is to understand how it gets to Him, a prayer, I mean. We're not talking about telephone wires and satellites and fax machines and e-mail, you know. He got messages from folks long before anything was invented to communicate at long distance. When you're talking to the Lord it just happens right there in His mind the second you're saying it, best way I can figure, and doesn't need to depend on the manner of conveyance.

So I told myself, He knew already, the Lord did, what I was about to ask for help on. The very second Archie reached up under the front of his T-shirt to pull that pistol out of the bellyband of his pants to use to hold up that Sac'n Pac on the Stephensville highway, the Lord was on to it. He knew what time it was (two in the morning), He knew what I was doing at the very minute my youngest son was breaking a commandment (I was sleeping), and He knew how that whole thing involving Archie and me was going to turn out and also who'd win every presidential election to come and every Superbowl, too, if He wanted to think ahead about such things. I don't expect He ever does, though. He doesn't enter into deciding the outcomes of trivial events like sports and politics.

That's why I get so disgusted when I see football coaches praying for victory during some old game. God doesn't give a hoot who makes how many touchdowns and whose side they might happen to be on. Let the Devil tend to sports, I imagine He says. I'm running a universe here. I've got to stay focused.

So I wasn't surprised when I heard what Archie had to tell me on the telephone at nine o'clock in the morning, but I've got to admit when I heard his voice at that hour, it took me back a little. He's never been one to do anything in the morning—get up, put on his clothes, eat breakfast, look for a job, nothing—before time for lunch for an ordinary person, but here he was, talking just as clear as a bell like he was full awake. And he was, of course. Being in a cell with a bunch of old drunk men and thieves and the kinds of trash they have in there had got Archie's complete attention.

Not much ever has before. So I figured whatever it was that had my boy inspired to speak up clear and alert had some up-side to it. Couldn't all be bad.

"Mama," he said, "this here's my one call they're letting me make out. See, you got to come down here and get me loose just as quick as you can."

I knew what that meant. I've watched plenty of TV shows and not just the made-up ones, neither. I prefer documentaries and news and real-life *COPS* and emergency response programs that act out what happened just like it was when it really took place. A little girl falling through the ice in the winter time, say, and a passerby saving her with a long stick, or a little boy whose mama had slipped down into a diabetic coma and him knowing already how to dial 911 and not even old enough to go to nursery school yet or graduate out of training pants. Some program like that, that's what appeals to me. The truth, see, with a capital T.

Anyway, when Archie said what he did, I knew he was behind bars talking on a pay telephone and the only thing that puzzled me right at the moment was that he had had a quarter to put in the slot to make the call. Maybe they gave them one to use for the telephone and then made their families reimburse the County later, I figured. A person who will get himself locked up does not think ahead to consequences, I can tell you, not even so much as to have a quarter in his pocket to call for help, so I answered that little question to my satisfaction right while he was telling me the first few words he said. He had borrowed the twenty-five cents, I decided, from somebody in charge.

"What have you done, Archie?" I said. "What have they caught you up to?"

"Nothing," he said. "Just showing the girl behind the counter at Sac'n Pac the pistol V. M. asked me to hold for him."

"V. M.?" I said. "You mean Francine Beasley's V. M.?"

"Yessum, and the girl she took it wrong."

"Took it wrong, huh?" I said. "I guess that little Sac'n Pac girl took you seriously, didn't she?"

"She ought not to have. I was just showing out, and here they have gone and put me in the courthouse jail."

"You're leaving something out," I said. "What else happened?"

"Well, she give me this big old handful of bills out of the cash register. I don't know why. I didn't ask her for nothing. I had already laid a dollar up there to pay for my bag of potato chips which was all I wanted."

"And you took it."

"The money? Yes, ma'am. I didn't know what else to do. She just shoved it at me and I walked on out the door and got in my car. I saved the potato chip bag. I can show you that."

"How long did it take the police to pick you up?" I asked Archie. I could just see him in my mind's eye, standing there by that pay telephone with his head thrown back to keep that messy hair out of his face and lying to me and to himself like a motor running.

"That was the thing, see," my youngest boy said. "I didn't know that car that come up behind me was the police. They were following real close and showing a flashing light, and I figured it was a fire department car telling me I was in the way, so I sped on up to get out of there and give them room to get by, and they took that wrong, too."

"What'd they think? That you were trying to run from them?"

"Yeah, mama," Archie said in this amazed-sounding voice that he has been using ever since he learned to talk. "I tried to tell him what I was doing once they got me blocked and pulled over, and you know what?"

"No, what?" I said, really sarcastic and sweet-sounding. Not that he could have figured out how I was saying it. Not hardly.

"They wouldn't listen to a thing I said. Can you believe that? Not even after I showed them the potato chip bag."

"Was it empty, your little dollar bag?"

"No, I never got the chance to eat a one of them, and they made me leave them in the car when they brought me down here."

"They'll be there when you get back," I told him, like it was important what had happened to his damned old chips, "if you remembered to lock the car."

"I don't know," Archie said. "They brought the car on in, too. A policewoman drove it right behind the car they put me in the back-seat of, and I swear she didn't shift it out of second gear the whole trip. Women can't drive a shift car. I could hear it just a whining. It sure wasn't good for my transmission, I know that much."

"Oh, yeah," I said back to him. "Son, you know all kinds of things and always have about how stuff works."

To show you what kind of a steel-trap mind my youngest son has got, he took that as a compliment. Thought I was saying something nice about him. He never has been one to recognize more than one meaning in anything he hears. Everything just lays out there to be understood the first time you run into it, he figures, I guess, if he figures anything at all. Sometimes I wish things were like that, simple, but they never are. Not for Louella Dowden they're not.

It must be a blessing to be mentally challenged, I suppose. But, of course, if you are that way, you wouldn't know you were being blessed so what's the profit? I reconciled myself a long time ago to having to just suffer along with being smart. If God can stand it, so can I.

Anyway, "Thank you, mama," Archie said in this real modest voice after I said that last thing to him. Then he went on to say something else.

"They say they'll let me out of here until it comes time for some kind of a hearing, mama. All I got to do is pay bail money so I'll be sure to show up."

"Oh, you'll show up, all right," I said. "If I have to get your daddy to tie you up with twine and tote you down there to do it."

"What they say they need is twenty-five thousand dollars," Archie said. "But it don't take but ten percent of that if a bail bondsman puts the money up."

"That seems like a lot," I said. "For buying a bag of chips."

"It wasn't the chips, mama. They say it's because of that old unloaded pistol of V. M.'s I was holding for him. That's why the bail's up there so much in price."

"You reckon?" I said in this puzzled voice, just entertaining myself as I talked, you understand, since I knew Archie wasn't about to catch on to what I was really meaning.

"Yeah," he said. "Uh-huh. And ten percent of twenty-five thousand, that comes to under three thousand dollars cash money they need, see."

"Can you get an exact figure on that ten percent?" I asked him, still enjoying myself the best way I could under the circumstances. "How close is it to three thousand dollars? Does it come to over five hundred total you got to pay that bail bondsman?"

"Oh, way more than that," he said. "They tell me it's twenty-five hundred dollars."

I swear they must have been using substitute teachers in every class of arithmetic Archie sat through in the Fayetteville, Tennessee Independent School District those years he was a pupil. And everyone of those substitute teachers must have been a pregnant lady knitting baby booties while she let the kids play hangman games on the blackboard instead of making them learn how to add and subtract and figure out percentages.

"Well," he said, "can you get the money down here sometime early this morning?"

"Where," I said back before he even got the last word out of his mouth, "am I going to get twenty-five hundred dollars to give away? Tell me that, if you please, Mister."

"I don't know," Archie said. "Sell your car? That'd be one way to go, I reckon. I tell you one thing, mama. It's some rough-looking customers they got in here with me. Tattoos all over them and real funny eyes when they look at a man. Don't take baths, neither."

"You ought to thought about what kind of company you were joining when you bought that bag of potato chips," I said. "The way you handled that transaction threw you into a whole new category of running mates."

"Or you might get daddy to sell his bass boat and trailer rig," Archie said. "I thought about that, too."

"Your daddy is not about to give up his weekends on Lake S. R. Butler," I came right back with, "and I am not going to start walking to and fro to town rather than riding in my Honda Accord. So you better figure something else. What about selling your car? You don't seem to have a use for it at the present time."

"I done said that to them down here," Archie said, sounding

proud because he figured he had got a step on me in some situation, "but they said no it was a vehicle used in the commission of a felony and that takes it off the market like."

He went on like that for a while, expressing in one way and another his total surprise with the police department and the criminal justice system of Polk County, just as amazed as could be that things had got all different for him once he'd carried that handful of bills out of the Sac'n Pac and crawled up in his car to make his getaway. Only, of course, he wouldn't call it that by its right name, a getaway, because that would have involved facing up to what something that had happened in his life really was. And my little boy never had wanted to do that in his entire existence, from now until way on back to when he was crawling around the floor sticking everything he could pick up into his mouth.

I mean he would really do that, I mean would cram stuff into his mouth, more than the rest of any kids in the whole Dowden family ever did combined. He was like a dog chewing on one of these rawhide bones in that way. Not satisfied until he found out whatever he came across was worth eating or not. And I don't just mean whether it tasted good. If he could find a way to worry it on down his throat, Archie would do it no matter what it was really intended for. Coins, buttons, cat food, pieces of the funny paper, match sticks, cigarette butts, just sheer old dirt and lint, you name it. If I didn't knock it out of his hand first or prise it up out of his mouth, that boy was going to figure out a way to eat it.

After I stopped talking back to him on the telephone and just stood there listening with one ear to his rambling on, he finally started to run down and in a minute or two, he stopped jabbering and we both ended up not saying another word, telephones at each end of the line jammed up against our heads, mother and son, so we could simply listen to the static whir and buzz, I guess.

"Well," I said, "it's been good talking to you, Archie. I hope they feed you nourishing meals there in the jailhouse and that you get yourself plenty of sleep."

"Mama," he said in this little wondering voice that he has been using all his life, "you not going to find that money and come on down here and get me out this morning?"

"No, Archie," I said, "I'm not. And I'm also not going to get up on that kids' trampoline in the backyard next door and start turning double back flips, either. No matter how much I might want to do that, I don't believe I got the ability to pull it off without breaking my fool neck."

"I don't see what that's got to do with anything," he said, kind of snappish. "I never have seen you up on a trampoline before anyway."

"Oh, yes, you have, honey," I told him. "You just didn't realize what you were looking at your mother doing, that's all. I have always been an acrobat."

"They're making signs at me to hang up the telephone," Archie said. "And they ain't going to give me another call to the outside until tomorrow."

"Those mean old things," I said. "And just when you were about to get into your closing argument."

About then, I heard a different voice coming over the receiver and then a click and then the dial tone, so I hung up the kitchen telephone which was the one I had been talking on and went over to the sink and drank me a glass of water. Then I drank me another one, though I didn't want it. It was either gain another few seconds to calm down or bust the glass all into pieces in the sink by throwing it down, and I didn't want to do that, not even to make a point. That glass is one of an evenly matched set, and one less would mean I'd have to throw away another one to keep the number from being odd. You invite over couples to eat a meal with you and your husband, usually, and I have always loved to keep things balanced when I'm obliged to count them up.

I unmuted the television set to get some noise going in the house—I had turned the sound off when the phone call came that had ended up being from Archie—and I sat down on my usual place on the sofa where I watch from, but I naturally couldn't concentrate. It wasn't that I really wanted to, of course. I had TBS on and they were running an old Andy Griffith show like they are nine-tenths of the time, either that or the Atlanta Braves, and it was one I had watched enough to be able to recite the dialogue. It was the one where Opie rescues the baby birds and has to finally let them go when they get grown. He doesn't want to, you'll remember, but Andy explains to him about how it's only right and proper to do it.

"They're about to fly off," I mouthed along with Opie as he and his daddy looked up into the tree there in the front yard to watch where they'd flown to after the cage door was open. You can't tell what kind of birds they are—sparrows, probably, or maybe miniature starlings, something common as dirt—but they've got them just a whistling away on the sound track. Don't try to see them the next time that episode comes on your own TV set, though, because you can't from the perspective the people that made the show put the viewer in. They're off-camera.

"Don't they sing pretty, though?" Andy Taylor of Mayberry and I said together, and then the screen went blank, and I hit the mute button again.

I couldn't leave Archie there in the jailhouse, I knew that, as much as I may have wanted to, and I needed to think about how I would be able to do to raise the money for his bail. Lord God Almighty, I hated to think that word, even to give it space in my head, much less to say it out loud. So I knew I wasn't going to be able to call anybody in the family up and then tell them directly why I needed the loan of twenty-five hundred dollars. My sisters, say? Ruth or Myra? Forget it.

Archie's daddy wouldn't say much, I knew that, of course, having been married to him for twenty-eight years, and whatever I wanted to do about the whole thing would be jake with him.

"You do whatever you think is right, sugar," he would have said. And he would have meant it, too, because he wouldn't have thought ahead to what the consequences might be—selling a bass boat and trailer, for one thing, or giving up an '87 Honda Accord that runs like a top. You can't even hear the engine when you're waiting at a stoplight. That's Japanese quality and the way I keep the oil changed and all the moving parts well-lubricated. That's what makes that true, my thinking ahead and doing what has to be done.

No, Arnold would have expected me to wave a magic wand and come up with almost three thousand dollars in a way that he never would have to feel in his own day to day life, and he would've turned his attention back to whatever new house he was inspecting the plumbing installation of for the Polk County Regulatory Board. That's what he does for a living, see.

But that morning, sitting there on the sofa with the TV remote in my hand and staring at a commercial with no soundtrack where not a minute before Andy Griffith had been teaching a lesson in life to Opie, I felt like I had misplaced that magic wand somewhere and wasn't about to be able to find it again to fix things up for my youngest child in a way that wouldn't affect anybody in the family adversely.

I let myself start to cry a little bit thinking about Opie and his birds and Archie behind bars for armed robbery, and in the middle of that a thought popped into my head and made me stop that business and laugh out loud. This come to me. Maybe I could root around in the closet in the back bedroom, the one we called the guest room, though the last ones to sleep in it were my cousin Virginia and her husband over three years ago now on their way that time to St. Simon's Island, Georgia, and see if I could find me one of my old mini skirts from 1967. Put that on, fluff up my hair and slap on some real red lipstick, and go stand on the corner of Franklin and Third in downtown Fayetteville and try to make that twenty-five hundred dollars by hustling. The only problem with that, I just could hear Arnold say if I was to tell him about it, was the kind of customer that would stop for a fifty-eight year old woman showing all her busted veins from her ankles on up to where the cellulite starts gathering in a serious way. That customer wouldn't be the kind you could rely on to honor his debts.

That was a good thing, that laugh I had, I mean, and it made me feel a little better, so I got me a piece of paper to write down some ideas on how I might go about raising Archie's bail. "How—" I said out loud to the TV set where Andy and Opie had been looking up at those two birds they had set loose, "how long would it take for me to make two thousand and five hundred dollars peddling my butt at a quarter a throw?"

I laughed some more at that, and by the time the next episode of whatever rerun it was had kicked off, I had begun trying to think of quick ways of raising money so I could write them down onto a list. Here's what I came up with in about fifteen minutes.

1. Raffle something off.

I looked at that for a long time and tried some thought, but I couldn't come up with a single thing I owned in the house or yard that anybody would want to buy a chance on. An old Sears lawn mower that wouldn't start half the time? A throw pillow and a matching scarf from Gatlinburg that said OVER GATLINBURG in

German on it in embroidery stitching? That's *ober Gatlinburg*, if you don't know the German language. That's all the words I know in German except *sauerkraut* and *blitzkrieg* and *mox nix*. That last one is something Arnold used to say all the time right before we got married and for a little while after. It means it doesn't make any difference, he told me. A buddy of his had taught it to him.

2. Set myself up as a seamstress to make wedding gowns and baby clothes.

No, not hardly. I'd sooner wade off into the Cherow River and drown in that nasty brown water.

3. Ask all our relatives to donate to a fund to spring Archie from the Polk County jail.

Who are you kidding? I wrote down to myself in the space left on the page right after that one. I wrote it twice in a real big hand and then I crossed it out so hard I tore the paper.

With that, I started feeling a little sick at my stomach so I got up and went into the kitchen and fixed me a cup of tea, but after it was brewed I took only one sip and had to put it down it tasted so bitter, even as weak as I had made it.

Help me, Jesus, I said to myself and let my head hang down on my chest. There wasn't anybody in the house to see me giving way to grief, so I felt all right about doing that for a few minutes and I let myself cry again for a little while as I tried to keep a picture of the Son of God the way He must look centered in my head. A full beard, you know, well-kept and worn by Him only because that was the way men let themselves look back when He walked on the earth among the people, and of course, those big soft brown eyes every artist who ever tried to imagine Him always draws in the painting. Sometimes they do make them blue, but not often. It was that, the eyes, how sweet they were always and full of love and understanding for the situation of anybody looking at His portrait, that made what happened next happen. I am convinced of that.

"Oh, my Lord," I said out loud and snapped my head up off my chest and looked straight ahead at the TV screen, though what was on it didn't register. I believe it was a *Dating Game* rerun or maybe that show where they do funny home videos. I don't remember. Anyway, I said that, *Oh, my Lord*, and then I said his name, because it was the face that popped into my head while I was thinking about the kindness in Jesus's eyes in all those portraits of Him.

"Pascal," I said out loud. "Pascal Richardson."

He, of course, was moved away from Fayetteville and had been moved out of town for over five years now, but I did know where he was living and most everything about his situation. He was residing over five-hundred miles away in Crawfordville, Florida, on what is known in that part of the country as a ranch. It's no such of a thing, of course, measured by any normal standards for what a real ranch is, but they like to call little truck farms that name in that panhandle part of Florida, so I don't waste time worrying about it. If it makes them feel better about their situation, why begrudge it?

It does burn me, I got to admit, a little every time Arnold and me get a Christmas card from Pascal's wife Monette with that return address of Whispering Pines Ranch printed on it, though. Not for long each Christmas season do I let it bother me, though, because I have learned a mental hygiene trick to put down that bad thought about the difference between our family status and their's, and it's this. I don't remember where I got it from. It might have just come to me.

If I start to get down on myself, I just make my mind remember the way Pascal always would beg with tears in his eyes for me to let him be with me just one more time, and that takes care of me worrying about him and his wife living on a so-called ranch in northwest Florida.

But don't get me wrong. I don't want to put Pascal down. His being so sweet and generous is for sure why God put him into my head when I couldn't figure anywhere else to go that morning I was studying so hard about how to raise twenty-five hundred dollars to get my boy out of jail. No, I'm not directing any bad thoughts toward Pascal Richardson. It's Monette I figure I got the advantage over, not him, not poor little Pascal who has never weighed in his life more than a hundred and forty pounds soaking wet.

It started out innocent enough, that little six-month thing that developed between me and him before they took off and moved out of the state of Tennessee, him and Monette and Blinky, their golden lab dog, on down to Florida.

They were at the house one Saturday night—it happened to be New Year's Eve, and that's important for what happened then and later and that's why I mention it—when the whole thing kicked off.

We had some folks over, not wanting to go out on the roads ourselves that holiday because of all the drunks sure to be driving up and down them everywhere, and everybody at the party was full of wine and margaritas and I don't know what all, and at midnight when the new year came in husbands and wives were kissing each other, and it come into my head to steal a little peck from Pascal, if I could do it and get away with it.

I don't know why exactly. I was just watching him and Monette smooch—she's a real pert little petite brunette—and I felt all of a sudden like I wanted a little of that kissing on display there in my living room myself.

So when everybody else had drifted off into the kitchen or out into the backyard or out onto the deck—they could because it was a real warm night that New Year's Eve—I fixed it so I was standing next to Pascal in the living room, talking about I don't know what, and I just leaned my head back a little and said to him, "I'm ready for my New Year's kiss now."

He reached over to peck me on the lips, saying something like he was glad to oblige, and I opened my mouth a little and touched just the tip of my tongue to his teeth so he could tell I'd done it on purpose. I could feel him just freeze when I did that and then kind of draw back and look at me close up enough to my face so that his features looked blurry. Then I said to Pascal Richardson, "That was nice."

To make a long story short, that's all it took. The next day he started calling me on the phone and inside a week we were naked together in my guest bedroom just going at it. I never did let him have me on mine and Arnold's bed, though. See, Arnold's my husband, and we've always had a real good marriage. But I did do it with him on his and Monette's bed in their house on Sea Foam Lane in the most outlandish ways I could think to come up with. Backwards, upside down, me on top, oral stuff, you name it. We gave Monette's little frilly Beautyrest a workout.

Then he wanted to get too serious, Pascal did, and I broke it off and he moved him and Monette to Whispering Pines Ranch in Florida because he couldn't stand to live in the same town with me and risk the chance of seeing me at Food Town or the bank or somewhere and listening to his heart break over and over again every time he did. He would say the sweetest things to me, and that was one of them.

So that morning there in my living room, looking at my little old silly list I had made to try to help me think about ways to raise twenty-five hundred dollars bail money for my boy, it was Pascal Richardson's face that popped into my head when I was thinking about the kindness artists always portray in Jesus's eyes.

I didn't let myself think about it for another minute, afraid I would find a way to talk myself out of doing it and knowing that when you pick up a sign from the environment after praying for an answer, you better act on it right then or risk never getting another one. I picked up the telephone and started punching in the number for long distance information.

I wasn't surprised, either, when Pascal Richardson picked up on the second ring and said hello into the receiver. Once God decides to go on ahead and put some process or another into operation, He makes sure all the pieces fall into place. That's how you can tell some series of events has a divine origin, in fact, I have learned over my years of battling around in this world. I'll put it to you this way, and check me out on it if you're of a mind to.

When things go wrong, that shows that people have had a hand in it. Human beings, I'm talking about. But when something clicks and falls together like crocheting a doily, one stitch after the other and everyone of them linked to the one before and the one after with no signs of a join, that's a sign that the Master is in charge and has taken an interest in the affair.

I will not argue points of theology like a bunch of Baptist preachers worrying about what the Trinity means, but I will profess the truth of what I just finished saying.

Anyway, here was Pascal Richardson saying hello through the earpiece of my portable phone, so I took it away from the base it had been sitting on and wandered toward the kitchen so I could look out the window over the sink while I talked to him. There was a birdbath out there next to a sycamore tree that Arnold had set up, and I sometimes like to see what kinds of birds might be drinking or taking a bath while I converse. It's soothing.

"Hello, Pascal," I said, "This is Louella." I could see one mock-ingbird on the edge of that concrete bath, and it was spreading its wings open and then letting them close real slow, over and over.

"It is?" Pascal said. "Are you here in Crawfordville?"

"No, no," I said. "I'm at home here by myself, looking out the kitchen window watching a bird preen himself."

"Why I asked," Pascal said, "is I thought maybe y'all was driving through, you and Arnold, on the way to Disney World or somewhere."

"No, I don't care anything about amusement rides. Neither does Arnold."

"It's good to hear from you, Louella," he said. "Anyway. It's just like you was in the same room with me, the way your voice sounds."

"Uh-huh," I said, watching that mockingbird do his wing exercises and wondering how long he would keep it up. "This is a portable telephone, but it's just as clear-sounding as if it had wires hooked up to it."

"We haven't talked since, you know, the last time we did," Pascal said. "Remember?"

"Yeah," I said. "We talked the last time we talked several years back now." That sounds silly and kind of dumb to me, I thought to myself as I was saying it. Of course, the last time you talked to somebody was the last time you talked to them. Could it be anything else? "Well, Pascal," I said. "I got a problem. I'm in some trouble. We are all here in some trouble."

"It's not Arnold, is it?" Pascal said in this real quick way. "He's not sick or something, is he? In the hospital or anywhere?"

"Arnold? No," I said, thinking how much power a woman gives herself over a man when she is the one who does the cutting off of relations. Let him do it, though, and he'll forget your name before he gets his clothes all buttoned up and hanging right on him again. "Arnold's as healthy as a race horse. He hasn't missed a day of work in eighteen years."

"Is his cholesterol count good?" Pascal said. "Mine is real high's why I asked."

"That's too bad," I said. "His is less than two-hundred, and he's fifty-nine years old."

"Oh," Pascal said. That mockingbird perched on the lip of the birdbath did one more wing exercise and flew off across the yard, chirping like a blue jay, and headed for the top of an oak tree next door at my neighbor's.

"No," I said. "It's my boy Archie. He's in jail over a misunderstanding at a Sac'n Pac store, and they're charged him with a crime."

"Well, I never," Pascal said. "He's just a little kid. Did he hurt somebody?"

"He's twenty years old, Pascal," I said. "You haven't been around for a while. And as far as hurting anybody's concerned Archie hasn't got enough gumption to kill a fly."

"But they got him in jail. My goodness."

"That's where they got him," I said. "No doubt about it."

"Well, what are you going to do, Louella?"

"Oh, get him defended by some jackleg lawyer when the time comes," I said. "But right now I got to find a way to raise twenty-five hundred dollars bail money to get him out of jail."

"You do ? Couldn't you just let him stay in there as a lesson to him until the court business comes up?"

"I would if I could, Pascal," I said, wishing another bird would volunteer to make use of our birdbath while I stood there looking out the kitchen window into an empty yard. "But it's bad people they got down there in the jailhouse, Pascal, and I'm afraid for Archie to be around that trash too long."

"I know what you mean," Pascal said. "I've seen TV specials on incarceration. It's rough as a cob in these holding facilities."

"Yeah," I said. "You got that right. So I have to find twenty-five hundred dollars to get my baby boy out of there." That was the second time I had said the number, so I made two little marks on a note pad by the sink with a ballpoint pen and then said the amount again on the portable phone and made one more little mark next to the other two. If I said it twice more, I could draw one at a slant across them, like I had learned how to do way back in the third grade when they teach you how to count by fives.

"I don't know how to get it," I said, "that twenty-five hundred dollars," and I made my fourth straight mark. "I have racked my brain. Is there any way I could borrow it from you, Pascal? I just hate to ask, but I'm at my wit's end."

Then I got quiet on my end of the telephone connection, and I could hear Pascal thinking as he sucked in a breath of air hard enough to be detected over five hundred miles of space between us. I remember I was thinking as I stood there, leaning a little against the edge of the sink so I would be able to see better out the window if another bird happened to fly up to our birdbath, that Pascal Richardson was breathing into a mouthpiece at his end which was connected to a wire, but I was listening through a receiver that was freestanding and unattached as one of those mockingbirds flying around outside.

You think about how something like that is able to work well enough to let me hear a man suck in a breath of air five hundred miles away in another state, and then tell me there's no mystery in this world. People will know something like that is possible and is going on every minute of the day, and they won't even blink at it. Yet they will doubt the divinity of Jesus Christ or even the existence of God. People are real funny. That's all I got to say about it.

Anyway, Pascal let that breath out and drew him the next one, I guess, but I couldn't hear it because he began to speak.

"Of course, Louella," he said. "I'll be glad to let you have that bail money for little Archie. Twenty-five hundred, you say?"

"Twenty-five hundred American dollars," I said and started me a new five-count pencil-slash arrangement on the note pad. "That's the ten percent of the twenty-five thousand bail bond I have to come up with for that fellow to stand good for it."

"Well, like I said, I'll be glad to advance it to you, and you don't have to worry about when it's got to be paid back, neither."

"Well, it will be," I said, "and quick, Pascal."

"Uh-huh," he said. "I'm not studying that part of it, Louella, though. I want you to know that."

"I appreciate it," I said. "Could you send me a check for that amount, twenty-five hundred, as soon as you can then, please?"

"No, I wouldn't want to have a check for that amount to show up in the bank statement, Louella," he said, his voice sounding the way it used to back when he was working the pharmacy counter at the All-Rite Drugstore downtown. Friendly, but all business. That's what Pascal is, see, a pharmacist. "I wouldn't want that, nuh-uh."

"Well, a money order, then," I said. "I see what you're saying about a check." I could imagine Monette's eyes bugging out when she went through the monthly statement from NationsBank or First Union or whatever financial institution they kept their money in. Bugging out, I say, right before they closed as she fell over into a faint from seeing my name on a check for twenty-five hundred dollars made out by her husband.

"No, Louella," Pascal said. "That'd present the same problem for me. See, what I'm talking about is avoiding a paper trail."

Lord, I thought to myself, Pascal Richardson's sounding like an investigator on one of these congressional committees looking into allegations of wrongdoing.

"No," he went on, "what I propose to do is all in cash, which I will deliver to you personally in less than twelve hours."

"Twelve hours?" I said. "You're going to bring it up here from Florida?"

"Yes, that's right. You got it, Louella," he said. "I'll leave here after I get the money together, and I'll drive to Fayetteville in the Lincoln, and I'll check into the Day's Inn on the bypass there off of route seventeen. It's still there, isn't it? The Day's Inn?"

"Last time I noticed," I said. "Yes, it was."

"You meet me there," he said. "I'll leave word at the desk for them to give you my room number."

"Well," I said. "I'd rather call the desk and not have to walk on in there in the office, Pascal."

"Whichever way suits you, sweetheart," he said. "That'd be fine with me."

"In twelve hours," I said, hearing that word he'd just called me ringing in my ears like an alarm hoot set off on one of these new cars somebody had knocked up against. "I'll call the desk."

"Good," Pascal said. "Don't you worry, honey. I'll be there waiting."

AND THEN HE HUNG UP, and I stared out the kitchen window at two blue jays splashing in the birdbath that I hadn't even noticed fly up while I was talking on my portable phone to a man located in a state completely different from where I was. Well, I didn't know what to wear, so I ended up compromising. I spent all that afternoon and way up into the evening looking through everything I owned that I could still get into. Time I had finally worked my way from 1967 up to the middle nineties, I was in such a state I had to take three aspirins and lie down on the bed with a wet rag over my eyes.

Lord have mercy, I said to myself, the stuff I used to put on and go out of the house in. Had I been out of my mind?

Finally, I chalked it up to changing hormone levels over the years—I've got that maintained nowadays by a doctor's prescription for estrogen replacement—and I got up from the bed, threw the wet rag which had got real warm into the bathroom sink and put on what I had finally ended up picking out.

It was loose-fitting, of course, and dark colored and high necked, and once I got it all assembled I looked like every other woman my age who might be fixing to go hang around a motel bar where they do stuff like sell beer and teach country line dancing to AARP members. Just desperate.

I told Arnold I had to go out and see what I could do about raising bail money for Archie, and he barely even looked away from the TV set.

"You want me to go with you?" he said and when I told him it was up to him he said he supposed he ought to stay by the telephone. I said all right and he looked relieved and started working the remote again.

I called the Day's Inn office from a pay telephone at Doug's Citgo there where the telephone's inside and the light's real bright, and I got Pascal Richardson's room number. Wouldn't you just know? Lucky thirteen, the same number as the dinner party during the Last Supper when Jesus got betrayed by a disciple almost two-thousand years ago.

I pulled my Honda Accord right up into a space in front of the door to thirteen, figuring there were so many models of that car on the roads that nobody driving by would recognize my '87, but to tell you the truth, by that point I didn't really give a good goddamn about anything. And I'm not one to take the Lord's name in vain, ordinarily.

Pascal Richardson opened the door at the first knock and stepped back so fast to let me in that he looked like a man who had just seen something to scare him. A Jehovah's Witness at the door, say, with a handful of *Watchtowers*, or a big black man wearing his baseball cap turned around backwards with a story about needing to use the telephone because his car had run out of gas.

"You're just as pretty as a picture, Louella," Pascal said after I'd got inside and he'd closed the door behind me and chain-locked it. "Just like you always were."

"That's nice of you to say, Pascal," I said, "to an old lady. Was your drive up here from Florida all right? No trouble?"

I didn't get to say anything else right then, because by the time I had got what I did say out of my mouth, Pascal was standing on tiptoe to start in kissing me.

I let him do that for a little bit, and then I broke him loose by pulling my head back and stepping around where he was standing. His breath smelled like a flower garden mixed up with Scope mouthwash.

"These rooms are a lot bigger at the Day's Inn than you might imagine, aren't they?" I said, making a big production of looking around me. It was a two double-bed set-up with a little table and two chairs and a TV set and a dresser up against one wall. I could see Pascal's shined wingtips sitting by the table, and that told me why he had seemed a lot shorter than I had remembered. Men, of course, do shrink as time goes by, though.

"They sure are," he said, coming up behind me in his sock feet and putting one hand on my back just below waist level. "I got the twenty-five hundred dollars and a bottle of Cold Duck chilling in the ice bucket, sugar."

"Oh, well, hell," I said and headed for the double bed that didn't have anything on it. Pascal had used the other one to put stuff on, a little suitcase and a carrying bag and a gray plastic sack from Wal-

Mart. I couldn't tell what was in that, or in anything else either.

"We'll drink that later," I said and let myself topple onto the empty bed as soon as my knees hit it, turning to face in his direction as he came toward me looking like a kid heading into a video-game parlor, eyes dancing like brand-new quarters.

THE NEXT MORNING when I paid Archie's bail and got him out of the Polk County jailhouse, he couldn't thank me enough for it.

"Mama," he said, "I have learned my lesson. I see now where carelessness and showing out will get you and the kind of people you get throwed in with when you let your morals down."

"That's nice, Archie," I said, steering my Accord back onto the highway in the direction of my house. I wanted to get back there as fast as I could and pour me some coffee in one of my blue mugs and look out of the kitchen window into my backyard for birds.

"Did you have to sell your car, mama?" Archie asked. He just couldn't stop talking that morning, it seemed like. "Did daddy have to put up his bass boat and trailer?"

"No," I said. "He didn't, and you can see what car we're riding in on our way home."

"Huh," he said. "How'd you get the money for the bail, then? All them hundreds of dollars?"

"From a man," I said. "A fellow I know."

"He must be a nice guy then," Archie said. "That's what I think about him."

"Oh, he's fine," I said. "He's a perfect specimen of a man." And then I stopped listening to my baby boy babbling on about what his experience had been like being locked up with scummy lawbreakers in the jailhouse, and I just set my mind to steering my Accord straight home.

They dropped the charges on Archie at a hearing about two

weeks later when the lawyer I had hired out of Tullahoma convinced the judge that the police had violated my son's constitutional rights to privacy. And I got refunded that twenty-five hundred dollars minus ten percent for the bail bondsman, when all charges were dismissed.

I never sent any of it back to Pascal Richardson down in Craw-fordville, Florida, where he lives with his wife Monette and their golden lab Blinky at the Whispering Pines Ranch, though. And he has not asked for it. Instead, I used it to have put in a Mirror-Lake Reflecting Ground-level Pool with Fountain in my backyard where I can see it out of my kitchen window over the sink, and everyday blue jays and mockingbirds and cardinals and gold finches and wrens and yellow hammers come from all over this part of Polk County to bathe and drink from that bubbling water while I sip my morning coffee and keep watch.

Believing in Memphis

Every time I travel it, I try to find ways to fool myself. It is the longest two hundred miles in the South, that stretch of interstate highway between Nashville and Memphis, and it seems to take twice as long to drive that distance as it would anywhere else in the country. And when I say that, I'm including that blank spot of geography between Dallas and Austin, Texas.

I'm not really in a car passing the exit to Dickson, Tennessee, I will tell myself, when I'm taking that road. I'm asleep, I'm dreaming, I'm dead. That's not really the eighteenth killed possum on the side of the road since I left Nashville heading west. It's a pile of trash, some old clothes somebody's dumped, an empty spot in the visual field, self-generated. It's nothing, it's this highway. It's a blind place on the map.

And that two hundred miles feels longer when you're heading west from Nashville toward Memphis, mainly because a normal person wants to get to Memphis, and nobody but an inflamed, line-dancing country music freak longs for Nashville at the end of his journey.

I take that back. Maybe a state legislator, representing Shelby County with his mouth watering for another go at the public trough in the capitol, wants Nashville as his goal to the same degree as a country music nut from the midwest, but I'm not talking aberrant behavior here. I mean to describe human beings with normally functioning central nervous systems when I say that two hundred miles is longer heading west toward the Bluff City than it is the other direction. Trust me until you try it yourself.

Anyway, I had finally reached Jackson, Tennessee, after what seemed like half a day, and was admiring the announcement of the road sign up ahead that the next four exits would spill you and your machine into that city if you happened to lose your senses at that point and leave the four-lane.

It was late in May and not yet officially full summer, but nobody was noticing what calendars said by that time of the year. It was the season of heat in the middle South and had been and would be right up to the time in late October when God might, for a spell, lift up the blanket off the bed everybody was smothering in to let in a puff of cool air. And then again He might not.

It doesn't pay to hope for relief that early on in the hot time. Like any dweller in that sore part of the country, you have to learn to take the long view. Give up on it. Abandon all hope. Expect nothing. And maybe you'll get it.

I have driven better cars, too, than the one I was in that day in May. And they have had better sound systems in them. More than an AM radio with only one speaker right in the middle of the dashboard full of static. That's for sure.

But it was picking up the right song out of those hot air waves, at least, that radio was, one that given the circumstances seemed to have been selected by a disc jockey blessed with synchronicity and clairvoyance. Because what I was hearing as I drove that twelve-year-old Buick past the first of the four exits to Jackson, Tennessee, steadily narrowing the distance between me and Memphis, was Carl Perkins singing one of his old ones from the fifties.

And, of course, Carl Perkins is a native of Jackson and had likely written that song at the kitchen table of some shotgun house which had stood not over two or three miles from where I was riding in that Buick with the nonfunctional air conditioner. The house itself, the birthplace of that composition and of "Blue Suede Shoes" too most likely, surely was in this world no more, victim to a highway widening or a fast food place installation years before, but it was a nice surprise hearing old Carl complain in song, and I began to sing along as he declared to anyone who had ears to hear that he was sitting there thinking a matchbox would hold his clothes.

I was warbling that next line, feeling a whole lot better in the process no matter how hot the air coming through the vents of the Buick happened to be and no matter how well the sentiments expressed by Carl Perkins fit my own condition, when I had my first view of the two of them up ahead on the shoulder of I–40.

"I got a long way to go," I said right along with Carl Perkins and then let him finish the rest of the tune on his own as I tried to see better what the two figures up ahead really looked like in the wash of air and dust coming off the semis blasting by them as they faced in the direction of my Buick, their backs turned to the way they were wanting to go, walking rearward in the classic stance of a hitchhiker on any American road. Thumb out, head a little twisted to the left to keep at least some of the trash in the air out of the eyes, hair roiled by the slipstream, and that look on the face. One I couldn't see yet from my range, but one I knew right down to the bone from my own experience of asking for and giving rides from and to strangers. I didn't have to imagine it.

Here's what it's comprised of, that look on the face of the hitcher, waiting on the side of the road. There's hope—maybe this vehicle will stop, this next one coming, a hundred feet or so up on the highway shoulder and let me run up there to it through the gravel and dust

and rank weeds, my kit bouncing against my back, my hand itching
to pop that door release and let me climb inside of something that
will pick me up and let me move on toward somewhere else other
than here. I don't know just where I might end up, but I do know
it won't be where I'm standing right now. Please, Jesus.

That's part of it, that's some of the hitcher's look, that expectation, that desire, that hope and need. There will be movement ahead
somewhere, to some place, maybe soon, maybe now.

But's there more to it, of course. And that comes out of motive:
the hitcher knows why he wants a stranger to stop his progress
and let the hitcher climb on board. He knows what he thinks he
needs. The real question on the dark side of the equation is why
is that stranger pulling over. Why is he willing to slow down, to
stop, to wait until the hitcher trots up and puts a face against the
window for inspection. What's motivating the driver? Are we talking Christian charity here? Or we into altruism and good will in
action? Are we really into a spell of emotional uplift on the open
American road?

That's the hitcher's dilemma, all right. But it's worth it for the
ride, the hitcher figures. Always worth taking that chance, always
a fair trade, right up until the driver shows his hand. Or his piece
or his knife or his length of rope.

Anyway, as I got closer to where the two of them were located,
shuffling backwards in the direction of Memphis, while Carl Perkins finished up singing "Matchbox" to me through the Buick's
radio, I began to slow down, and I did it for two reasons I could
name and for some more I couldn't put words to. The first one was
obvious: the two of them looked female, even at this distance, and
they looked to be that in an interesting way.

They were both tall, both of them wearing dark pants and shirts,
and they had hair almost the same color, although I could tell well

before I got close to them that one's crowning glory was assuredly a bleach job. Nobody but an albino had hair that shade of white. The other woman, the taller and slimmer of the two, the one holding the other reason for my stopping to take a look, had light hair, too, all right, but it probably hadn't come out of wrought-up chemical action in a motel sink. It still looked alive.

What she was carrying was a guitar case that looked new, and she had it held up in a position well free of contact with the gravel and trash on the shoulder of the road. It's not that I'm so interested in guitar cases or women carrying them, but I was struck by the fact that this guitar-toting woman was headed not toward Nashville but away from it.

You can see four or five guitar-carriers on the side of every road into Music City any time you drive one of them. They have their thumbs out, their heads up and that look in their eyes, and they're as much alike as a bowl full of ice cubes just popped out of the tray. Shining, slick, and not yet beginning to melt.

Come back tomorrow, though, and see what you find. A dull-colored puddle of water the same temperature as everything else around it.

But this guitar case and whatever was in it was not pointed toward 17th Street in Nashville and the dream of an appearance on the Grand Ole Opry and a big recording contract to follow, but the other direction. West toward Memphis on the big river, where the last studios where music was put down on acetate are now historical monuments without a tune, without a lyric, without a song anywhere in the air inside their empty rooms at all.

And that interested me as I rolled down I–40 in that shot Buick, because I have written songs back when I had the faith to do so, and I don't believe any more in dreams ending up being recorded on something tangible you can carry around in your hand and put into a machine to listen to. That recording won't play, it will not produce music, it will just make a buzz and a whirring noise.

Let me put it this way. I don't believe in Nashville any more. I believe in Memphis.

I slowed way down as I passed by the two women in black there on the truthful side of I–40, and I stopped the Buick a little distance beyond where they were standing, the wash of hot wind from a semi tugging at their clothes and hair as I looked at them through the mirror.

I figured they had to make the obligatory trot up the shoulder of the road to my car because I would be cheating them out of the full experience of hitching a ride from Nashville to Memphis if I left out that part. They ought to get all they'd bargained for, like everybody else has to do on that long stretch of road.

The shorter woman, the one with the dead white crown of hair, arrived at the passenger's side window of the Buick first, and leaned down to take a look at whatever was driving and had decided to respond to their signal to stop. We studied each other.

She had a short upper lip and appeared to be a mouth-breather, but that could have been because she had just trotted twenty-five yards in ninety-degree heat while carrying a suitcase in one hand and a duffel bag over the shoulder opposite. Her eyes were set far apart, and one of them seemed to be appreciably smaller than the other, enough so that she appeared to be half-winking as she stared through the window at me. She had been well-pierced, in what parts of her body I could see, metal and glass studs lining the outer edge of each ear and a small silver ring punched through the corner of the brow above the smaller of her eyes. What had been subjected to punching below neck level I could only guess at, but I had my suspicions.

I sat behind the steering wheel and stared back at her, waiting for her to make the first move toward opening the car door and letting her know by my posture that I was no more eager than she was to take the next step toward our becoming road companions. Squinting her smaller eye a little nearer to being shut, she decided, dropped the suitcase to the gravel of the shoulder and reached for the door latch.

About then the other woman, carrying the guitar case before her as though it were an offering she was about to make to someone, maybe one of the lesser gods of rock, came up from behind and stood waiting as the door swung open.

"You going as far as Memphis?" the artificial blonde said in a voice pitched lower than I would have expected.

"Just exactly as far," I said. "I sure wouldn't want to fall out of Tennessee and end up in Arkansas at the end of a trip."

"I'll sit in front," she said, without a smile, and turned to look at her companion. "You'll be all right in the back." Then again to me. "You got room in your trunk for our stuff?"

"Afraid not," I said, trying to look past her at the other woman, patiently waiting with the guitar case still held before her. "It's full of my own junk."

"That's O.K.," the guitar carrier said. "There's lot of room in the backseat. I can hold things in my lap."

As they loaded up and climbed in, I looked back and forth from the one in the front seat to the rearview mirror, checking out the visible differences between the women. The one in back had a head and face that had not been nearly so frequently penetrated by metal hooks and studs and rings. Only one set of hardware in the lobe of each ear and nothing else I could detect anywhere in the features of her face.

She caught a glimpse of me watching her in the mirror and flashed a smile that didn't get any higher than her upper lip, and at that I looked down at the side mirror as though to study traffic and then over at the woman in the passenger seat. "Ready to roll?" I said. "Everybody set?"

She nodded once, staring straight ahead, and let out a deep breath, and I put the Buick in gear and began looking for a gap between cars.

"Y'all are not starting out from Jackson, right?" I said as I eased the car on down the shoulder, picking up enough speed to be able to re-enter the flow toward Memphis.

"Depends on how far back you're asking," the woman in the backseat said.

"I know what you mean," I said. "Just today's what I'm talking about, though."

"Nashville," the front-seat rider said. "Back there."

"We've been there since November," the other one said. "Back before it got real cold."

"Y'all got an act?" I said. "You sing?"

"Now and then," the one riding beside me said. I could hear metal clicking against her teeth as she spoke, and I chalked up another piercing to her credit. A tongue-stud, too, for the little lady.

"What you call yourselves?"

"I'm Arizona Star," the one in the backseat with the guitar case in her lap said. "And that's George."

"Arizona Star and George," I repeated. "Catchy label. That ought to work."

"We keep hoping it will," said Arizona Star. "We sure are counting on it. We're trying."

She sounded like a woman who had been raised as a girl to be perky and optimistic, but I didn't say that to her out loud. Most people I run into, I have learned over the years, don't like to be accused of having been influenced by anybody or anything outside of themselves in their acquiring of an outlook on the world. They like to believe they are one of a kind, you understand. They have achieved the creature they are on their own and out of their own devising.

It's a view of personality that has a history that I'd like to be able to subscribe to myself. It has a real psychic attraction. But I know better. In that small respect, I've become smarter than either William Blake or George Gordon, Lord Byron. And, not counting song lyrics, I've written only one real poem in my whole life. Up to now.

"Are y'all *from* Arizona?" I said.

"No," said the one in the backseat. "I just like the way it sounds, the name of that state."

"That's a good way to pick," I said. "Find out what sounds right and latch onto it."

Nobody said anything to that, so after watching a few more cars catch up to and blow by the Buick I was driving, I tried again.

"Who sings lead?" I asked. "Who does back-up?"

"I do the lead vocals," Arizona Star said. "George does harmony and plays guitar."

"But you have to tote it," I said and jerked my thumb over my shoulder to indicate the guitar case in the backseat. "George makes you carry the load."

"Well, it's a whole lot lighter than the other stuff."

"It wasn't for Jimi Hendrix," I said, trying to see Arizona Star's eyes in the rearview mirror. I couldn't. She was looking down at the guitar case in her lap.

A double-trailer semi blasted by us in the inside lane, and I couldn't hear her response for the noise it made. "What'd you say?" I said.

"I said who's Jimi Hendrix."

"A black dude who played it left-handed," George said to her. "Upside down and backwards."

"How'd he do that?" Arizona Star said.

"Real well," I said. "He played it like the devil himself."

"You going all the way into Memphis?" George said, clicking her tongue-stud and twisting around to look over her shoulder at Arizona Star in the backseat. She was talking to me, though. I sense these things.

"Yeah," I said. "Down Union Avenue all the way to the river."

"You can let us out then on Front Street," George said. "There where it crosses Union."

"When we get there I'll be glad to," I said. I knew she had said that not because she didn't want to talk about Hendrix. Maybe it was because I had mentioned the devil. And for damn sure because I was talking a little too much to Arizona Star for George's taste. But that's not going to stop me, I told myself as I rode along at sixty in a ruined Buick with hot air pouring out of the vents. Let me see if I can make that tongue-stud rattle against the incisors one more time.

"What kind of stuff do you sing?" I said. "Mostly just a lot of covers, I imagine."

"No," said George. "We do not."

"We used to," Arizona Star said at the same time from her spot in the backseat. "All the time. You have to, starting out. Everybody does."

"Well, that's true," I said. "Even Elvis had his Dean Martin period."

"We don't cover nobody," George said, her tongue-stud giving off a hard click at the end of her statement. "Covering's for losers."

"We sing George's compositions," Arizona Star said, leaning forward a little in the backseat to be able to project over the road noise, I supposed. "She writes everything we do now."

"I could've predicted that," I said, giving a sidelong look over toward where George was sitting. She was staring straight ahead through the windshield as though she had a responsibility to watch the white lines pass beneath the Buick chugging toward Memphis. She had to hold it in the road for all of us.

"Really?" Arizona Star said. "How could you tell?"

"Your back-up looks like a real original," I said. "That's how I figure. I bet she hasn't done anything in her whole life that anybody else has ever done before."

I could see George thinking about that for about as long as it would take a Southerner to say *Birmingham, Alabama* three times out loud, and then her features pinched together and she spoke to the space between her and the dashboard of the car.

"Stop this goddamn car," she said, "and let us out of it."

"George," Arizona Star said, drawing the name out in a kind of wail. "What are you saying? We've been waiting by the side of the road for over two hours since that woman in the red truck put us out back there."

"Hey," I said, easing off on the accelerator and making a big display of looking into the rearview mirror and craning my neck to see into the blind spot before I would begin pulling off again onto the shoulder of I–40. "Anything to please a lady."

"I don't need this shit," George said. "Putting us down and saying about Jimi Hendrix and Elvis doing Dean Martin and all that stuff."

"He's doing us a favor, George," Arizona Star said, leaning so far forward in the backseat she was shoving the guitar case up high enough to bump me in the back of my head. "He's just talking."

"Yeah, hey," I said. "No offense intended. I was just passing the time of day. And I know all about the anxiety of influence."

"The what?" George said, turned by now to fix me directly with her mismatched eyes.

"Well," I said, giving the accelerator a nudge back to where it had been and keeping the steering wheel aimed straight toward Memphis. "You know. Feeling yourself obligated to somebody or something that came before you and needing not to think about it or not dwell on it so much it won't let you do nothing on your own."

"You called me a real original," George said in a voice that sounded like wire being dragged off a tight spool with pliers.

"So? That's not an insult, George," Arizona Star said. "I thought it was nice, him saying that."

"I ain't no fucking original," George said, fixing her gaze back now at the empty space that had been steadily moving ahead of her all her life.

"Whatever you say," I said. "Makes no difference to me. Y'all still want out?"

"No," Arizona Star said. "We sure don't."

"All right," I said. "We'll keep percolating on down the road. I won't say another word."

"Say what all you want to say," Arizona Star said. "It makes the time pass faster."

"I've noticed that myself," I said to her through the rearview mirror. "It's a good way to fool the clock, making noise is."

"Saying stuff is good," Arizona Star agreed. "When you're talking out loud, you don't have to listen to what your mind's thinking."

"Influence," George grunted in a low tone and clicked her tongue-stud against her teeth a couple of times. "Influence."

"The anxiety of it," I said in what I intended to be a mollifying tone, realizing I had to back off for a spell if I intended to be able to see what direction the two of them would take on Front

Street once we got to where Union Avenue crosses it in Memphis and I let them out of the car. "That's what I was meaning. How what's behind you makes you nervous about where you are now and where you might end up getting to. You know, when all the bets are called in."

"That don't make any sense," George said toward the passenger-side window. "Far as I'm concerned. Not a damn bit."

"Nothing makes sense the first time you hear it," Arizona Star said from the rear seat in a careful voice. "You have to think about it for a while. Or let it kind of sit up there in your head until you can get back to it. It's like learning lyrics."

"How's that?" I said to the eyes in the mirror.

"Well," Arizona Star said, "when you're first singing the words to a song, that's all they are. Just words one after another with no way of telling about what they mean. Then, after you get them by heart in a tune, it happens."

"You understand them then," I said. "Is that what you're saying?"

"Not when you're actually singing them in front of somebody," she said. "I don't believe it happens then with an audience. Like for me, it'll happen at night, say, when I can't sleep and a lyric keeps running through my head. Over and over, you know. Then, all of a sudden. Bam. There it is. The meaning."

Arizona Star clapped her hands together once when she said *bam*, and George jumped a little with the sound over on her side of the car as she rode in what's known to ambulance crews as the death seat of an involved vehicle at an accident scene.

"Then that's when you know what it means," I said in an encouraging tone. "The words to the song you're talking about."

"And you never did before," Arizona Star said. "Because you were too busy learning how to sing it."

"I believe you might be onto something worth writing down somewhere," I said. "What you just said about not knowing what stuff means until you already got it by heart."

"Why, thank you," Arizona Star said in a pleased voice and leaned back in her seat with the guitar case hugged up to her chest and began to hum something. It sounded a little like "Me and Bobby Magee," but not quite.

George kept silent, and remained so all the rest of the way into Memphis, never turning in my direction again, and it wasn't until we had exited I–40 and worked our way over to East Parkway by the Memphis Zoo that she stopped staring out the side window instead of the windshield.

Arizona Star hadn't much else to say, either, and I hadn't pushed her to talk the last fifty miles into the city. I just listened to her hum bits and pieces of tunes that were almost familiar, and tended to my driving.

As we turned right onto Union Avenue and began to head directly toward the Mississippi River, slipping past the fast food franchises and the supermarkets and the hospitals and the odd mansion or two still remaining from the nineteenth century and not yet knocked down but doubtless high on some middle South developer's hit list, she leaned forward and poked me again in the back of the head with the guitar case as she did.

"Will you know when we're coming close to the Sun Studio?" she said.

"I sure will. I'd know I was going by that if I was asleep."

"Tell me, please, when we're about to. I want to look at it when we go by. I never can place it. I always get lost in Memphis."

"That's a prevailing hazard in this town," I said. "It's coming up there about three blocks on the right."

"Get ready, George," Arizona Star said, laying her hand on the seat back so that she touched the short fringe of bleached-out hair on the other woman's collar. "Think Elvis. Think Jerry Lee Lewis. Think Roy Orbison. Think big time."

She was saying this to George in a voice I hadn't heard her use before. There was a purr in it and a depth and something that made it feel like we were riding along in that Buick sometime late after midnight, rain falling slow but steady, and the streetlights haloed by mist and the big river waiting at the foot of the bluff still to be seen.

And somewhere coming up from the Mississippi Delta was the faraway sound of an old blues number being sung by a black man accompanying himself on a twelve-string guitar, sliding the back of a closed pocket-knife up and down between the frets.

But, of course, it was actually the middle of a hot day in late spring and the traffic was bad on Union, not a hint of water or movement in the air, and the last thing I wanted to be reminded of any more was a cool late night in Memphis with everything around converging to a fine diamond point with me and a woman at the focus of all of it.

So to hold all that at bay, I threw in my two-cents worth.

"Yeah, George," I said. "Listen to your lead singer. Think about how that little studio room at the sign of the Sun was a launching pad to the stars. You know, a kind of a way-station on the path to heaven. But whatever you do, don't let your mind think influence. Don't let it think anxiety."

I was keeping my eyes straight ahead, watching the Ideal Bread truck I was following and trying to make sure I wasn't going to be rear-ended by the old clunker Cadillac from the seventies riding my tail if I had to brake all of a sudden, but I could see George turning away from the window to look in my direction, nevertheless.

As she did, I detected out of the corner of my eye Arizona Star's pressing down on her shoulder with the hand she had been using to reassure her backup singer, and George rattled her tongue stud but didn't speak.

"What?" I said.

"Nothing," Arizona Star answered in an ordinary voice, pitched a little high and girlish to show enthusiasm at seeing something she had been waiting for. "Look. There it is." She was pointing ahead and to the right, and I slowed to make the dogleg turn that Union takes at that point in its journey to the river.

"Yep," I said. "Sun Studio. Y'all want to stop for a quick look?"

"No," the two women said together and then Arizona Star went on to say they needed to get on downtown and would look at the birthplace of rock 'n' roll as we know it later on down the line.

"It doesn't say Sun on the sign any more," she said. "I thought I remembered it used to."

"Oh, no. Not now it doesn't," I said. "We're into a period of historical authenticity and revision these days in Memphis. We're getting back to the roots of the way things used to be. Back when Eisenhower was in the White House and Elvis was a little boy on Alabama Street."

"Are we almost downtown?" George said. "How many more blocks do we have to wait?"

"Just about a mile from the Mississippi bridge," I sang, doing my best to sound like Chuck Berry. "See," I went on then in my regular voice, "it was first called the Memphis Recording Company and then they changed the name after everything got historic, and then they decided to really make things be the way they used to be, so they called it its original name again. That's all it takes. Picking out the right word for something and making it fit."

"I didn't know they'd changed it," Arizona Star said, settling back into her seat and beginning to gather her and George's gear about her. "I thought it was always the Sun."

"Naw," I said into the mirror. "We talking putting things back together. We talking getting it right this time. The one true word for it is resurrection."

Nobody said anything else after that until we passed the Peabody Hotel, not even a tongue-stud click from George, and I pulled the Buick up close to double-park by a BMW just past the stoplight at the intersection of Union and Front.

"We're here," I said, "at the heart of Bluff City," but by the time I got that out the two women were already crawling out of the car and hoisting the suitcase and the duffel bag and the case full of guitar into carrying positions.

"Star," I said. "Arizona Star," and she stopped to look back at me through the Buick's open rear door and wave.

"Thanks," she said.

"Rock and roll," I said, "will break your heart," but by then she was looking around her to see which direction to go, I supposed, and George turned back to stick her head into the passenger-side window.

"I want to say something to you," she said, both eyes squinted against the sunlight coming down from between the buildings but one still giving the appearance of taking in more than the other.

"Let me guess," I said, giving her a big white-toothed grin. "*Fuck you*, right?"

"You got it, Jack," she said without even an audible tongue-stud click.

"How'd you know my name?" I called after her, "and where are y'all playing tonight?" but she was already turned to follow Arizona Star to the sidewalk and didn't respond. By the time I eased the Buick back into traffic, I could see that the two of them were headed in the direction of Confederate Park with its marble monuments to all those dead believers, Star with her head up looking around and George with the duffel bag looking down to watch where to put her feet. A corner of a building cut them off from view as I began to negotiate the last two blocks of Union before it would stop at the river and become something else with a different name, but I didn't have to study the route. I had turned that corner years ago and didn't have to think about how I'd get there now.

The Apple and the Aspirin Tablet

As their mother opened the door to leave the house, Harold and Nancy, sitting on the floor of the living room, began to quarrel. They were coloring with crayons in coloring books, and Harold, two years older than his sister, had reached across his book, the one with the cover of Spitfires blasting Zeroes out of the sky, and had scribbled red marks on the face of a panda bear Nancy had been laboriously shading green. She squalled with rage and slapped at Harold's hand and tore the page in the process. She screamed louder, kicked at Harold's color book and began to pitch around on the floor.

"She hit me first," Harold said, watching his sister's fit with interest.

"You kids behave," their mother said, sticking her head through the door to yell. "You mind Aunt Betty, you hear me. I pity you this old rainy morning, but I'll be back as soon as I can." She said the last part to her sister-in-law who was sitting on the sofa with her feet up. She had a newspaper in one hand and a cup of coffee in the other.

"Oh, you go on ahead. I'll take care of them. They won't be no trouble." The door closed and the aunt looked at her niece and nephew. "Harold, you leave your little sister alone. If you act right, I'll tell you some more about Leonard Allen after a while."

Harold dropped his crayon and said when.

"Oh, in a little bit. Y'all go on ahead and play right now. I'm reading this paper and drinking my coffee."

Harold turned away and walked to a window to look for airplanes. Outside the rain came down steadily from a sky so overcast he couldn't see above the rooftops. A wet bird sat on a branch of the tree close to the house, turning its head from side to side to pluck at its feathers. "Look, a bird," Harold said quietly so his sister couldn't hear. She would scream and run to see, and then he wouldn't be able to think about his cousin Leonard Allen.

Leonard Allen wasn't like most of his kinfolks. He was grown, a soldier fighting the Japs. The last time Harold had seen him, Leonard Allen was wearing a uniform with shiny buttons and ribbons, and he was drunk and carrying Christmas presents. Now when airplanes came over, Harold would run out to see them and pretend Leonard Allen was inside and hadn't been drinking so much that he laughed all the time. It amused Harold to tell Nancy, "There's cousin Leonard Allen." She really thought it was him every time, but Harold, of course, knew that Leonard Allen couldn't be on every plane that came over Nederland, Texas. Even the time the airplane wrote PEPSI in the sky Nancy had believed cousin Leonard Allen was the pilot when Harold told her so.

Harold sighed deeply and rubbed his nose against the pane. He blew out through his nostrils and watched the two little clouds of fog form on the glass. He drew a circle in one of the clouds with a fingertip and then another circle in the other one with a finger on his other hand. He couldn't see the planes come over now even if cousin Leonard Allen really was in one of them. It was winter, and it was cloudy. Harold looked again outside at the tree. The bird was gone, and where it had been sitting an empty branch moved up and down. Harold stared at it as it moved slower and slower and finally stopped.

Harold began to move his head back and forth in front of the window, watching his reflection in the glass. He narrowed his eyes and made a face so that his lips turned down at the corners. Leaning back and squinting, he suddenly noticed that he could make himself look like one of the artificial Japs he had seen in the two-man submarine on display in downtown Beaumont where Daddy and Mama had taken him a few days ago. Harold backed away from the windows in a hurry and turned to look at Aunt Betty.

"Were the Japs real?" he asked. She didn't answer. "Aunt Betty, were the Japs real?"

Harold moved up to stand by the sofa so he could look up into her face. Her glasses caught the light so that her eyes were hidden. They looked like searchlights or like the bottoms of green Coke bottles. Harold pulled at Aunt Betty's dress sleeve and repeated his question.

"What are you doing?" she said, pulling her sleeve away from Harold's hold. "Are Japs real? Of course, they're real. Haven't I told you over and over again about Leonard Allen fighting them Japs?"

"No, no," Harold tried to explain. "Them other ones. The ones in Beaumont in the submarine. The artificial Japs." Nancy looked up from her color book and tried to imitate what her brother had just said.

"Yeah," she said. "Them 'ficial Japs."

"Now look what you done. Got this baby talking about them mean old Japs." Aunt Betty held out her arms toward Nancy, and Nancy crawled up into her lap. "You leave this baby alone now, Harold. Go back there in the bedroom and play with something. Give me some rest."

Harold surrendered and started toward the back of the house. He was able to direct his path, though, so that he could step on

Nancy's box of crayons. After the satisfying feel of crunch and smear beneath his shoe, he looked back quickly at Aunt Betty, but she was still hugging Nancy and hadn't seen him. As he walked down the hall and prepared to enter his room, Harold imagined that the two Japs from the submarine were waiting for him, maybe in the closet or hiding under the bed. He looked cautiously into the room before going in and then went only as far as his rocking chair which still lay on its side where it had fallen after Harold tripped over it the night before. He had woken from a bad dream again and run crying to his parents' bed. Harold righted the chair and began to rock. Mama had said she was sorry they had taken Harold to see that submarine the Coast Guard had captured in the Gulf.

"Well, I'm not sorry," Daddy told her. "He's got to get over this scariness. He knows that wasn't real Japs in that two-man sub. They didn't even look real. Just store dummies painted up with Jap uniforms on. They didn't even have Oriental features."

"I don't care. It sure fooled Harold. And you know how scared he is of tight places. That sub was so little inside. I could just see Harold chewing on his fingernails while he looked at it."

"Leonard Allen doesn't chew his fingernails, and he's right in them islands in the front lines, fighting Japs from sun-up until the sun goes down everyday," Daddy said. His father had lain back down, and his mother had let Harold sleep the rest of the night beside her in the bed.

HAROLD STOOD UP in the rocking chair and faced the back of it. He held the rungs and rocked faster and faster, pretending he was diving in a fighter plane. He made engine and machine gun noises in his throat, tilting his chair to the right and left as he furiously rocked. After a few minutes, he allowed the chair to slow and stop. He could hear Aunt Betty singing to Nancy in the living room, and he walked out into the hall to listen. She sang in a high quavering voice one of the songs Harold had been taught in Sunday school.

> This little light of mine
> I'm gonna let it shine
> Ain't gonna let the Devil hide it
> No, I'm gonna let it shine

"Tell us about the Devil again, Aunt Betty," Harold said as he ran into the living room. Aunt Betty had finished her coffee and newspaper. Nancy was busy on the floor coloring one of the pictures on the front page with an orange crayon. She scrawled recklessly back and forth across the face of a general addressing troops. The soldiers had their faces painted black, it seemed to Harold, though he could tell they weren't colored people. Why? Aunt Betty was cleaning her glasses with a flowered handkerchief, holding them at arm's length to judge the effect of her polishing. She brought the glasses close to her mouth to spit on one of the lenses before turning her head to acknowledge what Harold had said to her.

"Little boys who pick on their sisters ought to be worried about the Devil all right," she said.

"She hit me first."

"That don't make no difference. She's little and you're big and she's a girl and you're a boy. Besides, you're supposed to take care of your little sister when your mama's not home." She finished wiping the wet spot off her glasses and after a last look lifted them to her face. She spent some time adjusting them on the bridge of her nose and settling the gold wires over each ear. Finished, she looked at Harold and motioned him to sit down in front of her on the floor. Nancy joined her brother in front of her aunt, jamming her left thumb into her mouth and beginning to twirl the curls above her right ear with the first finger of her right hand.

"All right," Aunt Betty began to say. "Little boys and girls who act up and do bad things are gonna get caught by the Devil." She reached down and pulled at Nancy's hand. "Get that thumb out of your mouth. Old Devil's watching you, everything you do." Nancy whimpered and put her hand under her dress. She twisted the hair above her ear faster, causing it to snarl into a puffy ball.

"Hair is bad, too," Harold said in a loud whisper to his sister. Aunt Betty didn't seem to have heard what he said or even that he had spoken, though. She seemed to be looking out the window at something far away.

"Do you see him, Aunt Betty?"

"What? No, I don't see him. I don't do bad things," she said. "Why should I be a scaredy cat? Nothing bothers me. It's if you do bad things you got to be worried. 'Cause everything you do that's bad when you're a little boy, the old Devil finds out about it. He's watching all the time. He don't know what getting tired is. Every time you bother your little sister or sass your mama, he's just outside the house looking in at the window."

"What does he look like? Like a Jap?" As he sat on the floor, Harold began to shift his weight rhythmically from one hip to the other. He waited until Aunt Betty looked back at the window and then bit quickly at his left thumbnail. Seeing him do it, Nancy opened her mouth to speak, but sat back when he gave her a mean look. Aunt Betty began to speak again in a comfortable sort of voice, the way she sounded when she talked about her boy Leonard Allen fighting the Japs.

"Well, he's big and he's red. He's got a long tail coming down from his hind-end, and it's sharp on the end of it. It's got a stinger in it that hurts worse than a thousand yellow jacket wasps if he ever hits you with it."

"What's his feet look like?" Harold spoke in a sing-song voice, continuing to shift his body back and forth. By this time Nancy had quietly slipped her thumb back in her mouth and was sucking hard at it.

"His feet," said Aunt Betty, lifting her own feet and extending them toward Harold and Nancy to demonstrate, "look like cow feet. Like hooves. When he walks, he leaves his footprints just like a two-legged bull behind him. Everywhere his feet touch the ground, they burn the grass off right in the shape of a old hoof." She stopped talking and nodded her head so that her glasses again caught and reflected the light. "Yes, kids, the ground is burned just in the shape of a old hoof. Notice sometime when you're outside walking by the windows where he looks in. See if you can't find a burned mark in the grass that looks like that."

"Does he get you when you're alive?" Harold said. Nancy echoed around her thumb, "Alive?"

"Sometimes. He can if he wants to. But mostly what he does is to wait until you do a lot of bad things and then when you die, he gets you in Hell where all his helpers stay." Aunt Betty paused to pull Nancy's hand away from her face and then went on. "Hell is the place where he lives. Under the ground where there's always hot fires and stinking smoke and not a drop of water and you can't get your breath. Where all the bad folks go when they die and don't get to go to Heaven where Jesus lives."

"Jesus," Nancy said and nodded her head knowingly.

"Yes, honey, Jesus," Aunt Betty said as she reached down to let the girl into her lap. "He loves the little children of the world." Harold spoke loudly to get his aunt's attention, and as he did, half-rose from his position on the floor.

"What does the Devil do to you in Hell?"

"Why, he just throws you on one of his griddles and sticks a pitchfork with real sharp points on it into you. Then he lets you burn and cook on one side and turns you over and lets the fire cook you on the other side. And he keeps on doing that forever over and over again. He don't get tired, and if he happens ever to, he's got his helpers to spell him and give him a hand. There ain't never no relief."

Aunt Betty leaned forward to put Nancy down and then stood up. "Where's your mama's sewing machine, Harold? Aunt Betty wants to hem a couple of dresses."

Harold led her to the bedroom and pointed out the machine behind the closet door. Aunt Betty adjusted her glasses and began to rummage in a shoe box filled with spools of thread as Nancy held on to the hem of her skirt. After watching Aunt Betty work the machine for a time, Harold grew bored and wandered down the hall toward the kitchen. He paused along the way to pick up one of Nancy's dolls from the floor. He held it in one hand, gave it a half-hearted punch in the face and let it drop. As he worked his way to the kitchen, he alternately kicked the walls on each side of the hall, making tank and artillery noises by humming through his teeth.

He stood in the doorway to the kitchen looking at the remains of breakfast. By standing on his toes he was able to reach across the front burner on the range and dip his fingers into the half-empty pan of cold oatmeal which his mother had shoved to the back of the stove. With the tip of his tongue he touched the pasty smear on his fingers. He immediately rejected it and wiped his hand on the leg of his pants and on one of the front burners of the stove. From his mother's bedroom came the drone of the sewing machine, and as it rose and fell in pitch, Harold attempted to hum in unison. He walked from place to place in the kitchen, and seeing a small paring knife on the cabinet near the sink, stopped to take a look at it.

The blade was shiny along the cutting edge, but blackened and rusty elsewhere. Harold thought about fastening it to the muzzle of his wooden rifle to use as a bayonet against the enemy, but then thought of Aunt Betty in the bedroom and shot a glance at the window nearest him. Nothing but gray sky, so he decided he would use the knife as he had seen his mother do, to peel apples for himself and Nancy.

He selected two from a brown paper sack on the floor near the refrigerator and began to turn one of them over and over in his hand. It reminded him of a clown's nose, red and shiny and too big. He picked up the knife from the floor where he had let it fall and made a tiny experimental cut. The skin of the apple seemed to open of its own accord, releasing apple smell and a thin thread of juice. "Blood," Harold said aloud.

He pushed the point of the knife into the apple and then made a twisting movement. A small section of the fruit fell out as he withdrew the blade. He retrieved it from his lap and replaced it in the cavity it had left. It fitted perfectly and, except for a fine line around the edge of the cut, the apple appeared whole and untouched. Harold shook the dollop out and replaced it several times, pleased by the secret he had created. He brought the apple to his mouth and stopped. He reached instead for the other one and bit into it. He ate slowly, pausing frequently to take out and replace the hidden door to the secret chamber in the other fruit. During one of these operations, he bit off the tip of the dollop of apple and was pleased to find that it still fit perfectly, though now with the advantage of a tiny empty space within.

Suddenly he scrambled to his feet, opened a drawer in a kitchen cabinet and after carefully placing the apple inside, ran through the living room, down the hall past where Aunt Betty was sewing, and into the bathroom.

"Are you going to wee wee, Harold?" Aunt Betty called as she heard him go by.

"Yes, ma'am."

"That's a good boy. Be careful now."

Harold quickly closed the bathroom door and closed the lid on the toilet bowl. By standing on top of it and stretching, he was able to open the medicine cabinet and reach the tin box which he knew Mama went to for aspirins. An aspirin wouldn't hurt Nancy, he thought, but he knew how bad it would taste. She would be fooled and spit and cry. He remembered to pull the flush handle as he left, and Aunt Betty congratulated him as he ran past the room where she and Nancy were, Aunt Betty pumping the machine with her right foot and Nancy watching the bobbin spin.

After putting the aspirin in its secret place, Harold began to call Nancy. "I got an apple. I got an apple." He heard the bang as his sister pushed open the door of the bedroom and slammed it into the wall. She ran into the kitchen, her hands stuck out toward him. Harold chanted and held the apple out of Nancy's reach, making her jump up and down as she begged for what he was keeping from her.

"Here, then," Harold said. "Bite on this side first."

She did, gnawing away at the special spot on the apple, and it wasn't until her third bite that she reacted. Nancy began to scream and splutter, rubbing the sleeve of her dress against her tongue.

"Bad, bad," she yelled. "Hot, hot."

Harold felt something give in his stomach, down low toward where it felt like he had to go to the bathroom, and he began to try to calm his sister by putting his finger to his lips and talking to her in a quiet voice.

"You just got a little bit," he said, pulling the apple out of her hand. "Look, most of it's still left."

"Harold, what are you doing? Why's that baby crying?" Aunt Betty was in the hall, then the living room, then the kitchen. Her face was red, and her hair looked as though she had been brushing it the wrong way for a long time. "I tell you I can't get a thing done this morning for you bothering that baby and getting her to going. One thing, little man, the Devil's sure taking notes on you today."

Harold looked up at Aunt Betty, trying to see her eyes, but again her glasses showed only a strange picture of himself, a Harold with a head bigger than it ought to be and no mouth, tiny eyes and what looked like flippers where his hands should be. She moved closer to him, so close he could smell the deodorant she used and feel the cloth of her dress shoving up against his face, and then he could see her eyes again as the light changed on the lens of her glasses. Harold looked down at the apple in his hand which seemed to have become much bigger than it had been before, even though it should be smaller since he could see the hole in its side where his sister had bitten into its secret chamber and taken part of it into her mouth.

"Well," Harold said. "She was eating this apple, and she started crying. I don't know why. Maybe she bit her tongue. Maybe it's a bad old apple. Maybe something's wrong with it."

"Let me see that apple," Aunt Betty said, pulling it roughly from Harold's hand and adjusting her glasses on the bridge of her nose. She squinted at the spot on the apple where Nancy had bitten, rubbed at it with a finger, and suddenly blew air out of her mouth as though something had hit her squarely in the middle of the back and made her lose her breath. "Oh, my God. It's poisoned." She poked at the residue of the aspirin and then wiped her finger on the material of her skirt over and over. The moisture of the apple had caused the aspirin to lose its tablet shape so that it now appeared to be a loose collection of grains. It looked to Harold like sugar melting in the morning on his bowl of oatmeal while he waited for it to cool off enough to be able to eat. His mouth suddenly watered with a bitter flood of saliva as he watched Aunt Betty sniff, touch and cautiously dab the tip of her tongue at the finger which she had been wiping on her dress.

"Oh, it's bitter, bitter. Some kind of poison stuff. Blessed Jesus in Heaven, hold my hand."

Aunt Betty wheeled around, laid the apple on top of the refrigerator and seized Nancy around the waist. Turning her upside down and holding her struggling and kicking under her left arm, Aunt Betty turned on the water faucet and thrust Nancy's head beneath it. While Nancy bubbled and squalled, Harold began to jump up and down in one spot clutching at the front of his trousers.

"Aunt Betty, Aunt Betty," he screamed. "I just counted the aspirins. One of them's missing. It's lost. It's lost."

"Harold, you hush. This ain't no aspirin tablet," Aunt Betty said, continuing to splash water on Nancy's face and into her mouth. "Blessed Lord, stand by me, please Jesus."

She was having a great deal of trouble keeping Nancy's hands away from her mouth as while she ran the water, so she half-laid, half-threw the girl into the sink, just as the front door to the house opened and Harold's and Nancy's mama backed into the room, shaking her umbrella outside the door. While he looked at his mother busily making sure not to make a mess and not yet aware of what was happening in the kitchen, Harold began to back into the narrow space between the refrigerator and the wall. This close to his head, the motor made a deep moaning hum interrupted regularly by deep clicking sounds. By the time his mother had realized something terrible had happened, Harold was already humming in tune with the electric motor, bouncing his head from the refrigerator to the wall, the wall to the refrigerator as each deep click came in the machine's rhythm.

The two women were screaming at each other in high voices as Nancy fought and spluttered beneath the stream of water from the faucet. "What is it? Is it lye? Did she swallow some lye?" Mama yelled into Aunt Betty's face. "My God, is it lye?"

"No, no, it's that apple. It's that poison apple."

"Where did it come from? Where is it?"

Aunt Betty pointed to the top of the refrigerator where the apple lay, the spot on it where Nancy had bitten already turning brown.

"Probably Jap spies," Aunt Betty said. "Or else the German prisoners of war they got working in the orchards. No telling what kind of chemicals that stuff is. We got to save that apple and send it to Austin to get that poison tested."

"Austin?" Mama said, looking around her wildly. "Austin?"

"Yeah," Aunt Betty said. "Like they do with mad dogs' heads after they cut them off."

"Where's Harold? Did he get any of it?" Mama was rolling her head from side to side as though stinging insects had crawled into both her ears and were driving her mad, stopping suddenly as she saw Harold standing in the empty space between the refrigerator and the wall.

"He didn't eat none, I don't think," Aunt Betty said, "but he touched that apple. He had it in his hand when I came in here." She turned abruptly from the sink and left Nancy in her mother's hands. "Here, you take care of her. I'm gonna mix up some dry mustard and egg white and hot water to make them take so they'll puke."

The dose was mixed, Harold was jerked from his narrow place and he and Nancy were led to the back porch to be force-fed the antidote. "I didn't eat none of the apple, I didn't eat none of the apple," Harold begged, but no one listened.

Holding a post on the post for support as he leaned over the edge to vomit, he mumbled over and over to himself between spasms, "Don't tell, don't tell, don't tell." The apple he had eaten, the oatmeal from breakfast, curdled milk and water fell in splotches on the dark earth near the porch. As it did, each patch of partially digested stuff seemed to Harold to be falling into a pattern, a design you might see in a coloring book, a shape which looked like something he should be able to know for what it was, but couldn't. Nancy retched beside him, Aunt Betty supporting her while Mama tended to him, praying aloud and pressing a wet cloth that felt like fire as it moulded itself to the exact shape of his forehead.

It was always that particular scene of the whole episode which Harold was to remember afterwards, on that morning when Aunt Betty had described the Devil at his work in Hell and Harold had found the secret hiding place which a knife could make—he and his sister Nancy vomiting off the edge of the porch onto the dark earth while he repeated again and again to himself the command not to tell what he had discovered and used. It was not until much later, after over fifty years had passed and many new wars had come and gone, that Harold realized one bright Sunday afternoon as he sat watching one of his grandsons play a video game buzzing with monsters why at the time he had known it was impossible to tell the truth about the apple and the aspirin tablet.

The Officer Responding

Quentin Vest had always trusted policemen, even back when everybody called them pigs, back when you weren't supposed to respect anybody in uniform. Even the cool kids in high school had believed the cops were just tools of the establishment, nothing but hired clubs and guns put on the payroll just to keep things the way the power structure wanted them to stay.

He never had said anything to anybody, of course, about the way he really felt about the police, the way his mama and daddy had raised him to, not even to Clarence Blackstock, his best and only real friend at Central High. Quentin had even joined in a couple of times when everybody in one of the peace marches to the state capitol building in downtown Nashville made oinking noises at the officers standing outside their cars along West End Avenue and then down Broadway after West End stopped being called that.

"Hey, hey," Evelyn Price had started yelling, "Nashville pigs, you think you are so damn big." Everybody started in hollering the same thing then, laughing and happy because Evelyn had figured out for them what would be a cool thing to yell as they marched along together to get peace in Vietnam.

Evelyn had spoken to Quentin once, passing him in the aisle

of the Candyland Store when he was there with his mother to pick up some peanut brittle for Mumu who was sick. She had said his name. "Quentin." Like that.

"Is that one of your girlfriends?" his mother had asked him, looking around to watch Evelyn Price walk on down the aisle, headed for the marshmallow chocolates, probably. His mother had turned and smiled real big at Quentin like she had found something out he had been hiding from her.

"No," he had said. "Mother, no. Don't talk so loud."

What if Evelyn Price had heard what she said, Evelyn the most popular hippie girl in high school. with her auburn hair all wavy like water flowing over rocks in a creek bed, Evelyn a girl who would never have spoken to him in the hall at Central High and had done it now because there wasn't anybody to hear her doing it but him and his mother, and of course his mother didn't count she was so old. And nobody would have believed Evelyn had noticed Quentin anyway back at the high school, so she knew he wouldn't be bragging about her saying his name.

And who would listen to him, anyway, but that overweight Clarence Blackstock who had no chin at all to speak of. Evelyn knew all that if she even bothered to think about it.

It had made Quentin's day, though, to hear Evelyn say his name out loud, even it was just in Candyland with no real people listening to verify it. He had gone straight to the bathroom when he and his mother got back home, and he had combed his hair into different looks for thirty minutes. That's not all he did, either, he remembered.

But he hadn't seen Evelyn Price in twenty years now, even though for a long time after graduating from Central High School, Quentin had watched for her name and picture in the *Nashville Tennessean* and even in *Time* and *Newsweek*. If anybody was going to make it big out of Central High, it would have been Evelyn, but no, nothing ever was mentioned about her that he was able to find out. Out of sight. Gone. Probably living in California or New York under a different name altogether, though there couldn't have been a sexier name for her than Evelyn was.

So when he called the police on the 911 line, Quentin had expected that probably a really nice one would show up at the house on Bellwood. Maybe one that looked like the officers on *COPS* on Saturday nights. One with a mustache like they all had, a pretty good-sized man with big forearms like he did a lot of arm curls everyday in the police gym, and just real calm about everything. Cool.

Quentin waited a long time before he called, expecting probably that Ruby would come driving back up any minute, the tires of the car making a crunching sound as she turned into the driveway that came in behind the house and the lights on high like she always had them.

He sat for what he thought was probably an hour out in the back yard in a lawn chair, as much as he could make himself stay still, looking up and down the street at every car that came by, expecting any minute to see the green Chevy slowing up to make the turn off Bellwood into the driveway. He fooled himself about every third car, jumping up when he did, and then walking back and forth in the wet grass that needed cutting until he was able to make himself sit back down to wait.

He wanted to smoke, but there wasn't a cigarette in the house, and he was glad of that, or he would have done it, even though he had been stopped from the habit now for almost a year, ever since the doctor had asked him if he intended to go on making his living by talking to customers in the paint store. "Yes," he had said, shocked at the question. "I do. That's what I do."

"I'll give you about six months more of having a voice, then," the doctor had said. "Then it'll probably play out for good. Maybe up to a year, if you're lucky, high-strung as you are."

Quentin knew the doctor was lying, but he was glad that he was, because now he could quit by scaring himself with what the doctor had warned him. Lying or not, maybe he was right, you know, unconsciously, Quentin had told himself, and his trained eye had seen something he didn't even realize he had seen. So he quit. But now, in the back yard of the house that Ruby had sneaked off from sometime after 11:30 pm when he had gone off to sleep, Quentin knew he would have smoked if he had the cigarettes to do it with.

Pall Malls, he told himself, watching a truck and a black Lincoln slide by on Bellwood, neither one the car Ruby had left in, that's what I would go out and buy a carton of to smoke if they said on TV that the world was coming to an end tomorrow or that missiles were coming in the next two hours and fixing to hit Nashville, aimed right at the Parthenon in Centennial Park.

But not until then, Quentin promised himself and leaned over in the lawn chair to pull up a blade or two of San Augustine grass to chew on while he waited for Ruby to come back home, park the car and try to sneak into the house without his hearing her because he was asleep. She wished.

The grass blades didn't help any, and Quentin spit them out, having trouble dislodging one that had gotten stuck to his lower lip and making a blowing noise like a horse while he did it. Something caught his eye up on the corner of Bellwood and Pace as he leaned forward in the chair to blow away at the grass blade, and he jerked as he realized it was Ruby, standing bent over from the waist and letting her hair hang down over her face.

But when he stood up to run toward her, knocking over the

lawn chair in the process, he could see before he took the second step it was nothing but the last one in a row of bushes in a neighbor's yard across the street, hard to make out the true nature of in the shadows but still just a bunch of unclipped twigs and leafy branches that looked like Ruby all doubled over.

Time to call that 911 number, he said to himself inside his head, I can't sit here all night waiting for Ruby to show up. She might be lying in a ditch somewhere, where she's been raped and run over by somebody she met at the Hound's Tooth or the Brass Scales. If we had another car, I could drive around and look for her, but we don't, so there. Besides I can't go off and leave Heather and Jason sleeping in their beds by themselves while I look for their mama.

The woman on the other end of 911 answered on the second ring. It seemed strange just to punch three times on the telephone rather than seven and have it begin to ring, Quentin thought as he stood by the wall set in the kitchen, the one the greatest distance from the kids' rooms so they wouldn't hear him talking and wake up. They didn't need to hear what kind of things got said on a 911 call.

"911," the woman said. Her voice sounded like she was black, and it was real calm, almost bored as she talked. You could tell nothing would faze her. "Can I help you? What is your location? What is the nature of your call?"

"Well," Quentin said. "Yes, ma'am. I'm at 2110 Bellwood, off of West End Avenue, and I'm calling about my wife. She's gone."

"Where is she?"

"I don't know, see. She just left when I was asleep in the car. I mean in the house is where I was asleep. She's in the car. I mean she was in it when she left. That's how she did it."

"Do you have any reason to believe she's in trouble?"

"No more than the usual," Quentin said. "See, she's mental,

kind of. Under treatment, you know."

"Do you want an officer to respond to your location?"

"That would be good, I believe, yes ma'am," Quentin said, listening to the 911 woman's computer keys tapping as he talked. "I'm worried a little about it. I mean actually I'm worried a lot."

"Stay there," the black woman's voice said. "A unit will respond."

After the connection was broken and all Quentin could hear was the buzz of the dial tone and the dead quiet of the kitchen, he hung up and tried to make himself sit back down in the lawn chair in the dark back yard, but he couldn't stay down more than a few seconds before he found himself walking around the house to stand on the front porch.

That would look funny to any neighbor who might be peering out of a window at the front of 2110 Bellwood, though, he knew, so he soon left that location and moved back to the corner of the house where he could crouch down behind some forsythia bushes and not be so easily seen. I can still watch from here, he said to himself in a whisper so low he could barely hear the words he was saying, and see the unit respond as soon as it gets here. I hope it won't be blowing its siren and flashing its lights.

It wasn't, when it pulled up to the front of the house in less than two minutes time, and the officer inside cut the headlights as soon as the vehicle stopped. The door opened, and the driver stepped out, and as Quentin straightened up from his crouch behind the forsythia bush he could hear the jingling noises of all the equipment the policeman, a rather small one, was wearing on his belt and attached to his shirt and collar.

"Hi," Quentin said and stepped out of the shadow of the vegetation and began moving slowly toward the officer, his hands held high in front of him so the policeman could see there was no threat coming at him. He was glad he remembered to do that, and he fixed a smile on his face to greet the man in blue walking toward him. "I'm over here. I'm the one who called 911."

The officer nodded and put the beam of a flashlight on Quentin's chest and then switched it off. "About your wife," the policeman said, "the mental case you called her."

"Not exactly a mental case," Quentin said, realizing something was not what he had expected about the responding officer, and as the distance between him and the person with the flashlight and the jingling noises lessened, knowing suddenly that the policeman was not a man at all. It was a female officer. "My wife," Quentin said, "she's just under treatment is all. That's what I meant."

"What kind of treatment?" the officer asked in what was definitely a woman's voice. "Psychological?"

"Yes," Quentin said. "That's it. For a good long time now. She's been seeing a master's degree woman for, oh, three years running now. But she's not, you know, crazy or anything like that. She doesn't see stuff that's not there or hear people talking to her in her head or believe in aliens or anything."

"Tell me what's happened tonight and why you're concerned," the officer said and stepped into the beam falling from the porchlight behind Quentin. "Has something unusual happened?"

The woman's hair hung from beneath the police cap just past her ears in a perfectly straight fall as though it had been cut using a ruler, and she was wearing eyeglasses with lenses large enough to cover the top half of her face. She looked up from the notebook she was holding in her left hand, a pen poised over it, and stared directly into Quentin's face as he stepped into the light.

"Quentin," she said, the same way she had said the word in Candyland twenty years ago in front of the stacks of peanut brittle on the aisle next to the one that held the various kinds of fudge:

vanilla, double Dutch, almond, cashew, peppermint, pecan, walnut, marshmallow, American Surprise, licorice, egg custard, and
Candyland Double Smash, the specialty of the store.

"Evelyn?" Quentin said. "Evelyn Price?"

"Eve," the officer said. "That's the handle I use now. And I've had
two other last names since Price. The full name is Eve LaMouse-
Shellaburger. How's it going, Quentin?"

"A police officer? You?"

"Just made sergeant," Evelyn Price said. "What's the situation
here, Quentin?"

Quentin felt like doing several things at once. First he wanted
desperately to retreat to the back yard and sit down in the lawn
chair in the dark and listen again to how many times Evelyn Price
had said his name in the last minute. Three, he thought it was,
maybe four, but probably one of them he was remembering from
that time in Candyland with his mother standing beside him. But
it was at least three times in one minute as compared to once in
twenty years.

The second thing he wanted to do was ask Sergeant Evelyn Price
to turn around so he could look at the back of her head to see how
her hair looked from that angle, all cut off and flattened out as
straight as a board. Third, he wanted to get her to step more over
into the light and turn sideways so he could see how her breasts
and her behind looked in silhouette, if they were of still the same
definition, if he could tell, that is, what with the uniform of the
Metropolitan Nashville Police she was wearing and the handgun
and handcuffs and leather sap and notebook bracket all attached
to the four-inch wide belt she had around her waist.

Fourth, he wanted to divorce Ruby and crawl into the backseat
of Evelyn Price's Dodge cruiser and let her drive him to Gatlinburg
or Memphis, one direction or the other on I–40, it didn't mat-

ter which, and he wouldn't care if he were being transported in restraints or not.

What he did instead was to stare, as deeply as he could in the dim light reflecting off Evelyn Price's glasses, directly into her eyes as though he might be able to catch another glimpse of the most popular hippie girl in Nashville Central High School his senior year. Leaning forward a little, Quentin opened his mouth to speak but found not a single word ready to come out and be pronounced. He swallowed twice, making a clicking sound as he did his mouth was so dry.

"Is it a domestic, Quentin?" the officer before him said. "Was there an argument between you and your wife?" She moved her ball point in a little circle over the pad in her hand as though encouraging him to give her something to write down. Then she nodded her head and looked up with a little smile on her face. "Do y'all fight? Did you tonight?"

"Why, no," Quentin found himself able to say. "We don't fight, Ruby and me. I mean, we pass harsh words now and then."

"Does it ever get physical, Quentin?" Officer LaMouse-Shellaburger asked. "Ever any hitting or slapping?"

"Some, yes," Quentin said, trying to keep count in his head of the number of times she's said the name again, but rapidly losing any sense of an accurate count. That was good, though. It meant it was a bunch. "I don't really mind, though. It never hurts me none."

"You mean when you hit your wife?"

"No, when Ruby she hits or kicks out at me," Quentin said in a shocked tone. "Why, I never would do anything like that to a woman. They're littler than a man, you know. And I was always taught to remember that. I mean they generally are. Women. Littler."

"So you're saying in these domestic disputes she's the offender, your wife?"

"Now she doesn't mean to be," Quentin answered Evelyn Price. "Just that she's always got a lot on her, she believes."

Feeling a little dizzy, not enough to want to sit down or anything, but like he wanted to move his eyes around some, or else faint, Quentin lifted his gaze from the surface of Evelyn Price's glasses and focused them on the silver badge or whatever it was in the center of her cap just above the visor. It had writing and some kind of a crest on it like you might see on a television screen right before the rerun of an episode from a 1960s' police program. *Dragnet,* maybe, or *Police Story.*

"Your hair," Quentin said to Evelyn Price. "You cut it off."

"No," she said. "It's always been like this."

"Not at Central. Not back in high school."

"Oh, I got rid of all that stuff years ago. Got in the way."

"Of what?" Quentin said in an amazed voice. He couldn't imagine.

"Doing what you have to do," Evelyn Price said. "You know, what you might be called upon to handle."

Quentin didn't answer back. He just stood in the front yard of his Cape Cod on Bellwood, his shoes getting soaked through with the dew from the San Augustine grass, and thought about clear water flowing over polished stones in a creek bed in dappled sunlight.

"So she just left for no reason you could ascertain?" the Nashville Metropolitan Police officer standing in front of him said. "You woke and couldn't find her?"

"Who?"

"Your wife," Evelyn Price said and wrote something on her pad of paper. "Ruby's her name, isn't it?"

"Do you know her?" Quentin said, surprised at the inside knowledge Evelyn Price was displaying as a police officer.

"No, you said her name already two or three times."

"I did? I thought I just thought it."

"You couldn't find Ruby when you woke?" Evelyn Price said in what sounded to Quentin like a patient tone.

"No," he said and shook his head vigorously. "And her name is Ruby. She was Ruby Fingerling. I mean before we married. She went to Hillsboro High."

"I see," Evelyn Price said, looking down at her book again, but before she could ask him anything else, Quentin pointed toward the street.

"Yonder she comes now," he said, narrowing his point to focus on where the driveway joined Bellwood, "in that Chevrolet."

Evelyn Price turned to watch with him a light-colored Nova pull off the street, surge halfway up the drive and stop with the driver's door right next to a forsythia bush at the corner of the house.

The woman driving the vehicle opened the door and had a hard time getting out, what with the branches of the forsythia pushing against it, but she worked at it until she was able to squeeze out of the small opening the parking position allowed.

"Woo," Ruby said, letting the door be slammed back closed by the pressure of the forsythia bush. "Damn if that ain't a tight fit."

Ruby's hair was pushed forward from the back of her head so that a big puff of it lay over her brow and hung down over the right side of her face. She pushed it up so she could look with both eyes at the two people standing in the wet grass of the yard as she walked toward them.

"What are you?" she said to Evelyn Price. "A meter maid?"

"No, ma'am," Evelyn Price said. "I'm a Metro police officer."

"Good," Ruby said and stopped three or four feet short of where the other two were standing.

She let her hair go, and it flopped back to where it had been in the first place. "I hope you're here in this yard to take him in for general sorriness. The little creep sure needs it."

"I was worried about you, honey," Quentin said and then added, "Ruby."

"Well, you sure ought to be," Ruby said, talking to Quentin but looking at the woman police officer in her front yard. "I about had it with you, I'm here to tell you, up to here." She made a quick slicing motion across her forehead with her hand.

"Are you all right, ma'am?" Evelyn Price said. "Is there anything I can do for you?"

"Nothing but haul Quentin Vest's jerky little behind off to jail. If you can do that, I'll be the happiest woman in the Nashville metropolitan area."

"Ruby," Quentin said, "don't talk like that in front of the police lady. You know what? She's Evelyn Price from Central High School. That's where I knew her from."

"Central High, huh?" Ruby said. "I'm from Hillsboro. I was a Lady Burro on the drill team. Let me tell you something, lady cop. Don't never marry outside your high school. That's my best advice to you and to anybody else that don't want a life of misery and sucky times."

"Ruby," Quentin said. "Honey, don't you want some coffee and then to go lay down?"

"Yep," Ruby said. "Set your sights on somebody in the class ahead of you if all the good ones in your own class have done got grabbed off by the cheerleaders. Get you a football player or somebody in the in-crowd with a real nice car."

Stepping back a couple of feet, Ruby squared her shoulders and let her hands fall to her sides, and then suddenly made as though she were drawing a six-gun from a holster on her right hip. "Pew," she said. "Pew, pew. Get him in your sights, the one from your own high school, and then give him whatever it takes to nail him down so you can make him marry you. By any means necessary, like it says on them rap-singers' T-shirts."

Relaxing her stance, she let herself collapse slowly into a cross-legged sitting position on the dew-soaked ground, replacing the imaginary six-gun in her play holster as she sank to rest.

"Don't never," she said, "lady cop, don't never marry some slack-twisted student-council French-club band-member from Central High."

"I'll get her in the house," Quentin said to Evelyn Price. "She'll be all right once she gets her some rest and talks to the master's degree woman."

"All right," Evelyn Price said, jiggling her note pad from one hand to the other. "Do you need some help?"

"No, no," Quentin said. "Not a bit. You're not going to write this up, are you?"

"I got to write a report, Quentin," Evelyn Price said, watching him walk around Ruby and set himself to pull her up off the ground from behind. "But it won't be specific. Take care now, Quentin."

How many times was that, Quentin asked himself as he duck-walked Ruby through the front door and listened to the Metropolitan Police cruiser pull away from the curb in front of his house, was it nine times or ten times Evelyn Price said my name tonight?

THE NEXT MORNING Quentin was up early and in the kitchen to get Heather and Jason fed breakfast before they left for the two-block walk to Ransom Elementary. Neither one of them wanted to take the lunch money he placed on top of their piles of school books and construction paper and crayons. They would rather take their lunch with them in brown paper sacks, they said.

"Well, you can't today," Quentin said as he buttered toast and poured orange juice and milk. "We haven't got anything to go in a packed lunch."

"I'd like to know why," Jason said, pooching out his bottom lip. "Us kids don't like that old mess they put on the plate lunch at school."

"It's got bugs in it," Heather said. "The meat part does. You can see insect body parts all broke up into pieces in it. I want my Red Devil potted meat sandwich from home in a sack."

"We're out of Red Devil," Quentin said to his daughter. "And peanut butter and Little Debbie Cakes, too."

"Why didn't she buy some at the store?" Heather said.

"Mama didn't get around to it, that's why. Now take this money and get you a plate lunch, and I'll get some Red Devil today at the store."

"Why didn't she?" Heather said.

"Drunk," Jason said and rolled his eyes around in their sockets like he was about to pass out and fall off his chair to the floor.

"Nuh-uh," Quentin said. "Mama's just tired, that's all."

"Again," Heather said and picked up the dollar bill and her books and construction paper. "We got to go, dummy," she said to Jason. "Shake it."

Quentin tiptoed back to the master bedroom after the kids had cleared out, and opened the door a crack to peek in at Ruby. The light was dim, what with the closed blinds and the bedroom being on the dark side of the house in the morning anyway, but he could see well enough to tell that Ruby was lying on her back with one arm thrown up across her face. He watched long enough to see the cover over her chest rise up and sink down so he knew she was breathing all right, and he eased the door shut again. The latch made a clicking noise as it re-engaged, though, and he was able to hear Ruby move in the bed at the sound.

"Quit," she said. "Don't you come in here."

He called home once from work, just after the lunch break, but the answering machine came on, and he didn't listen long enough to hear all of what he was saying to himself about neither of us being able to come to the phone at present, but please leave a message and we'll get back to you. He didn't like the way his voice sounded on tape, anyway, leaving no doubt about the part of the world he came from, a long way from where Peter Jennings or Tom Brokaw was raised.

When he got home, the kids were in front of the TV set, watching *Terminator II* on the VCR and eating Cheetos, and Ruby was gone from the house with most of her clothes and the checkbook and the Sears card and the Visa out of the dresser drawer in the bedroom and her black boots.

She must have taken a taxi, Quentin said to himself as he tore open the business-size envelope with his initials on it which he found on the sink in the master bath, or maybe somebody gave her a ride. I had the car all day, so she couldn't have used it. I know that for sure.

What Ruby had written on just one line in her small handwriting was two sentences run together, so he had to read the note twice to get the full sense of it. "This time for good I'm gone I will let you know soon."

Just as he was finishing reading what Ruby had left addressed to his initials, Quentin realized that the phone was ringing and about the time he reached to pick it up, one of the children answered it in the kitchen and yelled out that somebody wanted to talk to him.

"All right," he hollered and stuck the receiver to his ear with the same hand he was still holding Ruby's note in.

"Was that your daughter?" a voice said in the middle of the clicking noises of the receiver in the kitchen being replaced.

"It might have been," Quentin said, "or maybe it was Jason. They sound about alike on the phone."

"Quentin," the voice said, and he immediately revised upward by one the number of times Evelyn Price had called his name. "I wanted to follow up on the reported missing person last night."

"Ruby you mean," he said. "As you know, she showed up fine last night. And she's gone again right now, but she's not missing this time."

"Oh, I think I see," Evelyn Price said after a little pause. "You're saying your wife has left you, and she has announced her departure from your domestic arrangement in a formal manner."

"Well, she wrote it down."

"You have a document," Evelyn Price said, "in your possession informing you of her decision to leave her married state with you. With which you are in accordance."

"I guess that's what you could call it, all right, Evelyn," Quentin said. "Yeah, that's about it."

"Eve," Evelyn Price said. "I go by that name now. Is it a holographic text, and is it signed with your estranged wife's recognizable and verifiable signature?"

"Holo what?" Quentin said. "I don't believe I know that word, but yeah it's signed by Ruby, the note is."

"Holographic," Evelyn Price said. "Means it's all in her own handwriting."

"Got you. Yes, it is her name the way she always signs it. Real scrunched up and little."

"Well, then, Quentin," Evelyn Price said. "Have you ever gone to Vizcaya?"

"I don't believe I have if that's the place I'm thinking of. Is that that restaurant on West End past Vanderbilt? Past the musical instrument store?"

"Yes."

"Well, then, no I haven't."

"My advice to you, then, is to let me take you there to dinner tonight, Quentin."

"Why, I, I," Quentin said, rapidly losing any confidence in the accuracy of the name count, "sure, but I do have a problem with doing that."

"What's that?"

"Jason and Heather. I don't believe I could get a sitter this late in the same day on the night I'd be going off out of the house. These little middle school girls we use couldn't babysit because it's a school night."

"No problem, Quentin. We'll use Rainbow."

"Rainbow?"

"Rainbow LaMouse, my daughter by that first one. She's eighteen and works days, Quentin. No problem. I'll pick you up at eight."

EVELYN PRICE'S HAIR was still short and straight and she was still wearing glasses just as she had been last night, but she wasn't in a Metropolitan Nashville Police Department uniform as she sat across the table from Quentin in a part of the dining room of Vizcaya's next to a window. She wasn't dressed like the most popular hippie girl in Central High School, either, like in the old peace movement days, but the dress she had on suited her fine, sort of a mingled blue and green and red flowing outfit off of each shoulder enough so Quentin could see freckles dusted along her collar bone.

"I love Spanish food," she said. "Not Mexican. Spanish. Do you, Quentin?"

"Oh, yes," he said. "Eve, what does LaMouse mean?"

"It's a name," she said. "You're supposed to say it La Moose

Say, but I learned quick the truthful and accurate pronunciation is La Rat."

"Uh-huh. And Shellaburger?"

"There is not a translation for that one, Quentin. Except maybe pumped-up macho phony bullshit."

"Can I ask you one more thing?" Quentin said and popped a bite from his entree into his mouth. It was called Shrimp Costa Brava, it was hot and he waited for it to cool before he swallowed and went on. "You used to always hate the police back when you were at Central High. And now you are one. How come?"

"No, Quentin," Evelyn Price said. "I didn't hate the police. I just hated what they stood for back then. I have always loved law and order."

"I really like these Shrimp Costa Brava," Quentin said. "I never had anything like this before."

LATER BACK AT EVE'S HOUSE up on the tallest hill in Nashville on a curving street named Love's Circle, Quentin sat up suddenly and spoke. "What about Rainbow and the children?"

"Rainbow's cool," Evelyn Price said. "She's a big girl, and she knows what to do to fit any circumstance."

"Won't she be concerned?" Quentin said, still a little anxious. "Being so late and all?"

"No, Quentin," Evelyn Price said. "Relax and don't think about anything. Rainbow's smooth as silk."

"You know what I'd like?" Quentin said after a long while had passed. "You know what I'd like you to do for me?"

"Tell me if it doesn't involve a uniform. What would you like?"

"I'd like you to say my name."

"Quentin, Quentin, Quentin," Eve said very slowly, pausing a long space after each time she said the name. "Quentin."

"You know what else I'd like, Evelyn?"

"Eve. What else, Quentin?"

"I believe," Quentin said and stretched until every one of his joints popped, "I believe I'd like me some Candyland peanut brittle."

"Not me," Evelyn Price said in a kind of a low purring growl, "what I'd like me, Quentin Vest, is some of that special Candyland double smash fudge."

The Road to Damascus

I cannot for the life of me see why you want to go to that funeral," Hazel Boles said to her daughter. "He won't be around to make you do it, now, will he?"

Louise looked up from where she was sitting on the leatherette sofa against the far wall of the mobile home. It converted into a bed, and Louise had slept on it in that condition the night before even though the bedroom at the rear of the double-wide contained a queen-sized bed like one to be found in any traditional home. When you closed the door to the hallway you could believe you were in a ranch house in Central Gardens or a Cape Cod in Fairy Tale Acres or in any other housing development in the Greater Port Arthur area. With the door open, of course, the way the hall went directly down the middle of the structure as straight as a highway made it obvious the layout was that of a trailer house in the Sun 'n Sand Mobile Home Park.

There was no law that said you had to leave the door to the master bedroom open, though, so Louise didn't. Besides, she hadn't been able to bear sleeping in her and Dwayne's bed since the night it had happened in Beaumont. The door stayed closed therefore and she had spent the last three nights on the wall sofa and eaten every meal—soup, cereal, or vegetable—out of the same white

173

bowl with the design of cherries and blue birds around the edge, and she might keep on doing it forever. She had not thought that far ahead.

"How could he, Mother?" she said to the woman sitting at the dinette table sipping hot tea out of a mug. Her mother Hazel had been an English war bride back when God had been a little boy, as Dwayne would always say behind her back. And she would insist on doing things the same way fifty years after the fact. "That's a silly thing to say. It's *his* funeral."

"I've seen hands reach from the grave and cause all sorts of things to happen, love," Hazel said. "The past can lay a heavy burden on the present."

"Dwayne's not making me want to go to his funeral," Louise said. "He's gone and I know you're not shedding any tears about it. That's one thing for sure."

She got up from the sofa and went to the stove to pour some more coffee into her cup. Her mother stuck out her mug toward her for more tea as she did.

"To illustrate," Hazel said, "I know that though he's gone, Dwayne is still controlling your sleeping habits."

"What are you talking about, Mother?" Louise said, sipping at her coffee. It was microwave reheated and bitter, and it tasted just the way she wanted it.

"That," Hazel said, gesturing toward the end of the sofa where a stuffed animal sat staring straight ahead with its legs stuck out. "Clovis Bear is located on this sofa, and I don't expect he walked in here from the bedroom on his own."

"I slept in here on the sofa last night because I wanted to," Louise said weakly, regretting she hadn't remembered to return Clovis to the master bedroom before her mother arrived. "It's a very comfortable bed."

"Why haven't you sewn another button on his vest, love?" Hazel asked. "I've got one at home to match the other, if you haven't."

"I like him like that," Louise said. "That's why. Casual."

"Hmm," Hazel said and sipped at her tea mug. "Where is this funeral to take place?"

"Two places. They'll do the actual service at the Lopez Memorial Home and then a graveside ceremony after that, out where Dwayne's people bury."

"And that is?"

"Near Warren, out in the country in East Texas."

"Naturally," Hazel said. "Where else? I don't know why I bothered to ask."

"What's wrong with East Texas?"

"Nothing at all, love, if one keeps one's knickers on."

"And just what's that supposed to mean, Mother?" Louise said and picked up Clovis Bear to move him off the sofa. Where his vest button had been lost was a different shade of brown from the rest of his body fabric, giving him in Louise's estimation the look of a cartoon character on television. She liked to imagine that someday Clovis would get up from wherever she had placed him, say something cute and toddle off on his own toward the refrigerator or the bathroom or somewhere else of his own choosing.

"Nothing but what it says," Hazel said. "Just a feeble attempt to be funny. And accurate."

Both women sipped at their cups and avoided looking directly at each other for a minute or two. Hazel finished her tea before Louise got through the last dregs of microwaved brew.

"Surely, dear," Hazel said, "there's no practical reason for you to attend the part of Dwayne's funeral up there in that wilderness, is there? You don't know his family, surely, and certainly have no reason to become acquainted with them now."

"The pickup," Louise said simply.

"The pickup?"

"The pickup. It's in Dwayne's name, but I gave him the money for the down payment, nine hundred and ten dollars, and I've been making the note every month since he's been driving it."

"That is a consideration," Hazel Boles said and set her tea mug down beside Clovis Bear where Louise had put him on the coffee table. "Where is the title to it?"

"I can't find it," Louise said. "I've looked in the dresser drawer where Dwayne always threw stuff like that, but it's not there. What I'm afraid of is that he gave it to somebody in Warren to hold for him. Maybe his mother or one of his brothers or one of those other ones up there."

"Oh, dear," Hazel said. "You'll be in need of that, Louise. You can't sell it without the title."

"Well, I know that," Louise said with some heat. "I do know a little bit now and then about how to do. How things happen and all."

Hazel got up from her place on the sofa and began to walk around the confined space of the kitchen and dining area, picking up small objects from various shelves and surfaces, glancing sharply at them for a second or two and then replacing them in slightly different locations from where she had found them. A creamer in the shape of a brown cow with spots, its mouth open as a pourer. A ceramic thimble in blue and gold. A miniature football with the logo of the expired Houston Oilers. A pair of needle-nosed pliers and a roll of silver duct tape. Eighty-seven cents in change. A postcard picturing a shrimp boat in Pensacola, Florida.

"We'll go with you," she said, turning the postcard over to read the message on its back. There was not one. "You'll need aid with that business, love."

"You will not," Louise said. "I got that card when we went to Florida that time. I haven't sent it to anybody yet. Who's *we?*"

"*We* is, of course, me," Hazel answered, "and I'm going to have Charlie McPhee come along. He's the other part of *we.*"

"You will not," Louise repeated. "Why would you want to take that little old man with us?"

"It's always more impressive in situations like these," Hazel said to her daughter, "to be accompanied by a male, no matter how small he might be. It lends an air."

"An air? What kind of air? Don't drop that thimble. It'll break just like glass."

"Of seriousness," Hazel said. "Of implied force."

"Force? Ha," Louise said. "Your little boyfriend couldn't force his way out of a plastic baggie."

"People of the ilk of Dwayne's connections do not think that way," Hazel announced, as though explaining a recipe for candy-making to a child. "When they see a man, however slight physically, they believe he has the potential for all manner of violent response."

"Him? Little old Charlie McPhee? You could pick him up, Mother, and throw him out of the room."

"And have done, love," Hazel said. "But that's by the by. The way of thinking I'm referring to is the same reason Dwayne kept his name on the title of the pickup you paid for. What it is, see, is a man thing. You wouldn't understand."

"A man thing?" Louise said and reached toward the coffee table where Clovis Bear was sitting to touch his near foot. What if he had noticed and stretched it toward her, just like a person?

"A man thing," her mother repeated. "You wouldn't understand."

WHAT ARE YOU PLANNING to do Saturday anyway? his father had asked him. Lie around the house all day and pick at that guitar, a man your age? It'll only be from ten in the morning to two or three in the afternoon total, he had said, as Waylon watched a Discovery Channel special on insect larvae during the winter months. I suppose you're going to work on lesson plans for your substitute teaching, his father said. He would believe that when he saw it, his father said. I don't ask you to do much, his father said, and now you're saying no to this one favor. Do I even ask you to pay for what you eat or the electric bill for the air conditioning? his father said.

"All right," Waylon had answered finally, looking up from an explanation of galls on tree limbs (they are actually insect larvae, the voice-over was saying), "I'll go to that convict's funeral, as long as we're home before dark. And you got to drive all the way up there and back."

"Fair enough," Charlie McPhee said. "It's not over a hundred miles round trip to Warren anyway. It'll do you good to walk out of the house and let some air get to you."

"It's a lot further than that," Waylon said. The round protuberances on the branches of the longleaf pine are actually encapsulated beetle larvae, he learned, feeding off inner bark. "I thought Hazel hated old Dwayne."

"She does," Charlie said. "This funeral business is her last shot at him."

BY THE TIME WAYLON had had breakfast the next morning and put on a dark tie to go with his blue blazer and gray pants, Charlie McPhee had already taken his Chrysler to Jiffy Lube for service and was working on the windshield with paper towels and a spray bottle.

"Good," he said as he heard Waylon come up behind him.

"We're ready. We'll pick up Hazel and her girl at the trailer park. You ride in the front seat over yonder, but get in the back with Louise once we get there."

"I could just ride in the trunk," Waylon said. "And not have to shift around so much."

"And you could be a good sport, too," Charlie said and gave the driver's side of the windshield a last lick with a wad of towels. "And make things nice."

LOUISE'S EYES WERE RED and puffy, and she kept dabbing at them with tissue beneath the dark glasses she wore as Charlie McPhee steered the Chrysler north out of the coastal plain. Waylon had tried to talk to her for the first few miles of the journey, sitting as close to her in the rear seat as he was, but after she had met three or four of his comments with silence, he had decided to focus on the passing scene and listen to his father and Hazel converse.

Charlie described the housing developments they passed, read aloud from road signs, mused on the financial prospects of various small businesses along the way, and explained the feeding habits of the gulls, crows, red-winged blackbirds, and grackles working the fields between the stands of palmetto and eventually the pines reaching down from East Texas. Hazel nodded, murmured agreement and looked about her brightly as they proceeded.

I'll go to sleep, Waylon told himself, just doze off, but I'm afraid I might miss something. You never can tell what me and the Chief Mourner here could come up with on the way to the graveyard. Up around the next curve, there might be somebody selling squash and watermelons out of the back of his truck. Maybe a barn with a sign on it or a mockingbird on the telephone line. Maybe a run-over nutria.

"Do we turn off before or after Warren, love?" Hazel asked.

"After," Louise said in a lifeless tone. "Dwayne's mother said to look for a hardtop road two miles past the Piggly Wiggly. It'll say Damascus on a sign."

"I hope I don't get struck blind," Waylon said, "on that road to Damascus. I'd have to change my name."

"What?" Louise said, turning her head a fraction toward him, her mouth twisted down at the corners. A good portion of her lipstick was eaten off, he noticed.

"Nothing," he said. "A bad joke."

"Blindness is no joking matter, Son," Charlie called back from the front seat. "Remember how your granddaddy was in his last years?"

"He lost his sight, did he?" Hazel Boles said. "Your father?"

"All he could see was shapes," Charlie said, shaking his head sadly. "That, and a little light. That's what he would always tell us, at least, every time we'd think to ask him. That's what he'd say anyway."

"Would he have been lying, do you think?" Waylon asked.

"No," Charlie said. "Why would he have done that? Goodness sakes, Son."

"There's your Piggly Wiggly," Waylon said. "See its shape?" He pointed toward a pair of cavorting pigs high up on a sign mounted on steel girders the size of mature red oak trees, and everyone in the Chrysler leaned forward to watch for the turnoff to the Damascus burying ground.

"I see it," Hazel Boles said, gesturing toward the right side of the highway, "just there where the white car's turning."

The road to Damascus was paved for the first mile and a half, but quickly narrowed into one lane of red clay and sand, and until the Chrysler reached the cemetery, the occupants had to travel through a cloud of dust raised by the cars ahead.

"Times like this is when Chrysler recirculation comes in handy," Charlie McPhee said proudly, punching at a button on the dashboard. "We'll just keep breathing the same air over and over again until things clear up."

"Surely not," Hazel Boles said and lifted a handkerchief daintily to her mouth, coughing into it twice with a sharp barking sound.

"Just don't think about it, Mother," Louise said from the back seat. "The cough reflex is all in your head."

"That dust is all in the air," Hazel said. "And in my nose and in my lungs."

"Not for long," Charlie said, pointing ahead. "We're almost there. Everybody's pulling over yonder to park."

Up ahead a collection of cars and pickups lined both sides of the narrow road, not more than ten or fifteen in all, Waylon estimated, and a gray Cadillac hearse was pulled up into the graveyard itself, its open rear door pointed toward a heap of earth partially covered with what looked like a large swatch of AstroTurf.

"Oh," Louise said in a strangled voice, "Dwaynie's already here."

"He's one to get places early, huh?" Waylon said, but Louise didn't respond.

A large canvas covering emblazoned with the word PACE stood on the side of the grave opposite to the mound of earth, and four rows of folding metal chairs painted brown were arranged under the cloth roof, two-thirds occupied.

"Do you know any of these people?" Hazel asked her daughter as they all climbed out of the Chrysler and began to move toward the focus of interest.

"Mama Hazlitt," Louise said, waving at a large woman seated spraddle-legged in the middle chair of the row nearest the grave above which squatted a bronze-colored casket. "She doesn't see me, I guess."

"Dear God," Hazel Boles said. "Give me your arm, Charlie."

Waylon trailed behind the other three, looking first at the woman Louise had indicated and then at as many of the other mourners as he could observe before moving behind them to the last row of folding chairs. His and Charlie's were the only neckties in evidence, he noticed, save that of a huge man of about sixty standing beside the casket facing the occupiers of the seats.

He could hear the man breathing in strong puffs as he walked by him, and after he had found a chair on the end of the last row, Waylon could see that the man's tie, a study in red and blue, reached only to the middle of his chest. That was through no fault of the manufacturer, though, he judged, since so much of it had been used up in cinching the man's throat.

The eyes of the preacher seemed to be upon him, and Waylon dropped his gaze and settled into the chair beside Louise. As he did so, the preacher began to speak.

"At the request of Miz Hazlitt," he said and stopped to breathe for a space, "the mama of Dwayne, we'll begin the graveside service by all singing together Dwayne's favorite hymn as a child, 'Blessed Assurance.'"

As the first words of the song came from the preacher's mouth, a cappella, Waylon felt Louise seize his wrist in a grip so strong his own fingers flexed. "Jesus is mine," Louise was saying when he cut his eyes toward her to sneak a look, and he began to move his lips in unison with the sounds rising from the rows of metal chairs as though he were right on the beat and knew every syllable.

After that musical offering, the preacher called for another, this one favored particularly by some other member of Dwayne Hazlitt's family, and Louise relaxed her grip enough for Waylon to be able to pull his arm gently toward his body. She wouldn't completely relinquish her hold, however, in her crisis of grief, and Waylon spent the remainder of the performance of "The Old Rugged Cross" fastened to her. He could hear his father singing along in a robust voice, but he could tell that Hazel Boles was either lip-synching, too, or possessed a voice as light as the down on a thistle.

"Brothers and Sisters," the preacher announced after the last notes had died away, "we've come together today in God's great outdoors on this hot day to say farewell to Dwayne as he departs this world of sorrow to journey to his everlasting home."

A powerfully built man in a bluejean jacket seated immediately in front of Waylon twisted in his seat to look over his shoulder, and began to speak in his direction in a conversational tone. "Killed by a dirty coward," he said and seemed to wait for a response. Waylon smiled and nodded, and the man turned back, satisfied, to give his attention again to the preacher.

Louise jerked at his wrist, and Waylon turned toward her to lip-read the message she was mouthing in silence. "His brother," she indicated. "He's got the title."

"Oh," Waylon mouthed back and nodded knowingly, wondering what title the bluejean-wearing brother of Dwayne had laid claim to. Had he won some contest? Lifted the back end of a Volkswagen? Milked the most cows in a set time? Did he own a famous chicken?

"Dwayne Talmadge Hazlitt," the huge preacher was saying in slow tones, the projection of his voice toward the listeners powerful enough to cause the end of his shortened tie to twitch, "has fought the good fight, he has finished the course."

Must have been the G.E.D. at the correctional facility in Huntsville, Waylon thought. That, or one of these Can You Draw Me? programs on the back of a matchbook cover.

As the eulogy continued and the sun beat down on the canvas roof over the rows of folding chairs, causing any portion of un-shaded metal to rise steadily and uncomfortably in temperature, Waylon discovered that by leaning alternately forward and back in his chair he could observe first the full profile of Louise's face, then the tip of Hazel's nose and finally the right eyebrow and chin of his father. He entertained himself fairly well by that slight rocking motion, imagining a switching back and forth of these bodily parts into new combinations.

Charlie's eyebrow, for example, could be moved under Hazel's nose tip to form a small gray mustache for her. Hazel's nose tip growing out of the right cheek of Louise could be made to appear as a good-sized wart or Robert Redford-like wen. Maybe a coming together of these facial characteristics of all his companions at the funeral could be made to form a unity of bushy eyebrow, sharp nose, shaved chin and cosmetically enhanced cheek to create a countenance never before seen on God's earth.

By the time he had exhausted all the possibilities of transfer and rearrangement he could imagine, the preacher's voice had begun to take on a cadence which everyone in the audience recognized should be leading toward a conclusion. They all shifted in appreciation in their seats, and within less than a minute the preacher had said "Amen" and people began to stand and shuffle out of the shade of the canvas awning into the sunlight of midday in East Texas.

Louise had released her grip on his wrist, so Waylon felt free to head for an open space near a large cedar, unimpeded, his three companions right behind him. The row of people that had sat in front of him, led by the brother in bluejeans with the title, veered a little left and began to form their own cluster of mourners.

"He did go on and on, didn't he?" Hazel said. "That minister. Quite low-church."

"That's your old-time funeral preaching," Charlie McPhee said. "Let me tell you that takes me back a few years. He told them how the cow ate the cabbage."

"How the bulldog worried the kitten," Waylon said. "How the steamboat rounded the bend."

"I ought to go talk to Mama Hazlitt," Louise said, reaching into her purse for tissue. "But I don't know what to say to her."

"Ask her what Dwayne did with the title," Hazel said. "That will do nicely for a starter."

"Is that the title that fellow in the jacket has?" Waylon asked, gesturing toward the group to the left by nodding his head in their direction. "The one you told me about, Louise? The brother?"

"I think Darrell's got it, all right," Louise said into a handful of tissue. "Dwayne would have most probably asked him to hold it."

"It's portable?" Waylon asked. "Is it a family thing?"

"Of course it's portable," Charlie McPhee said. "How do you think you could ever sell the pickup if the title to it wasn't portable? Which one is he, now?"

"Oh, God," Waylon said, watching the man in question light a cigarette by touching the glowing tip of another to it. "A pickup. That's why we're here. Of course. Just what I need. A property dispute in East Texas."

"It's no dispute to it, Son," Charlie said. "It rightfully belongs to Louise, that vehicle does."

"And it would have to be something with wheels," Waylon said. "Something to drive up and down the highway in. Nothing matters more to these people than a means of transportation out of these woods."

"Go get his attention, one of you men," Hazel Boles said. "Let him know we want to speak with him about a matter."

"I don't know about you, Dad," Waylon said, looking sharply at his father, "but that fellow and I haven't been introduced. I never laid eyes on him to this day."

"Well, no, I don't believe I know the gentleman," Charlie McPhee began, but was cut off by Hazel before he could finish.

"There's a quick remedy for that," she said, pointing toward Louise and then moving her finger briskly in a circle which seemed to draw her daughter, Charlie McPhee and Waylon into a unit prepared to move forward together toward a common objective. "Louise will make introductions all around, and then we can get down to business."

Within less than a minute, Waylon found himself shaking the hand of Darrell Hazlitt, a hand hard with the calluses of labor in the physical world but strangely limp in his own. The man's obviously lived so far back in the woods and so low on the food chain he's never learned to white-tooth a smile and bear down on the flesh-pressing, Waylon told himself, and now I'm part of some scheme to convince him to give up a year-old Chevrolet pickup he believes he's inherited. He probably even thinks he's entitled to free gasoline for life now that his brother's been shot dead. Charlie and I will be lucky to get out of this graveyard without people carrying us feet first at a real slow pace.

"Oh, Darrell," Louise was saying, "I don't know what I'm going to do without Dwayne."

"Don't you worry yourself none," Darrell said, dropping Waylon's hand and wiping his own across one of the panels of his bluejean jacket as if to remove any trace of physical weakness it might have picked up from contact with Waylon. "We gone get some payback for what happened to my little brother. You can just rest easy on that."

Jesus Christ, Waylon thought, Jesus H. Christ on crutches.

"You know we'd been talking marriage the last couple of weeks, didn't you? Right up to what happened at that parts store. And you know something else, Darrell?" Louise said. "Dwayne was the one that brought the subject of marriage up himself, not me. I hadn't said a word about it."

"I ain't surprised none by that," Darrell said, getting another Pall Mall lit and then letting the butt he'd used for lighting drop to the ground where he covered it with the toe of his boot and began to grind it into the dirt. "He done told me many a time he thought you hung the damn moon."

"He did?" Louise said, brightening and lifting a hand to her cheek. "No kidding? Tell the truth now."

"Sure," Darrell said, "and like I was saying, we know where and how it happened, and we know right where that yellow coward that done it lives. We got his address. Set your mind at ease about that."

Turning his gaze away from Louise to Waylon, Darrell fixed him with a stare and bared his teeth in a smile intended, Waylon guessed, to express resolution and to seek a sympathetic response.

"You know what I'm saying, little buddy? You see where I'm taking this?" the brother of the shotgunned man in the bronze casket twenty feet away said. "How'd you like it if your brother'd been night-trapped at a auto parts store like Dwayne was?"

"I've only got sisters," Waylon answered, but seeing Darrell's face darken, quickly added, "but I expect I'd probably feel the same way if Terry or Beth got shot in a robbery."

"Robbery?" Darrell said. "Dwayne wasn't trying to rob nobody. He was just looking for parts after hours."

"Sure, right," Waylon said. "That's what I meant. If Terry or Beth was looking for parts is what I was trying to say."

"And got killed with a shotgun," Charlie McPhee stepped in to amplify. "One or both of the girls some night in Beaumont."

"Dwayne's and Louise's pickup," Hazel Boles said. "Is it parked here at the cemetery?"

That's easy for her to say, Waylon said to himself and eased back a step from his arms-length position near the brother. Her being a woman in her late sixties, he probably won't do more than backhand her a couple of times before he turns on me and Charlie.

"Ma'am?" Darrell said.

"Louise's pickup. The red Chevrolet. Did someone bring it to the funeral today?"

"You talking about the truck Dwayne was driving that night down yonder? The one he used to get himself around in?"

"That would be the one, yes," Hazel said in a tone pert enough to cause a couple of nearby mourners to look in her direction. "Louise's vehicle."

Hazel lifted her hand to shade her eyes and began scanning the collection of cars and pickups parked on each side of the dirt road leading to the gates of the Damascus Chapel burying ground. "Oh," she said, "I do believe I spot it, there behind that Japanese car—is it a Honda?—and in front of the grayish one. That Buick or Oldsmobile or something else American."

She turned back and made a questioning face at Louise. "That is it, isn't it, love?" she asked. "Do you see the one I mean?"

Waylon watched the heads of both Louise and Darrell swivel to peer in the direction Hazel had indicated, as though they were operating on a common electrical impulse. This is where it all starts, Waylon said to himself, right here at the end of a fat man's sermon on the Resurrection and the Life in the middle of a hot day in East Texas. As soon as old Darrell Hazlitt flips that cigarette butt off onto somebody's grave, he'll have both hands free for some payback.

"I believe it is," Louise said. "How I can tell is by that little Houston Oiler football helmet hanging from the rearview mirror."

"Yeah," Darrell agreed. "That's the Chevrolet pickup I drove out here in. Did you get Dwayne that little plastic helmet you talking about, Louise?"

"I wish I had," Louise said. "But no, I didn't. It was a Texaco gas station giveaway if you filled up your tank over ten gallons worth."

"Because I think it's real nifty," Darrell said, "is why I asked."

Nifty? Waylon thought. Nifty? This sworn avenger of his brother's blood said something was nifty?

"You know whose number it is on that little bitty helmet?" Darrell went on. "Warren Moon's, that's whose it is. 'Course, it ain't true now. Moon's done gone on to the Vikings these days, but I reckon Texaco made them little helmets up before he left." Dropping his head, Darrell dug at the ground in front of him with the toe of his boot. "You know what?" he said, uprooting several horseshoe-shaped divots as he kicked steadily at the earth of the Damascus Chapel graveyard. "That was the dumbest trade the damn Oilers ever did make. I'm just as glad the whole damn mess of them has left town for Nashville for them doing that. I hope to Jesus they never win another game."

Lifting his eyes to fix them on Waylon's face, Darrell spoke again. "Don't you think so, Buddy? That that was the sorriest trade ever was?"

"Bar none," Waylon said, asking himself who the Hell was Warren Moon and hoping Darrell wouldn't quiz him on what position he played or what records he'd set. "Dumb, dumb, dumb."

"Louise would be pleased if you were to accept that little helmet as a gift, Darrell," Hazel Boles said. "In memory of Warren Moon's time with the Oilers and your brother Dwayne's time here with you."

Darrell Hazlitt made a sound deep in his chest, and Waylon tensed to be ready to leap backward if the man in the bluejean jacket decided to propel what he was hawking up into his, rather than Hazel's face. Instead, Darrell made another noise, this one a high-pitched mewing whine, and began to weep great tears. Waylon saw at least two of them splash on a brass button of the man's bluejean jacket.

"That means the world to me," he said between sobs, struggling manfully to master himself. "You saying that, I see now what every thing means. It's like my eyes has been prised open. Come on over here and meet our Mama. I done give her the title to that truck to carry in her purse. I'm in the habit of losing stuff."

Later, transactions completed and earth returned to earth, as Waylon followed the two women to the Chrysler for the trip back out of the piney woods to the Gulf Coast, Darrell tapped him on the shoulder. "Little buddy," he said as Waylon turned to face him, "did you ever see anybody direct a run-and-gun offense the way Moon did it? Tell me the truth, now."

"Never," Waylon said in his deepest and sincerest voice, "not in my lifetime."

"Well, then," Darrell said, satisfied, and then leaning forward, spoke into the backseat where Louise was snuffling into a handful of tissue, "don't you worry none, Sugar. Payback is on the way. Big-time. It's a-coming like a freight train."

As Waylon pulled smoothly away at the controls of the Chrysler, Hazel Boles turned in the seat beside him to look through the rear window at Charlie McPhee shifting gears smartly and following closely behind in the red pickup. "I have the title," she said, patting at her handbag. "Right here."

"No doubt," Waylon said.

"That went rather well," Hazel said, cocking her head to one side as though she were about to peck at a morsel. "Rather swimmingly, I would judge."

"Just like," Waylon said, smoothly toeing the accelerator and leaning forward to punch the silver recirculation button on the dashboard of his father's Chrysler, "just like in the old days in the Astrodome before everything went to pieces. Just like when Warren Moon used to run and gun that two-minute offense."

Of all the cars returning from the burying ground at Damascus, their's was the winner, the first to climb back onto the hard-paved road where there was no dust left to settle.

Maryland, My Maryland

For Anne and John of the Eastern Shore

They said it was a river, some of the officers did, when we come up on it to cross over into Maryland, but it wasn't no deeper than a good-sized creek back in Mississippi. It was wide enough, all right, but it was plumb full of rocks sticking up and laying down flat so you could walk on them almost all the way across without getting your feet wet.

Major Sutcliffe now, he had to act like it was a perilous crossing, of course, so he put the spurs to his horse and made him rear up and splash water everywhere like it was a damn close thing a-coming through the flood over the river into the next state up from Virginia.

Cat, he was right behind him trying to keep up on that mule loaded with the major's campaign equipment, and he wasn't eager to try to run his mount up and down the stream and over and across them slick rocks. He give me a look when he come by me and the other boys a-jumping from one dry spot to the next one and holding our rifles up out of the water that was getting knocked up in the air by the horses' hooves. I give him a nod and he stopped his mule for a spell, like he was having to wait to get a better purchase in that streambed before going on after the major churning through the crossing up ahead of him.

"I believe, Willie," he said to me kind of out of the side of his mouth afore he plunged back in to trying to catch up, "that Jeremiah Sutcliffe thinks this is the Rubicon instead of the Potomac."

I give him a laugh like I always did, like I knew what he meant, and the old boy next to me, a fellow out of Franklin I believe it was, pointed up at Cat's back as he started into chasing after the major again, and looked at me real hard.

"Did that nigger just call you by your first name?"

This old boy had started off being a right fat fellow when we was all recruited up back in McNairy County, but now it looked like he was a little chap wearing his pa's clothes, just a-swimming around in them, what they was left of them by then.

"Naw," I said. "You misheard him. I known that nigger all his life, and he knows better than to do that."

"Well," he says, "I reckon so. But you got to watch when one of them gets off away from home like this. They'll take advantage." And then the once-fat man commenced looking for another dry rock to put them bare feet on.

Of course I was lying about Cat. He had always called me whatever he wanted to ever since I first known him there on the Sutcliffe holdings in north Mississippi, yonder where my old pappy was a kind of a helper to the overseer most of the time. At least when he wasn't laid up drunk or during one of the spells when old Mr. Sutcliffe had done discharged him for a while.

Cat was named for his daddy, the head house servant in the big place where the Sutcliffe folks lived. Catullus was the full name, but I always figured Cat was just the right thing to call the young 'un. 'Cause he was like one, see, a cat. You couldn't tell what he was thinking or what he might want to do next or say at you about anything about the place or about whatever wasn't about the place but just inside his head all by itself.

He was real private, what I'm trying to say, but that weren't all of it. Let me put it like this. A fellow lots of times will look at you when you're talking to him or even when you ain't, and you can see his eyes, and most of the time you might as well be looking into a real shallow creek bed. You can see the ferns at the bottom moving around in the current or maybe a perch or two or a tadpole or some other varmint swimming around as plain as day and there ain't a bit of mystery to what they might be up to. Looking for something to eat or trying not to be eat, most likely, all the time. Them little critters 'at swim, I'm talking about.

Now, Cat when he would look at you, and that was a seldom enough thing to remember whenever it did happen, he had a kind of a skim over his eyes, like that kind of a membrane that comes on sweet milk before it sours and before it's churned. They wasn't no fish swimming in that stream you could catch sight of, I'll flat guarantee you. Whatever was being eat or looking to eat, it was a mystery and a puzzle to the world outside of them eyeballs. It was covered right up.

We got on across that river, finally, all of us except for that bunch from Texas, that come on last like they always did, just a whooping and hollering like they had finally get there to save the day. Course there wasn't nothing to save, it was just time for the officers to let us lay down for a spell to rest before they got us up moving again. You couldn't a-told that by the way them Texans acted, though, running up to flop on the ground like they was salvation itself just arrived at the Pearly Gates.

One of them happened up to me where I was leaning my head against some kind of a oak tree, I guess it was, his eyes just a-dancing as he stood there looking down at me where I was resting.

"We gon' kill us some Yankees, Misssissippi," he said to me in a voice loud enough to hear across a cotton field, "right here in their own yardplace where they live."

"Yeah, I reckon," I said. "I expect we gon' shit, too, if we get to eating more regular."

"We got us some chickens," he said real boastful, "and four or five bushels of roasting ears of corn that ain't even got real hard yet, us boys do."

About then the Major come riding up to where we was talking, me and this Texas fellow, so I didn't say what I was fixing to, because Major Jeremiah Sutcliffe he thought it wasn't good for the troops to badmouth one another. Here's what I had thought to say, though: "Yeah, and you Texas waddies wouldn't share a single ear of that corn with your old granny if she was dying of starvation." That's what I was going to say back to him, but didn't get the chance.

"Hello, soldier," Jeremiah said to the man with all that corn and chickens, "welcome to Maryland, my Maryland. You men ready to strike a blow for the Confederacy?"

"Yessir, Major," the old boy said. "We gon' whip 'em bad if everybody throws in together."

"That's the spirit," the Major said. "With that kind of attitude, how can we not prevail?"

The Texan sloped on off to find somebody else to brag to, I imagine, and the Major looked down at me from his horse. He was a tall fine-looking man, I got to say, his uniform all brushed and kept cleaned up by Cat, and all the metal parts on his clothes were shining in the sun.

"Well, Willie," he said, "a long way from McNairy County and the old homeplace."

"I reckon so, Jeremy," I said. That's what I always called him when we was growing up there on the Sutcliffe holdings, and I knew he didn't like for me to use that handle now we was in a war. So I did it every chance I got.

He looked down at me hard and started to say something, but

then he throwed his head back and commenced to stare back down
that road we had all come up into Maryland on, like he was expecting
to see somebody coming that he knowed and was waiting for.

I watched him for a while as I was leaning there against the tree,
knowing he had something on his mind to say to me, but I wasn't
going to help him get it out and stated. I just listened to people
around us talking and hoorawing one another, lots of them snoring
there asleep on that hard ground in the middle of a hot day, some
of them milling around looking for somebody to talk into giving
them something they wanted. A chew off a plug of tobacco, maybe,
or a corn fritter or something, if they had one to spare. Nobody
ever did, best I remember.

"Willie," the Major finally said, getting off that big black horse
he was riding, one he had named Mercury just like he always done
whenever he got a new one. "I feel I need to speak to you about a
matter of some delicacy."

"What'd I do wrong, Jeremy?" I said. "You see me let down
somewhere or something?"

"No, no, of course not. You always act in a exemplary manner,
as you were reared to do. A real son of the Magnolia State."

"I was afeared you had done found out," I said. "Well as I tried
to hide it."

"What? What do you mean?"

"Nothing," I said. "I was just joshing you, Jeremy." For a man
that had gone off to school way up yonder at Princeton College, he
sure was always easy to fool. He never could tell when somebody
was joking him. Jeremy Sutcliffe, he always believed everything
anybody ever told him. Me and Cat, we never believed nothing.

"We are embarking on a perilous enterprise," he told me, taking
off his hat to let the wind get to his head, what little air there was
blowing there in the middle of the day. Jeremy's hair looked like

a woman's, always did, just like the rest of the Sutcliffes', kind of reddish-brown and real thick-like and curly. He was proud of it. All of them men of that bunch was. He shook his head back and forth so that his hair fell better and more comfortable and of more advantage to anybody who might be watching him.

I looked down at my right shoe to see if the piece of rawhide I had tied the sole to the upper with was still holding. It was. "You mean this here fight that's a-fixing to come up?" I said. "Ain't no more perilous than any of the rest of them, is it? I don't want to know about it if it is."

"The difference, Willie, old friend, is that we are in the enemy's home country," the Major said. "We are not defending home and hearth. We are involved in an offensive act of invasion."

"It looks about the same around here as it does on t'other bank of that river," I told him. "Ain't much difference I can tell between one side or the other, whatever it is that we are doing. Fighting here or back across yonder, it's the same, ain't it?"

"The distinction is of idea, Willie. Idea and symbol, not the comparisons of soil and vegetation and the slope of land mass." Jeremy made a big sweep with his right hand as he said that, like he was talking to a bunch of men all with their faces turned up to hear what he was saying.

"Uh-huh," I said.

"We will pay for this," he said. "This deviation from principle, and it will be in blood."

"We done seen a plenty of that, all right," I said to him and leaned back over to look at my other shoe and see how it was faring. Both of them was a little big, coming as they did off another man's feet and him dead, but better that than them being too little, I say. "Won't be surprised if we don't see a bunch more of it, neither."

"Some of that sanguinity will be mine, Willie," the Major said in a voice like a man who's just learned that the weevils has got into all the cotton, ever damn bit of it. "I feel it for a surety."

"Everybody's scared, Jeremy," I said and looked up at him standing there with his back to the sun and his hair floating about his head like he had his own little wind gust that followed him around even when the air was dead still as far as anybody else was concerned. "Right before a tussle, I mean," I went on. "That's all it is that's bothering you. I know it gives me the shake-leg if I let myself think about it."

"No, not this time, my friend. I'm not afraid for my own sake. I mean no more than is reasonable for a sentient being to be. It's for those who depend upon me in terms of sentiment and feeling that I dread the conflict to come."

I knowed who he was talking about, and it wasn't Squire Sutcliffe and the old lady and them three sisters, neither. But I weren't going to help Jeremy out by naming it for him. My feet was hurting me. "You as likely as any other man to come through it, Major," I told him. "Get Cat to cook you up something to eat, and take you a little nip of that whisky he's been toting for you from Tennessee all over creation. Things'll look different."

"Old Willie," he said, looking down at me where I was sitting on the ground trying to rest before they made all of us get up and commence trotting north again here in a few minutes. "You've always been the man of optimistic outlook and vigorous spirit."

Old, hell, I was thinking. I wasn't but eight months older than Jeremy was and had been all of my life, and he knew it, too. It just sounded better to him to call me that and believe it, too. He believed everything he said all the time.

"No, I've heard communication from a higher and wiser power than you and I, old friend, and it tells me I must prepare for the ultimate earthly loss in this coming battle. And when that consummation is achieved," he stopped talking for a minute and looked way off like he'd seen something fly up in the woods behind me, a big black bird, maybe, or an angel dressed all in white. I almost twisted around from where I was sitting to look, but I held steady, "I want you to convey this packet to Miss Sally Earl when you return to McNairy County."

He poked a little box or something wrapped up in a cloth and tied with string around it toward me, and I sat there looking at it for a while without offering to relieve him of it.

"I'm a lot more likely to get shot in the vitals or head or get my legs all blowed off than you are, Jeremy," I said to him finally, reaching to take the package before he got froze in that stance forever. "I got to scramble around on the ground afoot and run right up on them Yankees face to face. Least you got a horse to carry you around on."

"Fate does not wait on the manner of conveyance," the Major said and clapped his hat with the big feather on it back on his head and mounted up on Mercury. He gigged that big black horse a little with his spurs to make it look lively and then he said one more thing before he took off to find another officer or two to jaw with. "I have always relied upon you, and you've never disappointed me."

"It comes a first time for everything," I said to him as he trotted that big black off, but I knowed he constitutionally didn't hear me right then in the midst of his exit line and all.

I threw my head on back and dozed off and got to sleep for a full ten minutes before somebody kicked the sole of my sorest foot to get me up and moving with the rest of them Mississippians up towards where the Yankees was going to be, there in Maryland, waiting for us. The weather was still as hot as Drusilla's drawers at an all-night dance.

THEY LET US STOP MARCHING just about dark, them officers, hungry as they was themselves and ready to flop down for a spell, and I worked my way on over to where some fellows from Pearl County had got them a fire started and was cooking something.

"What you want?" a big black-bearded man said, giving me a real hard look as I come walking up. "It ain't nothing for North Mississippi river trash over here."

"I might want me a slice of that belly you carrying around underneath that blouse," I come back at him. "If you keep on being so friendly."

Some of the rest of them laying there by their big piece of hog meat they had rolled over half into the fire to cook laughed at that and started in hoorawing the black-bearded one.

"You better watch him, Tumber," a little quick-looking jaybird said. "Them up toward Memphis'll cut you, like he done said."

"And they ain't afraid to eat nothing," another one of them allowed. "I seen one eating goat meat once."

"What did it taste like, I reckon?" the little man that had spoke first asked the other one. "That old strong-smelling goat meat?"

"'Bout like dog does," I said, "but not near so juicy."

That made them all laugh, and the black-bearded one, Tumber, he cut me off a hunk of meat down toward the hoof end, and I thanked him and eat with them boys until I was finished and then went on back to where the McNairy County company was trying to worry down about a handful of parched corn apiece. I got me some of that, too, and walked on over to where I seen Cat standing by some kind of a gum tree, it looked like, and poked out the corn toward him.

"Thank you kindly, Mr. Willie," he said, talking like a slave would because that McNairy bunch could all hear him if they'd a-wanted to, then he jerked his head a little to the side to let me know he had something to tell me. I walked on off to where we was out of the light of the fire them McNairys had built up, and he followed me, putting that old hard corn up to his mouth like he was eating it.

When we got to where the rest of them was kind of out of range, he handed me the corn back and sat down on the ground yonder, and I joined him.

"I'll eat it," I said. "I ain't proud."

"You'll eat whatever you get your hands on, Willie," Cat said. "I've never seen it to fail."

"Yessir," I said. "I ain't gonna beg pardon for it, neither. I'll eat anything if it ain't jerking away too fast to hold down and get my teeth into it."

"Well," he said and just set there for a minute, watching me chew. I remember I was having to favor the teeth on one side of my jaw, so I was paying attention to that but I could see Cat was thinking about something, hard as he was to see there in the dark with his back to where the light was coming from the fire. It weren't never no moon none of them nights in Maryland that I can recollect.

"He's in a state," Cat said finally.

"The Major?" I asked him, but I knowed who he was talking about, of course. Me and Cat had spent years gauging Jeremy's feelings and trying to see where he was going to jump next, so I knowed, all right who Cat meant.

"No," Cat said. "I'm referring to Marse Robert. He called me into his tent for a consultation about tactics for the impending event."

"Bullshit, Cat. General Lee ain't talked none to you."

"Where is your sense of irony, Willie? Of course, I'm speaking about Jeremy Sutcliffe, like always."

"I don't know nothing about no iron," I told him, "but it's going to be plenty of lead flying and steel a-cutting here directly."

"That's the point. He is convinced he's going to be killed in this engagement, and he is about to drive me mad with pronouncements and exhortations and recitations of past events and predictions of future calamities."

Cat could forever talk, I'm here to tell you, and I always just loved to hear him get started to laying out a string of words a preacher couldn't understand. At least none of them foot-washers I was used to hearing ranting and squalling in meetings back in McNairy County. None of them had read every book on the Sutcliffe place like Cat had, neither.

"He done give me a little package all wrapped up in string to carry back to Sally Earl oncet he's been killed up here amongst all these Yankees," I said. "I reckon I'm supposed to be the message bearer of his death."

"Miss Sally Earl," Cat said in a kind of a sighing voice. "The emblem of Southern womanhood and all that's ethereal and pure."

"Huh," I said. "Remember that big wedding of that niece from Jackson two years back when every rich man and his old lady in the Delta was at the Sutcliffe holdings for a week?"

Cat didn't say nothing, so I went on a-talking to kind of jog his memory.

"You recollect," I said. "You was one of the ones serving, and I was there to be sure everything outside the house stayed right all week, and you and me, we seen Jeremy and Miss Sally Earl back yonder in that flower garden about midnight after most all of the rest of them was drunk and laid up in the beds and the yards and the sitting rooms on them sofas. Remember?"

"Yes, Willie," he said. "I do."

"She didn't look like no emblem of pure and that other word you just said. Aerial, or whatever it was. Remember, old Jeremy he had her up against the bole of that big fig tree, down in behind where all them limbs was all bent over until it looked like a little cave back in yonder. They was backed up in there, her just coiled up around him, and they was bowed up like two possums humping."

"Must you recount the entire thing?"

"Remember, she was saying every time he'd hit it, Jesus Christ, O Lord, Jesus Christ, O Lord."

"Yes, all right, it was very physical. Yes, I remember it. How could I not?"

"I tell you one thing, Cat," I said to him as I sit there eating that handful of parched corn. "It sure set me on fire."

"And your animal spirits are always so hard to arouse, I know, phlegmatic as you constitutionally are."

"It was automatic, all right, I flat guarantee you," I said. "Just like that big old German clock in the big house old Miss Sutcliffe puts so much store in. Them bells was ringing, Cat."

"Are you finished, Willie?" Cat said. "Is it appropriate to go on from this point to discuss the problem?"

"Yeah, I reckon. I just like to talk about it when it ain't nowhere around."

"And when it is, too, I warrant," Cat flung back at me. "But what are we going to do, that's the question, given what Jeremy's been saying to me and to you about the prospect of his imminent death?"

"Why, Cat, they ain't a damn thing we can do, way I see it. The Major's going to be just like anybody else. Maybe it's his time to get kilt in this here tussle, maybe it ain't. How're we going to have anything to do with that, you and me, I ask you now?"

"There is a difference to consider, though, Willie," Cat said, shifting around so the light from that big cook fire behind him kind of lit up one side of his face so I could see him some better.

"Let me see if I can present it to you. Think about this. What do you do, or what would you do, if you saw a man aiming a rifle at you or about to thrust a bayonet or knife toward you?"

"Hell, that's easy. I'd do my goddamndest to get out of the way, Cat," I said to him. "I don't have to ponder none about that, not even a little bit."

"Of course you would, Willie," he said. "As any sane creature with a sense of self-preservation would do as a matter of natural instinct. Right you are. Now, what would Jeremy Sutcliffe do in the same situation, and before you answer, add this bit to the equation. Consider him to be in a state of excitement and exaltation, and convinced that he is destined to lose all that is earthly in a great battle for his nation and for Miss Sally Earl, whatever she represents to him in that narrow little channel of self-consciousness that would be called a mind in another man."

Cat said that last part louder and louder as he went on, like he was making himself mad just giving voice to it.

"You know as well as I do, Cat," I said back at him, "what'd happen if you put it like that. Old Jeremy he'd run up closer to the man with the rifle or knife or whatever it was so's the fellow could have more of a chance to hit him slap-dab in the middle of where he was aiming. That there's the way I see it."

"Precisely," Cat said and slapped both his hands down hard on the ground in front of him where he was sitting there with me in the dark off to the side away from them McNairy County fellows. "Did you hear the truth of what you just uttered?"

I didn't say anything back, for two reasons. One was I hated to always be admitting to Cat that he was right and I was wrong about every little disagreement that come up between us, and the second was that he wasn't listening to me anyway and wouldn't have took no satisfaction in beating me again in an argument, if he was waiting to hear what I would say. He was used to it.

"Willie," he was saying, "you are accurate in your assessment down to the nth degree. Jeremy Sutcliffe is a self-fulfilling maker of his own destiny, and if he has concluded it is just and right to lose his life in this battle to come, he will find a way to have it happen. Rest assured he will."

"Well," I said. "Yeah, I reckon, like I said."

"You and I will have to prevent that outrageous fatalistic outlook from prevailing," he told me. "It will be our task to watch him like the very eagles of the air to assure that he doesn't encounter the dark mistress he will be seeking here on this battlefield in Maryland."

"Who?" I said. "Does Jeremy know a woman up here in this country?"

"I speak figuratively, Willie," Cat said. "But, yes, he knows that particular woman will be here and he will attempt to cleave to her wherever and whenever she may reveal her seductive shape to him."

Cat sounded to me like he was fixing to break down squalling or something, so I didn't say anything right then back to him. I just reached out one hand and kind of patted him on the shoulder, and then I got up to make like I was stretching so I could see if any of them old boys from McNairy was hearing what me and Cat was talking about. They didn't appear to be listening, sprawled out like they was by the fire, hard asleep most of them and the rest close to it.

"I'll keep an eye out then, Cat," I said, "best as I can, on the Major, if I can do it without getting my own self shot to shit."

"I know you will do your best, Willie," Cat said, "and I will not let Jeremy leave my sight until we're back across that river home."

With that, Cat got up off the ground he'd been sitting on and struck out for where the Major would be, puffing on a cigar and jawing with whatever officer he had found to discuss stuff with. Me, I just found a spot further on back from the heat of the fire and tried to go on off to sleep, but it took me a while longer than usual that night before I did, I got to admit.

THAT NEXT DAY started up like most of them did back then, way before sun-up with all of us fellows on the move fast, putting one foot in front of the other one, and the officers trying to herd us all in one direction, at least most of us, that is. Some of them fellows was falling out, sitting down and holding their feet in both hands, some sloping off whenever they found a bend in the road to hide them while they did it, but the great majority was coming on fast enough to satisfy the men riding horseback, and we just marched steady toward wherever it was they was heading us.

Barns was built big on the places we passed by there in Maryland, nothing like what I was used to seeing in Mississippi or Tennessee. Rock foundations to the buildings, fences made out of rocks, too, and house places with grass growing right up to the front doors. Everything prosperous.

Now and then, folks would come out to the road to watch us coming by, children and women mainly. I reckon the menfolks was hanging back to keep from having to take a lot of ragging from us boys as we walked by their farms and little settlements, knowing they was going to be called all kinds of things and asked rude questions and such.

Our officers had done told us to behave ourselves like proper folks there in a foreign country, and General Lee hisself, he had done passed word down through the chain of command to get as many of us as could to sing that song "Maryland, My Maryland" whenever there was people to hear us. Most of us didn't know the words for it, nor the tune either, of course, but that didn't stop a bunch of the boys from butchering it up. See, that was supposed to make them folks that lived up yonder to realize we was friendly to them and wanted them to join on in and see that what we was doing there was the justified thing.

We was also told to pay for everything we took to eat, and we did too, every time we run into somebody that'd take Confederate script.

So we sung, eat roasting ears out of the fields, recruited the odd pig and chicken, and had ourselves a high old time marching up into Maryland.

We hollered things, too, at the folks standing there to watch us go by. "Here's your played-out rebellion," some of the boys'd say. And, "Where's General McClellan? He owes me money and I been chasing him all over Virginia and now Maryland to make him pay up." Such stuff as that. Ignorant, but some of it funny enough to make us laugh, anyway, us boys from Mississippi and Alabama and Texas and Georgia and I don't know where all.

We commenced to getting quiet, though, before the sun was too high up in the sky, when we started hearing the cannons up ahead, booming like thunder way off just before a real heller of a summer storm comes on late of an evening.

"Pelham," some of them Alabama troops started calling out. "Major Pelham. Him and Stuart has done got there and he's got that horse-artillery stinging like a yellow jacket."

By that time, officers was dashing up and down the lines of troops walking there in the road, and directly I seen Major Sutcliffe coming at a lope on that black horse Mercury, hair standing in the breeze he was kicking up and that big feather plume laid back at an angle to his hat. Cat was right behind him on his mule, cooking pots a-jangling and saddle bags a-flopping as he tried to stay in range of Jeremy. He looked like a jockey at the Jackson races perched up there leaning forward and drumming that mule in the ribs with both heels.

"Ride him, hoss-fly," some river trash from close to Memphis yelled out, "you about to win." Nobody laughed, though, and he never said nothing else.

"Mississippians," Jeremy said about the time he got even with where I was located in that bunch, his voice lifted up like some kind of a damn bugle, "wheel left and proceed to that line of trees." He pointed off toward the horizon, way yonder across a bunch of open fields and in the direction of where you could see a church steeple sticking up into sight like a toy a child would play with. "I want you to be in line of battle at that grove in twenty minutes. It's three miles and a little over, men. Let us strike a hard blow."

It takes a while to turn a bunch of men out of a line of march, and them sergeants and lieutenants flung in and began doing it, and I looked up at Jeremy right before I was fixing to stomp my left foot and veer left with the rest of them. Our eyes caught, and he flashed me a big grin just below his mustache, teeth shining white, and I could see his lips say *Willie*, but I couldn't hear him, of course, in all that racket and jostling.

He touched his spur to Mercury, and that big black horse reared up, and Jeremy swept his hat off and waved it at us Mississippians, the sun gleaming off all the bright parts of his clothes, and the boys all give him a big yell, like he wanted, and as we moved out of the road and he loped off, I found out I was hollering, too, and never even wanted to, nor meant to do it. I shut up quick when I discovered that. I have always tried to keep my head.

It was a long trot to them trees, and a hot one, but we went at it hard enough, jumping over corn rows and tearing out the stalks as we went through them, most of us not even trying to snatch at a ear or two as we went by. I wasn't hungry, anyway, but I was sure

wanting me a good long drink of water by the time me and the rest
of them boys had run three miles in that sun, hotter than blazes,
no matter if it was a Yankee state we was in where it was supposed
to be lots cooler than home, I had always heard. It weren't.

It looked like that the shade of them trees wasn't never going to
get there, as we was running toward them, but finally the ones of
us in front reached to them and flopped down to rest and then me
and the others got up yonder, too, and joined them on the ground.
We didn't get much of a chance to get our breaths and take a drink
of water, though, before the officers got us on up again, seeing to
our firearms and forming ranks and what not.

I remember I had just said something to the fellow next to me
on the left side. I believe I might have asked him if he had a spare
piece of twine or rawhide string to let me have to tie that damn
shoe sole back to the upper again where it had tore loose in the
last hundred yards of that three-mile trot. He was shaking his head
no, and I remember believing him because I had learned he wasn't
one to lie like a lot of them jaspers that came from down south
of Jackson in there toward Columbia, when I saw his eyes get real
big all of a sudden.

I looked back to the far side of that grove of trees, and I could
see way out into the cornfield that bounded it, and something was
wrong with the cornstalks on the far side. It was something happening to them, like a big slow wind had come up and was pushing
all of them forward and down, and it hadn't got to where we was
yet, so we couldn't feel the cool of the air stirring.

For just a spell, I didn't know why them head-high cornstalks
was acting like that, laying down all together, and then, of course,
you could see the banners sticking up above the green of the corn-
rows and the sunlight flashing off the muskets and the tips of their
bayonets and the metal parts on the uniforms, and then here they

come, and I knew what it was then, all right.

The officers commenced to yelling and giving orders and running back and forth in front of us where we was ranked up in the
middle of that grove of trees, and I kept my eyes on that line of
corn falling toward us just as regular as a steady wind off a big
body of water, and when there weren't but just four or five rows
still standing between us and that big push headed our way, they
give us the order to fire and we got a volley off.

It was a big coughing sound, and it made that wave coming
toward us shudder a little, like if you'd just throwed a dipperful of
water onto a big fire, but it didn't stop it, just a little steam rose up,
and here they was, busting right into the stand of trees where we
was lined up, not even yelling much as they come, just firing and
pushing like men in a big crowd at a cattle auction or on a voting
day at the end of a campaign.

We broke and ran, us Mississippians, back on out of the other
side of that stand of trees, the ones of us that was still standing up,
and headed back the way we had come into them fields we had just
run across in that hot sun there in Maryland. Some of the boys was
trying to run backwards, not wanting to take a ball in the back,
but it has always been my experience that you can run a lot faster
if you face the way you're going. So I did, along with a bunch of
otherns from down around home.

It was a swale up ahead in the cornfield, must have dipped down
four or five feet below the level of the ground around it, and I set
my sights on that, and about the time I run up on it, I could hear
horses' hooves pounding right behind me and the rest of them
boys. I remember hoping to the Lord it wasn't no Yankee cavalry
they had done sent up ahead of that infantry that had busted into
us in them trees, and sure enough it wasn't.

It was Jeremy Sutcliffe and a couple of other officers, captains

I guessed, at a dead run calculated to put them between us Mississippians on the lope and where we was aiming to get to, as far away from that blasted grove of trees as we could make it afoot. Like to Virginia or East Tennessee.

Time we got to the middle of that swale of ground they was turned and waiting on us, facing toward us and trying to make us listen and look up at their eyes. Not a one of us wanted to, running at them officers and staring down at the cornfield like we was afraid it was going to get away if we didn't keep a good hard watch on it there in the middle of that scalding hot September day.

"Mississippians," Jeremy said in a voice loud enough you could hear it over the rattle of firearms behind us and what little noise we was making as we run. Just hard breathing was about all that was. Nobody was yelling nothing, I flat guarantee you. "It is time to rally, men. Time to rally. You have made your withdrawal, and now you must form ranks."

The lead soldier of us, an old long-legged boy from Holly Springs that I had never talked to much, was right near up to where the Major was setting his horse when Jeremy got them first words out. He kept on going, the old boy did, on a track that was taking him right by Jeremy's right leg, acting like he hadn't heard a word that officer had said, and when he come up even to the crop of that big black horse Mercury, Jeremy reached out and kind of slapped him a good lick with the flat of his sword on the left shoulder.

"Halt, soldier," Jeremy said, and the long-legged fellow did, grabbing at his upper arm where the sword had hit it and rubbing it real hard like you will do after something gives you a stinging lick, maybe a limb on a bush that somebody ahead of you in the woods has let snap back quick on you.

"Willie," Jeremy said, "Willie Magee," and that stopped me for some reason, him saying my name like that. I sure as God didn't

want it to and hadn't planned on it, but there I was all of a sudden
dead still in that swale with a bunch of other men slowing up and
stopping, too. And the next thing you knowed we was all standing
there, waiting for the officers to tell us to turn around and look back
to where we had been running from. They did, and we did, and
then I seen that what I had thought was a captain on horseback a
little ways behind where Jeremy Sutcliffe was sitting on Mercury
was really Cat on his mule, instead.

"The enemy is regrouping," Jeremy said to all of us Mississippians standing there like hogs waiting to be knocked in the head
with sledgehammers on slaughtering day in November. "See to
your arms and prepare to receive a charge. We've plenty of time
to get ready to repel them. We'll be firing out of this depression
when they breast the hill, and they will not stand it. They will not
be able to bear the blow you will deliver."

I looked down at my hands and was surprised to see I was still
carrying my rifle, and so was the rest of them boys, I reckon, because here in a little bit we was all lined up again, facing north and
breathing like we had been chasing bobcats for two miles through
a river bottom. The officers let us lie down in place in the bottom
of that swale, and I appreciated the hell out of that, but when I
looked up at Jeremy again he was sitting his horse on the lip of
that swale with a smile on his face like he was at a dance in some
planter's ballroom, Cat on his mule right beside him leaning over
to hand him a canteen of water.

"You ort to see the mark that son of a bitch put on my arm,"
the fellow lying next to me said. It was that long-legged runner
from Holly Springs. "It burns like fire. See here where little drops
of blood has done come out all in a line."

I didn't look, but he kept talking. "He's crazy, ain't he, that
major?"

"As a boar hog drunk on rotten peaches," I said. "Now hush." We all laid there for a while, not too long by a clock, probably, if somebody had one to look at, but judging from the way the sun was stuck in one place in the sky, it seemed to me like the earth had done forgot how to keep on turning, and it was always going to be that same time of day there in the middle of a cornfield in Maryland waiting for a bunch of people to come up and shoot us all into pieces.

"Who was them folks?" Holly Springs asked me directly. "Come up on us there when we was resting in the shade?"

"Soldiers," I said. "Fool. Yankee soldiers, it appeared to me."

"Oh, it was?" he said, like I had told him something didn't nobody but me know, sounding satisfied he had learned something and better able now to rest easy in his mind.

Then here they come again, up over the lip of that little hill, but this time our bunch didn't run. I don't know why exactly, except maybe it was because they didn't give us time to. It was just all a confusion, like you had dropped a bucket of slops over the fence into a pen of hogs and they was all coming to fight over which one got to eat the most, falling and scrambling and getting back up and slipping down again in the mud but never forgetting to keep their jaws working. The squealing and grunting and the snapping and breaking sounds was all over me and all in my head and ears and teeth, and somehow I found myself backed up underneath something big and solid, and then I seen by the hoof lifting up in front of my face that it was a horse. I looked up at its belly, it was coal black, and the stirrups had the toes of a man's boots in them, straining up like he was pushing hard, and I recognized them boots before I knowed the horse.

It was some footwear that Jeremy Sutcliffe was awful proud of and that I had seen Catullus working on with a brush and grease many

a time back in Mississippi and then around all them cookfires after
we had got into this rebellion mess way back spring before last.

I kind of liked being up under Mercury out of the way of what
was going on all around where that big black horse was pawing
up the ground, but then he made a bigger move real sudden, and
I knowed it was just a matter of time until he stepped all over me
and maybe kicked my brains out.

So I rolled on out the far side of him and was fixing to stand up
when I seen that mule of Cat's pushing on up through a bunch of
fellows pawing at each other like they was in an all-out wrestling
match.

Cat was leaning over frontwards with his body almost laid out
flat on that mule's neck. I remember his name now. Tiber was what
Cat called him, and that animal's eyes was walling around like they
will when one has been snakebit somewhere high up on one of the
legs above the hoof and shin in a soft part. Ready to jump out of
his own hide.

I moved aside to get out of the way of a big yellow-bearded man
in a blue uniform who looked like he was fixing to coldcock me
with the butt of his rifle, and when I got that done and let him go
on by to pick on somebody else, I looked back at Cat on his mule
to see what he was up to, and I seen where he was headed.

It was toward a spot right in between the withers of the Major's
black horse and a fellow to the left and behind who was reaching
up with his rifle and about to stick the bayonet on the end of it
into the small of Jeremy's back. He was having a hard time a doing
it, this fellow, because Mercury was pawing around and jerking
from one side to the other there in the middle of all them folks
tussling with one another and swinging their rifles to and fro and
poking and pulling at folk's arms and faces and clothes and what
have you, but he was about to get himself a good angle and room

to do her with that bayonet when Cat he pushed himself on off the front shoulder of Tiber like he was diving into a big hole of water in the Etowah River.

Lots of things happened then all at the same time, it appeared like to me where I was hanging back there by the rump of the Major's horse. The fellow shoved his rifle up and forward, Cat he come flying in front of it before it got to Jeremy's back, and the point of it took him in the left side high up toward his shoulder, and an actual puff of dust flew up from Cat's shirt when that blade hit it.

Cat he landed on the back skirt of Mercury's saddle, kind of bowed up and the Major twisted around to see what had hit him in behind him and reached back his left hand and grabbed aholt of the collar of Cat's shirt, and Mercury he jumped sideways it looked like four feet, and the end of that rifle flew up out of that fellow's hands where he had poked it up yonder.

That man stepped back, looking up like he was somebody who had just throwed his gigging stick at a big bullfrog and was waiting to see if it had run true. Interested, you know, to see if he'd had any luck.

I reached out to take his shoulders and pulled him down to the ground, and I swear it wasn't two heartbeats later that all of us Mississippians was throwing our firearms down and quitting, it was too many of them to keep on a-fighting, and me and that fellow who had been frog-gigging was rolling around in the knocked-down cornstalks in the bottom of that swale, the last ones still trying to kill each other on that part of the battlefield.

Directly, somebody made us stop and we sat up and looked at each other in the face, and I tell you that fellow that had tried to stick Jeremy and had hit Cat instead didn't look no different after it was all over than if he had just finished a hard day's work in the cotton field rather than just having put a bayonet into a man's side.

"See what you done?" I told him, but he acted like he hadn't even heard what I said.

Jeremy was off his horse by then and had laid Cat on his back up against the angle of the rise of that swale, and him and a Yankee officer, a colonel, was staring down at him where he was lying, breathing shallow and fast, looking no bigger than a child.

"You people," the Yankee colonel was saying in a loud voice to Jeremy, "have certainly done a job of conditioning your slaves. If I had not seen it, I would have called the man who recounted it to me a liar."

I squatted down beside Cat and looked him in the face close. His eyes was open, and he knowed me. I could see that in them.

"I got his little wrapped-up package," I said, patting the front of my blouse where I had stuck it when Jeremy gave it to me that first day in Maryland. "Right here where I been carrying it for Miss Sally Earl." I was lying, of course. It had done slipped away somewhere in all that running I had been doing.

"It's over now," Cat said real calm and blood bubbled up in his mouth so I could see it, but none of it come out on his lips or showed on his teeth. That's good, I told myself, that's a good sign. But I known it wasn't. I couldn't talk myself into believing it.

"Naw, it ain't about over," I said. "You going to make it. We'll be on back to McNairy County before you know it."

"I don't mean me," he said. "The war. Jeremy's war's over. He'll be paroled back home. Preserved."

"I reckon you're right," I said and watched the blood bubble up in Cat's mouth every time he drawed a breath.

"It is not conditioning," Jeremy was saying in that big voice to the Yankee colonel. "Sir, these people are loyal to us in the manner any man is loyal to his family. To any member of his family."

"Well," the colonel said. "You will see it and understand it the way you must. I prefer to face the brute fact. This behavior is from learned reflex, nothing more."

"Loyalty, sir," Jeremy said. "The noble instinct for family."

Both of them officers arguing in their different colored uniforms about what to call it was wrong, dead wrong. Neither of them knowed the right word for it. They didn't have the reason. I understood it, though, down to the bone, why Cat done what he did, and I kneeled there by him the whole time and watched his eyes flare up and clear until he finally let them close there in Maryland on that hot day, until they was finally shut for good in that state so far from home.

Redemption

That affair of honor started in Blue Water Chapel, there in the southwest corner of Sabine County, close to where all those baygalls and marshes set a limit to farming. The church building at Blue Water is not standing anymore, having burned down over twenty years ago, but the graveyard there is where a lot of the Holts are buried, Papa and Mama among them. We don't bury there now, since almost everybody has moved out of that part of the country. All those clearings they put so much effort into to grow cotton have grown up now into a regular jungle of yaupon and saw briers and slash pine. It appears to me like man has not trod there when I go back now to visit the graveyard.

But that Sunday morning in Blue Water Chapel found Papa preaching in the pulpit on the theme of redemption, and people had come from all over those little communities around in that part of Sabine County to hear him do it. There were folks from Cold Spring, Standard, Rock Hill, Horse Pen, and all up and around Ellis Landing, back there on the river. I do not know all that part of the story on my own, why there were so many attending worship that day, since I was just a yearling girl at the time, but when people have talked about it over the years I have learned more of the names of places and the families that lived around them and who was there to see it start up.

Papa had built himself up a real reputation for preaching the gospel by that time, though he hadn't really started good at it until after we came to Texas in 1867. Something happened in his mind and in his soul crossing that river and leaving that life back in Louisiana, and he just started in reading the Bible every day in earnest, though he had read it plenty before. Something just took him over in Texas, though, once he got to living and farming there with Mama and the children that kept coming, and he felt the need to tell people about it, that new thing that had him. I reckon it was the grace of God, I don't know. It was one of those things preachers talk about, I imagine. Grace, salvation, eternal life, conviction, whatever they call those ideas that plague them when they get to worrying about something other than wringing a living from the sweat of their brows and that of everybody else around them.

Redemption was the main theme of all his preaching, he always said, no matter what in particular he talked about in one sermon or the other, but it was not always the subject matter of what his talk treated on. He saw a difference, and he declared it, and when he would explain that difference in one of his messages to the congregation that was when he was at his best as a preacher. Everybody who saw him preach more than two or three times always said that about Papa, and they felt the Holy Ghost moving when he would get into explaining to the congregation why he was preaching what he was preaching and doing it in the way he was.

That Sunday morning in Blue Water Chapel the singing had gone on for longer than usually it did, I don't know why, but all those folks there had sung on for a long time as one and then another among them lined out the verses for them, enjoying it, I reckon, or feeling the spirit beginning to move as they thought ahead to the sermon on redemption that Amos Holt was going to preach. I figure lingering over the hymns was like the way you will put off doing a thing you know you want to do for longer than you need to, because thinking about it and knowing it is there for you to take whenever you decide to do it makes it sweeter. Contemplation is a relish.

That was the kind of mind folks at the Blue Water Chapel worship service were in that morning, at least most of them, while they sang hymns and listened to another offer up prayers. Putting it off to make the having of it better.

I was sitting about halfway back from the front of the chapel building near the end of one of those old split-log benches country churches used back then, and during all the singing and praying that went on, I could tell Font Nowlen right in front of me was not in accord with the way the congregation was feeling—satisfied, looking forward to what was coming, joining in together with each other in the worship, all manner of that.

His people come from down in there close to the Romayor settlement, river bottom land that flooded out pretty bad every now and then, but they were the kind of folks that just put up with that happening and never had enough gumption to move when conditions didn't suit. It was good land, rich enough for cotton to grow quick and make big in a season, I'll grant them that, but it was a gamble every year, even more than is ordinarily true for anybody bound and determined to try to make a living off cotton.

The old man, Alton Nowlen, was always talking about how their bunch was from Georgia before coming to Texas, not Louisiana or Alabama like were behind most families who moved to that country after the war, and he meant by that Georgia business to set a premium on him and his somehow. I never could figure out why he believed that or why he broadcast it around, nor could anybody else in Sabine County. As far as I'm concerned, Georgia is not any place but Alabama put further off. It is certainly not a distinction worth making to a Texan.

Font Nowlen kept craning his neck around to look behind him while everybody was singing hymns, which part he did not join in, and a couple of times during the offerings of prayers by one and then another, he looked up from bowing his head like a buzzard trying to see where something dead might be lying. How I could tell he was wobbling his head around doing that was that I have always had the ability to keep my head down but roll my eyes up really far, far enough to see what's happening around me and not give a sign of my doing that. No one's ever complained about that regarding me, because I assume they can't tell it.

One reason Font Nowlen, as old as he was to be acting that way in a worship service in Blue Water Chapel, was doing so much to call attention to himself I figured out as soon as I saw him in front of where I was sitting that morning. He had on a new-made shirt with an extra big collar that stuck up from the neck of the dress coat he was wearing, and it was not white in color but a shade of blue. And that on a grown man with a full set of whiskers. Font was as proud of that piece of apparel as a jaybird stretching its wings out to fly from one limb of a sweetgum tree to another. Both Font and that blue jay constitutionally want to be seen, and they would make enough ruckus to assure that notice took place. I figured some girl had made that shirt for him, not his mother, the way he was acting, but I don't know that to be true.

Just at the end of a prayer that old man Adolphus Collins had offered up, all quavery and high pitched and as mixed up as a jar full of stray buttons, Font Nowlen twisted his head around to look behind him and then he said something to me. I remember when he did I could see his bottom teeth and they were an ugly shape and color.

"Abby Holt," he said. "Here to see her old daddy rear up and holler." He had cast his voice low to keep people sitting to each side of him from understanding what he was saying, but people around could tell he was talking in the middle of worship, no matter what he was saying.

I didn't say a word back to him, but something must have showed in my face because I could see that Papa, standing up there in front of the congregation to preside during all that would go on before he started his sermon, was looking straight at me. Usually, he would not look at any one of his children or Mama during a service, because it was not the proper thing to do, I suppose, though he had never expressed that in my hearing. I just figured out on my own that a preacher during a worship service in a church is not really part of his own earthly family while it's going on—the service, I mean. He belongs to the party of the Lord during that spell of time and is no more a member of his own family than he is of any other family of people in the congregation. He is of everybody and above everybody at the same time.

Papa's eyes were on me, when I looked up toward the front where the preacher stands in a church, and I had not answered Font Nowlen when he made that low-minded statement to me, but I was fearful that people, and most especially Papa, might have thought I did. I was in a predicament. I wanted to stand up then and there and announce to everybody in Blue Water Chapel something to this effect: "I did not invite this piece of trash to speak to me during worship, and I most assuredly would not and did not exchange remarks with him."

That's what I wanted to say, or something approximate to it, but all I could do was just turn red as fire in my face and throat like a sign board declaring my guilt for a misdeed I did not commit. Thinking that made my coloring become even more of an intense shade, and I sat there with my own father looking at me, convinced probably that one of his daughters was talking in church to a jaybird-looking excuse of a man while he was fixing his mind and soul to preach a sermon on redemption which people had come miles to hear.

And with another part of my mind, I was envying my sister Maude once again for having that dark hue of skin she got from Mama while I was blighted with the pale skin of Papa which showed every emotion that went through me, no matter how trifling, and magnified it for all to see.

Like I said, this rude and ignorant action of Font Nowlen's took place at the end of Mr. Collins's prayer and before Papa had begun to say anything toward commencing his sermon, so it had grown perfectly quiet in Blue Water Chapel, while Papa fixed his eyes on me. They were snapping like blue fire.

And then the fool sitting in front of me did it again. Twisted around, showed the bottom inside of his mouth to me—but he wasn't thinking about that, it goes without saying—and said something else.

"Did you bring a dinner bucket with you, Abby Holt?" he said, the sound of his voice louder this time in that quiet after his prayer ended. "I'm going to be hungry when all this hooting and hollering is over."

I began to entertain two thoughts at the same time, both of them amounting to the same thing, though a little different, these being "Has Font Nowlen gone crazy?" and "Is this fool in front of me drunk on a Sunday morning in Blue Water Chapel?" But by the time I was coming to the conclusion that whichever was the case it made not a hair's distinction between them anyway, Papa began to speak directly from the pulpit right in our direction, mine and Font's. Not that he and I were in any way, shape or fashion part of any kind of a combination. I would not be mistaken in that matter.

"Mr. Fontaine Nowlen," Papa said in the voice he used when preaching before a gathering, one with a kind of ringing note to it, "I would request your full and undivided attention."

I remember the church got quieter than it had ever been in my memory, at that moment. You could hear a dirt dauber buzzing somewhere up close to the shingles of the roof, working on building its mud nest, though I did not look up to verify the truth of what I knew the insect to be. I knew it was not a wasp, though, because the sound of the wasp buzzing is different, being a higher pitch and more energetic sounding than a dirt dauber.

"You want what?" Font Nowlen said back in a kind of a drawling tone, lengthening the words so they didn't carry their true meanings, the ones they would have if you read them off a page of print. The way he said those words was nasty sounding and insolent, apart from and in addition to their substance and content. Then he added this statement: "I know what this girl of yours wants."

"I had meant to inquire if you wished to speak to this congregation," Papa said, "but let me amend that. I would state now that I do not know the name of the man you would have second you. But I assume you will be able to find someone willing to perform that office. I request that you have him consult with my second, Mr. Wayland Austin of the Cane Creek community, as to date, location, and choice of weapons. I will be at your service at the time appointed by them."

Font Nowlen rose up from his seat on the split-log bench, and he did so slowly, shrugging his shoulders a little to make his coat set better, I suppose, though to an interested observer it might have appeared he was fixing himself in a pose.

I thought that, sitting there behind him as close as I was, though what was happening right then kept getting mixed up in my head with the sound of my heart pounding and of the dirt dauber buzzing away at its work above us. I can still hear that exact insect drone today or any day, if I want to call it up in my head to listen. I reckon I always will.

"Reverend Amos Holt," Font Nowlen said in that same drawling tone, "I will attend to your wishes, and I will do so with pleasure."

And then he walked down that space between the benches, reached the aisle, put his hat on his head before he got to the door, and left Blue Water Chapel in a strut.

Everybody in the building just sat there, not saying a word, and we all could hear Font Nowlen outside getting up on his horse, the saddle creaking as he did, like leather will do, and the horse groaning. But before we began to hear the first hoofbeats as Font commenced to ride off, Papa had begun his sermon on redemption, the one everybody had come to hear him preach at Blue Water. And it was what folks called a stemwinder, then when he delivered it and all the years since when people have talked about it. They still do, the ones left, that few of them.

I do not hold with dueling, now and back then when so much of it went on, being a Christian and a civilized person and most particularly a woman. But I knew, sitting there in Blue Water Chapel listening to Amos Holt quoting scripture directly from the Bible without having to refer to the book and then explaining to the congregation what it meant as regards redemption, that I was going to find the way and the means to observe my father meet Fontaine Nowlen in mortal combat.

I knew where it would take place. Every soul in Blue Water Chapel did, and that was Honeysuckle Island, in the middle of the Sabine River, about three miles downstream from Sabinetown. So while I sat there, listening to Papa line out the necessary and inevitable steps toward redemption, I was calculating how to find out the time the seconds of the involved parties would set for the duel to happen.

It came to me fairly quick who to ask, as I sat there beneath the buzzing of that dirt dauber still at work and the sounds of Papa's comments on the scriptures from Matthew and Luke and John. Maude could find out from Drusilla Austin who was bound to hear her father Wayland talking about arrangements for the duel with her mother. Wayland Austin couldn't keep anything private from his wife, Myrlie, who could and would prize information out of anybody as neat as she could get the meat out of a black walnut shell.

It would be no real project for me to get over to Honeysuckle Island, whatever day the seconds picked for the event to take place, since like all the young folks around Sabinetown, I had been there to picnic many a time. I could find some boy to paddle me over to the island in a skiff or canoe or on the off-chance I could not, I would do it myself. Through the course of my life to that point, I had found that boys generally liked to do favors for me. That has not changed yet, though it has slowed considerably.

The time of day for the meeting would be just after daylight, just like when most every settlement of an affair of honor was held back then, so all I needed to find out was the date itself. And from the offense Papa had taken from Font Nowlen's act and the way he had called him out there in Blue Water Chapel, I felt in my bones it would not be many days off from that particular Sunday.

The way it worked in those days in Sabine County, Texas, in such matters was that if honor could be satisfied by just a show, why then the seconds would go through a lot of palaver and arranging and arguing for a long spell and set the date several weeks off. Everything could kind of die down by the time had come for the parties to meet on Honeysuckle Island, and satisfaction could be gained by one of the parties not showing up because he was taken sick or his wife was in a sinking condition of some sort or another, or one of the children, maybe, was at death's door. And the opponent would forgive that, as a gentleman.

And if both parties ended up facing each other finally at the appointed time, there in that clearing on Honeysuckle Island, back in behind those stands of water oaks with the Spanish moss hanging down from their limbs, the weapons of choice would have been settled on as pistols. Then, nine times out of ten, with one of these agreed-upon dates set by the seconds long after the triggering offense itself, the first man would miss his shot and the other one would shoot up into the air or into the ground after that miss, and everybody would be satisfied with the outcome. Then they all could go separately home and eat breakfast and listen to their folks go on about how honor had been fulfilled and bravery demonstrated and a lesson learned by the other fellow.

And the combatants would avoid seeing each other from then on, or sometimes they might even shake hands as time went by and even get to be friendly toward one another. I have seen that happen, as have other people in those days when the name of Honeysuckle Island would send shivers down people's spines, men as well as women, not even to mention children.

The settlement of the affair of honor between Amos Holt and Fontaine Nowlen would not fit into that category, I knew. What had begun in Blue Water Chapel that Sunday morning right after the praying stopped and before the sermon began would not lend itself to a lot of talk between seconds arguing and speechifying about arrangements and choice of weapons. It would be settled in one sitting, as soon as Font Nowlen named his man as second and as soon as that man met with Mr. Wayland Austin of the Cane Creek community.

I knew that by two things, and as I think about it today, I remember saying those two things to myself as Papa coolly worked his way through his sermon on redemption before the congregation and that dirt dauber above buzzed away at molding its mud nest together in the rafters of the church. Not Papa's words, I kept hearing my voice in my mind say over and over to me, not Papa's words to Font Nowlen, not his words but the way he said them. The cold in the words, the cold in the words, and the heat in the eyes, the fire blazing up in the eyes.

THAT AFTERNOON, after dinner around the table with Mama setting the vessels of food out to feed all of us and her completely silent and the rest of us the same way, the only sounds that of the knock of the bowls as she set them on the table and of the utensils clicking on the plates, I put my sister Maude to work on learning the day of the week the duel would occur. Told her who to talk to, Drusilla Austin, swore her to silence, which I knew she would observe, and readied my mind to allow me to watch my father meet a man in combat some morning soon on Honeysuckle Island with the air still cool, the light steadily growing, and fog coming up from the ground like tendrils from a fern or tatters from a woman's veil.

It would be Wednesday, only three days after the offense made and taken, and the settlement of honor would be accomplished with Bowie knives.

When Maude told me that, she did so on Monday at the schoolhouse after Professor Runnels had let us out to eat our noon meal. Since I was one of the older girls and Professor Runnels had early on learned how much sense I had, I had been sitting with some of the little ones in one corner of the room helping them recite their words, as was my habit and duty. He depended on a couple of us to help him out when we could, given that it was a large school with over a couple of dozen scholars to teach.

So when Professor Runnels hit the little bell on his desk at the front of the room to signal all of us to line up to leave the building and go outside to eat what we had brought with us to school that morning, I looked up to see that Maude was trying to catch my eye. I nodded at her real quick, just one little bob of my head, so as not to call attention to the fact that two of us Holts were communicating with each other in school, and I went to my place, at the front of the line.

As I walked toward the door of the building to let the rest of the scholars get in behind me, I felt a little something kick up low in my stomach, not like I was about to get sick, but more like a message my body was sending me, telling me to get ready to hear a thing I wanted to know but dreaded to receive.

Outside, by the bole of the sycamore under whose shade the older ones liked to sit while we ate our dinner on those days nice enough to be out in the open air, Maude looked at me with a piercing gaze.

"Well," I said, "did you talk to Drusilla?"

"I did," she said. "Is it some more of those crowder peas?"

"What else?" I said. "That and some corn pone. Here." I handed her the tin vessel we carried back and forth between the old place and the Double Pen schoolhouse every day lessons were in session. "What did Drusilla say?"

"Drusilla heard her Mama and Papa talking last night after supper," Maude said and lifted up a spoonful of peas toward her mouth, hoping I'd break down and ask her to get to the point. I did not. So she put the peas in her mouth, chewed them more than needful, and swallowed them down.

"Mr. Austin met with Fontaine Nowlen's second on Sunday afternoon. It's John Milton Redd who's the second. That's who

Font Nowlen picked to speak for him."

"I don't like to hear that," I said. I didn't have to explain to my sister why. Everybody in all the settlements in Sabine County knew the reputation of John Milton Redd for hotheadedness and a rowdy nature. He would rather argue than eat, and he was way too young to be acting as a second to a party involved in an affair of honor with a man of our father's substance.

"He is disputatious," Maude said, showing off a word she had learned, which she has always been bad to do, though I do give her credit for always being a girl eager to increase her vocabulary. I don't question that urge, but I do have an opinion about the manner in which a woman chooses to offer up the accomplishments of her mind.

"John Milton, I am speaking of," Maude went on. "He is ever eager to fight."

"I know what that word means," I told her, "and he is not eager to fight himself, but to talk about fighting and to encourage others to do so as he watches the battle."

"That is what I meant, of course," Maude said and took another bite of crowder peas, adding a portion of corn pone to her mouthful.

"All right," I said, breaking down, finally, in my desire to know what my sister had learned about the matter at hand. "When will it happen? What are the conditions?"

That was all Maude needed to hear from me, a sign of surrender, and she ceased parceling out her information in dribs and drabs, and told me the rest of it in one burst of speech. Wednesday morning on Honeysuckle Island at dawn, Bowie knives because as Mr. Wayland Austin reported John Milton Redd's statement to him, "Font Nowlen wants either to kill that damned Amos Holt or cut him up so bad he won't never preach another lick."

"Damned, indeed," I said to Maude, the words bursting out of my mouth, "Papa will show Fontaine Nowlen what damned means. That jaybird will rue the day he crossed Amos Holt at Blue Water Chapel in the middle of a worship service."

With that, I immediately felt hungry and took the tin of crowder peas and corn pone out of Maude's hand and pitched in. She was through eating, anyway, and she was beginning to cry, not loud, but enough so you could see the tears starting to streak down her cheeks.

"I'm going to be there to see him do it, too," I said. "Want to come with me?"

Maude didn't answer, but I knew she wouldn't be on Honeysuckle Island that morning in any shape, form, or fashion. She has never had stomach for such matters as duels. Sitting under the sycamore, my sister weeping beside me, I ate with relish every last pea and swabbed the bottom of the tin container with the last bite of corn-bread until the metal shone clean. And then I ate the bread.

IT IS A STRANGE THING to admit, but I must report that I don't re-member how I got to Honeysuckle Island that Wednesday morning before daylight, nor how I returned across the water of the Sabine River after the events that took place that day were over. But it's true. When I cast my mind back to then, what I recall first is how wet the leaves of the undergrowth on the island were as I kneeled at the edge of the clearing where I knew the meeting between the opposing parties would take place.

That I remember clearly as my first impression of that day, that, and the dress I was wearing, a light-colored one which showed every drop of water from the leaves which spotted it as they dripped. The morning was cool, and the sky was beginning to brighten in the east and the outline of the limbs and foliage was becoming more visible. Birds were tuning up their songs, and from somewhere in the shallows of the river flowing about the island came the croaking of a couple of bullfrogs looking for each other, there in no-man's land between Texas and Louisiana, a location nobody claimed and a place subject to no law.

As Mama had said to me back on the very day the Holts first came to Texas, the place where I now knelt in concealment on an island between two states was nowhere. By nature, it was between places.

Papa and his second arrived in the clearing first, and I could have predicted that. He was always a man prompt to get where he was appointed to go and determined not to keep others or any business waiting.

He and Mr. Wayland Austin walked out together well into the open space at the heart of the stand of water oaks, not talking and making little sound as they pushed through the low grass and weeds of the clearing. Mr. Austin was smoking a small black cheroot, the plume of smoke from it disturbed a bit by a light breeze that was coming from the east and stirring the fronds of Spanish moss on the limbs of the water oaks. Papa was not smoking, since he seldom used tobacco, and when he did, not in a smoking form. He would chew a small amount now and then of bright leaf, but only as a tonic. He had, in fact, ceased doing even that many years before he died in 1906.

He was wearing dark pants and a dress coat, over a white shirt fastened at the neck with a black string tie. He was carrying nothing in his hands, but Mr. Austin had a black leather valise, the sight of which made my throat constrict when I saw it, enough to cause me to begin swallowing over and over with difficulty as though I had bitten off a mouthful of something too dry for me to get down.

I put my hand over my mouth to help me swallow with no

sound, and I was instantly glad I had done so, because at that moment Papa took off his hat—he was wearing his black dress one—and shook his head a little, causing his hair to move in the breeze. The gray I could see in it, even at that distance, in the growing light of the morning was what affected me, and I believe I would have made a sound if my mouth had not been fortunately covered already by my hand.

Wayland Austin said something to Papa, which I could not make out, and Papa nodded and answered him, and I could hear and understand what he said back, "Oh, he will be here, all right," and it was just then that Fontaine Nowlen and John Milton Redd stepped from the stand of water oaks and yaupon bushes opposite, making their way into the clearing where what had begun in a worship service in Blue Water Chapel would meet its termination that cool morning on Honeysuckle Island.

"Gentlemen," Mr. Wayland Austin said in greeting and nodded his head in their direction, but John Milton Redd didn't answer, choosing instead to turn to look directly into the face of Font Nowlen beside him, as though checking to see if his companion had heard the same noise he just had.

Fontaine Nowlen didn't look back at his second, but instead continued swiveling his head around from side to side as he appeared to be inspecting the complete circle of the clearing he had just stepped into. I remember wondering at the time as I peered between the boles of two water oaks and just over the top fronds of a palmetto bush if Fontaine Nowlen was afraid he was walking into an ambush. No chance of that existed in an affair of honor involving Amos Holt, I knew, but a man will always fear the possibility of what he knows he himself is capable of.

So Font Nowlen was revealing his character in every particular of his behavior that morning, just as he had in his violation on the

Sunday before in Blue Water Chapel. That's what was making him suspect the underhand on Honeysuckle Island that morning.

"Reverend Holt," Font Nowlen said in a pert voice, "I see you have chosen to show up."

"I have," Papa said, but he didn't bob his head as Mr. Austin had done earlier, and he kept his gaze fixed on Font Nowlen, not choosing to survey the scene from side to side and in all dimensions as the man he faced continued to do.

Neither of the principals spoke again, but waited in silence as Mr. Austin and John Milton Redd walked up to each other in the middle of the clearing and began to converse in their roles as seconds.

As they talked in murmurs low and indistinct, I watched the morning breeze lift and move my father's hair, and I kept my hand pressed to my mouth. It was not that I felt any longer that I might make an untoward outcry or groan, but I remember thinking that if I kept the pressure of my hand applied to my face I would be able to forestall any shaking or tremors which might move the leaves behind which I shielded myself. That does not make sense now, but it did then and was a comfort to me.

After Mr. Austin and John Milton Redd had said a few words, each of them opened the valise he was carrying to show its contents to the other, and both looked intently within. I knew what they were examining, though I myself was in no position to see. It was the Bowie knives.

I thank the Lord the Bowie knife has largely passed from the scene in Texas these days, but back then it was of great moment in situations of dispute and reputation in the state.

The Bowie was a knife in name only, in a realistic sense. It was actually a long, heavy blade, more like a hatchet with a razor-sharp edge, attached to a handle which allowed its wielder to employ it to chop as well as to thrust and slice. It was serious, it was deadly, it was Hell held in the hand.

Thinking of what those two men in the middle of the clearing filled with birdsong were considering as they peered at the contents of their valises, their heads together as though they were a team studying a water moccasin's fangs, I knew I had to look away from them or collapse into the saw briers and underbrush around me.

I fixed my gaze first on Papa, but I could not maintain it there, with the breeze continuing to ruffle his head of hair, revealing the silver mixed with black. So I focused instead on Fontaine Nowlen, now standing with his head back and his eyes fixed on something higher up, the tree line maybe, or the sunlight touching the leaves, or the empty sky itself.

He was wearing that same new-made, light blue shirt with the oversized collar, the garment which I took to be at the bottom of all this before me, the reason that Font took it into his foolish head to strut and flare and forget where he was in a given location and how to behave in that place. I believed to my soul that was the truth of the matter there on Honeysuckle Island that morning, I believe it today, and I will go to my grave with that conviction.

Around the neck of that oversized collar, Font Nowlen was sporting a canary yellow tie, which in a situation other than the present one, would have made a nice contrast. Say at an all-night gathering in a house full of young people dancing on a floor cleared of all breakable furniture, or at a church singing outdoors with dinner on the ground to follow.

Here on Honeysuckle Island with seconds approving weapons of choice at daybreak and Amos Holt standing across the clearing, prepared to rectify an insult to himself and to the honor of his family, the yellow tie and blue shirt Font Nowlen wore did not fit the circumstance.

But seeing the yellow tie and being able to consider the thoughts it brought to my mind eased and calmed me enough to allow me to bear and endure the situation I had got myself into so I would not faint, I would not cry out and reveal my presence, I would not shame Papa in the performance of the duty he had no choice but to owe himself and accept.

The seconds finished their conference, looked each other in the eye, shook hands, turned and walked back to their principals. Every bird on the island was in full song, the sun rose steadily above the tree line to the east, and its beams lit the clearing like a stage.

A duel fought with the Bowie knife, for those who have not seen one, is in its progress slow at first and then lightning quick. I watched that entire struggle between my father Amos Holt and the provoker of the affair of honor, Fontaine Nowlen, and I choose not to describe it in detail.

I will say this much, however. At the end of the encounter, Papa was cut to the bone on his left arm, high up toward the shoulder, enough so that arm was not the same in its strength and use to him ever again, from that point until the day of his death. He favors it in the photograph taken those years ago, three months before Mama's death, and he continued to do so, learning to use his back muscles and his right arm more from then on in discharging the duties of farming and all other physical labor. I am convinced his rheumatism, severe in his last years, came as a result of that morning's struggle, as well.

His shortage in that arm, as he always termed it, began that day on Honeysuckle Island. Fontaine Nowlen's yellow tie at the end of combat was yellow no more, nor was it intact about his throat, and his new-made light blue shirt was cut into ribbons of red. Amos Holt walked to the small boat he had used to cross from the Texas bank of the Sabine River to Honeysuckle Island, but Fontaine Nowlen was carried by John Milton Redd, assisted by Mr. Wayland Austin, to the skiff he had rowed to Honeysuckle Island that morning in a state of perfect health and strength. He departed his life on earth before he arrived at his home near noon in the Romayor settlement and before he had opportunity to say farewell to his mother.

His last words, uttered in the skiff to his second in the affair, John Milton Redd, I do confess, included my name.

The Bliss of Solitude

Today is Tuesday, the day they bathe the Cuban Chili Pepper. I can hear them getting ready in the hall outside my room, Lawrence grumbling and sighing as he gets the chair unlimbered and the straps unfastened, Rolando whistling and making noises with his mouth like a drum and a steam engine and a tire going flat. And all in one and the same breath. Amazing.

I tilt my good ear toward the door to listen, but she in the next room hasn't cottoned on to what's coming down the pike for her, what's on her immediate horizon, so she hasn't started up yet. With the screaming and the swearing and the spitting and the sobs and squeals, I mean, and all the other noises the Cuban Chili Pepper was so well-known for back when the screens were black and white and the light was always silver.

Mainly silver, I mean. That silver light. There was color too then, I know, I know, but that's not the part I want to think about. If I want to remember color, I can turn my head and look out the window at the sun lighting up everything outside like a Howard Hawks set, day after day after day every minute, every hour, from six in the morning until after six at night.

There's your color, all right, as real as oatmeal, and you're welcome to it. Eat it while it's hot down to the last grease mark. I'll wait until it cools first and gets a little darker, thank you.

Lawrence doesn't really enjoy it, I can tell, the getting them up and the undressing and the pulling them out of bed and the pushing them down into the chair while Rolando makes his mouth noises and fiddles with the straps and buckles and Velcro binders and waits for just the right time to pinion a hand or a foot and then another and another until they're all fastened down and ready to roll.

Lawrence, as I said, doesn't enjoy the first part, the getting them ready to take that trip down the hall, then roll left at the intersection and on through the extra-wide door that lets into the bathing room. Water World, I've come to call it, because that's a name most of the crew living here can still recognize and know what I'm talking about. I tried calling it the Esther Williams Commemorative Spa for a while, thinking some of them would like that, maybe see a little wit connected with the title. But none of them did, not even Tory Mimsel, who worked in three of Esther's pictures and was Best Boy in at least one.

He's here, Tory is, and has been since the early eighties, and doesn't even know his own name anymore, much less who or what Esther Williams was. Is. She's still outside somewhere, I believe, moving around on her own. Finding her own way to the refrigerator, taking naps on her own schedule and flushing her own toilets, too, as far as I know.

What I was talking about, though, was Lawrence, how he doesn't enjoy the prep part of the bathing job, the waking them up and strapping them in. What he appreciates, and I know this fact from paying attention and making close observation, is what happens once he and Rolando get them rolled into Water World and one of their chairs hooked up to the dipping mechanism.

It's like a crane, you see, a long metal arm that bolts to the back of the chair and that swivels around and lifts things up and sinks things down. Once that contraption's hooked up to a chair it's got as much flex and movement as a camera crane. And it's hydraulic and one man can handle it with no more effort than he would have to use to lift a fork from a plate to his mouth to take the next bite of sautéed veal. Or field peas and cornbread and okra. It depends on the circumstance and just where you find yourself. It's all timing. You eat what's before you.

So Lawrence is at the controls, and the man or woman Velcroed into the chair, ex-first lead or ex-second lead or background or production crew, it makes no difference in Water World, swings out over the pool full of bubbling warm suds and gets dipped right down to the chin line. Sometimes it's further, sometimes as much as a foot below the surface for a second or two, if Lawrence so decides. It's up to him. He's the one pushing the buttons and figuring the shot and measuring the focus and the duration of the close-up.

And what the director decides, the director decides, and nobody anymore of our whole bunch can pull any rank as regards exposure to the elements of the scene. Box office and bankability don't apply any longer. You go where he puts you, and you stay there until he decides he's got it right. And there is no agent or legal counsel involved in establishing the scene.

The Cuban Chili Pepper's trip is underway now, and the procession of her chair down the hall toward the turn to the left and then the turn to the right is in hard focus. We've already got past the wide shot, and we're in deep close-up now. We're tight on the Cuban Chili Pepper's face, and she is working her mouth for all it's worth. Or almost all it's worth. At least what's left of that million-dollar set of lips, teeth, and tongue. It was quite a unit in its day, that mouth.

"Barry," she's calling my name as Lawrence and Rolando wheel her past my open door, "Barry, for the fucking love of God, don't let them take me out of my cottage. Not again, not again."

And so on and so on, she goes. Most of the rest that I'm able to hear is simply a series of whoops and moans and squeals and sobs, all delivered at the rate of speed which earned her her name in the first place.

The Cuban Chili Pepper! Hot, hot, hot. Fast, fast, fast! A Latin spitfire who takes nothing from no man. Nothing but love, that is, if she so chooses.

That's the way some of the copy read, as I recall it, some of the first stuff the studio used right after the war when they used her in *Havana Nights*. Her breakthrough vehicle, I guess they'd call it these days.

"Hold on, Elsie," I call toward the door, "Stay with it, girlie. It won't last long."

"Barry," she interrupts her cries and moans and screams to say, her voice fading as Lawrence trudges along, "these assholes are going to do things to me. Things I can't bear."

"Relax," I say, "enjoy it." But, of course, no one's close enough to hear me and appreciate the wit. Nobody but Tug Sanders, my neighbor on the other side, so far gone by now he thinks Cream of Wheat is lamb chops.

"Hang in there, Elsie Flattman," I say to the empty air. "Bend your knees and spread your toes."

That makes me laugh a little out loud, myself alone as audience again and the best one I ever had, and I feel better, good enough to let the weight of my legs dangling off the bed pull me halfway up toward a sitting position.

My ears pop, and the wall across from my bed does a little swoop to the left and then one in the other direction, but the scene rights itself by the time I'm sitting all the way up, and that wasn't too bad. Not bad at all, in fact, for the first resurrection of the day, and I even allow myself to test the stability of the room in which I sit and the world in which I live by wagging my head back and forth like Johnny Weismuller used to do on the set when he would get water in his ears.

Everything sticks in place despite the maneuver, the wall across the way and the framed print in the middle of it and the small bunch of plastic flowers Myrtice has stuck onto the wallboard with some sort of substance tacky to the touch, like chewed gum.

That temporary stability of all I'm seeing, short though it's likely to be, is cheery enough to cause me to remember and sing the next line of the old blues number I just quoted to the Cuban Chili Pepper, née Elsie Flattman. "You know I love you, goodness knows."

And I did at one time, goodness knows, as the song says, goodness knows, Lord God, I did, I did. Back when she answered to Elsie Flattman when called, and I was still Lester Moye from LaPlata, Maryland, and not one Barry Foxmoor from parts unknown.

She was a child, and I was a child, but where we dwelled was no kingdom by the sea. No, Elsie Flattman and Lester Moye did not enjoy their first encounter in a magic land far removed. It was not a fairy tale setting, but it did happen to take place by water, and that has remained a constant, the water part, for as long as I've known her.

Even now as I listen to her last squeals coming from down the hall as Lawrence and Rolando bump her chair through the swinging doors to Water World, the wet stuff is playing a large role in the story line, upfront and in hard focus. Wetness is motif, as a screenwriter would say.

It was off and on, that relationship we had. I suppose I should say, to be truthful, the relationship I had, because for most of the time I knew her and have known her and do know her, Elsie Flatt-man was all pure object in reference to me. What I mean by that is I was here, and she was always yonder. Somewhere out there just within the range of touch, at least on a part time basis, but just barely, barely, and not enough in evidence even for her to have to admit to it.

So while the Cuban Chili Pepper screams and bubbles and strains at her Velcro bindings in that room full of dampness down the hall, let me remember the first time I saw Elsie Flattman by water.

It wasn't standing still, contained in a man-made concrete pool that first time. And it wasn't intended for bathing, that water. It was a river, and it was wide and it was moving, though you couldn't tell it was by looking at it. The Potomac by the time it gets to George Washington's house in Virginia is almost a mile wide, and it's prac-tically tidal, flat and dark in the summertime and slick enough to skip rocks off of.

It has picked up and is carrying all the filth of the District of Columbia by then, and that is a heavy load to bear, so it's just easing its way down between Virginia and Maryland as it oozes toward the Chesapeake Bay. It doesn't make a ruckus, and it doesn't make a sound. It's already been flushed, thank you, and by this time in its journey the tanks of the commodes that gave it the kickoff are al-most all filled up again. Geographically, we are talking aftermath.

I wasn't on the good side of the Potomac at the time I met the Cuban-Chili-Pepper-in-training. I wasn't lounging on the green-sward of the ancestral home of a national forefather large in American history, gazing at a vista as I sipped a meaningful drink.

No, I was on the Maryland side, across from Mt. Vernon, sit-ting on the end of a dock with my feet dangling over the edge and watching one of the ride wranglers fishing with a cane pole.

His name was Bud Pickle, and he operated one of the most

popular rides at Marshall Hall Amusement Park, the Whip 'Em, and he had no idea that the moniker he answered to could be considered by some people as funny. He didn't have the capacity to understand that fact. Whenever Bud laughed, it was always tentative.

It was midweek, and the time of day was just after supper. The cruise boat that brought passengers down from Washington, D.C., the SS *Mt. Vernon*, had left at four o'clock, local customers came to the park only at night and the weekend, and everybody who worked at Marshall Hall Amusement Park—the barkers for the games of chance, the ride operators, the bottle boys and the ticket booth girls, the bosses and the security guards, the keepers of the hot dog stand—everybody but me and Bud Pickle, were all holed up in small rooms resting up for the spasm of visitors to come later that evening, if they did. There was not a customer in the park.

"You know what I'm using for bait?" Bud Pickle said to me as he detached something he had caught on his hook. I forget what it was. Not a fish exactly. Something small, dark, and nasty looking.

"No," I said, to be sociable. I still thought at that time in my life you had to respond to everything that popped up and confronted you with a demand, mild though it might be and however inconsequential its source. "What?" I said to Bud Pickle, though I didn't want to talk to him.

Bud turned away from fiddling with his hook to look at me, the expression on his face the same one that must have appeared on D. W. Griffith's when he regarded his work and thought it good. Bud's eyes were closer together than D. W.'s probably were, though, and I don't imagine the T-shirt Bud was wearing, heavy with grease from close acquaintance to the engine of an amusement park ride, was anything Mr. Griffith would have ever pulled over his head.

And the best I can remember from photographs I have seen and stories I have heard, D. W. had all five fingers on each hand, clear down to the nail. Bud Pickle kept getting parts of his nipped off.

"Nothing," Bud said and dropped his mouth well open to wait for my surprised response, his eyes dancing.

"Nothing?" I said, giving him what he wanted, puzzlement mixed with a smidgen of awe and a good dollop of eagerness to be enlightened. "How can that work?"

"Nothing," Bud said, looking back at his hook and poking it with the remainder of one of his digits. "Just a little piece of my shirt tail I tore off and stuck on the point of this hook right here."

"Fish will bite at a piece of T-shirt cloth?" I said, though I wasn't looking at the hook or at the shirt tail Bud had pulled up out of his waistband for my inspection and verification that it was missing a piece.

"Things hungry," said Bud, "will bite at whatever they see in front of them. They'll worry about where or not they can chew it up and get it down later on."

"Later on."

"Later on," Bud Pickle affirmed and flipped his hook and line back over the guardrail into the waters of the Potomac. "After they get whatever it is into their mouth. Then that's a new job, see. They done got the hard part done."

"So you have caught some fish like that," I said.

"What do you think's in this bucket?" Bud said. "Rhubarb pie?"

I didn't deign to answer that example, though it was Bud's best attempt at wit, but I did get up from where I was hanging my feet over the water and walk over to look into Bud's bucket. It had a little water in the bottom, and it was moiling with several dark-colored fish of a small size all fighting to get their noses down into the element which had sustained them at one time.

None of them appeared to have much hope evident in their

eyes, but all but one or two were still in the struggle.

I was leaning over, getting closer to the scene and attempting to identify one of the lead actors, a snaky looking thing with what appeared to be two underdeveloped legs near the front of its body very close to its popped eyes, when it happened.

Somebody laid a hand on my left shoulder and tugged at it as though the owner of the hand wanted me to get out of the way, push me to the side, make room for himself or herself to get at what was of interest and worthy of consideration before us. Move, it said. Shake it. Now.

It was a herself, of course, and not a him, and it was the first time that action was to take place, though I was to experience it in one form or another for the rest of my days, and I mean right up to now, the present moment, where I sit in a well-lit, two-person room in the Spencer Tracy Wing of the South Florida Retirement Facility for Motion Picture Personnel.

It's got a ring, doesn't it, that label? It was explained to me once by Mr. Gilpin, a superintendent or two before the one now, Caughran the Drunken Gnome, as I call him, why the name for where we all live doesn't have more punch to it, more marquee value.

"No metaphor," Mr. Gilpin said, his eyes bright as he peered out at me from the big swoop of hair that lay across his forehead. "The Board decided unanimously and to a man at the founding that people like you, Mr. Foxmoor, would want it that way. In his wisdom, Sol Golding put it best. 'They're sick of stuff being called what it's not, these show business veterans. They want reality up close and in front. Call it what it is. No more B.S. for these troupers.'"

"No more secrets," I said to his pompadour, "no fancy names. No make-believe. That's what you're saying."

"None," Mr. Gilpin said and slapped his hand down on my shoulder hard enough to sting. "A spade is a spade, right?"

"And a cemetery is a boneyard," I said. "Call it that and be done with it."

But I wander, and that I don't like to do, unless it's late at night and my actual eyes are closed and I'm watching the credits for some production roll up on my own personal screen for viewing, and I'm the projectionist making it happen on my inner eye. Which is the bliss of solitude, as the poet said.

The hand, that's what I'm supposed to be telling about, the hand on my fifteen-year-old shoulder, and the first touch from it as it pulled me aside so its owner could get a good look into that bucket full of creatures fighting for a little more of the life-prolonging properties of water.

"What is it?" the voice said. "Let me see. Let me see it now."

So the first time I heard her voice, my first experience of that instrument, was by the dark flat wet sheet of the Potomac on the Maryland side, late in the day in the summer of 1939, about a month before Adolph Hitler invaded Poland.

"Yeah, sure," Bud Pickle said, moving to claim his rights to the bucket at the focus of attention, "let the little lady see into there at what I caught, Lester. Let her get a load of it."

So I did, though I hadn't completed my study yet of what was inside, the strange snaky creature with the legs by its eyes where there shouldn't be any legs, none at all. I moved out of the way, I dropped everything and stepped aside, and I focused on the person tugging at my shoulder.

Actually, I looked at her hair as she thrust her head forward to look into Bud Pickle's bucket, and I found myself rubbing my shoulder where her hand had been a second before as though it was bothering me, the way you'll do if something physically sudden has stung you a little.

Where she had touched me didn't really hurt, and flesh has no memory, but I could still tell where her hand had been, despite that fact.

"Why, there's nothing in there," she said in that voice, its direction this time all the way down, nothing at all like the way it had first sounded when I heard it ordering people out of the way so that its owner could get at what she wanted to see. "Just some ugly little fish."

"Well," I said, "what did you think it was going to be? What else would come out of the Potomac this far downstream?"

"Wait a minute," said Bud Pickle, snatching the bucket back toward him as though it was a child he had been carrying proudly down Main Street and someone had spoken against it somehow. Called it bug-eyed, maybe, or asked when it was going to grow some hair.

"These here," Bud Pickle said, peering hard into the bucket which he had lifted chest high in a protective instinct, "is real good eating. See that eel? You couldn't buy nothing like that booster in no store for no amount of money. He's prime."

Her hair was what I kept staring at, as I said, and I was doing that for a couple of reasons. First, there was so much of it. Not that it was especially long, I don't mean that. Girls back then were all wearing it controlled and bobbed with the general appearance of its just having been stamped out by some kind of machine that produced a uniform product.

No, her hair was the required and accepted length and up to the standards of the national hairdo licensing board, if there had been such a thing, but it was dense, thick, concentrated. I swear, at the time I had my first glimpse of it, her hair must have had twice the count of individual follicles per square inch of scalp than the standard woman would have had. And every one of those follicles was filled to capacity, no vacancies to be observed.

The other thing remarkable was the color, and as she stood toe-to-toe with Bud Pickle downgrading his catch from the black water of the Potomac on a hook with no piece of real bait, merely a sketchy symbol of one, I found myself trying to determine precisely just what hues were present in that mass of curl and swoop of tress that would cause the late afternoon light to continue to shift the message it was giving my eyes.

The predominant color here is brown, that river light in Maryland would say. No, it would amend its statement in the next second, not exactly. Auburn, maybe, just now. Wait, darker than that again. On towards true brunette, maybe. Is that an authentic reddish glow that beam of sunlight just picked up? At least we're not seeing blonde, for certain. There's color here, there's pigment a plenty, not an absence of anything. What it appears to be is not a lack, but an abundance, too much of lots of hues and shades and colors, and they're all fighting to dominate, and the outcome remains in grave doubt.

"I wouldn't put any part of any one of that bunch in my mouth," the girl was telling Bud Pickle. "I'm particular about what I eat and where it comes from."

"Huh," Bud Pickle said in what he obviously thought was a tone of killing rejoinder. "Huh, huh, huh," he continued as he backed away, his bucket full of trash life from the river flowing by the home of the Father of Our Country. "I ain't asking you to. These is all mine, every damn last one of them. Huh."

Then she laughed and turned to look at me, and the sun shot forth a final beam to attempt to solve the riddle of the color of her hair, but failed again and quit trying. I give it up, the light said. You figure what to call it. I've got appointments on the other side of the world. "Why aren't you fishing?" the girl said. "Afraid you might catch something?"

"I don't like fish," I said, my eyes still fixed on the abundance of hair before me. "They don't smell good. They taste funny."

"Real fish don't. Just what comes out of this old river is what tastes bad."

By this time Bud Pickle had moved his bucket and his pole and line as far down the pier and away from us as he could without leaping into the Potomac itself, so I felt emboldened enough to attempt to change the subject. That was the first time I tried that with her, and it never worked for long, though I have been employing that strategy from 1939 up until today.

She does not like that, being redirected, and has always insisted on considering what she has selected for discussion, not someone else, and she always will. Right up until the entrance interview at the Gates of Paradise, I expect. Or, to be fair, at the alternative, Hell Mouth.

"Are you visiting Marshall Hall for the first time?" I asked her. "Did you miss the boat back to D.C.?"

"Who'd visit this place?" she said and put a hand to her hair to push it back. It returned immediately to where it had been. "I mean after they'd turned twelve years old."

I didn't say anything to that, but continued to focus on the hair while now and then letting my eyes jerk down to get a glimpse of her face. I was afraid to do much more than that, because I had sensed already that if I let myself go too far in that direction I would be in jeopardy of becoming riveted into a stare on the spot. Struck dumb on a pier poking out into the Potomac, eyes glued on some portion of a strange girl's face, while a thin line of clear saliva worked its way out of my slackjawed mouth to gather on my chin and drip onto my shirtfront. Not an attractive scene. But an attention-getter.

"I wish I had missed my ride on the *Mt. Vernon*," she was saying. "And that I was really upset about not getting back to D.C. in time to arrive back at my apartment to get dressed to go out to dinner."

"You live in D.C.?" I said. "I thought from what you said at first you didn't."

Her lips are thin, one of my little eye sorties told me, but before I could register that thought well and adjust to it, the next little glimpse my eyes allowed me revealed that rather than being thin, her lips were pale—full enough, certainly, but pale to the degree that no obviously visible boundary existed marking where the skin of her lips began and the facial skin ended.

She always has hated that, all her life, and that's why in every close-up in every scene in any movie she was in, her lips look either glossy black if the picture's not in color, or deep crimson if it is. She always kept the make-up people slathering away before every take, no matter how many the director called for.

If you remember her at all, you know that the Cuban Chili Pepper had a mouth, and it was a trademark one of the species, and anyone who saw it could have no doubt about the fullness of the lips which formed its body and gave it life. There was a line, my friend, which marked it off from the rest of the face, and it stood out. Got that? her mouth said. Understand? See me? I am here. Do not mistake it.

"No," she said, shaking her head back and forth with enough vigor to put a mild thrash into the density of that hair whose color I had yet to be able to categorize. "I'm imagining this, goofy. See, I've got to get back in time to get ready to go out to a cocktail party in Georgetown, and then to a restaurant, a French one, and then to another party that starts at midnight. Understand?"

"Yes, sure," I said. "I guess so."

"And the problem is I've come down here to Marshall Hall

because somebody told me to, recommended that it might be quaintly amusing for an idle hour, and I've never been here before, so I didn't know any better. And now here I am, on this dock, and I've missed the fucking boat back to D.C."

To that point in my young life, I had never heard a woman say the word *fuck* or any variant of it, so I stood there on that Marshall Hall dock completely astounded. That's not the right word for it, exactly, *astounded*, because that implies more consciousness on my part than I actually possessed at the moment.

What it was really like, the way I felt watching her getting into the part she just conjured up and hearing that word come from that mouth, was not awareness, astounded or otherwise, but a sensation that somebody or something had slipped up behind me and hit me on the back of the head and neck with a large flat object, hard enough to deaden for the moment and to warn that the pain when it came had better be prepared for. This is going to hurt, it said. For a long time. Get ready. "When is the next boat?" she was asking while I stood there watching the word *fuck* float in the air between us. "When does it leave?"

"Ten-thirty," I said after a time. "Are you going back on the boat to D.C.? I thought you said you weren't."

"No, goofy," she said. "I told you. Not me. I'm asking for her." She jerked her head to the right and back a little as though pointing out some other person standing a little distance away from us. I actually looked over her shoulder to see who she meant, despite trying my best not to.

"The girl who lives in D.C. in the apartment on Capitol Hill," she said. "With the sheers in the windows. The one with the date with the congressman. You know, that good-looking young girl from out in the Midwest somewhere. Tennessee or Texas or one of those places."

"That's not the Midwest," I said, saying that because it seemed to offer the opportunity to speak about something I knew to be real. I wanted to seize on a verifiable fact. "That's the south."

"All I know," said the girl before me, lifting both hands toward her face as though she was about to touch some fragile and precious object someone had just presented her for the purposes of admiration, "is that I have missed the boat, and I've probably missed my chance at true happiness, too."

After reaching her destination with her hands and saying that, she lowered her face toward the cup of her fingers and sobbed twice, quick intakes of breath which, though muted, seemed to me totally real.

The numbness down the back of my head and neck caused by my first experience with that word coming from a person who was female and looked the way she did was wearing off, and I braced myself to begin feeling the pain it had promised. It didn't come, of course, actually, but the sense of dislocation stayed right there with me where I had first felt it on that amusement park dock shoved out over the edge of the Potomac.

After those two small expressions of despair, the girl before me straightened her head again to look at me, no sign of grief evident on her face and her hair as lively and dense as ever.

"Well," she said, "I feel sorry for her, but she ought to be more careful who she listens to."

"The girl with the apartment in D.C.?"

"Yeah. People will tell you anything when they want something from you. I learned that years ago." I was in no position then to doubt anything she said, so I nodded a lot to show I was in agreement with what she'd just told me, though the fact was at that point in my life nobody had yet to want anything from me enough to lie to me to get it. I had a lot to look forward to.

I remember I looked away from her face to gaze out at the Potomac, thinking if I didn't, she would rapidly come to believe I was even dumber than she already seemed to categorize me those two times she'd earlier called me "goofy."

A boat was passing, a small cabin cruiser outlined black against the setting sun, and I watched that while I tried to think of something else to say. Somebody at the rear of the cruiser threw something out into the air, and a gull swooped down and made a successful grab at it before it hit the water. After seeing that transaction completed, I turned back toward the girl who'd been facing me, but she had begun walking back up the dock toward the shore, and she had almost reached the big arch built over the end of the dock to indicate to folks that they were entering Marshall Hall. I forget what it said now, the tag line under the name of the park, something like "Step into Pleasure" or "Enter into Pleasure." Pleasure was in it somewhere, I do know that, but I don't know the precise claim that was made about the concept all those years ago. I did watch her walk through that arch, though, and continue her progress.

And I do remember, as well, even at that time being suspicious about what was being promised by that sign to lie just beyond that brick and wooden construction which marked the end of the journey down the Potomac, up the dock and into Marshall Hall. I wanted to believe it then, don't misunderstand me, and I did my best to for as long as I could. Enter and receive. Ask and it shall be given. Seek and you shall find.

I have endeavored to live my life expecting great and enduring changes whenever I cross a boundary, announced or unannounced, wherever and whatever it is. I have always lived with the hope that I'm just one step away from wherever it is I need to go.

They are coming back down the hall now, Lawrence pushing the wheelchair and Rolando strolling along on one side or the other of it putting a little extra flourish in his step to show the residents peeping out of their doorways that he has assisted once again in breaking one of them down—he has removed all of somebody's clothes, no matter who they were, first or second lead, male or female, camera crew or grip, best boy or makeup girl, costumer or director, horse wrangler or caterer's assistant—and he has dipped them in warm, soapy water up to the level of their mouth and beyond, and then he has scrubbed the living bejesus out of them with a long-handled brush that stings like fire, no matter how much Mr. P. U. Caughran, Ph.D. and Executive Superintendent of the South Florida Retirement Facility for Motion Picture Personnel, says it doesn't.

She is in the wheelchair, of course, being pushed and accompanied by her attendants, but the Cuban Chili Pepper is now huddled in a terry cloth robe, wet, weeping, and small. She has cursed until she has cursed herself out and has nothing more to say, and I can see through her damp hair all the way down her scalp, pink as a cooked shrimp. She doesn't look into my room as she rolls by in her chair.

"You look like a million bucks, Sweetness," I call out into the hall as soon as I see her. "Back from Water World, looking like a dream."

She automatically starts to lift one hand toward that damp head of hair, but she can't, of course, because of the Velcro strap binding her wrist, and she lets go the struggle and doesn't bother to look in the direction the words are coming from.

"You the next," says Lawrence in that deep lazy voice, slipping me a glance by lowering his head a fraction and tilting it sideways. He could have played a great heavy, a real menace in one of the late-forties B movies, maybe a Mitchum vehicle, but of course they didn't use blacks back then. Now his type is a dime a dozen.

"I can't wait," I say through the empty door. "I'm as dirty as your socks, Lawrence. Come hose me down. Do your worst, Big Boy."

Nobody can hear me, the people in the hall have moved on by, and my roommate's last response to the world of sound took place years ago. That doesn't stop me from delivering my line, though, with the words coming from way down deep at the level of the diaphragm. What I say booms in all that empty air.

Here's what we're eating today, this is what's for lunch at the SoFloRetFac on a Tuesday, round about eleven thirty. I am limiting my description of the grub and the enumeration of the vittles to the Spencer Tracy Wing, of course, and I'm not including what's being served to those of us entertainment folks with special feeding needs.

I don't know what that gray stuff is they pump through feeding tubes inserted into the throats of the ones that are trying to die by not eating. Or in some cases, where the throat approach won't work for one reason or the other, directly into little plastic valves cut straight through into the stomach cavity.

No, what I'm talking about is the bill of fare for all of us still able to sit up, open our mouths and make chewing motions before we gulp down whatever it is we're having to deal with.

I had listened to the Cuban Chili Pepper cry for a few minutes after Lawrence and Rolando had unstrapped her from the wheelchair, slipped her into something more comfortable, as women used to say in motion pictures, and tumbled her back into bed. She didn't cry long, though, Elsie didn't, and evidently drifted off to sleep because I never heard her radio come on all the rest of the time between then and right up to now.

But it was the food I was telling about, lunch today in particular, a Tuesday, wash day for the Cuban Chili Pepper, and the cart is rolling from door to door of those able to feed still, and it is an important time of the day just as it is everyday. I can hold my breath and listen, and through the white noise that has been buzzing in my ears ever since Duke Wayne clipped me up beside the head repeatedly during the sixteen takes of a saloon brawl in *Red River* come the sounds from up and down the wing of the boys and girls rousing up to sniff at the trough one more time.

It is baked beans today, and coleslaw chopped so fine it couldn't choke a canary, a slice of white bread, and at the center of the plate which Myrtice puts on the handy-dandy tray before me, a wiener boiled and sliced bite-size. It is plumped and red from the boiling water where it has been at swim, and it says to me now as its ancestors have all my days, eat me. "Here's your wienie," says Myrtice. "I know you always like your wienies, Mr. Foxmoor."

"Myrtice, you are right," I say. "I have always appreciated a waitperson who remembers my preferences. But please call me Barry, won't you?"

"Shoot," she says. "All right. Enjoy, Mr. Foxmoor."

It is a game we play, as much for her benefit as for mine, and Myrtice deserves a little special attention and a perky hello from all who can muster one. Most of us troupers can't these days, and those who're still able generally conserve their energy to complain and threaten and beg.

"I'll have your job for such impertinence," an ancient director will say when Myrtice has moved the bedpan wrongly or committed some other breach against protocol on the set.

"The light strikes through the window in a peculiar way and puts me at a disadvantage," a former female lead will opine. "Adjust it now, or I walk."

"Look, please call my agent," another old fool will whine. "I can't get to a phone, and he's Morris Morris at Whitehills seven two-thousand."

As if, as the young actors on daytime television today continually honk at each other. As if.

But not me, not Barry Foxmoor, that's not the way I come on to the currently most important woman in my life, Myrtice Jefferson, when she comes into my room and brightens my day. When I say important, I'm speaking of practicalities, you realize, and not emotional history. I keep hoping that maybe someday Myrtice will slip a hand beneath the coverlet for me, you see.

We don't go a long way back, Myrtice Jefferson and I, to a past of close relation and lost passion or anything like that. Don't get me wrong. I've only known Myrtice for a little over two years, back to the time she came to work here at Slow Motion Acres, which is what I call the facility in which all us retired motion picture personnel now dwell. That's not original with me, that designation, but most everybody now here thinks it is, those of them who can still think, and most of them still smile or make an attempt at it whenever several of us are gathered in a clump for one reason or another and I use the phrase.

No, it didn't come from my fertile imagination originally. It popped out of the mouth of Eddie Jarman, who spent most of his career being a stand-in and stunt double for Cary Grant in long shots and chancy situations on the sets of yore. Eddie had Grant's carriage but not his chin.

Eddie and I were sitting outside one day, frying in the late afternoon sun on the west side of the Spencer Tracy Wing of our E-shaped facility and watching the parade of stars, supporting staff, grips and best boys, and the odd camera man or two and all the rest of the assortment shuffle by on their way back into the building. It must have been close to suppertime or maybe the beginning of a rerun of *Gilligan's Island* on the television set in the lounge, I don't know. All I remember is that they were on the move, they had a destination, a great long procession of them, and Eddie and I were the audience.

Here they came. Some on walkers, those metal contraptions you clump ahead of yourself and walk up to and then clump ahead of yourself and walk up to, some rolling themselves in chairs by reaching out with one foot, or in some cases, both, to scrabble at the sidewalk and draw it to them, some using their hands to push at the top parts of the wheels for purposes of rotation, several walking on their own as they tottered along amid the walker-assisted and the wheelers. There was all manner of locomotion on display for me and Eddie Jarman to observe as we lounged in our Adirondack chairs.

"You know what this reminds me of, Lester?" Eddie said, making a gesture with one hand to indicate his subject matter, the parade of ruined talent before us. I didn't bother to answer since I knew he would tell me whatever he had on his mind, unprompted.

"It's a premiere, see, and they're all turned out for the big night, the whole damn kit and caboodle of them that worked on the picture. And if your eyes are as bad as mine are, and if you squint them just a little bit, enough so you don't see what kind of get-ups they're actually wearing, you understand, if you do that, it almost looks like it's real, like it's something happening in the actual world."

"The actual world?" I said, unable to keep myself from responding aloud to Eddie, which was always a danger.

"Yeah, the world before this one," he said. "Back there where we all lived before we got swept into the waste bin. You remember, Lester. When things were real. Before the shitcanning."

"How do you make that distinction, Eddie?" I asked him. "Right now seems real enough to me to satisfy. Just as real as the wooden slats of this chair cutting into my aged ass."

Throwing in that last little reference to my ass would please Eddie Jarman, I knew. He is a man hungry for entertainment, and it doesn't take much to gratify him. The odd obscenity now and then is a delight and a comfort to the old double, accustomed as he was in his working life to long waits while nothing was going on. Any little variation, even linguistic, was to be appreciated, then and now.

"I'll tell you the difference," Eddie said. "If you want to know. Back then was real because a lot of it was being filmed, and you can still watch it if conditions are right. I can show you my picture in *Bringing Up Baby*. You know the scene when I fell over that little dirt cliff. You know the one. The big one."

"Yeah," I said. "Yeah, right," hoping he wouldn't sketch out the whole sequence for me again. I was lucky. He didn't.

"See," Eddie went on. "I was real, see, we all were, because we were filming or being filmed or helping the filming get done. Got me?"

"Yep."

"Now, today, right now, nothing's being filmed, and you can't tell today if you were even around this morning, much less yesterday, because you can't point to nothing to prove it."

"O.K.," I said, seeing the dangerous area he was straying into. "Got you."

"Now is not real," Eddie said as he flopped to a better position in his Adirondack chair. "Then was. Now's not. That's the difference. And that difference is a son of a bitch." And then he said it. Twice. "Slow motion acres, slow motion acres."

The wiener Myrtice has presented me is real, though, and I know that by another way of testing evidence, one different from the visual that Eddie Jarman swears by. And it's this, because over the years I've perfected it.

If I can get a thing into my mouth, like this wiener dyed red here before me, say, and it bites back, it's real. By bites back, I mean resists, of course, because the difference between really biting into something in the world and doing it in a dream or a fantasy or somewhere imagined is all in the resistance.

Here's what I've learned. Anything worth really having bites back at you, it resists, it puts up a struggle. It says not so fast there, friend, I'm sorry if I'm in your way, but this space is taken.

What comes in at the eye, the sense on which most people like Eddie Jarman depend and live by, will fool you. It's just light and shadow, after all, and all that shadow is, is the absence of light. So it's a nothing, a deceiver of children and the mentally weak. It's film, it's motion pictures, it's sitting in a dark room with a bunch of other solitary fools watching the wall flicker.

It's what I grew up on and what I made a living doing, and it's what put me here in the Spencer Tracy Wing where I'm living out the remainder, waiting for the big projector to click off and the real light to come back on, the one that burns your eyes to see.

So what's real is this wiener, dyed falsely to appear more zestful though it may be, and I know that not by the look of the meat but by the way it fights back when the caps on the good side of my mouth bite into it.

Yes, and yummy. I win. I cut through, I masticate, I swallow, I digest. I'm here now, my bite says, converting something other than me to my use. I bite harder. I'm winning once more, one more time finding myself on top.

It's so good, my bite of this wiener, that it brings Elsie Flattman's face swimming up into view from somewhere deep in the brainpan, and the face is Elsie's as she was when I first knew her at Marshall Hall Amusement Park on the Potomac in Maryland all those cans of film ago.

The face is hers as she was that day on the dock where Bud Pickle caught fish on an unbaited hook from a stream so slow it seemed not to move at all. And her hair is that color so rich and dense that not even the sun can fix it nor my eyes focus to classify. And that picture is just beginning, the credits still to come. Always.

"Elsie," I call out, loud enough, I hope, for her to hear as she lies now one door down in a whimper on her single bed between silver-colored protective metal bars. "Elsie girl, have you tried the lunch entrée yet? It's done to a T and fit for a queen."

She doesn't answer, of course, and I don't expect her to, here in the post-Water World where we live at the end of the day. Now her gaze is fixed on something moving far off toward her, a thing she can't identify but knows the shape of, and I'm speaking again to make her look away from it.

"Try it, Elsie," I call out. "It's the dog you love to bite. Come on, girl. You can do it one more time."

And now I'm straining to be heard and to have that notice from her I've forever craved to be directed at me. "Let's do it again, girl. Hit your mark, and let's show them. We'll do it in one take this time, you Cuban Chili Pepper. Don't be afraid to look in Bud Pickle's bucket at all that life swimming in the bottom. Stare them down, Elsie. They're only fish, dark ugly fish, and they're drowning like you'll never do, girl, like you'll never do. You catch the light, Elsie, you always catch the light, and it holds on to you."

The screen is fading now as it always does, the silver light is going, and I'm offering her all there is.

I go on telling her all I can.

Charm City

When Benford Ferguson's wife told him she was leaving their marriage, he thought at the time that she had said it was because of his lack of sensitivity. That was distinctly the word he heard. Sensitivity. The two of them were sitting at opposite ends of the sofa in what natives of Baltimore call the club room of their row house on Calvert Street, though it was just a den, watching a documentary on the poetry of Robert Lowell. Benford was giving closer attention to the screen and the voice-over than he ordinarily would have accorded a PBS cultural offering because Robert Lowell, like he and Karen, had been a graduate of Kenyon College.

"How can you say that, Karen?" he asked. "I am, too, sensitive. Sensitive to a fault. Here I am with a lump in my throat right now, thinking about Robert Lowell walking down Middle Path. You know, I'm remembering Kenyon stuff. Gambier. Corn fields. Sunsets. Poets reading their poems out loud to people sitting on the floor. The wine afterwards. Those little chunks of cheese."

"I said *sensibility*," Karen said. "Not *sensitivity*. That's your problem, Benford. Sensibility. You want sensibility, not tear ducts."

"Sensibility," Benford had said back to her, several times, more loudly each repetition since Karen was moving steadily up the stairs toward another floor of the row house as he spoke, further and further out of range of his voice.

He had not been able to finish seeing all of the documentary on Lowell, of course, having to leave to follow his wife upstairs to beg and plead and weep for her to stay with him and their marriage until they both fell asleep on the same bed together for the last time, and months later with property divided and decrees signed and conditions agreed to and the row house on Calvert Street sold and emptied, Benford still felt the lack of not having experienced the last twenty minutes of the PBS show, *Robert Lowell: A Poet's Poet.*

WHAT HAD BEEN the last visual, he wondered. What had the documentary maker used as a final image to capture and sum things up? Probably a superimposition of Lowell's face on the Kenyon College seal, while one of the old college songs sung by an all-male group welled up. That would work, Benford thought for about a minute, and then changed his mind. No, not that. Too conventional, too trite, too expected. Maybe instead a grainy shot of Ascension Hall where Lowell had taken all those classes from John Crowe Ransom, or an old photo of Lowell among his fellows, wearing a badly fitting suit with pants too short for his height, his eyes behind his glasses as staring and ancient as Rome. Benford had felt himself beginning to tear up at the thought and had forced himself to turn his attention back to the set of figures before him on the monitor of his computer at work. I have got to get a date, he said to himself and to the cursor blinking steadily away. I have got to talk to a woman.

THAT NIGHT, A WET and gusty one, he had stopped his car on the way home on Charles Street at the first empty parking space he saw near a bar, a place named "The Bust of Pallas." Inside to the left of a line of stools was a small stage with a lectern, a lamp, and a microphone, and gathered before it were a dozen people, most of them women, and as the door pushed against Benford's back, a gust of wind lifted the hair on the backs of the heads of everyone in the row of metal chairs nearest the door, causing several to look his direction in annoyance.

"Sorry," Benford said, and someone shushed him as attention refocused on a woman stepping toward the lectern, clutching a sheaf of papers to her breast with one hand and carrying several thin volumes of a muted shade in the other. Her hair was a large mass of graying curls, she was wearing a blouse covered with representations of what seemed to be china cups, and her skirt was either black leather or a high-quality imitation which convinced. She tilted her head back, closed her eyes, and then lifted one hand to her forehead.

Poetry, Benford thought, it's a poetry reading. She's going to read her poems out loud to us, just as sure as her bunch of papers is about to slide off that lectern.

The poet (Mistene, she gave as her name) had done that at some length, Benford Ferguson had asked her to re-read one of the shorter ones of her offerings after she finished, which pleased her greatly, and later that evening he ended up seeing her to the door of her apartment, just two blocks from the George Washington monument at Mount Vernon Place. After several cups of coffee and some thin cookies, Benford placed his arm around Mistene's shoulder and inclined his head toward hers, a sizeable swatch of her gray hair, prematurely that shade he concluded, rising up in his face and slowing his progress.

"No," Mistene said gently, and Benford began to withdraw immediately toward his rightful share of the sofa. "This is what I do," she went on, and firmly pulled Benford's right hand off her shoulder and toward her lips.

She then proceeded to place each of his fingers, beginning with the pinky, in her mouth and to suck first gently and then as she warmed to the task, more robustly at them. Benford allowed her to continue, not wanting to offend, but he wondered what he should be doing in the meantime. When at about the time Mistene had finished the middle finger on one hand and was shifting to the index next to it, Benford offered to touch her breast. Like kissing, that was not allowed, either, however, and Benford considered other options. Was it appropriate to begin sucking at the fingers on one of her hands at the same time she was doing his, or was it like oral sex, where it was better to take turns at giving and receiving so one could concentrate and be more effective?

Benford didn't know, couldn't decide, and after Mistene had finished with each of the fingers on both his hands, he left her in the apartment after pleading fatigue and a busy day ahead, all her fingers unsucked and dry, and on the way home he held his own fingers awkwardly away from contact with the steering wheel, as well as he could. He drove a little faster than he should have, given the fact that he was maneuvering the car with only the palms of his hands, but he wanted to get home as quickly as he could so that he could get his fingers properly washed with liquid soap and dried with a real towel in the master bathroom of his own house.

It wasn't that he harbored any repulsion for female secretions as such, he told himself. It was just that his fingers had been in the mouth of a woman whose last name he didn't even know, and he needed time to get used to this aspect of dating in the new millennium, if it happened to be a general practice, and also it could be the case that Mistene was singular in her habits and likings and might even be considered dangerous by people younger than he and more in the know. How many less common ways than anal sex did HIV get around anyway?

Washing up after midnight in the all-white bathroom, Benford Ferguson had a line from a poem by W. B. Yeats pop into his head, something that hadn't happened since he was a senior studying in the last week of college for the comprehensive exams at Kenyon. He had walked around then for several days with all manner of words written by other people roiling through his head, but that had been understandable because senior comps week was a time of trauma. To have the lyrical words of a dead poet surface now, however, was beyond weird, in Benford's estimation, but he supposed he was in a sort of trauma again. He had to be, as cut loose from life with a woman as he now was.

It was only part of a line, really, and it wasn't a nice one, either, but Benford knew where it was coming from. Somebody in the poem by Yeats had "liked the way his finger smelt," the poet had declared, and it took Benford half an hour in the public library the next day to find the full reference. He read over the entire poem several times, and still couldn't understand what Yeats was getting at or why he had written something which surely would have been terribly shocking back when it was first published. Not only was the poem sexually bold, it seemed to Benford, it must have been sacrilegious as well since St. Joseph was the man who had sniffed at his finger and liked it.

Thinking about why the poet might have been impelled to say such a thing and what it might mean coming from somebody who usually wrote such nice-sounding lyrics about loving that woman, Maude Gonne, who never would let him have her, did lead Benford in a new direction, however, that he had not anticipated. He checked a collection of Yeats's poetry out of the Pratt Library, along with one of those thin little yellow-backed books containing the works of some contemporary woman poet—it was called *What Is Round Can Be No Rounder*—and read through both books in about three nights of sitting on his living room sofa.

He found the experience oddly soothing—he was able to go

right to sleep after slowly reading eight or ten poems and somewhere during the third night, he discovered himself dreaming that he was actually writing a poem of his own. He could read the words, see the lines in which they were arranged, and they came into his head in the dream with no effort, unbidden. The poem grew in his mind like a flower.

It wasn't that way when he woke and tried to remember what he had composed while asleep, however. Not a syllable of his production remained, and as Benford sat with a legal pad and a pencil at the breakfast table waiting for something to happen automatically, nothing did. He drew a complete blank, his memory of what he been shown while asleep nothing now but white noise in his ears, and after five or ten minutes, he gave up on the idea of trying to be a passive receiver of communication from the unconscious, a simple recorder of verse data.

He let himself be late to work that morning, in fact, for it came to Benford to try to write a poem on his own as he sat with a cup of coffee and his legal pad at ready. Maybe he'd do one influenced by Yeats, as he remembered reading somewhere that apprentice painters in the Renaissance did as they copied works of the masters while waiting to become major themselves. He would try perhaps a lyric in praise of a lost love, a woman who refused to return his affection but in so doing raised the level of his feeling to something universal, gave his pain meaning and direction, made his anguish art.

"Step softly, Karen," he wrote carefully on the legal pad, "for you tread on my dreams," and then he stopped to study the effect. He could see that it was not good. The name *Karen* was not one which lent itself to mystery and romance, he decided, for one thing, and the image of his departed wife stepping softly anywhere was ludicrous. She weighed well over one hundred and forty muscular pounds and had been on a championship women's swim team at

Kenyon. In fact, when Benford thought back to Karen in those days, he remembered her as being intensely robust, always slightly damp, and smelling faintly of chlorine.

And, as angry as she had grown to be with him over the years together in Baltimore, Karen if asked to tread softly on his dreams would most likely have kicked them into little pieces and ground them under the running shoes she wore while doing her three miles a day.

No, not Yeats, Benford said to himself at the breakfast table, feeling disappointed that he would not be able to write a poem after all about lost and despised love raised to the universal level of myth.

Still he didn't leave the breakfast table and start for work in the Monumental Insurance offices on Charles Street that morning. He felt a little paralyzed for some reason until he would at least have begun a poem after the strange poetic visitation in his dream state during the night. If not Yeats as master, who? What, for example, Benford said to himself, taken by a sudden thought, would the feminist author of the little yellow-backed book from the Pratt Library have done in his situation? If she were a man, that is, who had been abandoned by a large, health-conscious wife who did stretching exercises before and after each of daily long-range runs. What language would Molly Kratz use that had not been available to William Butler Yeats in his day?

Benford Ferguson picked up his mechanical pencil, looked deep into the surface of the top page of his legal pad and wrote the first two lines of the first poem he was to complete since his twentieth year. "Love lies flattened beneath the tread marks / Where the rubber meets the road."

That completed poem, which was a verse explanation of those first two lines, now resided in a manila file folder in a canvas carrying case Benford had purchased especially to hold whatever poems he might decide to write in the new phase beginning in his life. Two weeks after the birth of what Benford called in shorthand his "road kill" poem, the canvas case for poems lay on the table before him in the Bust of Pallas Coffee Shop and Bar, and Benford touched it every now and then with his fingertips as he waited for the Thursday night poetry reading to begin.

He didn't know why exactly he had brought the poem with him to the occasion, which he had learned of through reading the cultural events calendar of the *City Paper*. It had seemed appropriate somehow to bring it along, though, much the same way a father might take a sports-minded child to a baseball game to see the professionals perform. Being in the presence of competence, paying witness to acknowledged accomplishment, watching the real thing being done—all this couldn't make his own poem any better, Benford knew, no more than the sight of a big-league second baseman turning a double-play could cause a ten-year-old to keep his head down on a hard-hit grounder.

But it couldn't hurt, Benford said to himself. It might inspire the novice to witness the real thing. Who knows what causes motor neurons to line up and fire away successfully? What rough beast slouches toward Bethlehem to be born? That line, that bit of mental furniture was from Yeats, not Molly Kratz, certainly. Maybe someday, though, Benford heard a voice whisper deep in his head, some person somewhere will try to remember a line of poetry written by Benford Ferguson. A new Benford Ferguson, one with sensibility.

Up on the stage, the small man who had just been introduced by a much larger one, an announcer with a thin and graying ponytail, approached the microphone, a black loose-leaf notebook held before him in both hands as though he were about to offer it in tribute to the god of sound systems. On his face he wore the look of a shy man entering an establishment where women took off their clothes and danced around to loud music while staring off into the middle distance. He wanted to be there, he wanted to see everything, he wouldn't even mind a table dance by one of the smaller women, but he was hoping desperately that no one in the place decided to ask him just why he was there.

When he began to speak, Benford was surprised by the man's voice, however, and it wasn't simply the amplification provided by the Bust of Pallas's sound system that explained it. Ray Tone, as the announcer had named him, may have been small, but he had a public voice that might have belonged to a Hollywood leading man of the 1950s. Charlton Heston, say, or maybe even Howard Keel in one of those old musicals.

The voice boomed, it sank, it rose, it soared, it rattled the beer bottles on the display shelf behind the bar. It caused Benford Ferguson to lift his hands instinctively to his eyeglasses to make sure they were firmly seated in the face of the blast coming from the poetry-reading platform.

And Ray Tone made Madeline Peacock, co-reader for the night, in her chair a few feet behind the man at the microphone, feel once more the resentment which always welled up in her breast when she had to endure the evidence of the unfairness of physical differences between the genders. Here Ray Tone stood before a group of people, reading aloud the same poem he always began with, the one about his father losing him in a marsh somewhere on the Eastern Shore while hunting ducks or dipping crabs or strangling muskrats—Madeline never remembered the details of the poem from one hearing of its recitation to the next—and the physical power of Ray's male diaphragm and vocal cords and the rest of the speaking apparatus was investing his words with a significance and scope the words themselves on the page did not possess in the least.

The one thing, Madeline said to herself, looking out into the audience from where she sat on the platform waiting her turn at the microphone, this is the one thing, the one disadvantage of doing a co-reading with a male. The physical disparity in voice alone. That and nothing else, she thought as Ray Tone bugled on about father/son separation anxiety. I'll match poetic insight, my ability to read meaning from image, my depth of feeling with any man, no matter how loudly he can bray. If you want to speak of poem *qua* poem, that is, and not shouting contests.

But the audience now, unless it was a very special one, and those are few and far between, increasingly, the audience is deeply impressed by broad resonance and vocal thunder, and the female reader of verse is at a decided disadvantage when it comes to shouting out poetic feet and baying forth the tolling effects of rhyme.

Take, for example, that interesting solitary man at his table alone, hunched over some sort of parcel before him. If he were a text—and indeed isn't each phenomenon and each sentient being precisely that—I would judge him to be an unemployed steelworker from Sparrow's Point, this his first time at a poetry reading. In his agony of pointless television watching and beers at the neighborhood bar and a harping wife starved emotionally and educationally and a clutch of dulled and resentful children, somehow something has dragged him to the Bust of Pallas this night of all nights, Thursday reading night. He knows not where he is, he feels he should leave, but something in the power of the word has spoken to him, and he lingers, for what reason he knows not.

His shoulders betray him, his baffled expression, his shy clutching of that bag filled no doubt with unfinished employment applications—all these speak of a lost creature hearing in the distance a faint sound of hope. When Ray has reached the end of his rant—let it be soon, dear God—perhaps that awakening steelworker will hear something that speaks to him in what I'll read this night.

But in the meantime, having to follow that blare of sound from Ray Tone's lament for the lone duck, there's nothing to be done but to make a weakness a strength, Madeline reminded herself. By indirections, find directions out. When my time at the microphone comes, I'll speak softly, yet clearly, as always. They'll lean forward in their seats and hold their breaths to be certain they don't miss a syllable of each line I read. These words are precious, these vibrations falling so gently on the ear, the audience's inner monitors of stimuli will tell them. Be still and listen, and you will hear.

The gale of words from Ray Tone had now reached a height and was declining, and the listeners could tell from the lessening of energy and tension that the poem was moving toward its close. The sensitive young boy depicted in the narrative structure had reached a new understanding of how he must face the future and measure the impact of his male parent on his prospects. The wild duck had been killed or perhaps had recovered from its wounds, it was difficult for Benford Ferguson, harking to the words from the platform, to determine just exactly what had befallen the central symbol of the poem, but he knew the status of the duck was important somehow to find resolution to the situation of the poem, so he strained to hear and appreciate its final lines.

"A feather floats freely on the breast of the Chesapeake," Ray Tone said in that Moses-like or Mississippi River gambler-like voice, depending on whether it was most similar to Charlton Heston's or Howard Keel's, "and it shall ride there forever in the flow of my dreaming heart."

That image does not make sense, Madeline said to herself as she joined in the applause from the eighteen-person audience, just literally. It doesn't. It never does, every time he reads it. An image must be logical in its carrying out, no matter how fantastic the original conception. Look at that poor downsized steelworker alone at his table, trying to puzzle out what he's just heard from Ray Tone's umpteenth recital of his rite of passage from innocence into experience. After attempting to sort through that vision, he's likely to turn back from his newly awakened interest in poetry and hit the remote button for daytime TV again and leave the tube on for good.

"Something a bit lighter," Ray Tone was announcing into the microphone, "after that insight into the marshy darkness of solitude."

If that's what it takes to be able to read poems to people in public, Benford Ferguson considered as he applauded politely and stared at the little man and his loose-leaf notebook before him, they should sign me up. I can do that kind of stuff easy. My road kill poem I brought with me tonight is better than that.

TWENTY MINUTES LATER, her reading ended, the sharing of a portion of her heart's work once more given others, Madeline stood with her head tilted a bit to the side, her eyes cast downward, the beam of the baby spot catching highlights in her hair. This was when it was best, this was the true reward, she confessed to herself as she listened to the applause of the audience in the Bust of Pallas reach a crescendo and begin to moderate and decline. Stealing a glance toward the bar to her left, she could see that not only was the bartender joining in but a random drinker who had earlier attempted a cheap put-down of the whole event was also clapping and nodding his approval in her direction. He who comes to scoff remains to pray.

Yes, this is the reason to present one's work publicly, to lift a part of one's soul up into the light that it may be seen. Not for the applause itself—Ray Tone's presentation had received nearly as much display of approval as hers had, though not quite, thank Athena, and anyway people were always polite, no matter how they really felt about the poetic acts they had just witnessed—but for the experience of appreciating the immediate effects one's work had on individuals. Seeing someone awakened, seeing them get the point of something she had written, touching them with the fire of her imagination, that was the real payoff, the true money shot. No, not the applause itself but what happened afterward, if anything did, and it almost always did happen, if the audience in the Bust of Pallas was attentive and not too drunk yet.

The reward was this: the procession of people coming up to the poet, one by one to say a word or, in the case of the women usually, to put out a hand to touch the poet's. And the beseeching looks, the long stares, the attitudes of hunger from those famished for insight.

Especially gratifying were the males who attended, though, because they approached always, if they did, not simply to be polite, unless the female element in their nature happened to be strongly present, but because they were in the grip of a strong emotion, some impulse which overwhelmed their constitutional reticence, their inability to demonstrate having been moved, and their paying of respect was all the more meaningful thereby.

Here, for example, Madeline considered as she listened patiently to the final few words of praise by the last of the six women who had come up to the platform after Russell Masden had declared this Thursday night of poetry in the Bust of Pallas officially completed, here at the edge of the circle waits the economically isolated steelworker, the solitary man who had brooded alone at his table during Ray Tone's reading and who had appreciably become more enlivened as Madeline had read her selections to the audience.

In the grip of metaphor, he comes unknowingly to speak with a woman for the first time in his life about the effects upon his sensibility of a verbal construct.

Gratifying. Gratifying beyond measure.

Lifting her gaze above the head of the woman before her, Madeline Peacock looked directly into the eyes of the man and smiled. She signaled non-verbally to the woman speaking to her that their conversation had reached a natural conclusion by gathering her sheaf of poems into a neat bundle and inserting them briskly into her book bag. This she then hung on her left shoulder by its strap.

"Well," the woman said, "I know you must be exhausted after that delightful reading. So emotionally draining it must be. I do so want to hear more someday soon."

"My next appearance, if and when, will be announced in the usual place," Madeline said, brightening her smile in farewell to the woman. "I do hope you'll be able to come."

"Not if, but when," the woman answered cheerily and moved away to join two others waiting for her near the exit to Charles Street.

"Hello," Madeline Peacock said to the downsized steelworker after waiting until the woman was fully turned away. "Is this your first trip to the Bust of Pallas?"

"I've been here before for lunch," Benford Ferguson said, smiling and nodding as he drew near the platform from which poetry had been broadcast just minutes before. "I work just up the street. But it's my first time at a poetry reading here."

Not a laid-off steelworker, Madeline Peacock told herself, after all. A security man, perhaps. A man who had worked in law enforcement for twenty years, the son of an Irish-American cop on the beat, now retired from duty, living on an inadequate pension and working part-time as a rent-a-cop for a security-minded corporation. His shoulders told the story, his shoulders and his chest and the eyes, those eyes which have seen all manner of human depravity through a lifetime of watchfulness. They have grown old, like the rivers. "I see," Madeline said. "You must have popped in for a quick drink at the end of your shift and happened upon us, warbling our wood notes wild."

She smiled to show that she was being consciously over the top in her choice of words and dropped her gaze a couple of inches down from the policeman's eyes. "I hope you enjoyed some of the poems you heard read. I expect you found Ray Tone's first piece, the one about hunting ducks on the Eastern Shore, quite moving. Most men do."

"Actually," the retired policeman said, "that was my least favorite of all the ones I heard tonight."

"Really," Madeline said in a voice that allowed more surprise to show than she liked. The time to be demonstrative of inner states of feeling was in performance, not in casual speech. Besides, there was weakness in admitting surprise, an admission of innocence that confirmed stereotyped views of gender difference. "Why is that, may I ask?"

"That particular poem I found a little sentimental for my taste," the retired policeman said. "It didn't seem to earn the feelings it expressed, if I'm making myself clear. I mean not sufficiently."

"Oh? I believe Ray would question your judgment on that point."

"Don't get me wrong," the deep-chested ex-policeman said. "I don't question the depth or the quality of the emotional impact the episode had on the poet. I'm speaking of the poem itself apart from any biographical content."

"Biographical content? You mean Ray's?"

"His, yes," the man nodded, "and of course the audience's experiences, too. They shouldn't get in the way, either. The poem stands as a construct on its own, don't you think? Or it should."

Where was all this coming from, Madeline Peacock asked herself. Were courses in poetry appreciation part of the curriculum at the Baltimore Police Academy? Or had this man before her, standing as solidly as a parked police cruiser, happened somehow upon an anthology of poetry and perused it those long nights of inactivity when it became too cold and wet in Baltimore for even the muggers and drug dealers to venture out of their row houses? And where was he coming from with this weirdly antiseptic view of the communication between poet and audience? How old was the poetry anthology he had been reading anyway?

She could see him in an alley, stopped near a streetlight, rain misting in thin sheets as he held an umbrella, a blue one issued by the police department, over a book of poems, hunched against the elements as he puzzled away at the meaning of some flight of metaphor. Donne, perhaps. Marvell. Or maybe a contemporary. Robert Pinsky. James Seay. Elizabeth Spires, perhaps. Far away, a ship hooted on the storied reaches of the Chesapeake, and a dog howled plaintively at the lowering sky, unseen in the somber bowl of the dull atmosphere crouching over Baltimore. A few blocks away, Edgar Allen Poe lay moldering in his tomb at the heart of this vexed and vexing city, a fool for death and beauty.

"I find your comments fascinating," Madeline said, her voice catching a bit in her throat after her momentary vision of Poe, dead yet alive, like a poem itself, at once simple ink marks on a page and yet a sacred fire forever burning.

She moved toward the edge of the platform, stepping down to stand on the same level as the poetry-struck policeman, noting with a slight but quite perceptible tingle that he was a good half head taller than she. She clutched her sheaf of manuscripts in their leather case to her breasts.

"Why, thank you," the ex-policeman said, extending a hand in acknowledgment of Madeline's descent to floor level in the Bust of Pallas. "I enjoyed your reading, especially the new poem."

"The new one?"

"Well, yes. I guess it's new. The one that's going to be in the magazine. The one with no title."

"Oh, it has a title," Madeline said airily. "By default, of course. The first line, I believe I mentioned." She knew damned well she had mentioned it, it being her policy to remark always on the title of any of her compositions. In titling a work, it is there the poet comments on her own work and comes as close to giving away her own assessment and perspective as she ever does in an explicit sense. Readers must pay attention.

"It's not a new poem, though. Not really," she went on. " By the time they appear in print, poems always have some age on them. Would that they did not."

"Well, that makes sense," the burly ex-policeman said. "When you think about it. Not that any true poem ever really gets old."

"I need a coffee," Madeline heard herself saying. "Would you care to join me?"

"AND YOU SAY it's your first poem?" Madeline was saying two hours later, tipping her head to peer over her reading glasses at Benford on his end of the sofa. They had worked their way almost through an entire carafe of coffee, and had turned off all the lights in the room save for one reading lamp. "You've not attempted to write before?"

"Not since college," Benford said. "I've had no reason or need to until recently."

"Reason not the need," Madeline said. "You say college. Are there college curricula to prepare for your line of work?" She looked back down at the sheet of paper covered with Benford's road kill poem. She had read it twice and was prepared to read it all night as though it were a charm, if need be. "I suppose there must be degree programs in all manner of practical areas. I mean particularly in state universities or community colleges which must be all things to all people."

"I suppose, yes," Benford said, and took another sip at his coffee, a blend from somewhere in Sumatra as Madeline Peacock had explained it. The taste was on the edge of being both bitter and overly sweet, and it was beginning to make his ears ring. "Look at the University of Maryland. Lots of offerings."

"Would you say that this poem, 'Love Lies Crushed Beneath the Treadmarks,' is the result of playfulness or trauma?" Madeline said, tapping the sheet of paper with a tiny silver spoon. "Do you see it as a verbal construct primarily, or is it an outcry of pain?"

"Both, I think," Benford said, cocking his head to one side and staring at a corner of the room occupied by a cabinet filled with what seemed to be miniature bouquets of flowers made of colored glass. "But I guess mainly the pain outcry thing. That would be it. A little yowl."

"So mad Baltimore hurt you into poetry?" Madeline said and began to read Benford's poem again, this time aloud in a low voice with an undertone which thrilled Benford, and also at the same time made him want to giggle like a teenage girl in a television ad for personal products. He had written these words, and now a woman was mouthing them as though they amounted to something, caressing the syllables he had joined together as though they had a particular taste she was attempting to identify as she savored it. They're my words, Benford thought, and I put them into her mouth. And she makes them her own. He made a mental note to write that phrase down before he forgot it. It might come in handy for a future poetic venture.

"Yes, Baltimore," Benford said. "Charm City. It's hurt a lot of people over the years."

"And buried a good share of them," Madeline said, tilting her head back to minimize the bit of slack in her throat of which she had been becoming increasingly conscious for several months now. "You must have seen your portion of that over the years. In your work, I mean, of course. The burying."

"Protection is my business," Benford said, wondering whether or not the poet before him was going to turn her attention back to art and go ahead and read some more of his road kill poem aloud. He found himself wanting to rock back and forth in expectation on Madeline Peacock's nubby sofa as he waited to see if what he wanted to happen happened.

"Insurance, you know," he added, restraining himself from the impulse to reach out and seize the back of Madeline's neck gently but firmly and physically turn her head around and down, forcing her to focus on the sheet of paper she held so carelessly before her. "Trying to make sure that if bad things happen, somebody's there to clean it all up afterwards."

"The way you put it," Madeline said, "I've never conceived of the kind of work you do in those terms. So matter of fact, yet somehow—I don't know how precisely to phrase it—somehow dedicated, humble, selfless."

"It's not glamorous, certainly," Benford said, looking directly at his road kill poem in Madeline's hands. Maybe if she noticed where he was focusing she'd cut out the chatter and put some more of his words in her mouth. Let them form deep in her chest cavity, flow over the vocal apparatus and slide between her lips, moistened.

"But there's some satisfaction at times. People do thank you once in a while, and when they do, that's nice."

I'd thank him, Madeline heard herself say deep in her head somewhere near the physical center of where consciousness resided, this member of the thin blue line. If he had revenged in some fashion an insult against me or my property by a Baltimore perpetrator. I'd throw him an expression of gratitude long enough and strong enough to make Walt Whitman blush.

"So the ending image works for you?" Benford said, choosing a direct approach at herding Madeline's attention back to what he had written in the road kill poem. He was coming to believe it was going to take either that or some kind of direct physical action to get her to focus. "I wasn't sure whether it tailed off too much or not. I want the reader to feel that's it's finished, that it's got there."

"It works well," Madeline said, letting her gaze drop to the paper she was holding before her. Better that than yielding to her real impulse to throw the poem to the floor, freeing her hands to rip the shirt on this sensitive cop open down to his navel. She could imagine his top button breaking loose to fly across the room and skitter beneath a table with a rattling sound, the cheap cloth of the garment tearing at some point of weakness, a tangled mat of chest hair springing into view, a deep groan bursting from someone's throat. God, it would be her own. Had she in fact just groaned aloud? She couldn't remember.

"The ultimate image is synesthetic," she went on, and then paused to ask the retired policeman if he knew what that term meant, but she couldn't get the question phrased properly in her mind because he had seized her near hand and was pulling it toward him, and as she tried to come up with the proper way to begin to phrase the query, he placed the thumb of her captured hand between his lips and began to suck it like a hungry child at nurse.

"Oh, God," Madeline said, involuntarily crushing Benford Ferguson's roadway love poem into a wad in her free hand, "what you must have experienced on these mean streets. What you must have gone through."

"I want to make it into a poem," he said, finishing her thumb and beginning a shift of attention to the index finger.

"Your protection of others?" Madeline heard herself say in a changed voice, but a familiar one, the one she used when reading poems aloud. "The way you clean up the messes people make?"

Before her, an image arose of him in his uniform, a long-sleeved winter issue all in blue decorated with patches for service and bravery, the cold rain of Baltimore whipping his face as he refused to seek shelter, restless as he was to take another perpetrator off the streets of his city.

"Where the bee sips," he was saying now, the words moving past the tip of her glistening middle finger, his breath hot on her dampened cuticle, "there sip I."

"Already with thee," Madeline said, collapsing backwards into her corner of the sofa and finding herself unable to sort out the lines of one Romantic poet from another since all things around her had become swimmingly synesthetic, "I fall upon the thorns of life."

"I bleed," Benford Ferguson said, finishing her thought, as engulfed in sensibility he moved steadily in his progress toward the next digit, at one with the poem of Baltimore he had been born to write.

Texas Wherever You Look

Carolina

I am named for a place where I never lived, a state so far away I cannot think it. It lies behind, beyond the mountains and the forests and the rivers, and the widest one of all those waters is the Mississippi and that one I have seen, though I have not in my knowing had to cross it.

When I came to myself as a child and could hear my name called and know the sound *Carolina* meant me, I was already on the Louisiana side of that big water and did not have to fear going over it. That had been done, the coming through it, and one of my brothers or sisters must have held me in their arms when whatever boat or raft we were all on had floated us over.

And when something happens and you in your mind do not know it is happening, that is the same as if it were not. There is a comfort in that, and I have always felt it, and it has made parts of living easier to bear. What comes from a thing's happening which you do not know can later cause you pain. I learned that, and I know it in my heart. But you have missed some of it by not knowing where the start was, and I have made it my custom to think of that instead, that blank spot in my head. The stillness of it, the quiet, the nothing that's there for you to see and hold to, when you need.

The faces of my people, the Camerons and the Holts, have always been turned to the west, and what is behind us, the little clearings of land in the forests with the marks of the plow and the house places and the wagon ruts and the springs that are muddy, some of them, and the ones that are clear, and the dug wells for water are all things of the east. And our backs are toward them, and we never go back there, though we may remember them for a time, a time, a time.

When land is played out and a river is crossed and people moved away from and left behind, the thing is finished and the sun is low in the sky and my people journey toward it.

The stream before us now is called the Sabine, and where we are standing with the mules hitched to the two wagons full of our goods and the children is still Louisiana. But across the water which is dark and so slow it makes not a sound, not a whisper, not a splash, is another state. It is where we are going. It is waiting, and it does not notice us from its side of the water. We look at it, but it is studying nothing of us. It is Texas.

"This here is the ford all right," Amos says, pointing to the wagon track which leads into the water and goes underneath it as though it were a road people would take to go live in a land under the river. How would they breathe, I ask myself. How would they build their houses. Would they wash away?

"See yonder you can tell."

He is talking because he has come to a thing he is afraid to start grappling with. He is not ready just yet, and until my husband has given himself enough time to talk to himself and to whoever is there with him, he will not begin the thing he knows he has to do, want to or not. He is always that way, and must allow the words he speaks aloud space enough in his own hearing to make him know he will take the path there before and go on. Go on because he has to, toward the one thing before him with all the nothing behind him to turn back to.

Before I allowed him to speak to me of marriage back in Livingston Parish when I lived as a girl in my father's house and was a Cameron, Amos first talked to me in his way. Throwing his words out into the air before me like a scarf so light it floated in the sun open for all its colors to be seen, the weaving of them together light and dark, bright and muted and dim.

And when I let Amos say enough to satisfy himself, I let him speak of our marrying and then we did that before the preacher and our families gathered beneath the brush arbor in that hot day, and we made our own house and the first two children came, Abigail and Maude. And they lived, and the next did not, and I do not say his name or let others, though he was in this world for almost one year and knew his name when I called it then.

When Amos had to speak aloud at length the next time to me and himself about what he must do about a thing before him was when the war came in the east, and the states fought with each other in Virginia and Tennessee and Maryland and Pennsylvania, a place so far away I could not dream it.

"Louisiana," Amos said to me and to himself, and "the South" and "my country" and these were the words and the ones around them he used to make himself be able to leave me and the two girls in Livingston Parish and to go back in the direction from which we had come, the Camerons and the Holts and the Ellises and the Dowdens and all the other families living in that parish, and make himself stay away those years living in that fight.

And when he came back after Clytie and Mose and the Broussard boys and I had made the plantings and the three harvests, walking from Virginia with no shoes, his feet were so ruined he could not stand on them to work in the fields. I lanced them finally with the point of a heated knife, the deep carbuncle and knots and boils, to make my husband whole again.

He did not speak the name of the state where we lived again, nor the words *country* nor *South*, and after the next planting and the harvest, Amos talked only of one place aloud as he made himself ready to be able to do what he believed he must. That was to move us and the girls, but not Clytie or Mose who were gone in their own direction by then forever, belonging to nobody but themselves anymore.

The word now was Texas, another state, and the location in it was to be Bandera County where the land would be cheap and unplowed and rich.

We are standing for the last time in Louisiana, watching the ruts which wagons have made as they vanish beneath the waters of the Sabine River, and Amos is wearing the same coat he had on when he walked back from Virginia two years ago. He has torn off a marking it had, and I can barely tell where it had been on the sleeve.

"Look, Carolina," he is saying, laying the words out in the air again for me to look at and admire, "there on the other side. See where the road comes out of the water in Texas? All we must do is aim ourselves in that direction, and when we are yonder, we will be in a new place."

THE BABY IS MOVING strong now within me, as though it had heard its father's voice and wishes to see across the dark slow water to the other side, too, and I give Amos the nod he is waiting for, and he begins to move toward the head of the lead mule of the first wagon. I put my hand on my belly and feel a knot rise up and shift, but I will not let myself think of the other, the one who is gone and whose name I cannot say.

"I figure," Amos calls back to me, "to lead both wagons over while you and the girls wait. Then I'll carry you over one at the time."

"We'll stand here and wait in Louisiana," I say, "for you to go to Texas and come back for us."

"What did you say, Carolina?" he says, pulling at Dex's head to get him moving forward. The mule does not trust the water and looks away from it. "I couldn't tell what you said."

"Nothing," I say. "Go on to Texas, Amos, and then come fetch us. We'll wait here on this side of the river."

Amos hears what I'm saying, and he knows what the words are I said, but something in him is uneasy. He knows I am saying more than I seem to be, and he never likes for me to talk in two ways at once. It is my way, though, and I like to do it.

"It's just a little old muddy river," he says. "You can't even tell it's moving. One bank of it is the same as the other, whichever side of it you're looking at or standing on."

"No, Amos," I say back to him. "Over yonder is Texas, and Louisiana is where I'm standing with the girls."

"Where will Papa be when he's in the water?" Abigail says, "After he steps off the bank and ain't in Louisiana?"

"He'll be nowhere, Abby," I say to her as she hangs to the skirt of my dress and leans her head back to look up at me. "Your Papa will be between two places, and he won't be anywhere then."

"Don't tell her such things as that," Amos is saying as the mule finally begins to move forward slowly, blowing its breath out through its nose as though something has got up inside its head and won't get out. A fly, maybe, or a wasp or a piece of trash the wind has lifted up into its face. "You'll scare the child, telling her that."

"It's the truth," I say to him. "A little bit of it she needs to hear. Abby must get used to it, to the truth, by drips and drabs."

"Oh," my husband says, "Carolina," and then his feet are wet, and he's knee-deep in the Sabine River, out of Louisiana into a moving stream, and Texas is over there waiting on the bank as solid as a green tree stump just after it's been cut. What would it feel like to the inside of a tree for the air to get to it for the first time, I am wondering, as Abigail watches her father lead the mule drawing the wagon deeper into the black water and Maude whimpers in my arms. Would the tree stump know it was dead yet, or would it like feeling the air move over it for the first time while it sees light and open space which it never could have imagined touching it inside where it's always been dark and safe before?

It would be good, I decide, to the tree stump, as I watch my husband reach to the middle of the river deep enough now that the water is halfway up his chest. It would appreciate the experience, even if it took the time to realize it was coming at such a great expense.

"But it wouldn't be thinking about that part," I say aloud to the top of Abigail's head as she observes her father moving away from us. "No, sugar. It would be enjoying the view too much to let such thoughts as that bother it."

My daughter nods and says yes, mama, still looking toward that wet place between us and Texas, always agreeable as she is, wanting to please whoever takes enough notice of her to say words in her direction. "I know I would," I tell her. "I'd want to feel that air and see that light and know there's something else outside me besides me. Wouldn't you?"

Yes, she says again, and now Amos is at the deepest part of the river and the water is touching his throat and trying to float him off his feet, and Flony, our best mule, is snorting so loud we can hear it back here in Louisiana, and I expect Texas does, too, but it's not making a sign it does or not or that anything is happening. Just some more folks coming to me, coming west, headed for here, that's all that state is thinking, probably, but I'm not going to show any interest or surprise. I'm Texas.

SHE COMES UP out of the dark into the light of the cook fire and stands there so I can see her, swaying back and forth a little from side to side as though she's tired and wants to lie down but can't find a place to do it. She is old, and her hair is all white, hanging down in two thin braids worked with beads and string, and I can tell by that she is not some white man's wife who has gone to settle in Texas but something else altogether different. She is an Indian, and she is carrying a bag that looks like it has come from the inside of some animal. There is no hair on it, so maybe it is just cured hide, I'm thinking, but something about the way it looks in the firelight tells me it did not come from cattle or deer or any creature I know.

Both our wagons came across the Sabine River without losing wheels or breaking loose from the harnesses holding them to the mules, and the water that rose inside them did nothing but wet our goods. Nothing was washed away downstream, and the flour and cornmeal sat high enough in the wagon bed not to be ruined. Amos is proud of that, the way he brought his family and our belongings safe from the river's bank in Louisiana through the flood to Texas, and the fire he built, his first one in Texas, is bigger than it has to be because he wants to show how bright and warm all prospects are for us in the new country.

The mules are eating leaves off the lower limbs of the hardwoods at the edge of the circle of light, making blowing and chewing sounds, and the girls are asleep in the little wagon after the supper of corn dodgers and smoked pork I cooked for my family. My husband is looking into the heart of the fire as though he can see something, maybe a map of the way we must travel south and west to Bandera County where the land will be new and unbroken, and he is making the little groaning noise he utters when he is content and rested in himself and where he is.

He does not hear these sounds he makes and will not believe me when I tell him he does, so I no longer note them to him. I learned soon after we were married, even before he left for the war in the east and the part he thought he had in it, not to make him know that I saw how he felt about what happened around him. Amos does not want to know he has a state of mind that changes and that allows others to see when it does. He wants always to think he is the same, no matter what he is facing, or thinking of facing, or getting over having faced. I allow him that. It comforts him, and it is a small thing.

Because he is looking into the flames, lost already in tomorrow, and making his small grunting sounds, not that different from the noises the mule are making as they graze, he does not notice the Indian woman standing at the edge of our circle of firelight, her animal-hide bag held before her.

"Do you reckon she just now walked out of the woods," I say to him, "or has she been watching us all the time we were crossing the water and setting up for the night?"

"What, Carolina?" he says without looking away from the story the fire must be telling him, "who?"

"The old woman yonder," I say and look back at her. She has not come any closer, but she lifts her head now in my direction as she sees me turn toward her. "I think she's by herself. I don't see no other Indians with her."

"Indians," Amos says, beginning now to look up at me and then, when he sees where my head is turned, in the direction I am looking. "There ain't no Indians left in this part of Texas. They all been drove out of this country."

"One at least," I say, "is still here." This causes Amos to hop up from his squatting place and spin around to look toward the darkness at the edge of the firelight. He has stopped making his little groaning sound now, I notice, but the mules have not quit pulling and chewing at the leaves they can reach. It has been a long haul so far and farther to go and they are hungry. They eat when they're not hungry, though, I know. They're like we get when we're around something to put in our mouths, ready always to do it.

"What?" Amos is saying. "What do you want?" He says this toward the old woman with white braids and the animal-hide bag, and then to me he directs the next words, the scared ones. "The rifle's in the little wagon with Abby and Maude. I didn't think to get it out. I ought to know better than that."

"You don't need to," I say and nod my head toward the old woman. "She's not fixing to hurt us. She just wants to sit down, I reckon."

"Mother," I say in a louder voice to her, "are you cold? Do you want to get closer to our fire?"

I do not expect she will understand what I am saying, but she seems to, all right, because when she hears me say that she begins to come toward where we are standing by the fire, Amos and me. She takes small steps and keeps holding the animal-hide bag before her as though she is about to offer it to somebody who has been waiting to receive it. Her face is plainer to see now as it picks up the light from the fire, but she has no expression on it, neither that which a body might have when she is meeting people for the first time nor the one to show she is uncertain about how she will be greeted by those she is coming toward.

As she comes our direction, taking those small steps like somebody weary after a long journey but knowing she is nowhere near the end of it, Amos moves to the side and cranes his neck to try to see behind the old woman, way back into the darkness from where she has come. His beard is shining in the firelight, and his eyes are popped wide open to let all come in that might be out there where he can't see. There is nothing. I know that, but Amos is afraid there might be and is now trying to catch up with seeing what's around him, as though that could be done to satisfaction.

Once a thing is over and behind, you can't reach back into that time before now and pull it up before you again. I have learned that and written it on my heart, because I have had to live in this world each and every day it comes to me, sliding away steady as it does. Amos looks before and behind, as though *now* was a stile built up to a fence between two fields, a place to stand where you can get the advantage to look in both directions. At the field behind you, and the one you're coming to. Where you're going and where you've been. The advantage to stop the world and hold it still.

There is no such stile. There is no stopping point of advantage between the two parts of your life, the before and that which is coming. All that is is *now*, a little word and a narrow place where you must stand and one which crumbles off beneath your feet on both sides, of what was and what will be. You cannot reach either place from here.

"I don't see nobody," Amos is saying to me in a voice higher and quicker than his usual one. This shows me where his mind is now. "They could be hiding back in them woods, though. In the dark out yonder somewhere. I got to get the rifle."

"Leave it where it is," I say. "Say howdy to the lady coming to visit with us. She's all the Indians there is out there."

"You don't know that, Carolina," he says. "You can't tell that."

"I can," I say and put my hand on his arm. It is tight and jerking a little as he moves forward and then back, not knowing what to do next. "It's all right," I tell my husband, there on the bank of the river where we are, in Texas for the first time. "It's all right, Amos."

The old woman is close to us now and stops taking her small steps, but she is looking deep into the fire, not at our faces. I wonder what things she is seeing in it, how different they are from the map of our journey I imagine Amos had been dreaming before I made him look away from it. Her animal-hide bag is before her, and she shifts it a little to one side and says something out loud, a word I do not know, of course, because it is in her language, not ours. She says it again, and then she speaks a word I do know.

"Hot," she says and looks toward us for the first time since she has been standing inside the circle of our firelight. "Hot."

"She knows how to talk," Amos tells me. "That old woman has been around people."

"Yes," I say to her and draw my arms in across my chest and above my belly where I am so big with the child inside me. "But it's cold, the wind," I say. "It's cold tonight."

The old woman nods, her white braids swinging so they brush against the bag she is holding. I can see that what I thought were strings are really strips of rawhide woven into her hair along with colored beads and small pieces of carved wood.

"Baby," she says and points toward my belly upon which I am resting my arms.

"Yes," I say. "It's coming two months from now."

"No," she says and then she speaks another word in her own way of talking. Reaching out her hand toward me, she touches just the tips of her fingers to the cloth of my dress and then slow, slow draws the hand back to help support the animal-hide bag.

"Now," she says and looks back into the fire. "This night."

The first pain comes.

Amos

I like to think I don't scare easy.

When a thing threatens to happen that will throw me or mine in the way of destruction, I do not turn tail or show the white feather at calamity's first notice. I try to stand up and put my face toward it, let it know it has a man to deal with, that it can't just go on its path and not show no mind of what might be opposing it. It's got to move something first, whatever it is and however strong it might be in its furtherance. Somebody is in its way.

Saying all that, though, I will admit that there have been times when I have run. It has been things before which I have quailed, I have faltered, I have give ground.

Sometimes it's happened in front of other men who could see me beginning to back up, needing to tend to that feeling that has come all down in my liver and lights, like the voice of a small thing whispering a message only I could hear, telling me to lift foot and turn tail and seek a place somewhere other than here.

Those men that could have seen me give way and remarked upon it were generally in a situation too close to my own to notice what was happening to me, though. They didn't have no advantage, such fellows, because they were getting the light-foot and the shake-leg themselves.

I'm talking about being in battle, of course, and I'm thinking back to all them scrapes we were in up there in Virginia and Maryland and Pennsylvania during the years we gave up to rebellion on the part of our country.

We didn't know then we didn't really have a country, though we thought we did. They showed us that and taught us a lesson. And in a way I'm grateful for learning it. Once you understand you don't have something you thought you did, why you are set free to go on and do something else. You don't have to think about things near as hard as you did before you learned that lesson and got it by heart.

You can watch what you considered to be your property walk off the place, never looking back, and it does not bother you near as much as you thought it would. In fact it makes you easier in your mind than you have ever been before. You can leave the home place yourself. Head on out, and every step you take you feel lighter. You can float right on off, like one of them observation balloons they used against us up yonder back then.

Hell, you can pack it all up and go to Texas.

I don't talk about such things to Carolina any more. I don't mean about the times I showed the white feather. That subject I never brought up to her because a woman does not need to hear about the occasions on which the man she is married to broke and ran. Talk of that subject will unsettle a wife. No, what I mean that I do not bring up to her any more is such confidences I used to try to speak of when I told her how easy I found it to move on. To turn my back on where I lived and had been living for a while and to do it without feeling the need to look back once.

I remember the last time in particular when I spoke to Carolina of such a subject, back in Louisiana in Livingston Parish on our place twelve miles from Denham Springs. It was a cold night, up in December, way after sundown and the children all in bed asleep. I remember that Thomas, the littlest one, had been gone for several months already by then and wasn't the littlest one no more, and she wouldn't let me talk about him. She would just hold up one hand when I would say his name or mention something about the ways he had already got about him before he sickened and died. She would hold up that hand, Carolina would, like she was trying to knock down something I had just flung at her face. A little stone, say, or a piece of rotted fruit.

I would never do anything like that, of course, throw something at her, but the way she would raise that one hand toward me puts that kind of thing in my mind.

I had already got in bed that night on her side to warm up the bedclothes for her before she would come to lie down beside me to sleep. She had taken all the pins out of her hair and let it fall down her shoulders and back so she could brush it.

I was watching her hair as the brush moved through it, how the fire reflected from the hearth was picking up spots in it that looked lighter than the rest, though I knew that was a trick of the shadows. Carolina's hair is an auburn color, as people call it, not a speck of gray in it even today and her a woman with three children and another one coming.

"Carolina," I called to her from where I had moved over to my side of the mattress. It is a good one, combed cotton with not a seed in it and covered with a smooth ticking. I have never wanted my wife to have to lie on a bed made of shucking. "What are you thinking about, combing your hair so long over yonder in this cold room? You better come over here and get warm."

"I'm thinking about how I might plant me some more flowers by the door come springtime, Amos," she said after running her brush through her hair a few more strokes. "Dig some up from off the side of the hill at the back of the place and put them there by the front stoop."

"You ought not to spend much time studying that, Carolina," I said. "We might likely not be here by the time September comes. Flowers'd just be wasted work."

She stopped brushing her hair, I remember, and sat there for the longest spell, not moving or saying a word, her back turned toward me and the only sound in the room a noise a chunk of firewood made when it burned through and fell in on itself with the rest of the embers. "Why do you say that?" she said finally and made one more lick at her hair with the brush. I had bought that brush for her off a drummer up from New Orleans. It was a good one. I had paid top dollar for the best one he had in his valise. "What are you meaning when you say that?"

"Well," I said. "I figure if we make one more good crop out of this gumbo clay, we might ought to be thinking of moving on."

"Moving on?" she said and turned slow to look at me, lying there in the bed. I couldn't see her eyes in the dark with her back turned toward the fireplace the way she was sitting, but then a little flare-up happened in the embers and a glint of reddish light come over her face for about as long as it takes to tell about it and say it happened.

"Yes," I said. "Moving on, you know. West to Texas. This here Louisiana is about all used up for us, sugar girl." That's one of the things I like to call Carolina when we're by ourselves just talking.

"Texas," she said. "That's a long ways off, Amos, and it's not anything there we hadn't already got here in Louisiana."

"It's got possibility," I told her. "Texas has. There's land in Bandera County that's never been broke by a plow. It'll grow crops as high as your head. All you got to do is just throw seed at it, they say."

"They say," she said and laid her brush down. Then she said that same thing again. "They say."

"I seen a flyer there at Turner's store in Denham Springs. They begging folks to come settle out there in Bandera County. They'll give a man a quit-claim deed for just a little bit of money on enough land to put this little old Louisiana farm down on it eight or ten times and have space left over to spare."

"No," she said, but it didn't seem like she was saying it to me. She was just saying it. "No."

Again, and then she let her head drop down like she was noticing something on the floor she had never seen before and now had to figure out.

"No, what?" I said. "I tell you I seen it. There on the flyer in Turner's nailed up there. Everything you'd need to know about it to be able to decide to move to Texas. It'd convince anybody."

"Convince anybody," Carolina said. "You mean convince you, Amos. You, that's who you're talking about."

"Why, yeah," I said back to her. "I'm talking about myself as being the one who read the thing. I'm a man open to persuasion."

She didn't talk any more about it that night, nor the rest of the winter or during the planting time in the spring. But after the crop was made and the time come to load up the wagons with the goods I didn't sell and the consumables we'd need for the journey, Carolina pitched on in and helped and got the children and the household fixtures ready to move.

But it wasn't on that night when I first told her about Bandera County in Texas that we got the next baby started for us. Then she just laid down on her side of the bed in the warm spot I had made for her, and she kept her back turned toward me and wouldn't face my direction until we both fell on off to sleep, no matter that I had put my hand on her hip which had always told her what I wanted. She could always tell that.

Up to then.

WE ARE ACROSS the river now in Texas, and naturally the Sabine is nothing up beside the Mississippi. It takes a big raft and men pulling on ropes close up to the bank and praying all the time in the big open water of that stream, the one you cross to get to Louisiana. It is muddy, and you can't see into it, and it has waves on it like you was on an ocean instead of fresh water, and you lose sight of where you've been and where you're going because all you can do is look right at where you are and nowhere else and hope for the best.

But that Mississippi crossing was way back yonder and years before in the time when the Holts were coming to Louisiana, and now I am in Texas with my wife and my children and my goods.

And the Sabine was not wide, and the mule pulled hard and nothing much got wet, and I can look back now in the direction I want to without worrying about some force of water washing me away.

That old Indian woman who walked up on us out of the dark was by herself, just like Carolina said she was as soon as she saw her, and what they say is likely true. The bad Indians, the Comanche, have all been driven out of this part of the country and killed off and are out there somewhere in the Staked Plains, a part of Texas I am not headed for. And it's fewer of them all the time, and that is a blessing to the people who are trying to make a decent living out of plowing and planting the land and harvesting the increase.

If the old woman herself is any sign of what the Indians still left in this part of Texas are like, they are not much and nothing to worry about. All they'll want from a white man is just something to eat and some whiskey, if you'd give it to them. I for one will not give them that. Not because I will not share what I own with the next fellow, though. I like to consider myself an open and a generous man. If somebody is hungry, he is welcome to eat some of what little I have and to take a sup of my whiskey, if I've got some and he has a medical need.

But not the noble red man. Not Lo, the Poor Indian. Him I will not give whiskey to, because it is no telling what he will do when it hits his belly. He is not built the same as a white man is, and the whiskey turns to a fume as soon as it hits the back of his throat and it rises up into his head, the fume I'm speaking of now, and it paralyzes any sense of right and wrong he may have had before he supped it.

I learned this account of how whiskey works on an Indian from a man who come through Denham Springs several years back. He had lived among the tribes in the West, and now he makes a living telling folks what they are like and how it is to be around them in their natural setting. That is what he called it, their natural setting, and I felt like the ten-cent piece I paid to get in the hall to hear his lecture was one of the best I ever spent. Natural setting, a good way to put it. A man that does not want to learn and that keeps his mind closed is little more than a beast of the field. I believe and know that to be true. I like to study a thing out.

So when I see a creature like the old Indian woman with her medicine bag all hugged up to her chest, I understand her in ways Carolina cannot. I do not fault my wife for her lack of understanding of matters like this. I simply state a fact.

Carolina sees an old woman who appears to be tired and hungry and needing to get close to the fire, and it is the softness of her heart that will not allow her to judge the truth as it stands before her. She sees only the particular thing and not the meaning behind it, like I am able to do. Like I try to do and must do.

The old woman with her hair all twisted into knots with little pieces of trash worked into it represents to me her race. A tribe of beings like us in shape only, as the lecturer explained they was back there in Denham Springs, a people who have never produced nothing of value and whose idea of worship is to dance around in circles and mumble prayers to a bunch of rocks or a tree or a cloud or a wild animal.

The Christian thing to do is to convert the ones who are worth saving and to get the ones that's not out of the way of us folks that are trying to make something out of this country. I explain this notion and its truth to Carolina in bits and pieces that are not beyond her comprehension. I try to, anyway, and she does attend to what I am saying most of the time, as she is able to understand.

When the old woman talks the words that she has heard some white man use, Carolina looks into her face as though she is conversing with anybody else. Sleetie Woodson, say, back in Louisiana, or Carolina's own sister before she died, Myrtle Cameron.

I look away from this, back toward the wagons like I am being sure there is nobody else sneaking up out of the woods to try to pilfer something of ours, but what I am really doing is wondering how little a woman pays attention to what her husband tells her about different things. Such as what I explained to Carolina over a good long period of time about the nature of the Indian and his prospects. I think it is that her mind will not rise to general principles. That is not her blame, though, and I do not fault her for it. She is made that way and could not choose it.

The old Indian woman, close up to the fire now, says another word to Carolina and puts out a hand to touch it to the swell of my wife's belly. When she does, Carolina looks up at her in the face, sudden, and an expression comes in her eyes like she is hearing some noise far off that she has to attend to so as to be able to understand. It is faint, this sound, whatever it is, that has spoken to Carolina, but it is one she needs to hear, and I can see her listening to it for all it might be saying.

"What is it, sugar girl?" I say and move to put myself between her and the Indian woman. "Is it something bothering you?"

"Amos," she says, speaking my name slow and careful like she is telling somebody who has just asked her what her husband is called and she wants to be sure the person hears the word right the first time she gives it voice. She does not want to have to say it again.

"My baby," she says and turns partway from my direction to

face toward the old woman warming herself by our fire. "Its time is coming now."

"I'm not sure about that," I say, making my voice a little louder than need be so my wife can tell I know what I'm talking about. I notice that the wind had picked up some and is cutting me a little on the side of my face away from the fire. "It's way too early for that, ain't it? You just ate too much of them corn dodgers, I expect. That's all you're feeling."

But the women, the two of them, my wife Carolina and the old Indian woman with that white hair all twisted up into knots, appear to have quit listening to me and are moving closer together there before the fire I have built up.

"It can't be that time," I tell her. "We left Louisiana in plenty of time to get to Bandera County, Texas, before you have to do any laying in."

They are moving off together now toward the wagon Carolina has pointed to with the hand the old woman is not holding, and my wife is stepping like she has just all of a sudden got many years older. Now she leans against the old woman hard, putting a good bit of her weight on the woman's shoulder, acting like she has gotten not only older but a good amount heavier in her body in the last little time that has passed.

"I thought ahead to that," I call after them, "I planned in enough time to allow for us to get where we're going first before any birthing has to come. I have made sure of that. I am telling you now."

They don't give any sign they have heard me, neither one of them women, and they are now far enough from the light of the fire so that you can't tell which one is the white woman and which the Indian.

"I'll build up the fire," I am saying to them. "I'll build up the fire real big."

Carolina

Here is what the pain tells me. I do not speak of the discomfort or pressure or the little hurts that come once and then go, say when I am holding myself wrong or when a small change is taking place inside me. No, not those. I mean the first real pain that comes, the sharp one that lets a woman know it is but the first of many that are to follow, the one that foretells a separation to come.

It says you know me when I come. It says I am here. It says get ready. It says I am final.

At that time any woman knows what it speaks to her, and I would not place myself apart from all the others of my kind, but I know that pain carries another message, too. Maybe it is true all women hear it, this thing the pain speaks in private to the one who contains it, but I do not know that. I can see only what is within me.

And I would not be proud. But no one who has borne a child has ever told me she has heard the thing the pain tells me. Maybe it is a secret each woman has for herself and can see it only on her own alone, but if she were to say it aloud all other women would agree. They forget it later or they believe it vouchsafed to them alone, and they hug it to their bosom in the dark like a jewel given them by a man not their husband in the eyes of God and all others.

It says this. Another came into you, into your body, and that is where you live, but it is not your home. A hope for pleasure caused this thing, whether pleasure was found in the doing of it or not, and that portion is the joy which feeds the growing of another life within you.

That is the side which profits, that part which leads on to something of you still being alive after you are gone, after you are nothing in the earth. But there is a loss to be reckoned, too.

That is what the pain is reminder of, the letting into yourself of another, the entrance of a self into yourself where you dwell alone and secret and satisfied with the person you are. To let another inside the body in which you live for the mere pleasure of a moment, a thing that does not last, is to betray that part of you which lives alone and above all change and shift and dislocation. That is to be Eve, and that is to suffer the pain which announces the separation to come.

If you had not been joined, you would not now be left behind. You would not have ever to bear loneliness. That pain says greeting and farewell together in one.

She is old, but she is strong, the Indian woman, and as I lean against her she gives no sign she feels the burden of my weight. I think she is like a walking cane, a crutch such as the one Drewie Watkins used to get around on back in Livingston Parish. As we walk toward the wagons, I imagine her gray hair to be the cushion Drewie had placed on her crutch to soften where it came up underneath her arm, and I lean my head against the top of the woman's head for support. The Indian woman does not pull away or seem even to notice my doing it.

The pain comes again, harder this time, and I let out a groan before I can stop myself, and the old woman says something to me as we hobble along together. I wonder how a walking cane can talk, and I know that is foolishness, but I let myself think it again because doing that seems to help me walk. What if every tool or support we use could talk to us, I ask myself. Would a crutch or a cook pot or a broom say I have reached my limit now and you must ease up before I break?

I laugh at my thinking that, and the old woman laughs, too, and I tell myself that the things which help us, which hold us up and let us work, those implements can be happy, too. They can take pleasure in getting a job done, just as a woman can do, and if that is true that they can be satisfied, they can also sorrow over something not accomplished or a thing lost and broken.

Thinking this makes me cry a little, only a sob or two, and the old woman says something, whether in her own language or mine I cannot tell, and we are at the wagon now, and she is turning me around so that my back is against the tail of the wagon, and she lifts me up so that I am sitting on the edge of the wagon bed. She does this with no strain and gives no sign of what it costs her but for one deep breath.

"Mother," I say, "you will hurt yourself. Call Amos to help."

"No," she says in English, "he must do what a man does when he tends a fire. I do my own work."

I am lying on my back now with my feet planted on the wagon bed, and the pain has come to me like a house moving down a road on its own. It is too big to fit between the trunks of two oak trees on each side of the road just ahead of it, but the house does not falter in its progress, and I open my mouth to scream, thinking that will cause whatever is moving the house to notice and stop before it is too late. The old woman is beside me in the narrow wagon bed putting something in my mouth under my tongue. It tastes like dirt, but I suck at it as though it were as sweet as a piece of honeycomb, and the house keeps moving toward the place where the trees are standing so near to each other.

I cannot scream through the sweet dirt in my mouth it is so dry, so I close my eyes to shut out the sight of the house and the oak trees coming together. For a space I can still see them on the inside of my eyelids, dark as it inside the wagon, but then they are fading, and the last thing I know is the sound of the Indian woman saying something close to my ear in her language, which I can now understand though all I have known before in my life is my own tongue. I wonder at that, at how it can be, as I leave my body, and now I am not worried about the moving house and the trees anymore.

Abigail

It's not crying.

Maudie when she came, now she did cry. I heard her hollering as soon as Mama hushed. So loud she was, Maudie, that I opened my eyes when I hadn't wanted to, wanting them to think I was asleep so nobody would take me out of the place where it was all happening. But I couldn't keep them closed when I heard that first holler from Maudie, like the little possum that time Papa had let me keep it, the sound it made when it was mad or hungry and wanted something to eat.

It didn't live long. It got out of the house once, and the dogs got it. One of them did, I don't know which dog, I think it was Belle.

It's not crying, not making a sound, and that makes me want to open my eyes even more than I did the time when Maudie was born. That was in Louisiana, and this is Texas, everything on this side of the river is. That's what Papa says. Texas wherever you look.

I picked up a rock just before dark and showed it to Maudie when we were lying down in the wagon.

"You know what this is?" I said to her, her with her fingers in her mouth so she couldn't have answered me even if she knew how to do it. "You know what it is?" I said. "Texas," I told her, and she didn't say anything. "Texas all over the place," I said. "This rock, them woods, the dirt the wagon's standing on, that water Papa put in the bucket. All Texas. Everything Texas."

"I ain't Texas," Maudie finally said, after she had pulled a couple of fingers out of her mouth. "I ain't."

"Now you are," I told my sister, "and don't you forget it. You used to be Louisiana, and now you're Texas, little girl, like it or not."

"Nuh-uh," she said and started into crying. "I'm not. I'm not Texas."

"Are, too," I said, "and don't go bothering Mama about it, neither. Go on to sleep." We was in the sleeping wagon where the bed stuff is, and Mama and Papa were outside by the fire. "Might as well get used to it. You're just Texas, that's all. Like this rock, like everything. Texas wherever you look."

Maudie didn't say nothing else, just kept on crying, wanting to still be Louisiana, until finally she went on off to sleep, worrying about being part of Texas, I reckon.

It doesn't bother me none. I like it all right. Like Papa says about things that happen to us, I have to live with it.

But it's not crying. I know. I'm listening for it, and it ain't made a peep yet. Maybe it's because it's being born in Texas and hasn't got to worry about getting used to it. It already is part of everywhere you look. I'm holding my breath to listen and hear it when it does. I'm just waiting to hear.

It's not crying.

The Way a Blind Man Tracks Light

They're saying my name in Maude's room, but that doesn't mean I'm the topic of conversation among all the women watching my sister on her deathbed. Abigail is just using me to talk about something else that's on her mind, some kind of angle she's working to get at one or the other of that bunch in there waiting around and putting in the long hours of the job they're undertaking.

Abigail is entertaining herself by referring to me by name, the way a cat will knock a sweetgum ball or a cotton fluff or some other piece of trash around the floor with first one paw, then the other one. Just keeping in practice, working on its style with whatever's before it for a target, not really serious about what it's doing but not wanting to pass up an opportunity to hone its skills for the time ahead when something actually worth killing and eating will show up. And it will, because something always does, and it's just a matter of time until the chance to pounce arrives.

When I feel my way in there into Maude's bedroom, everybody will look up and say howdy to me, even Maude, the one who's doing the dying and has the most serious job of all of these women waiting ahead for her alone. I say even Maude, but I should say particularly Maude. Particularly, because that's the way Maude is,

taking time away from her dying to say howdy, and that's one of
the things that's eat away at me all these years of being around her,
most of all. It won't let me alone, that feeling my sister's treatment
of me has built up inside me over time, and I have never been able
to get it outside and shut away from me for good.

I have tried, though. I give myself credit for that. I have tried
to expel it and get it out of my system the way your body will tell
you to do when you've taken something into your stomach that
it can't abide, can't digest, and is being poisoned by. Even when it
was sweet at first and easy to swallow on down and you felt like it
was doing you good, there came that time, that little uneasiness in
your chest and gut that said now wait a minute, are you sure you
want this, are you positive it's going to benefit you on down the
road, are you counting on this to stay with you?

Why is it, I asked myself at first way back when I was a young
one trying to get out from underneath Papa, the preacher and
teacher and the farmer who ran everything, the man everybody
everywhere respected and looked up to, why is it that I get this
sick feeling inside me when Maude sides with me against him and
Mama and Abigail and everybody else in the country busy taking
notice of me and all the rest of the Holt family?

Shouldn't I be grateful to my sister for standing up for me,
for finding excuses to explain why I wasn't doing the things Papa
wanted me to, for supplying reasons why I wasn't making myself
into the man he wanted me to fit into the shoes of?

But, no, I never could explain it to myself and for sure not to
anybody else why it was I never felt like thanking Maude a single
time when she did something for me in all those times I didn't
satisfy Papa and all those fights I had with him about every little
thing he found wrong with me, every little way I wasn't being the
right and true son for Amos Holt to have.

Maude would look at me when I did something that got me in trouble with the man who always had the right word for every occasion, say one of the times when I came in drunk from some play party or busted some piece of harness or forgot to feed some damn mule or another, she would look at me not like she was mad or disappointed or surprised but like she was sorry for me, like she loved me. That was what was always in her eyes when she'd come to me to try to talk to and comfort me after Papa had punished me however he'd done for whatever particular offense of mine it was this time.

Maude loved me, she forgave me, I was her brother, and that's what I never could stand about the way she has always treated me. I couldn't do anything wrong enough ever to stop her from judging me in that way.

How, though, at the same time could I blame her? That is what I'm talking about when I say it's like taking something into yourself you believe and know is sweet and good and nourishing, and then discovering when it hits the pit of your stomach that it is poison to the system and must not be let to abide within.

That is Maude and her nature and the way it's been to me all these years to have to live with, the ones when I could see to walk around and want things, and the years I've spent where the light can't reach to show me what I still want.

Big Sister Abigail now is another proposition, and always has been, and what she provides and represents I have always been able to handle. I've even come to like her—though I'd never let her know that—in a way I've never been able to like Maude.

I don't like Maude, I never did from my childhood in Amos Holt's house all the way up to now where I'm living in her house. But I love her. And that's what makes me feel sick inside, always on the verge of throwing everything up and having to think all the time, every minute of my life, how to keep going in a way that will let me hold it all down.

I don't tell Maude I love her, and I won't. And I don't tell Abigail I like her, but I do.

I love my sister Maude in the way a man loves the air he takes in to let him live and the way he loves the light when he's allowed to see it. Just benefiting from it, and not having to think about the good it does him. And I like my sister Abigail the way a boxer in the ring likes the man he's fought who has just beat the living hell out of him. That man who's whipped him, made him know he's the lesser in the match, and let him feel down to the bone that he's not won and can never, that man is owed a debt by the man he's beat. He has taught him a lesson he needed to know.

Abigail does that for me. She keeps me whipped down and mad enough to keep going, and she always has, damn her soul.

They're looking up as I feel my way into Maude's bedroom, all of them, each one in her own location that she could point to exactly, like it was a place on the map, if somebody asked her to do that. Why, here, she could say, here is where I am, and yonder and yonder and yonder is where the rest of them are.

Now when they speak to me, and all of them do, even the one dying by slow degrees on her final bed, I can tell where they are, too, more or less, and I know they are all sitting down and in the case of Maude, lying down, and I know they're looking up at me standing in the door with my head higher than any of theirs. How do I know that, how can I figure the angle at which a man or woman's aiming words at me, and me blind, somebody might be curious enough to ask?

It's one of the blessings granted me, Abigail would say and has said many a time in my presence, a compensation God gives a blind man, a special development He allows to take place in the hearing of the one who can no longer see. What happens, understand, she will say, is that my brother's hearing has got so strong he can locate where you're sitting and how you're holding your head while you talk to him. Just watch Lewis's head while he's hearing what you say to him and you can see him turn it to face you, tracking where the sound is coming from, almost like he's trying to see the true location of the one speaking to him. You close your eyes and try to do what he's able to do, and set somebody to watch you while you're trying it. You won't even come close to matching up with him, I guarantee you. Abigail will say that and look around like a banty hen, just daring somebody to contradict her.

And explanations such as that are what I'm talking about when I say enduring a session with my big sister is like getting in the ring with that superior boxer, the one who whales the dickens out of you from far off and from close up, from way across the ring up to right inside in all the clinches.

I will say this about Abigail explaining the way a blind man will track sound. If that's the best method God has figured out to improve the sense of hearing in a man, put out his eyes, that is, and teach him to follow vibrations in the air like a dog sniffing at a smell of rot the wind has blown up, God needs to take building lessons from somebody else better equipped. And if what's going on beneath the surface when a blind man is tracking sound in that fashion is no more than God just dishing out some more punishment for misdeeds and sorry behavior, it is my opinion that God has stepped over the line and needs to be reasoned with. If there was somebody to reason with Him, I mean, and if there was such a thing as reason.

But they are all looking up at me from their particular spots here in Maude's bedroom, and saying hello and asking how I've slept and if I've had breakfast and the other things they are supposed to be uttering in the middle of the morning of a warm day in Coushatta County, Texas, and I know where each and every one of them is sitting. Pretty much.

"Well, Lewis," Abigail is saying, "I see you've shaved this morning."

"I have made that my habit over the years," I say, not swiveling my head in her direction though I could if I wanted to. She needs to be denied the satisfaction of visiting that tried and true topic for conversation first thing this morning. That one's too easy. "I do it most every morning."

"How come you never seem to miss a patch of whiskers?" Abigail says. "Just looking real close at your face, I swear I can't spot a single place you haven't shaved all the beard off of. Now all of y'all know that an older man like Lewis is now, even if he's got good eyesight so strong he doesn't even need to wear glasses, why he will miss a patch or two of whiskers on his face when he shaves. I see that all the time on old fellows."

"I hate seeing that," Abigail's granddaughter says, getting her oar into the conversation, "on a man. It looks real ugly and like the man doesn't care enough how he looks to people to even do a good job of shaving."

Maude and her granddaughter don't add anything to this part of the discourse, as they generally don't when Abigail is just limbering up, but I know where they're located in the room anyway. Maude's bed is where it always has been, and she's not leaving that piece of furniture ever again, it looks like, and Dicia, by a process of elimination, has got to be over in the corner of the room next to the window in that straightback chair sitting up against the wall.

"The reason a man misses a patch of whiskers when he's shaving, Abigail," I say, turning my head not toward her but toward where I know Dicia's got to be, "is not because he doesn't see it, but because he doesn't care. Isn't that right, Dicia?"

"I suppose so, Great-Uncle Lewis," she says, not right off, but giving herself time as though she's according due consideration to what I've just said. "It depends on the man and the circumstance, I expect."

"That's right, girl," I say. "A man who's got good eyesight doesn't have to prove anything to anybody by the way he shaves his face. He's got seeing ability to spare, and he doesn't need to apologize to a soul for anything. All he's doing is shaving his beard in the morning. He's not having to show he can be neat and clean, even with his eyes put out, in every little thing he does. Understand what I'm saying, Dicia? I imagine you do."

"Maybe so," she says. "But sometimes things we do we do just because we do them. We're not trying to prove anything."

"That's exactly right," I say. "The man with good eyesight don't have to prove anything with the way he shaves his face, or the way he does anything else of a domestic nature, neither. He just does it and don't have to care how anybody looks at it or if anybody looks at it. The blind man, now, has to prove things to people every minute of the day in everything he does."

"You shouldn't say 'don't' when the subject of your sentence is singular," Abigail says. "The proper grammar calls for 'doesn't'."

"See what I'm saying, Dicia?" I say. "A blind man has got to watch everything, even how he says his sentences, or folks will think less of him."

"You used bad grammar long before you lost your eyesight," Abigail says, "and you did it not because you didn't know better but because you did know better. You were taught correctly."

At that, Maude speaks up right in the middle of me gathering myself for the next shot at Abigail, and I let that one go for now.

"Lewis," she says, "will you pour me a little water into that glass on the table? I don't want to have to sit up."

I do that, and I don't spill a drop, and I put the pitcher back down where it comes from, nobody saying a word but Abigail drawing a quick breath like people do when they see a danger all of a sudden present itself. That does not rattle me. It steadies my hand.

"Do you want a chair to sit down in?" Maude says, and I hear Norma Mae get up from where she's located, seeing the chance to leave the room while kindly giving up her seat to her old blind great-uncle.

"Here," she says, "take my chair. I've got to go take care of something anyway."

"Why, thank you, Norma Mae," I tell her. "But you got to give me a big old hug first and show me where you've been sitting."

She is not going to like doing that, I know, hugging up tight to a blind man and him just old kinfolks, but she'll step on in there and do it, all right, like a little soldier, and the girl is a full-grown woman just come into her prime. Unlike Dicia who is compact and slim and no matter how close you grab her up to you for a hug, not really there at all because she doesn't want to be, Norma Mae pushes right into you, strong arms and high-set breasts and a smell like perfume from a store in Houston.

Norma Mae is not really there, either, in her mind, but she lets her body be present for admiration and a touch or two, even if the man benefited in this case is just old blind Great-Uncle Lewis. My grandniece Abigail's granddaughter Norma Mae has the heart of a whore, though she'll probably never use it.

I hug her up to me.

One thing touches on another one, always, all the time and I've come to know the truth of that during these years of feeling my way along these walls between me and daylight. That was there for me to learn by sight if I'd wanted and been willing to look, back then before it happened, but I didn't, of course, care anything then about wasting time doing that.

Now I've had time sufficient and plenty to learn it not by sight but by feel, and that is the surest and most solid way to comprehend any lesson. You get it by touch, and you get it by heart, and it is written in letters carved into stone which you trace in the dark with your finger. It comes into you at a point where the flesh barely covers the bone, and it moves into your system the way a dram of whiskey moves out from the belly to all parts of the body, steady and sure and not to be denied its path.

One thing touches another. It is a single wad of string balled up into a knot, and there is no end to take hold of and pluck and no unraveling ever to come.

Papa knew that, and he knew that he knew it, because he had learned it on his own. What he came to understand about one thing always touching another confirmed the teachings of the Bible, in the way that Papa saw to be true in his own life. I want to be particular and precise in thinking about this matter, and I don't want to mislead my own understanding. Papa's experience confirmed the truth of the matter as explained in the Bible, not the other way around. The prophets and teachers and apostles and Jesus Himself had their statements made true by Amos Holt's experience in his life in Louisiana and Virginia and Maryland where the Civil War was and in Texas where he ended up living and dying.

Papa didn't have to look to the Book to support his own understanding of what means what in this life. If Jesus and the apostles and the rest of them that put those words into the Bible had had the advantage of foresight into the career of Amos Holt, they could have saved themselves some trouble and a lot of effort and wasted motion.

The life he lived and his measuring out of it into portions small

enough to bite off, chew up, and worry down allowed him to judge
which parts of the Bible to take seriously, which parts to question,
and which to just glide right over. He held up the rule to himself,
not himself to the rule. It didn't measure him. He measured it.

So when they brought me back to the home place in Sabine
County after what happened to me in Beaumont, carrying me in
a truck that passed for an ambulance, wobbling all over the roads
and hitting every hole in every one of them, my head feeling like
it was floating somewhere about a foot above the rest of me, like
it was tied to a thin string frayed and close to snapping, I knew
Papa would be waiting in the room where they put me, the Bible
in his hand, ready to read out the scriptures that showed how Amos
Holt was right on the money about how one thing always touches
another. "You are home now, Lewis," was the first thing Papa said
to me where they put me on a bed in a room I couldn't see and
never would, "The prodigal son has returned, and we will kill the
fatted calf. Listen to the word of the Lord."

And that I did, and I did that for over a month right up to the
point when one morning I woke up remembering that Papa had
been dead for over twenty years. Abigail had been doing all the
talking, and I had been listening to her but hearing Papa, and I had
been counting it a blessing every day he read to me the explanation
and support for the truths he ladled out to me like soup from a
pot never emptied. I couldn't escape the sound of his voice and the
way the mind will listen to words spoken to it even though you're
telling it not to, but I couldn't see his face, at least. I didn't have
to reach judgment about the difference between what Amos Holt
said aloud and what his countenance told of the feelings behind
whatever he said.

You can't see the dark, only the light. So if and when you say a
thing like, "I can see it's really dark tonight," you're speaking non-

sense. What's really the truth is that there's less light than usual, not more dark. It's always dark as the pit everywhere all the time, and when you're able to see something it's not an absence of darkness coming into your eyes. It's a relief from it.

The night was dark in Beaumont when it happened, and I remember saying that to Clay Whitehead when we were walking along Crockett Street looking for the Maryland Hotel that evening. I wouldn't say it like that now, after learning what I have all these years of touching the wall and reading what it has to say through my fingertips. Maybe instead I'd say, "Clay, there's not much light available to us this evening. Be careful, lest all of it leak away."

And then I'd say to old Clay Whitehead, "One thing touches on another, Clay. Keep that in mind, always." But, if I'd had sense enough to know that and to have said anything like it, there'd have been no occasion to. One thing touches on another, like I've testified, and that includes every second and minute of time, but time is a snarl of string with no end showing to grab hold of. Pull at one place or another of that rat's nest of string, and there's no telling what will rise up coming toward you.

By then, Darlene was gone, stolen away from me by my own damned nephew Richard, and she had been the only one for me where things were working out between us for more than a month or six weeks in a row.

I'm not talking about some permanent arrangement when I say that, naturally, not that there is such an animal as a permanent arrangement between a man and a woman not kin to each other by blood. That is a whole separate subject and one you can't get away from while you still have body and what moves it around yet hanging together.

But, Lord, I did love to touch her and look at her hair with the sun on it and the shape her face had when seen from the side.

I say Darlene Simmons was stolen from me by Richard Black-stock, Maude's only child by that first husband, but I'm using the wrong word, I admit, when I say stolen. That would be an accurate description of what happened that night when she stepped into the light from that lantern Richard was holding up on the porch of Maude's house and the two of them got that first full look at each other, accurate only if the word stolen would apply to what takes place when a prize possession just walks right through the wall of your house or the fence around it built to keep things in and climbs on the truck itself to be carried off.

One thing touches on another, that's what I'm pronouncing as a truth learned by moving my fingers over the carvings on the wall between me and the light. So if that lantern held up on that porch in Coushatta County those years ago had not shown two people what it did of each other and what at least one of them thought was wantful and necessary at the time, I'd not have been on Crockett Street in Beaumont, Texas, looking for the Maryland Hotel not two years later. Maybe.

But I was, and I found it, and Clay Whitehead and I walked through that door at the bottom of the stairs and started up to the second floor where everybody and everything in my future was located and waiting to say hello.

I had been to the Maryland before, and that was why I wanted to find it again. It's not hard to find things in Beaumont, Texas, so the search I was undergoing should have been an easy one, but I was naturally drunk the first time I'd been there and was being led by somebody else. So finding the Maryland Hotel the second time was a satisfaction to me, and I was the man leading the way on this occasion, and for some reason that was a cheering notion to me. We went up the stairs at a trot, me and Clay, and I pulled the string that made the bell on the other side of the door ring hard enough to make it jangle like it was about to come unnailed from the wall.

I have made myself remember exactly the way that string looked hanging out there waiting to be tugged at, and I can see, anytime I want to, my hand reaching out to grab it. When a man is blind, he has plenty of time to call up the way light once fell for him on most any object at almost anytime. When you can see, you don't really care what the light shows exactly about most things you happen to let your eyes move over. You just waste all that light touching things in the way a man at the end of a meal, crop full of food, will throw away the last bite of steak on his plate or the crust left after eating a slice of pie. It's more coming, he thinks, if he thinks at all, and I don't need to give these leavings any scrap of my attention.

The string to the bell of the Maryland was about a foot long, what you could see of it hanging before you, it had been broken by some fool anxious to get inside with all those women, and it had been tied back together in a granny knot, it was black with dirt and sweat and grease from people's hands grabbing at it, and it was the last piece of string I ever saw.

Going into a whorehouse always made me feel two ways at once, from the first time I visited right up to the last. The first way was what might be expected—all wound up and nervous and excited and popeyed to see women ready and willing to crawl into bed with you with their clothes off. Any man working in the oilfields and shipyards around Beaumont or Orange or Port Arthur would agree with that understanding of the way you felt when that eye looked at you through the hole cut in the door where you'd just rung the bell and then the eye went away and the unlocking and opening up took place.

But I never heard anybody talk about the other feeling that door opening caused, the one opposite from being all keyed up enough to walk across broken glass in stocking feet and not notice the cost of a single cut nor one drop of blood drawn. And that feeling to me was always a sensation of relief, a relaxation, like that feeling that comes on you akin to water seeping and rising and beginning to lift you off your feet, or the way the second drink of whiskey takes hold and you start feeling it in the tops of your thighs and in the muscles of your neck.

What I felt like each time I walked into a whorehouse, apart from the sense of something good happening low and deep in my belly, was the same way I would feel when I was paying the bill at the end of a cooked meal in a café or restaurant in a town where nobody knew me. I had done a job of work, I had been paid for it, I had the money in my pocket to show it, and I had not had to see the meat and potatoes and beans and bread I had eaten planted and cultivated and raised and slaughtered and picked and cooked and brought to the table. I had had no part in any of the preparation. It came complete.

I had just to point to the words on the menu or on the blackboard behind the counter and say I'll take that. Then they had brought it to me to eat, and I'd paid for it with dollars out of my pocket, and we were settled up. Nothing was left to consider.

The same way obtained in a place where women were selling what I wanted for straight cash on the table. I hadn't seen a one of them before, including the one I ended up following out of the big room down the hall to one of the little rooms with a bed and washstand in it, and I'd never had to talk to them before, or during, or since, if I didn't feel like it. And yet they would treat me the same, no matter how we talked or didn't or wouldn't. They'd take my two dollars, put it up somewhere, pull their clothes off, crawl into bed, and put their legs up.

Knowing that was coming was what gave me that feeling, the

one opposite from being as keyed up as a stallion around a mare in heat. I was relaxed, relieved, ready to do business, and I didn't have to say a word.

So when we popped through that door of the Maryland Hotel on Crockett Street in Beaumont that February night, I was ready to see what I could, and I wasn't thinking much about Darlene Simmons for the first time in a while, and I could feel the sense of water seeping in around me and beginning to lift my feet from where they were planted on solid ground. I was about to float. I was almost tiptoeing, walking across that flowered rug in the big room to sit down on a sofa up against the far wall and wait to see the women come traipsing in with what they had to sell.

"What y'all do for a living?" the colored woman who'd let me and Clay Whitehead in the door said. "Work in a insurance office?"

"Why you think that?" Clay said. I could tell he liked what the woman had said.

"Way y'all dressed," the woman said. "Them nice duds."

"Nah," Clay said. "We just like to dress up a little when we go out for some fun. You not going to find us sitting behind a desk in a office somewhere."

"We like to work in the open air," I said, helping Clay make conversation with the woman as I looked around the room. The first thing that caught my attention was a victrola in one corner with a woman bent over it doing something to its knobs, making it ready to start playing, I guessed, since there wasn't any sound coming out of the machine.

Her dress was short, way above her knees, and split up the back, and as she bent further over to move something on the victrola, I could she wasn't wearing any underclothes. Just as I saw that, the sound of a musical instrument came out of the victrola, a trumpet, maybe, and the woman began to move her hips back and forth in rhythm to it, still bending over as she did that.

"Good God," I said, loud enough to cause Clay to stop in the middle of something he was saying to the colored woman who'd let us through the door to the Maryland Hotel. "I believe we come to the right place. Look up way underneath and deep inside yonder. That thing looks like a skinned rabbit trying to back out of a hollow stump."

I figured that would get Clay's notice, pussy hound as he always was, so I just kept my attention focused on what I saw in front of me and waited to hear what Clay would come back at me with. He would always try to outdo the other fellow, top whatever'd been said with something better of his own. Sometimes Clay could, sometimes he couldn't. He would take a stab at it, though.

But before he could get anything said back to me, somebody else spoke up. "What'd you just say to Velma?"

I had missed seeing him when we came through the door into the Maryland Hotel, paying attention as I was to the colored woman letting us in, and besides that he was sitting across the room from where the whore was messing with the victrola, and I hadn't looked anywhere but in her direction. He was dark complected enough to be colored himself, but the light was bright in the room, the better for customers to see the women by, I guess, and I could tell by his features he was a white man, though probably a Cajun.

"I didn't say nothing to nobody," I said. "I was just remarking on that wad of hair I see moving back and forth over yonder."

"You ain't been here what—two minutes?—and you already low-rated Velma twice like that."

He was sitting back in a straight chair when I first saw him, but now he leaned forward so that the chair legs hit the floor with a bang. I remember thinking it wouldn't have sounded so loud and made Clay Whitehead jump like he did if the rug in the room had been bigger and could have covered more of the wood floor. The man rubbed the back of his hand against his chin as though he was wiping something off his mouth left over from chewing a bite of something greasy and too big to get all of it down in one swallow.

"I don't know her," I said, jerking my head toward the woman he'd called Velma, now standing straight up beside the victrola, her head turned to look over her shoulder. "I was just talking about what all I could see when she was bending over that music machine."

"Her name's Velma," the fellow said, moving his head from side to side like his neck was stiff, "It ain't skinned rabbit, and it ain't a wad of hair." He moved his head slow, like his neck was bothering him bad.

"I was talking about her pussy," I said, "what I could see of it. I wasn't trying to call her name."

"Her pussy," he said, like it was a question he was asking, "her pussy? Where you from, friend?"

"Hardin County," Clay Whitehead said, as though the man talking to me actually wanted to know the location of my home. "That's where Lewis is from. Me, I'm from Orange, Texas."

"Hardin County," the Cajun-looking man said, "That makes sense. It's coming together for me now. What do you peckerwoods use for women up in them woods? Shoats?"

"Dane," the woman by the victrola said. "We're in business here. You know that, and I want you to think about it."

"You heard what this peckerwood called you, Velma. Didn't you hear that? Have you lost your hearing, too, along with the rest of it?"

The woman turned a knob on the victrola and it made the music get louder. Somebody on the record was singing along with the music, and I could tell he was colored, but I couldn't make

out what words he was saying, even though it was the same ones
over and over.

"He didn't mean nothing against this lady here," Clay said.
"Lewis didn't. Did you, Lewis?"

I tried to say no, but words wouldn't come out the first time, so
I cleared my throat and did it again. It worked that second time,
my mouth did. "No," I said. "No, I sure didn't."

"You got to give a man some leeway with what he says," the
colored woman said to the man called Dane, though she was not
looking at him, but at me. "A man come in that door from way
up yonder in one of them counties in East Texas, and he see Velma
bending over, he bound to start saying things he ain't thought
through yet. Ain't that right?"

"Yes, ma'am," I said, even though she wasn't a white woman.
"Yes, ma'am."

"Well," Velma said, and looked at me. "You going to want to
do anything about it this evening? You want to take a little walk
down that hall yonder?"

I looked over at Dane, who had settled back into his chair again,
far enough to let the front legs rest again on the floor, and he was
not looking at anybody now, his eyes closed in fact, and his mouth
drawn up as though he was whistling a tune under his breath. I
remember thinking that he was probably imitating the music of
the song coming from the victrola and probably knew what words
the colored singer was saying, the ones he was repeating over and
over, every one of them.

"I sure would," I said, looking back at Velma. "Just show me
the way."

"I'll show you where that rabbit lives," she said. "Back in here
behind all that underbrush. Come on now, Hardin County."

Clay Whitehead laughed at Velma saying that, giving it a lot more credit for being funny than it deserved, but I knew he thought he had a good reason for doing it. I appreciated what Clay was trying to do by giving the woman's words the acknowledgment he did, but nobody else joined in with him, and that made the room seem quieter than if he hadn't laughed any at all or made any other sound.

I followed right behind Velma into the hall, not close enough to touch her but wanting to get as quick as I could out of the room where the man called Dane was sitting in a straightback chair with his eyes closed, rolling his head back and forth.

Leaving the room, I didn't look at him, nor at anybody else, just kept my eyes fixed on the spot on Velma's back where her hairdo stopped and her skin began, dead white against the dark hank of hair bouncing on it.

I don't remember following her into one of the rooms off the hall, but I do know it was the end of the corridor because it seemed to take a long time to get there. Once we got inside, Velma did what whores always did back then and still do, I guess, told me to take my clothes off, shucked her dress in less time than it takes to tell about it, and then took a long look at my pecker, holding it up and squeezing it to see if anything suspicious came out or if I flinched like it hurt.

Then she washed it with soap and water from the jug on the stand by the bed, and I was surprised by what happened to me when she did that, which was nothing. Always before in a whorehouse when a woman handled me, I'd get hard while she was doing it without even thinking about whether I was going to or not, but this time when Velma had finished, it was showing no more interest in what had been going on than if I'd just taken a short leak through it.

She didn't say anything at first, nor look me in the face, but of course a whore never does that. Even if she has her eyes on you,

you can tell she's looking through you, not at what's in front of her, the man about to climb on.

"Well," I said, "that's never happened to me before," and then I reached for one of her tits, but she put her hand up to keep me away from them, and then she looked at me.

"Not for two dollars," she said. "That's not part of the deal. You don't handle my breasts for that."

"What if I give you another dollar?" I said. "Then can I get my hands on them?"

"No," she said. "I don't care how much extra you might offer me. Nobody plays with me like that, but just the one man."

I figured I knew who she was talking about, but I didn't ask her his name. Instead, I just reached out for her belly and ran my fingers down until I found what I was paying for.

"All right," Velma said, looking at me again but this time not letting her eyes see me, "let's lie down on this bed and see what happens."

By the time we got situated, I could tell it had got over whatever was holding it back, and I was able to start in putting it to work on what I had come there for. Velma didn't say anything while it was going on, like some whores will do and like some men like to hear. All that talk about how it's feeling so good to them, and how fine you are giving them what they need, and they never had it like this before, and please come by tomorrow so they can have something to look forward to that another man can't give them and never has before.

That's all lies, and if a man can get some satisfaction from that, not even to say believe it, that's all to the good, I suppose, but I never liked hearing that from one of them. Just keep your mouth shut and let me get to where I want to go. That was my policy.

We finished up with it, and got up off the bed, and she gave me a rag to clean myself off with, and that's when it came into my head to do what I did, while I was watching her hold out that wet cloth toward me, looking at my face like she was doing, but actually staring right through me toward some spot on the wall behind my head, I figured, some place she thought was better to study than me. A crack in the paint, maybe, or a nail hole, or a blood spot where somebody had killed a roach with a shoe.

I grabbed her by one of her tits, it was her left one, I know, because I was facing her and I'm right-handed, and I squeezed it hard enough to feel my thumb opposed by my fingers through the flesh.

"I told you not to do that," the whore said and knocked at my hand with hers. "Don't touch my breast."

"What about this one, then?" I said, the idea coming into my head to say that like it was automatically given to me, something I didn't even have to think to be able to come up with, and then I reached out for the other one and squeezed it harder than I had that first one.

She hit that hand, too, my left one, but slower than she'd done the right one, and then she stepped back and looked directly into my eyes, seeing me this time, I could tell, as she settled her eyes direct and steady on mine.

"Get out of here," she said, slow and deliberate. "Don't come back here again. Not ever."

"Oh, Velma," I said, trying to make my voice playful as I looked into her eyes, "didn't I just give you the time of your life on that bed over yonder? Didn't you just fall in love with me when I did you so good?"

"Don't call me Velma," she said. "The only name you get to call me is whore. That's the one you paid for. Now you get the hell out of here."

By the time I had put my clothes and shoes back on and had got back down the hall to the room we first came into, Velma was already out there, standing close to where the Cajun-looking man Dane was sitting in his straightback chair, and looking down at him.

He had a beer bottle in his hand and had drunk about half of it, and he was holding it partway up to his mouth, as though something had interrupted his train of thought and he had forgot to finish the action of taking another drink from the bottle. Six or seven other people had come into the room since I had left to go with Velma down the hall, four of them customers, I guessed, and the other ones new women looking to make a sale.

I didn't see Clay Whitehead anywhere, and I started looking around for him, thinking as I did that if he were to suddenly appear before me I would knock hell out of him for not being there ready to leave when I got back. But, I couldn't do that, since he wasn't there, and if he had been there'd be no reason to feel like doing that to him. You want to do what you can't do when there's no reason to do it if you could.

"Where's Clay?" I said to nobody in particular, speaking out loud, almost yelling so I could be heard over all the noise of the victrola, which somebody had turned up high, and the talking going on between the whores and the men trying to get up the nerve to do some serious bargaining with them. "Where's the fellow that came in here with me? Has he done left?"

"You talking about that little fellow wearing them big red-colored boots, he gone back in the room with Dolly," the colored woman who had let us in the Maryland Hotel said. "He might be a while, too. Dolly she twice as big as he is."

"Suppose she going to have to hold him up to it?" said one of the new men in the room, looking from me to the colored woman and back again. "So he'll have a fighting chance to hang that thing in her?"

The rest of them laughed big at that, though not any of the whores did, and I joined in, too, as I began to work my way toward the door to the stairs leading down to the street. "Tell him I'll be outside waiting," I said to the spot where the colored woman had been, though she was not there now, and I turned to look back toward the corner of the room where the whore I had been with was talking with the man in the straightback chair. The chair was there, and Velma was there looking down at the seat of it as though there might have been somebody still sitting there saying something to her. But there wasn't. The man she called Dane was not in sight, and seeing that chair empty was like feeling cold air moving across my face on a hot day in August. I could not get my full breath.

I fumbled the lock open on the room side of the door, and I was halfway down the stairs before I heard it slam behind me. It seemed to me that somebody must have turned out the light bulb in the stairway because I remembered it being easy to see the steps when Clay Whitehead and I had climbed them on the way up, and now it was so dark I couldn't see my feet in front of me as I came in a half run down, down, down toward the square of light in the door at the bottom leading to the street.

The quiet on the stairway got so different so quick when the door to the Maryland Hotel at the top had slammed shut between me and the noise of the victrola and the whores and the customers, so different in my ears, that the absence of sound seemed loud to me. My head was roaring with a noise like a big wind blowing through cedars in a cemetery somewhere, and I couldn't get outside the building fast enough to suit me.

I ran at the door at the bottom with my arms lifted to knock it open, and I stumbled on the threshold on the way out, half falling

FIRE ANTS

as my feet hit the concrete sidewalk.

That stumble was why when he swung the hand holding the knife at me he didn't catch me with it in the belly or chest, but in the right temple, lodging it so hard in the bone that it twisted out of his hand when I went down to the pavement. And I heard a click when that steel hit bone, though I never felt it as a pain but as the sound of a thing shutting off, the way a radio will when you twist the knob and the music and the talking stop coming out, and the light in the tubes that make it run dims down to nothing and winks out.

I couldn't see anything of where I was, anymore.

But I've found where the light is now, though I can't see it, and I don't need it to tell me where things have got off to and where they touch and where they finally are. Everything is right there, just outside me and behind that wall, and I can stand in this room, not one hand having to feel the facing of the door to tell me the direction where I need to turn my head so I'm looking toward Maude, my sister in her bed waiting to die.

"I'd like a little more water," she's saying. "Lewis, could you pour me a little in my glass?"

"Sure, sister," I say, reaching out to touch the smooth cool glass and the pitcher beside it on the table. I pour the water all the way to the top, not spilling any of it, and hold the glass toward the place in all that empty air where her hand has to be. It's there, it always is, and I never miss.

About the Author

Gerald Duff is a native of the Texas Gulf Coast, and has taught literature and writing at Vanderbilt University, Kenyon College, and Johns Hopkins University. The title story of *Fire Ants* won the Cohen Prize from *Ploughshares Magazine*, was cited in *Best American Short Stories*, and republished in *The Editors' Choice: New American Stories*. His novels have been nominated for the PEN/Faulkner Prize, an Edgar Allan Poe Award, an International eBook Award, and a Texas Institute of Letters Award. He has published two collections of poetry, *A Ceremony of Light* and *Calling Collect*, and six novels, including *Indian Giver*, *That's All Right, Mama: The Unauthorized Life of Elvis's Twin*, *Memphis Ribs*, and *Coasters* and *Fire Ants* from NewSouth Books.

Coasters

BY GERALD DUFF

featuring characters from the Fire Ants *story*
"The Road to Damascus"

Waylon McPhee, middle-aged and divorced, moves back in with his widowed father in hopes of coasting through another year. But his father is dating again, and his sisters are trying to manipulate Waylon into asking their father for their inheritance before he gives it to a second wife. The sarcastic Waylon, juggling his relationships and responsibilities caustically but light-heartedly, hopes to recover something he lost in his youth: enough momentum to reach escape velocity.

By turns humorous and melancholy, this novel cruises to a conclusion where all its characters satisfyingly reap what they have sown. Gerald Duff has perfect pitch for the ennui of contemporary life in the suburbs of the petroleum-chemical corridor that stretches along the Gulf Coast from Texas to Mississippi.

"Gerald Duff's *Coasters* is a wild carnival ride to the rocky bottom of the New Economy—ferociously funny all the way through, and washed in a shade of deep poignancy."

— MADISON SMARTT BELL

"Deft, often droll comedy is at the fore in Duff's story . . . Hilarious scenes of family outings and school play rehearsals round out the realistic depiction of life in the oft-neglected other New South . . . wit and subtlety as simply satisfying as a tall cold one on a hot Gulf Coast afternoon."

— *Publisher's Weekly*

ISBN 1-58838-029-7 • Trade Cloth • $25.95
WWW.NEWSOUTHBOOKS.COM